BRIDGING GLOBAL INDIAN DIASPORA

A Journey from Dharmashala to New York

BRIDGING GLOBAL INDIAN DIASPORA

A Journey from Dharmashala to New York

Bhishma Agnihotri

PRABHAT PRAKASHAN
ISO 9001: 2015 Publishers

Published by
PRABHAT PRAKASHAN
4/19 Asaf Ali Road,
New Delhi-110 002 (INDIA)
Tele : +91-11-23289777
e-mail: prabhatbooks@gmail.com

ISBN 978-93-5322-594-0
BRIDGING GLOBAL INDIAN DIASPORA
by Dr. Bhishma Agnihotri

Edition
First, 2020

Price
₹ 900.00 (Rupees Nine Hundred only)

Printed at
R-Tech Offset Printers, Delhi

Dedicated to

Shri Atal Bihari Vajpayee

The Visionary of Global Indian Diaspora

Remembering all the great souls of India who inspired us to love India, the land of wisdom and world harmony.

In appreciation of my life-partner
Krishna and
three brilliant children Shailly – Gauri – Arvind

I acknowledge
the valuable and sincere advice and support
provided by my dear friend Dr. Leonard Hochberg.

Preface

This book is not my autobiography; I had never intended to write my life story anyway. This book principally revolves around my appointment as the first global Ambassador-at-Large for the Indian diaspora, from 2001 to 2004. The position was quite unique and challenging, and I enjoyed it.

As it happened, I was attending a get-together with my friends and associates known to me for many, many years. One of them asked me why I did not write anything about my experiences as an Ambassador for the diaspora. A few others joined in and encouraged me, if not pushed me, to share with others what our office had accomplished. Many other leaders of major organisations, like American Association of Physicians of India (AAPI), occasionally made similar request. I had worked with AAPI, almost since its inception, as their honorary legal advisor and their demand for me to document my tenure was affectionately persistent.

The creation of the post of Global Ambassador for the Indian diaspora was the first initiative taken by Prime Minister Atal Bihari Vajpayee. I was the one he chose to become the first Ambassador-at-Large for the Indian diaspora in order to harness relationships with the Indian diaspora to increase India's connectivity. It is true that my position was new. Our mandate was general. We established our goals and kept on moving to accomplish those goals.

The story of this voyage started with the wisdom of the Prime Minister. The position was a challenge to the forces opposed to the Prime Minister. There was also opposition from various sectors led by the media. In addition, the retired Indian Foreign Service (IFS) officials' group was opposed as its sympathy lay with the IFS cadre so that the 'purity' of the Indian Foreign Service could be maintained intact. This allowed the anti-BJP politicians to pick the opportunity to attack the government. How could the Leftists remain behind? My RSS connection had caused pain to many. It was interesting to observe a walkout in the Parliament upon my appointment. The President of India was also reluctant to approve my appointment initially.

I attracted a lot of attention, a lot of press coverage, a lot of interviews. In a few weeks, I was a well-known person in India. Despite all that, I accepted the challenge. I accepted the position, not because I wanted a job; I wanted to serve India. At that time, I had a very rewarding and unique position as the head of the Southern University Law Center. I didn't hesitate to leave all this earned to serve India's cause in connecting the Indian diaspora. In fact, I had officially written a letter to the Foreign Secretary of Indian Foreign Service, requesting him that I be paid only one dollar as my salary. This could not be done, so I ended up donating the amount earned as a fund to charity.

I discovered as time went by that the work of my office in establishing a great rapport with the diaspora, not only in America, but all over the world, was being appropriated by the people at large. The innovative and glorious effort on the part of the Prime Minister and our staff in building bridges with the diaspora was praised by many.

I took upon this writing project to highlight the achievements of our efforts. We connected the Indian diaspora all over the world, treating them as members of one large family. On going through documents relevant to this book, I was overwhelmed with the amount of material in my possession. My staff was very diligent in maintaining all the records for me. I had difficulty in sieving out what to use and what all to leave out. This book will help the readers to understand how, with the help of a very small staff, we could realise our established goals beautifully. The various sections of the book, including the appendixes, shall reflect on our achievements.

The program arranged by our office on September 21, 2003, at Jacob K. Javits Center in New York City in honour of the Prime Minister showcased our attainment in establishing unity amongst almost all the social community organisations. Leaders of different organisations came on the stage, one by one, to offer their commitment to serving the cause of India as one.

Workshops were arranged in different parts of USA to discuss and disseminate issues concerning various segments of the society. Notable amongst these were issues related to women. Topics included: 'A Diaspora Perspective' in New York, Atlanta, Baton Rouge; Indo-American Students/Youth: Their contributions and concerns' in New

York; 'Leading Financial Institutions to improve the quality of financial services aimed at NRIs and PIOs' at New York; 'Inter-Religious Leaders' in New York and 'Evaluating India's Image in Western Media' in Los Angeles, New York, Atlanta and Houston. It was refreshing to notice the energy amongst all participants for serving the diaspora and their country of origin. One of the most gratifying programmes saw the involvement of the youth in our efforts. Many of the second generation's youth volunteered to help us achieve our goals.

I visited various countries to interact with the Indian diaspora; the meetings with the diaspora in every country were very rewarding. The countries visited included Surinam, Guyana, Trinidad and Tobago, Canada, United Kingdom, Japan, Hong Kong, Thailand, Spain, Netherlands/Amsterdam, France and Mauritius. There was eagerness on the part of Indian diaspora to stay connected with India and this was very apparent as seen in their theme – 'Love India, but always be loyal to our country of adoption'. It indeed worked very well.

—Bhishma Agnihotri

Contents

1

Harnessing Soft Power

In the latter part of 2000, rumours began to circulate in many circles of India that I was going to be appointed Ambassador to the United States, though nobody talked to me about that development directly. One of my friends, who was once in the Indian Foreign Service, told me that I was top on the list for consideration to that position. He also told me that the then Foreign Secretary of the Foreign Service, known as Ministry of External Affairs (MEA), was actively seeking the job. I ignored these rumours as I was not officially contacted for any position by the then Government of India. In the beginning of January 2001, when I was on a visit to India, I received a call from the Prime Minister Atal Vajpayee of India. He invited me to come to his residence in New Delhi for a meeting. I was away from Delhi, so, it took me some time to get to New Delhi. I went to the PM's home and was immediately led to the Prime Minister, who was very warm. After a few pleasantries, he offered a very novel and dynamic position. I had interacted with him many times, even before he came into power. I knew he was a great poet, a great thinker, a wonderful speaker, but his administrative skills and his presentation to me in selling the job were unique. He told me that he wanted me to be the Global Ambassador. He then laid out the details of the new position, explaining that a lot of efforts had to be made in connecting the Indians living abroad. I was a little embarrassed when he said I could do it and that I was the best to accomplish that task. He also discussed my job details as the Global Ambassador for Non-Resident Indians (NRI) and Persons of India Origin (PIO). Additionally, I would be Ambassador Advisor to India's Ambassador in the United States. The Prime Minister also went on to say that I would have a status of Cabinet rank. He spent close to an hour in discussing all these issues.

It was clear that he had planned to reach out to the Indian diaspora in his vision to enhance soft power for India.

I could not believe that he could be so thorough and convincing. He expected some answer from me. I told him that I had to talk to my wife, who was in America, before I could make any commitment. He asked me to go to the other room to call her and I did. Of course, she would not have said no and this was what I expected. Then I was asked by the Prime Minister to see Shri Brijesh Mishra, his Chief of Staff. I went directly to Mr. Mishra, and he enquired about the conversation with the Prime Minister. I gave him the details. When I came to the point that the Prime Minster mentioned Cabinet status for me, Mishra interjected, "Did he say that?" I responded in the positive. I told him that the Prime Minister of his own accord mentioned that without my asking for it. It appeared to me that Mishraji was not in favour of my receiving the Cabinet status. I could not fathom him nor did I care because I had not asked for what I was offered. I enjoyed the concept and opportunity as it entailed the pleasure of working with over 20 million people of Indian origin living outside India and through them, serving India.

Prime Minister Vajpayee in appointing me to the newly created position had in mind the soft power, or use of non-coercive means to influence others, of the Indian diaspora and their potential to contribute to the development of new India. He knew that Indians, wherever they resided, had emotional attachment to the land of India, to the values of India and the culture of India. He had appointed me to tap that resource. Indians all over the world were occupying, at that time and even now, very attractive positions in all fields of life. They were known by their adopted countries as smart, cultured and loyal citizens of the country of adoption. We all knew that wherever an Indian went, he kept in his heart the welfare of his motherland while staying loyal to the country of adoption. Prime Minister Vajpayee wanted them to be part of India's glory. He had faith in me, as he had known me since the days of Dr. Syama Prasad Mookerjee.

Currently, India's soft power approach is open strategy. Prime Minister Narendra Modi's various programmes on a worldwide basis are geared to promote the soft power of India. For example, yoga is one such initiative. Celebration of International Yoga Day by 170 members of the United Nations and yoga public exercises is now a welcome sign for almost all the countries of the world.[1] People are embracing it for their health and spiritual uplift. Subliminally, they are also appreciating the great culture, history and knowledge of India from ancient times until today. Articles on 'soft power', as the phrase was coined by Dean Joseph S. Nye Jr. of Harvard Kennedy School of Government, are serving as the beacon light to statesmen from various countries in presenting their soft power besides their hard power. Even though some countries, like USA, China, and Russia do not need a soft power approach in international affairs, they understand the role of softness played in marketing their countries. For example, China has currently established hundreds of Confucius Institutes around the world, to spread the eminence of Chinese culture. India has still a lot to present to the world from its rich historical wealth of culture, music, wisdom and what not. Prime Minister Modi is promoting goodwill and love for India all the time. Recently, Prime Minister Modi's approach to extending soft power was seen in his commitment to the grand *Kumbh Mela* at Prayagraj, where 70 countries participated with their flags aloft. The *Kumbh Mela* was celebrated from January 15 to March 4, 2019, where millions of people had assembled.

During Australian Prime Minister Tony Abbott's visit to India, he was asked to justify Australia's reason for signing a deal to sell uranium to the country. In response, the Prime Minister said, "India threatens no one and is a friend to many." This was not a mere diplomatic nicety, but a carefully chosen answer based on India's international image – an image that is rare amongst great powers of India's size and strength and which will give Delhi a unique soft power advantage in the future multi-polar world.[2] Dr. David Frawley, American Hindu teacher and author, also says, "India's potential soft power and cultural diplomacy is reflected in its vast and unique heritage that is already influencing the world by its own intrinsic value."[3] Harsh V. Pant, professor of international relations, writes thus of India's soft-power strategy: 'The Modi government is striving to not only revive national pride in the country's ancient values, but also enhance India's hard power by using its soft-power advantages.'

During his travels, Indian Prime Minister Narendra Modi makes it a point of promoting India's soft power, including Bollywood, Sufi music and yoga as well as a shared heritage in art, architecture, cuisine and democratic values. It's too early to assess if India's efforts are having any substantive impact in meeting the nation's foreign policy objectives, but for the first time, a coherent effort is underway to raise India's brand value abroad. This is likely to have significant implications for the conduct of Indian diplomacy and the broader role of India in global politics in the coming years.[4]

India has a lot of wealth resources in spirituality with the world's religions—Hinduism, Buddhism, Sikhism, Christianity, film industry, music and diversity, and much more to share with others in the world. Though at this time, India is not ranked in the top 30 countries in terms of soft power as indicated in the list released by Portland Communications, it is expected that India will be moving upward in view of its targeted movement in harnessing soft power in addition to hard power.[5]

□

2

MEA 'Well-Wishers' Unhappy

A few months passed after my meeting with Prime Minister Atal Bihari Vajpayee, but nothing happened. I was informed by various friends that the Indian Foreign Service 'well-wishers' were not pleased with my proposed assignment and were anxious to stop it. In the meantime, expecting the new assignment, my wife had resigned from her job as a professor, effectively from May 2001. I called the Prime Minister for checking the status of the position. He told me that the President of India, who was technically the final authority to approve of such positions, did not agree with his decision. President K.R. Narayanan was once Ambassador in the USA and was reportedly from the political affiliation not generally favourable to the Bharatiya Janata Party (BJP) before becoming President. The Prime Minister also told me that under the Indian law and norm, the President could not say no to the recommendation when sent back again for approval. So, ultimately, the President had no choice but to concur with the Prime Minister. During this period, inspired by Ministry of External Affairs (MEA) 'well-wishers', old timers and new aspirants for plush jobs had joined hands to campaign directly or indirectly against my proposed appointment. Many retired foreign officers used their professional skills in writing letters to the media, condemning the appointment. I happened to be in New Delhi in August. The media somehow or the other was informed of my presence. They came to the hotel where I was staying and began shooting all kinds of questions at me. To be honest, I was enjoying it because I had not received such attention in India for a long time. I knew they were wrong. I knew the Prime Minister was right, and I knew I was equally qualified, if not more, than most of the persons serving in the Foreign Service. I also knew that the opposition to my appointment was spearheaded by the Opposition parties. In fact, one of the former political leaders in the previous government, who was friendly to me at one time, invited me to his house and told me that everything was being leaked out and engineered by some people in the MEA. They were feeding the information to the media and attempting to make me not accept the job.

□

3

Negative Role of Indian Media and Others on My Appointment

In order to apprehend the furore sparked by my appointment as Ambassador-at-Large, it is essential to appreciate the role of the press in India. When compared with the press in other post-colonial societies, the press in India has enjoyed since Independence a remarkable degree of freedom from direct governmental intervention and control. With the fall of the Berlin Wall and the intensification of economic and other forms of globalisation, Western news outlets have entered the Indian market and offering competition in both readership and viewership via television and the internet. Likewise, Indian-owned newspapers and entertainment outlets are now using traditional and modern means to reach the readers and viewers to influence the Indian diaspora. Here, too, globalisation has had an impact. The press and media are a vibrant sector of the Indian economy.

By 2005, India boasted of 5,000 newspapers printed daily, in English, Hindi and vernacular or local languages. "The print media reach approximately 300 million readers each day."[6] Thanks to the improvement in the standard of living and the expansion of the Indian middle class, "newspaper sales in India increased 14 per cent between 1999 and 2004, which made the country second only to China in the number of newspapers sold everyday." Reinforcing the increasing consumption of news is the trend in expansion of advertising and consumerism, with the Indian media showing an increase in the percentage of its revenue from advertising from 25-30 per cent in the early 1990s to 45-55 per cent some 10 years later. "Some larger newspapers, such as *The Times of India,* claim that advertising constitutes close to 70 per cent of their revenues." A quest exclusively for profits either through increased readership and/or advertising threatens, in India as elsewhere, to undermine professional ethics of the journalist.

As to whose code of ethics should be advanced is a question with which many journalists in post-colonial societies must grapple. Is there a universal code of professional ethics that should apply to all journalists without regard to their country of origin, their culture and local values, or their political affiliations? Or is the very claim that there is a universal code of ethics merely a smokescreen behind which hides a demand that Indian and other post-colonial societies adopt Western journalistic values? As one senior reporter of the *Times of India News Service* is reported to have said: "Who will develop these universal principles? Will it be the age-old story where the IFJ (India Federation of Journalists) tells us what is good and bad journalism and what we should do to win awards to be called a 'good' journalist? Or is it to be American professors writing about Plato and Aristotle who will tell us what the universal principles are?"[7]

Two American university-based professors, Shakuntala Rao and Seow Ting Lee, have recommended such a universal code, 'the principles of which include such fundamental ethical precepts as displaying (1) autonomy (from government and political control), (2) tolerance for religious and cultural diversity, (3) respect for others, and (4) honesty, accuracy, impartiality, objectivity, and non-fabrication.'[8]

Although India does not lack promulgated codes of journalistic conduct, adherence to their precepts remains wanting. Private organisations, NGOs and even the Parliament in India have advanced codes of professional conduct; nonetheless, political, economic and educational factors militate against a widespread and intense personal commitment. As of 2005, although India had more than 30 departments devoted to the training of journalists, the need for journalists far outstripped the supply: "There are fewer than 1,500 journalism graduates from universities in a year, but the manpower needed in the mass communication industry is somewhere between 84,000 and 155,000 every year."[9] Few practicing journalists have been exposed to courses devoted to observance of professional ethics in journalism. As a result, there are limited countervailing forces blocking the impulse to sensationalise and personalise the news.

Recent research into the way in which news is presented to an Indian readership reveals that journalists themselves are concerned over the close ties the press maintains with political parties, with such ties often resulting in conflicts of interest and a loss of credibility and objectivity. Indeed, journalists have noted that their editors receive valued gifts from government officials and party leaders – a practice which permeates a profession whose practitioners are, in general, poorly paid. A relative absence of highly remunerated and trained journalists accounts for lack of evaluating, collecting and checking facts. Learning to verify facts occurs on the job, if at all; and the final product of the journalist, that is the report itself, is rarely subjected to a systematic checking of the facts contained therein. Regrettably, facts are sometimes of less import than coming up with a way to personalise important political and economic developments, thereby sensationalising the news at the cost of offering accurate information to the public.[10]

Many of the general features of the Indian print media described above were all too present in the run up to and in the aftermath of my appointment as the Ambassador-at-Large. Most of the prestigious national news outlets failed to report accurately on my credentials, qualifications and connections; and when those facts were reported, they were distorted by individuals whose professional and/or political commitments prompted them to distort the record in a vain attempt to embarrass me into declining this post.

Consider, for instance, the titles of some of the articles that appeared concerning my posting to this position: 'Agnihotri posting a weird move; All the PM's men,'[11] which calls to mind the old politically satirical English poem, 'Humpty Dumpty' 'Agni Diplomacy';[12] 'New Czar of the Diaspora' – a title attached to a picture of me that accompanied an article titled 'Privileged Posting'[13] and my personal favourite one, which inadvertently praised my skills even as it sought to call into question my likely impact, "Super Ambassador-at-Large: Will this new envoy become a fifth wheel of our diplomatic cart in Washington?"[14] Although many articles were titled with a fairly standard summary of what followed in the body of the text, some displayed a marked tendency to personalise their critique of the appointment or sensationalise the impact I would have as the Ambassador-at-Large.

Perhaps the most virulent attack was launched by Praful Bidwai, in his lengthy article 'All in the Family.'[15] Bidwai, a well-known peace activist, journalist and foreign policy analyst, dipped his pen in venom when he wrote the following racist comment about Louisiana and attributed the attitudes expressed herein to the Rashtriya Swayamsevak Sangh (RSS) and, by implication, to me: "Agnihotri might be a poorly known academic at a supremely obscure university in Louisiana, a state known for jazz, Creole food and all those positively non-Aryan, mleccha-and-mongrel things the RSS despises." The fact that I was the only NRI to serve as the Dean and then as the Chancellor of a law school in the United States was denigrated; my effort to build this law school into a regionally followed by a nationally prominent institution was ignored. What bearing my having lived in Louisiana might have on my ability to serve the needs of the NRIs and PIOs remains a mystery.

Beyond such personal assaults, the press launched four lines of attack on my appointment. First, I was personally attacked for my connection with the RSS and then dubbed an RSS appointee. Second, the Leftist parties and their affiliated papers condemned me for ideological reasons. Third, the foreign service 'well-wishers' were not pleased with the appointment of an 'outsider'. And, fourth, the 'well-wishers' alleged that the appointment of an advisor to the Indian Ambassador to the United States would affect the operations of the Washington embassy.

□

4

An RSS-Connected Ambassador

The first line of criticism suggested that my affiliation with the RSS disqualified me for the post. Although I did not hide my ties with the RSS, those who sought to block my appointment accused me of seeking to advance an agenda that would favour religion and values of practising Hindus over the other religious communities living in India – specifically, Sikhs, Christians and Muslims. Curiously, the authors of these articles failed to note that among my credentials were awards for service to a Christian organisation and to Israel – an ample indication that my political and religious commitments never stood in the way of respecting religious pluralism.

One particularly egregious and unbalanced article cited a letter written by the president of the Indian National Overseas Congress, which was addressed to the Indian President, Mr. K.R. Narayanan and subsequently leaked to the press, stating that the government's intent in appointing me was to 'saffronise' the NRI community in the U.S. 'Saffronise' was the term used by the Bharatiya Janata Party's (BJP) political opponents to condemn its policies and appointments which sought to honour the values and sensibilities of the majority of voters. The letter accused the government of promoting a 'hidden agenda' of communalising the NRI community. 'This appointment', the letter stated further, 'is a sublime message to NRIs to get into the hold of the RSS (or its affiliated groups) if they wish to communicate with the embassy, consulate and the Government of India.' The implication of this assertion was that it was my 'sublime' mission to turn the NRIs in the United States (and by implication throughout the world) into a power base for the BJP by requiring these individuals, who are known for their independence of thought and their varied political commitments, to join the RSS or its associated organisations. 'This country (USA), like India, is a pluralistic society' – the letter stated; it is 'a mosaic of different religions, ethnicities and cultures, but, at the same time, is secular when it comes to governance, that is, it strongly believes in the separation of Church and the State'. The letter – copies of which were forwarded to the Prime Minister Vajpayee and the Congress president, Ms Sonia Gandhi suggested that 'India's secular profile in the USA[16] would be placed at risk with my appointment.'[17]

The source of their irritation with me was my affiliation with the Rashtriya Swayamsevak Sangh (RSS), which is an organisation committed to revitalisation of the spiritual, moral and traditional values of Hinduism. It was founded in 1925 by Dr. K. B. Hedgewar. Many individuals who have done well in economic and social life in India were inspired by the ideas of the RSS, which serves as a higher education facility for those who wish to serve in various allied organisations, including the BJP. Although there is no formal membership as such in the RSS, I attended their programmes during high school and college days, inspired by their dedication and commitment to a nationalistic view of the people of the world. I was particularly inspired by those RSS members who had given up all their professional commitments and confined themselves full time to implementation of the organisation's national ideals, which include a forthright desire to unify Hindus who have the greatest stake in the unity and development of India. All my contacts with the RSS, at all levels, promoted the sense that every human being has the right to realise his or her potential within India, provided they were loyal to India as a nation-state.

This line of attack was deployed by many in the political arena and the press. In the press, my appointment was characterised as that of an RSS ideologue, as an effort to placate the RSS lobby[18] and as a passionate RSS soul-mate of the Prime Minister.

It was left to the government spokesman, Parliamentary Affairs Minister, Pramod Mahajan, to defend me against the charge that the government was seeking to advance Hindu nationalism (i.e. Hindutva) through my appointment: "Being associated with the RSS is no crime; if an RSS member can be Prime Minister of the country; what's wrong with this appointment[?]" Another newspaper described the reaction to Mr. Pramod Mahajan's defence of my appointment as follows:

"Almost the entire Opposition staged a walkout from the Lok Sabha (Parliament) on Thursday (August 30, 2001) when the government justified the appointment of Bishamber [sic] Kumar Agnihotri...on the ground that the incumbent could owe allegiance to the RSS."[19,20]

Obviously, there is a world of political difference between owing 'allegiance' and having acknowledged an affiliation with and attended meetings of the RSS – a difference that the 'Our Special Correspondent', that is, the anonymous author at *The Asian Age* ignored.

The persons in opposition to my appointment were concerned about my closeness to RSS. It is very unfortunate that the so-called intellectuals or at least educated persons have no love for the truth; at least, they didn't have the desire to find the truth. It is true that the basic goal of the RSS is to organise the Hindus, who are not united and have to be brought to one common platform. Mahatma Gandhi once visited the RSS camp and was surprised to see the participants eating in one line without a reference to their caste or creed. The same thing happened when Dr. Ambedkar witnessed the RSS programme.

The critics of RSS should figure out what binds the members of RSS to the organisation. I have been a very disciplined and organised person, and I know this is because of my RSS background. I am never late for any work as a student, as a judge, as a professor, as a Chancellor or as an Ambassador. This is because of attending the RSS shakha. I only attended RSS activities during school and undergraduate studies, but the sincerity of the RSS functionaries, their sacrifice and their commitment are overpowering.

During President Bill Clinton's visit to India, I asked him and his accompanying Congressmen, especially Congressman Gary Ackerman, Chairman of India Caucus in the Congress, to visit the place where the persons, who are responsible for the appearance of BJP on the national scene, reside. Chairman Ackerman agreed to visit the RSS office/ residential section of the full-timers of the organisation in Delhi. He had a good talk with Shri Sudershanji, the Sarsanghchalak or head of RSS as the latter was in Delhi then. Then I took him on a tour of the place. He was almost shocked to see them living like hermits, and he mentioned it to President Clinton. They talked about this to everybody wherever they went. Chairman Ackerman took a picture with the RSS Chief, which he displayed in his Congressional office all the time. This is why, RSS has been prospering day-to-day because its leaders/prime workers/Swayamsevaks embody the spirit of *sannyasis*. Thousands of well-educated young men have given up their professions to become full-timers with RSS expecting no compensation or reward. I owe a lot to various other forces in life, like mother and teachers, but nothing comes closer than the RSS Shakha regimen in instilling in me the values, commitments, sincerity and honesty in performing my *karmas* in every aspect of life. The petty talk indulged in by the media or former IFS retirees had no effect on my thinking. I knew they were misguided and misinformed, if not mischievous. In fact, I thanked the media attention because without paying any marketing fee, I had acquired popularity. Now, almost everybody knew me, and for a good reason.

Leftist Ideology and the Press

Nationalism has generally been an anathema to Leftists who view it as a form of 'false consciousness' designed to mislead and distract the 'working classes' from realising their historic mission to engage in a revolution to fulfil the socialist or communist programme. On rare occasions, nationalist sentiments may be harnessed to suit an anti-imperialist agenda, as was the case in Vietnam, provided nationalism (in the form of 'national liberation') was merely a means to realising a transformation in traditional society and the introduction of public ownership of the 'means of production' National sentiment, in the Marxist understanding of history, is often based on religion, distracting the working class from the realising its revolutionary potential. As Marx once put it, 'Religion is the opiate of the masses', thereby implying that even as religion induces unconsciousness in the believer, it also overwhelms him or her with pleasure. These so-called 'primordial sentiments', undermine the revolutionary fervour of the oppressed and downtrodden, by advancing sentiments of community and social solidarity. At best, nationalism, according to Left-wing ideologues, creates an 'imagined community' and never a real one that is worth defending. The attacks on my affiliation with the RSS were part and parcel of a wider Leftist ideological stance that denigrates nationalist and religious beliefs as being neither revolutionary, nor secular, nor progressive and nor modern.

In addition to this ideological attack, I was also subjected to a populist attack directed at the ambassadorial office. From September 23, 2001, the time of the announcement of my appointment, through May 30, 2004, the approximate time when I resigned from my post, the *Indian Express* occasionally mentioned how my office was administered in its news reports, though it rarely mentioned my activities in a favourable light. Typical of its reporting was the following claim: "Not content with travelling the world first-class to ostensibly pursue the interests of the Indian diaspora, Ambassador-at-Large for NRIs, Bhishma Agnihotri is now said to have asked for a $3-million special grant (equivalent to Rs 1.5 crores) for use by his mission." Although the reporter for the *Indian Express* noted that I denied requesting 'a discretionary grant,' no effort was made to check the anonymous claim. My responsibilities included, not 'ostensibly' but in reality, the necessity of travelling the world to make contact with NRIs and PIOs in the Indian diaspora. My staff, assigned by the Ministry of External Affairs, repeatedly reminded me that when representing India, it was absolutely necessary never to bring the State into ill repute by an illegitimate display of parsimonious behaviour. In fact, the *Indian Express*, in the same article, allowed that I 'had the world...[as my] portfolio [and that over the previous several weeks, I had travelled to] London...Canada, Surinam, Trinidad & Tobago, even Fiji.' Obviously, such criticism also incited me to get out from behind my desk in New York City and build contacts with the Indian diaspora. Later, on January 6, 2003, the *Indian Express* finally conceded that the Ministry of External Affairs had funded my travels so that I might fulfil my responsibilities as Ambassador-at-Large to the NRIs.[21]

Opposition by the Foreign Service 'Well-Wishers'

From the very first announcement of my nomination to the position of Ambassador-at-Large, the media reported opposition by the Ministry of External Affairs and the Foreign Service of India. The *Economic Times* noted: "The empire is hopping mad. By nominating Bhishma Kumar Agnihotri as an adviser to the Indian embassy in the US, the politically determined appointment has raised the hackles with the Foreign Service corps who anyway find themselves having to yield ground to an increasing tribe of political appointees."

Although the members of the MEA did not speak for the record, at least two prominent retired members of the Foreign Service prepared editorials attacking my nomination. J.N. Dixit, the former Indian Ambassador to several countries, including Afghanistan, Bangladesh (first ambassador), Chile, Mexico, Japan, and Pakistan among others, served as the National Security Advisor to the Prime Minister of India during the first years of the Congress Party-led United Progressive Alliance, which came to power after the fall of the BJP-led coalition – the National Democratic Alliance.[22] S.K. Singh, Ambassador and former Foreign Secretary of India, authored the second editorial; he served as Ambassador to Pakistan, Afghanistan, Jordan, Lebanon, Cyrus, etc.[23] Both authors reveal, perhaps inadvertently, but nonetheless explicitly, a sense of loss of status as a consequence of the Indian Prime Minister exercising his legitimate power in making this appointment.

Both Mr. Dixit and Mr. Singh noted that their evaluation of my credentials and likely actions might be motivated by unwillingness to see an 'outsider' attain the position of Ambassador without having been first admitted to the Foreign Service club. Dixit apologised for the institutional conflict of interest inherent in his attack on my appointment. He stated that he did not want his negative and 'sweeping value judgement' on my appointment to be seen as emanating from the 'careerist psyche of a former[24] Foreign Service officer'.

Singh revealingly quoted Ambassador Charles W. Freeman on the undesirability of appointing an outsider to a diplomatic post, which after all is the closest position in a democratic republic to an aristocratic title. He said, "In republics which do not confer titles of nobility, the title of ambassador comes closest to such an honour. Many who should justly be recognised for notable achievement in fields unrelated to diplomacy, therefore, seek ambassadorships. As they are without experience to prepare them for the multiple duties of the office, such men are only seldomly able to discharge it with full dignity.

"The appointment of such men, therefore, risks damage both to their own previously distinguished reputations and to those of the states and governments they represent. It would be kinder, both to them and their nation, were a less onerous honour found for them."

Singh, in offering this quote from Freeman, was highlighting the nobility and dignity attached to anyone appointed to the diplomatic corps and was struggling to reserve such honours for the members of the Foreign Service club. Thus, it was entirely appropriate that Singh felt "a little squeamish raising here the question of [the proposed] precise grade and rank [of my position]." Singh demanded to know what the government intended to do regarding 'salary and allowances and frais [i.e. daily allowance]' He asked if they would "be those of a Grade-I, or Grade-II, or Grade-Ill envoy" and what would the "entertainment responsibilities and allowances be?" After suggesting that 'outsiders' should not be afforded the dignity and remuneration accorded to members of the Foreign Service club, Singh resorted to an undiplomatic attack on the government and the appointee: "This government has, thus, shown unprecedented decisiveness and commitment to innovation by insisting on having an undistinguished, superannuated, party functionary made an ambassador..."[25]

It must be noted that *The Hindustan Times,* the paper in which these two editorials appeared, did offer a dissenting assessment of my appointment by Vir Sanghvi, the editorial page editor. Sanghvi noted, "The Opposition has walked out of Parliament over Agnihotri's appointment, editorials have criticised the decision, former Foreign Secretaries have condemned the move and the Foreign Service has been busy doing its best to undermine Agnihotri before he takes up his appointment. Nevertheless, it is to be expected that Agnihotri will find innovative ways to show off his newly endowed diplomatic status." I was extremely grateful for this endorsement and over the next three years, sought to find 'innovative ways' to advance my mandate from the Government of India.

Bureaucratic Complexities

My appointment was not without its bureaucratic complexities. I was appointed Ambassador-at-Large to the NRIs and PIOs worldwide and as an advisor to the Indian Ambassador to the United States. Though it was widely appreciated that my appointment was a 'political appointment' made by the Prime Minister in order to facilitate closer ties between India and the NRI and PIO communities and among those communities scattered across the globe, there was widespread, if not deliberate, confusion over my brief. Although my efforts were to be directed exclusively towards the NRIs and PIOs, the Foreign Service 'well-wishers' were convinced that there would be an overlap in responsibilities between the US Embassy and my mission, such that the US Embassy (and other envoys around the world) would find their authority undermined by my activities and by the conflicts among the NRI organisations plaguing some of the NRI communities for many years. S.K. Singh raised these points in a succinct fashion: "Will this new envoy become a fifth wheel of our diplomatic cart in Washington, DC? Could he become a source of embarrassment and pinpricks to our ambassador, by importing into the embassy the unfortunate rivalries and petty disputes which afflict some of our 26 NRI concentrations abroad?"

The editorial by J.N. Dixit presented a far more complicated picture of my role vis-a-vis the Ministry of External Affairs and the Foreign Service. His overall assessment was, "The government has taken an unprecedented decision which will have a negative impact on the general functioning of one of India's most important embassies abroad, our mission in the US. This is apart from the negative ramifications of this decision on other Indian missions."[27] Although Dixit recognised that there was ample precedent for the Indian government in handing out the 'personal rank of ambassador', he made an issue of my appointment on the grounds that there was no precedent in any Foreign Office of an outsider being appointed as an ambassador, parallel to the regular appointee as ambassador of the country. Dixit proceeded to highlight the potential for bureaucratic turf battles by raising a series of rhetorical questions:

With Agnihotri's political linkages, will he be functioning under the jurisdiction of Ambassador Lalit Mansingh, or will he be a parallel and equal centre of authority in the Indian embassy? What would be his relations with the senior most officials dealing with political, economic, information, technological and cultural matters? Will he be advising them also or overseeing their work which is the responsibility of the Ambassador and the deputy chief of mission? Will he claim equal access to the higher echelons of the US government which is the prerogative of Lalit Mansingh, because he (Agnihotri) has the personal rank of Ambassador?

Such questions were rhetorical precisely because my appointment as envoy to the NRIs and PIOs was indeed 'unprecedented'. Only experience, well thought-out institutional arrangements and goodwill between the members of the Foreign Service and me could ultimately address and resolve the issues raised by these questions.

Conclusion

Since I too was aware of these possibilities for bureaucratic confusion, I publicly sought to reassure the Indian Ambassador to the United States, Mr. Lalit Mansingh, of my intent to complement his efforts:"He (Mansingh) is a wonderful guy and we are good friends. We will complement and supplement each other and function as a team because we will all work for India's betterment, for better relations between India and the United States and between the NRIs and India. We will be glad to step back, or forward, as required. We are only individuals serving a cause. That's the way I operate and that's the way I will operate."[28]

Mansingh concurred. Commenting on the need for an ambassador to the NRIs and PIOs, Mansingh stated: "'It was an appointment which was long overdue. [Agnihotri] is highly respected among the NRIs. I couldn't think of anybody better for this job. We will be working very closely together. I look forward to his help and guidance on matters related to NRIs and persons of Indian origin."

Meanwhile I was appreciative of the publicity this controversy over my appointment had brought to me. As I laughingly stated in one interview: "...the PR (public relations) I am (now) generating has never happened to me before. I think I am getting very important (laughs). I tell my friends, in just three days in India, I have wiped out 25 years of distance."

□

5

Educational and Professional Background

Some of my friends approached me off and on asking me to highlight my educational background and other experiences in professional and public life before I became a global Ambassador-at-Large, especially because of the controversy raised by some adversely affected people regarding my appointment and my qualifications for appointment. This exercise, some stated, will also validate Prime Minister's vision in selecting a person of my background as the Global Ambassador. It was for the first time this position was created and it was the first time the government in power had taken such a step. My opponents were either misinformed, ill-informed or didn't care to be informed. In any case, let me introduce myself briefly for the benefit of my readers.

Schooling

I went to Arya School, operated on the principles of Arya Samaj. The school was a regular institution of learning. In addition, once a week, we had the opportunity of chanting prayers in Sanskrit before the *havaṇ/yagna*. It was very rejuvenating. My family members were not followers of the Arya Samaj system, but they liked the exposure of their son to Vedic prayers, which were part of *havan* ceremony. I started my schooling in the Pakistan side of pre-Partition India. I finished my high school after Partition and vividly remember a few highlights of my earlier schooling. I was a good speaker. I was awarded prizes in extempore presentations and one of the events of my pride was when during a huge prize distribution ceremony, the headmaster of the school introduced me by saying that I was the grandson of a great scholar and thinker, who had been a teacher in the high school where my grandfather was headmaster. He also added that he had been greatly influenced by my grandfather's leadership qualities. I felt very proud and that was the first time when I decided to take up the responsibility of furthering my family name. Another incident occurred when I was late in reaching school. It was customary for the headmaster to hit the latecomers with the ruler. Seeing me in the queue, he said that he couldn't hit me and let everybody else go without punishment. I became popular with the students thereafter. I used to play hockey and organised a group of students to play every evening after school, and then keep the sticks at one place. Additionally, we created a library by putting some money from our meagre allowances. The library operated from my house and the students took turns to run it. There are other incidents which made me more responsible as I was given various responsibilities in the school programmes. In the high school exams, I finished with a very high grade. My mother had a great influence on my upbringing. We used to recite prayers in Sanskrit on a regular basis, besides discussing issues related to religion and politics. My mother, being well-read and well-informed, guided our locality girls who sought advice and guidance. I used to daily fetch milk the milkman at his farm. It was about a mile away from our house and my mother made me utilise time while walking to and fro for reading the *Gita*. She encouraged me to memorise the *Gita*, and I did. I remember reading a lot of religious literature together on a regular basis.

Dharamshala College

My father was in the audit department of the Army. He was stationed in upper Dharamshala with the army regiment in the cantonment area of Macleod Ganj. Our family had a rented house in lower Dharamshala. My government college was located in lower Dharamshala, which today is famous as the abode of the world-renowned spiritual leader, the Dalai Lama. The Dalai Lama and his close associates, as we all know, had to leave his kingdom and spiritual home of Tibet and seek shelter in India. He established his government in exile at Dharamshala, which is today a place of pilgrimage for visitors from all over the world.

The government college at Dharamshala was situated at the foothills of the glorious Himalayan Dhauladhar range, presenting one of the best views to humanity. I completed four years of college with honours. Honours courses are taken in addition to the normal load. The main attraction of Honour courses was that they were conducted by the college principal. He was an erudite and established scholar on Aristotle and Plato, about whom I wanted to know more. The honours classes were small – in all six people and we read the writings of these philosophers in detail in the class. I completed my BA degree with honours, maintaining my regimen of participating in sports.

Next to the college was a big ground for police use. Our hockey team used that ground for playing hockey and soccer (football). I was also on the college debating team and won trophies by participating in debates and declamation contests.

In the peaceful and divine environs of the college, some tension was created by the principal when in a fit of anger, he blurted that the backward women of the hills sent their stupid kids to college for wasting everybody's time. I heard it. All the students were mad, and they decided to go on a strike until the principal apologiesed for his ugly remark. The student body went on strike for days. The city leaders intervened and the principal had to apologise. Not only that, he was transferred to another government college in another city. Incidentally, the principal had been partially educated in England.

Prof. Chaman Lal joined the college as a professor. He was interested in yoga. He organised a yoga group in the college. I was secretary of the group and we offered yoga classes to interested students on a regular basis. Prof. Chaman Lal, after retirement, constituted a big non-profit yoga group in another city. He died at the age of ninety-five.

Another memorable event took place when we invited Prof. Harivansh Rai Bachchan, a great poet, to share poetry with the students. His books, like *Madhushala*, were great literary works. After the programme, he wanted to walk going to upper Dharmshala. I, with another student, went along with him. After seeing the full range of Dhauladhar, he stopped, while we stood behind him. He stood totally engrossed in a meditative posture, appreciating the beauty of the snow-clad hills. He softly murmured some poetic verse, as if conversing with the mountains. I was young, but I can remember even today his expression as if he was in sync with the mountains overlooking the humanity below.

Close to our college was a World War II Italian cemetery for Italian soldiers who had been confined in the Yol jail as prisoners of war. Yol was a town very close to Dharamshala and the soldiers who died were buried in the cemetery close to our college. I visited that cemetery quite often because it presented a wonderful view of the entire Dhauladhar range. I enjoyed the solitude and would close my eyes and imagine walking on the top edges of Dhauladhar. It enthused me with a lot of ideas for my speeches and poetry. The entire region surrounding Dharamshala and neighbourhoods of Kangra, Palampur, Baijnath and others were very attractive and exciting places which I often visited with my friends. Once we went to Palampur (25 miles away) on our bicycles. It was a hilly area and the roads were steep and serpentine. We were four students and two of our bikes broke on hitting against the rocks. We somehow managed to reach Palampur where we spent few days, exploring the beautiful tea gardens and mountain ranges.

While I awaited my college results, I decided to visit upper Dharmshala with a friend of mine. We reached Bhagsunath, which boasted of a Shiva temple and pure spring water. A well-known astrologer often visited the temple during the summer months. My friend Ramesh Sharma asked me to take along my horoscope to consult him. He studied my horoscope and told me that I was going to be a lawyer or in the field of law. I detested law and wanted to be a political science professor. I ignored his advice and took admission at a college in Hoshiarpur to study for a Masters in Political Science. I had a few days before my classes began. So I visited the city of Jalandhar to meet my uncle, who was the Mayor of the city. He asked me to join the law school in Jalandhar besides continuing to study for Masters in political science. It looked like a good deal: free food, free residence and uncle to take care of me. I joined the law and evening classes for Political Science at D.A.V. College. I completed studies in political science and law. However, only law has been with me ever since then. It appeared the astrologer knew the best.

Debating Skills

I participated in regional and national debates, representing D.A.V. College as also the Law College. I won more than twenty trophies in those contests, invariably winning the first prize in both English and Hindi competitions.

This reminds me of an interesting episode that happened at the law school when participating in a United Nations mock session. The professor in-charge assigned the members of the selected group one country each which he/she would represent in the debate on the issue of world peace. I was selected to represent USSR. Everybody in the group was preparing his or her role very diligently, while I started going to the office of the Communist Party in the city to read the material on communism and USSR. Everybody was well-prepared and as an established debater, I was seriously ready and prepared. My presentation was quite powerful in praise of communism and deriding the evils of capitalism, especially of America. I still remember I said, "One day, America's dollar dance will end." An interesting by-product of my presentation was that the communist comrades attending the debate, were so impressed by my presentation that they were ready to honour me as one of them. I had to tell them one day, "Look, that was only a drama. I was playing the role of the head of the USSR. I don't approve of communism. I like democracy and freedom." It was then that they stopped bugging me (see Appendix II for details).

Memorable Events During College Days

1. **A.B.V.P.**: I was elected president of the Students Union at D.A.V. College. I was also elected first state president of Akhil Bhartiya Vidyarthi Parishad (A.B.V.P.), a students' organisation in the state of Punjab.

2. **Kashmir Delegation**: I was selected as chairman of the team to visit Kashmir. It was a team of twelve student leaders from different colleges in the state. We visited the entire region of Kashmir and talked to students in different institutions. We also interacted with the officials of the government. In an interesting incident, we visited a cabinet minister of the government. We started discussing the various aspects of life in Kashmir. The minister began to explain the concept of mobile schools for Gujarwals or wandering tribes, who moved from place to place along with their herd. On being asked who provided the finance for mobile schools, the minister replied that India provided the funds. I bluntly remarked, "Sir, you mean the Centre helps you?" He

became nervous and corrected himself. That encounter displayed the common mindset of the rulers of Kashmir. Our official visit covered almost all parts of Kashmir Valley. One of the memorable events was our presentation to the all girls' college in Srinagar.

3. **Dr. S.P. Mookerjee**: As president of A.B.V.P., we organised a programme in honour of Dr. S.P. Mookerjee, the founder president of the Jana Sangh. He was on his way to Kashmir. A huge crowd of students and professors came to hear him, who was once the youngest Vice Chancellor of Calcutta University. I shared the dais with him along with another leader from Jammu, Shri Prem Nath Dogra. I introduced the speaker to the huge audience and then requested Dr Mookerjee to speak. He came to the microphone and started in Hindi, "Brothers and sisters." I had advised him earlier on his arrival to speak in English and to which he had agreed. I promptly reached the microphone and covering the mike with my hand, requested Dr. Mookerjee to speak in English as agreed upon earlier. He then switched to English and gave one of the historic speeches of his time. At that time, Shri Atal Bihari Vajpayee was seated below as secretary of the Jana Sangh. He commented that it was the best ever speech given by Dr. Mookerjee.

Selected as a Judge

I was selected as a judge when I was 24-years old. Here it may be relevant to explain how judges are selected. The selection for trial judges was based upon examinations somewhat similar to bar exams in America. The applicants were tested in writing in six subject areas. The selection was then based upon the ranking of the applicants on their performance in the examination. For example, if there were ten vacancies in a particular state for which the exam was conducted, then the High Court would select the top ten performers.

At that time, I was teaching political science at an all-girls' college in New Delhi. A friend of mine informed me that there was going to be an exam for selection of judges at Shimla, a mountain retreat. As a fresh graduate of the law school I had just started teaching in Delhi. Anyway, I took the exam for judges, primarily to enjoy a Himalayan holiday. The exam was taken by many professors and senior lawyers. Under the rules, I could take the exam even though I was not experienced as a lawyer because I was under 25 years of age. I appeared in the exam, returned to Delhi and resumed my teaching, almost forgetting about the exam for judgeship.

After a few months, I was busy in college, rehearsing the girls for a play. The play was based upon Shakespeare's 'As You Like It' and one of the students came running to me to tell, "There is a telegram for you, sir." When I opened the telegram, it stated, 'Selected as Judge.' As it happened to be April 1, I thought the telegram was engineered by the girls to make fun of me, the professor. Later on, I was duly informed about my selection and I could not resist being happy at my selection as a judge, though I loved to teach at the college. It appeared as if Bhagsunath astrologer's forecast had come true.

I was appointed a civil judge and magistrate at Mansa, a town in Punjab. A judge could be transferred to another station in the state after three years. Additionally, promotion to the appellate level was made on the basis of seniority and performance. A person of my age, based upon the official document recording the standing of every judge, could be nominated to the High Court as a justice before becoming a Supreme Court judge.

I must have decided hundreds of cases in ten years of my judicial work. There were some substantial and important cases, out of which some stayed in memory for simple humane reasons; not for judicial eminence or scholarship.

Memorable Cases

1. The first case that I tried as a judge was a criminal case. An accused person was presented in my court by the prosecutor and was accompanied by a defence attorney. The accused was arrested by the police for illegally brewing liquor, in violation of the Indian Excise Act. The accused was poverty ridden, scantily clad and stood with folded hands, as if pleading for mercy. The prosecutor explained the charges to the court. When asked to plead, the defendant's attorney communicated that the defendant pleaded guilty. The family of the accused – a wife and four children, stood in tears. I fixed a date for pronouncing the sentence. On studying the documents of the case and the law of the subject, I found that the minimum sentence for the offence was two years of rigorous imprisonment without any exception. The court had no discretion or leeway, even in the case of a guilty plea.

The prosecution charge was very simple. The accused was a very poor man who made his living by brewing one or two bottles of country liquor as he had no job or income to live on, I feared his family members would become beggars or die of hunger, etc. I was a young man, hailing from a cosmopolitan city of Delhi, with very idealistic views. I kept on researching by reading all kinds of material on probation, etc., to find a way out for the accused. I discovered I could not do anything within the legal framework to help the accused.

On the day of sentencing, everybody from the lawyers' bar chamber was assembled in the courtroom as it was my first case. The prosecutor was smiling and the defendant's lawyer, who I thought was stupid because he should not have confessed the guilt, was present too. I gave my decision. "I hereby release the accused on probation and he will have to report to the police station once a month." The prosecutor jumped up and said, "Your honour, you cannot do that." I told him, "Look, Mr. Prosecutor, my decision is the law of the land at this time, until it is overturned by the Superior Court." He looked at me and interjected, "But..." I interrupted, "Do not say 'but'. If you say anything else, you will be charged with contempt of court." After this, the news spread like wildfire and the lawyers began talking about a young judge and his first decision prompted by intuition rather than the law. The appellate judge heard the news and asked me in the evening, at the club house, "What did you do, Judge Agnihotri?" I replied, "I could not do anything else. This was my first case and I could not send one man and his entire family to virtual death. You may overrule me." However, no appeal was filed.

That was the first decision and I felt good about it. I was pleased that I could do real justice with mercy in my own way. I could not have done it any other way.

2. Another interesting criminal case filed in my court involved two important persons from Mansa Mandi, the seat of my court. The established procedure for arguments was followed, then the case was fixed for judgement. I gave a date after a week for judgement/decision. From that day onwards, I received so many recommendations from both the parties and from top leaders of the state, including the Chief Minister. The other judge in town stopped by my house and had the audacity to tell me that I could make a lot of money if I were to tell

a day before the decision date as to who would win the case. I was shocked. I couldn't throw him out of my house because he was my senior. I went to the court on the date fixed for judgement. Everybody in the court was looking askance at me. I had figured out the problem: both were leaders, both were millionaires both were political enemies of each other. Both had strong connections and it appeared even the community was divided. When they appeared in court, I looked at them. They appeared ready to go to jail, but I acquitted the defendant.

3. I was later transferred to Gurgaon, where too I had a very interesting experience. Two lawyers came to the court and one said that he wanted a declaration that his client had divorced his wife. I saw the wife and the file. She was a Muslim girl, whose lawyer said that she was not divorced. I had acquired recent knowledge of Muslim law and was surprised why they had come to court for this determination. I told the lawyer of the husband, "Your client has just to say, 'talaq' three times and the divorce is done under your law by which you claim to be governed." The lawyer looked at me, while the other lawyer smiled. He asked his client to say 'talaq' three times. I just wrote two lines on the file indicating that they were divorced. Thereafter, I talked to the lawyers and asked why they had not studied the case properly before coming to court. In all eventuality they wanted to make money.

4. I used to conduct a court in Sultanpur Lodhi at Kapurthala twice a week. It was a beautiful place and the courtroom was at the top of a fort. One day there was a large crowd in front of the court, and they came in with the lawyers. One set represented one party, that is, the boy; the other set represented the girl. I was curious and I asked them what the case was all about. They gave me the documents and I glanced at the parties. The plaintiffs, the boy's party, were asking for divorce from the girl. The boy and girl were hardly in their twenties. Under the Hindu Marriage Act, the judge has to do some counselling before trying the case. I asked both the girl and the boy to come to my chamber. The lawyers wanted to come too but I told them, "No, it is only for the boy and the girl and me." I asked the boy and girl, "What's the problem. Don't you like each other?" They were bashful as they were recently married. After drinking tea and eating some sweets, which I asked my assistant to bring from the shop across the court, in about ten minutes, they blurted out their whole story. The crux of the

problem was that their families were pushing for separation because of family pride. Under some custom, after the marriage, the girl's brother was expected to escort his sister back after the first visit to her new family. The brother of the girl could not do so and this gave rise to a dispute. After a few more minutes of pleasant talk, I asked them if they loved each other. They said, "Yes." I said, "Why don't you just go and live independently somewhere?" They asked me how they could do so. I told them to go to their uncle's home, which was close to the boy's and to work and start living till the family took them back. I asked my assistant to give his bicycle to them and let them go from the back-door and that they would return the bicycle the next day. I asked my assistant to stay in the chambers until they had gone away. The clerk came after some time to say, "Sir, the lawyers want to have the case heard." I asked, "Which case? Oh, that case is gone." I had made the complainant, the boy, to make a statement on record withdrawing the case. Then I went into the courtroom and told them, "They have gone somewhere and the case has been withdrawn by the plaintiff." The lawyers became red with anger. I said, "Don't be mad. You are only the lawyers, not the parties." I also gave my own advice to them that lawyers should not be disrupting things, but should figure out how to resolve issues. This episode became the talk of the town.

5. I was a judge in New Delhi. In a case of eviction of a tenant, I decided that the tenant must leave the property immediately. It was based upon evidence and history. The bailiff took the order to the property for execution but before he could serve the order, the other person standing in the house asked the bailiff to get out. He mentioned that he was a police chief and he would not let him evict the tenants, who were his relatives. The bailiff came to court the next morning and reported the incident in writing. He told us that the person who stopped the process was the police chief of Delhi. I studied the file and issued a warrant for arrest of the police chief for interfering in the judicial process. The news spread like wildfire about my handling the issue. Before evening, people started calling me, warning me not to go along with the warrant because the police chief was very influential. I told them, "Forget it." Some higher-ups in the government called me. I told them, "I am sorry. I can't help." Then arrived a group of prominent lawyers to request for leniency. I told them that the police chief has

to come to court and apologise in writing for his behaviour. The next morning, the police chief came and apologised. He said, "Your Honour, if I were to give it in writing, I would lose in my job." I said, "Okay, go. Don't do it again in future."

6. In another memorable case, one lawyer came to the court with an application that despite the fact that I had decided his client's case against the Government of India, the government did not pay the amount owed in the judgement, despite multiple requests and reminders. He showed to the court all the documents with copies of the request in his effort to execute the court order. As I was a judge with a difference, I asked the lawyer to do something unthinkable. I asked him to get the details of the engine of the Frontier Mail, the train which leaves the New Delhi station in the late evening. He understood what I was trying to say, and within an hour brought me the details and filed a petition to attach the engine, which belonged to the Government of India. I issued the order and suggested the lawyer to go to the railroad station half an hour before the train time, and hand over the attachment order to the head of the Railways. The idea was that the train, full of passengers was ready to leave within minutes and the engine was attached but couldn't move. In this short time, they could not arrange for the kind of engine needed for a long journey. It worked. As soon as he handed over the court order to the station master, he had no other choice but to immediately arrange for payment of the amount owed by the government. Of course, later on, the law was amended to say that the property of the Government of India couldn't be attached without notice, etc.

7. The Chief Justice of India, as administrative head of the Supreme Court, fired his stenographer perhaps for some good reason. He didn't give the reasons. The case was filed by the stenographer against the Chief Justice with a request to reinstate him. Under the Indian Constitution, no such government servant can be fired without due process under the law. As required by procedure, I asked the lawyer representing the Chief Justice where the defendant was. He had to be present in court in this case. The lawyer said, "Your Honour, please don't expect him to come to the court." I said, "Why not? He is not the Chief Justice of India in his judicial capacity in this case. He is an administrator firing a government servant working for him and the requirement is that he

has to appear in the court." The lawyer said that he needed some time. I am sure he persuaded the Chief Justice of India and the person was reinstated in a few days' time before the next hearing in the court.

8. I was known to be a very fast judge. Many old cases were pending in the courts of Delhi. The Chief Justice decided to establish a special court to expedite those cases efficiently and quickly. Out of all the judges in Delhi, I was selected by the Chief Justice to be the head of the Old Cases Court. All the cases which were considered very old were transferred from the different courts to my court. I looked into the history of all the cases duly prepared by my staff, spending day and night. I had asked them to prepare the list according to seniority of oldness. I found one case which needed my immediate attention. I immediately summoned the lawyers of that case. They were all senior lawyers, mostly practising in the Supreme Court, but they had to come. I told them that I was embarrassed that not only it was a very old case, but the case was older than I was! I told them that I couldn't tolerate that my age seniority was being challenged by a case, which was 35-years old. I knew the reasons for the delay because I had read the case history. The lawyers reacted in a half serious manner about their inability to do anything about it. I told them that they were very senior lawyers and that I had been asked by the Chief Justice to clear the embarrassingly old cases as early as possible. I further told them that case would be tried on a day-to-day basis from that day onwards. The lawyers jumped, "Sir, we have cases in the High Court and the Supreme Court. We cannot just be tied up." I told them that I was tied up and they had to be there. If not, I would take appropriate action under the law and procedure. They threatened that they would approach the Supreme Court at which I told them, "You be here the next day." They did approach the Chief Justice and he said he could not do anything because I had been following his directions. He suggested that they should make some alternate arrangements for representation. The next day, the lawyers appeared and I told them, "Look, there is one way out. You sit down and come to a compromise. You have made ample money from the case over the years because it is a big estate and you are earning fees on an appearance basis, and, that is why, the case is not decided. Generations have gone by and the estate is still feeding lawyers." That was not fair. They put their heads together and in a few

days' time, settled the case. They knew I meant business, and I had the backing of the Chief Justice.

9. A divorce case was filed in my court by a boy. The family was very actively involved and were citing some flimsy grounds against the girl. I called the lawyers to the chamber and asked them what was going on. They explained that the couple was not getting along with each other and primarily it was the boy who wanted to get rid of the girl. The boy's party was richer than the girl's party. Weddings in India are very expensive, especially for the girl's family. A lot of money is squandered on dowry and receptions and ceremonies. I went to the courtroom and asked the boy if he wanted a divorce. He said 'yes'. Then I told them, "You can have a divorce if you repay every penny spent by the girl's parents for this marriage, including dowry, receptions, parties, clothes, gifts and anything else." I asked the girl and his father to prepare a list of everything to the penny that was spent. I gave them two weeks' time to come back with a list. The plaintiff ended up paying a lot of money, and the divorce was granted.

10. I had become an Appellate Judge before I came to the USA. I was in the courtroom until 4 p.m. on the last day, working as a judge. A case was presented to me at about 3 o'clock against a young man for stealing. The boy was hardly 18 years of age. I asked him, "Why did you do it?" He admitted that he did it, and that he stole because his family needed some money. I told the prosecutor, "I am going to let this boy go on probation." He asked, "Sir, why?" I said, "Because this is my last case in the court." He didn't know that. He told everybody in the courtroom that I was leaving. Lo and behold, before 4 o'clock, hundreds of lawyers came to my courtroom and began to compliment me and asking me why I had not given them enough opportunity to give me a party, etc. Anyway, I had decided my first case in Mansa ignoring the law, but doing social justice. In the last case also, I did the same thing: I saved the young man's future by giving him a pep talk and letting him go.

Transfer Challenged

The trial judges in the state judiciary are transferred generally after three years. The purpose is that a judge should not get too close to the people and the lawyers, which may affect their honesty and fairness. At one time, I worked at Kapurthala for a few months when I got the transfer order to go to Mansa. I was shocked. Kapurthala was a desirable station. Every judge wanted to go there because it had good houses and a good environment as it was capital of a former kingdom of Maharaja. I was upset. I inquired from the High Court where the Chief Justice was. They told me that he was holidaying at Manali in Kulluvalley. I took the plane for the first time in my life from Chandigarh to Kulu and went on horseback to the upper mountains of Manali where the Chief Justice was camping. I told him who I was and that I was there to offer my resignation in person from the position of judgeship. He said, "Why?" I told him I was transferred in a few months' time from one place and sent back to the place I started and for no reason. I thought he figured out that the Registrar who ran the High Court administration must have obliged somebody. He told me, "Please don't do any such thing. Just go back to your station. I will handle it." I came back and my transfer orders were cancelled.

Justice William O. Douglas and Berkeley, California

When I was at Dharamshala, I developed a liking for mountaineering. At that time, Justice William O. Douglas was a Justice on the U.S. Supreme Court. He was on a trip to the Himalayas. He had been afflicted by polio in early life, but he was a very determined person. Ignoring his infirmity, he climbed mountains in different parts of the world. On his trip to the Himalayas, he was planning to go all the way to the Rohtang Pass after crossing Kullu and Manali. I had the opportunity to be with him. I was 17 years of age at that time. I was anti-capitalism at that time and harboured a very poor impression of America. We used to have long discussions on it. He tried to convince me that America was not all that bad, that there were all kinds of people in America and the beauty was that America was a democratic and free country. He encouraged me to come to America for studies.

Later on, when I finished law and became a judge and had worked for 10 years, I wished to go to the USA for higher education. I wrote to Justice Douglas about my plans to come to USA and apply to a law school for an L.L.M. He welcomed the idea and recommended joining the University of California at Berkeley law school, known as Boalt Hall. He wrote that Berkeley was the best place for exposure to real America. I decided to attend Boalt Hall. I applied and was accepted.

I landed in California in 1967. Interestingly, when I told the Dean of Boalt Hall about the recommendation of Justice Douglas regarding Boalt Hall, he was very anxious to get the letter from me. I declined by saying that as it was a personal letter to me, I would not like to share it with others without his permission.

Interesting Experiences in California

I secured assistantship to work for 15 hours at the library of University of California. I was assigned to do research on the cross-cultural study of world leaders through computers. I knew very little about computers. There was only one computer at the military facility off the campus. I reported to Dr. Rose, who was head of the faculty. I received an interesting shock when I asked Dr. Rose about my working hours. She said, "You can work any time." Coming from India, it was strange. I had another problem: I was concerned about my image, so I had to work at least twenty hours per week to be sure I was not considered deficient in my work. It was also unusual for me that despite coming from New Delhi and being a judge, I was given by Dr. Rose the keys to the whole library for entering at any hour of the day or night. I asked her, "How can you trust people like that?" She said, "We may have one in one hundred who would cheat, but why should we punish 99 others? The system should bear the misdeed of one deviant person."

Another instance of my surprise was when I went to a telephone company to get a connection for my apartment. A young lady at the reception counter asked me if I had the necessary deposit fees to pay. I told her that I didn't have the money, but would receive it in a month's time. She looked at me and waived the necessary deposit. It was unthinkable in India to provide that kind of a waiver. I was impressed, and I could see why America was what it was.

It was the hippy era and it was fashionable to smoke marijuana. Some of adventurers would even try LSD. I was invited to many groups/parties and I could see most of them smoking. They would offer me a smoke, but I would reply, "No. I am on a student visa." They could understand my predicament.

I was sharing an apartment with another law student. He was very smart. We shared a kitchen. Mostly we spent our time studying. One day, his girlfriend came almost running to my apartment. She looked panicky and said, "Bhishma, Dan is on a trip! He is on the road almost dancing. Please do something!" I went down and saw where he was and managed to get him inside the apartment. It took about a day and a half for him to come to his regular senses. I asked him why he did it. He said he had to experiment LSD. Later on, we came to know how many young people destroyed their lives by getting into those kinds of trips. Haight-Ashbury was the area where every such activity went on. I went to that area along with my friends to see what everyone was talking about. One could see all kinds of mixed-up people. We could also see the slowly driving big cars where parents were peeping out to see whether their kids who had left were anywhere visible on the streets, which were filled with hippy crowds. Many young people had left their posh homes for a wayward life in that region. Though the law college was not really into that kind of drug culture, many students were awkwardly dressed or had grown long hair.. One of our friends told us that his parents had given him the offer that he would get a Cadillac (car) if he shaved himself on graduation day. They had come from Los Angeles. It was a wild environment in San Francisco/ Berkeley/Oakland.

Working with CRLA Programme for Native Americans

Come summer, I began looking for a job. I was told that a newly formed CRLA (California Rural Legal Assistance) programme may have an opening for a person like me. I talked to them and they offered me a position in Santa Rosa working in a program providing legal aid to Native Americans. I liked the idea. There were three lawyers working with CRLA. We travelled occasionally Berkeley to Santa Rosa. One of the three, son of Ambassador John Kenneth Galbraith, gave us a ride whenever we went to Santa Rosa. We shared our expenses. Later on, the three of us rented an apartment together. Working on this programme was a great experience and an eye-opener for me. Before going to Santa Rosa, I knew nothing about the conditions of Native Americans. I had heard stories of their misery and misfortune. In the reservations, they had lack of basic facilities, lack of clean water, and the children had to go to school on foot. The police did not cooperate with the Native Americans, even if they were wronged. There were cases of girls being molested, but no action was taken. It was enough to make me sick. However, our activities made many officials of the government angry. I remember one instance when the Secretary of Interior came to address the Native American group and ended up commenting in a paternalistic way that Native Americans should consider America to be their country. I couldn't resist interrupting by saying, "Please don't say that. These are the only people in America who have no other country. I could go to India; somebody can go to England; somebody can go to France and so on. But this land belongs to the people who have nowhere else to go. They have been maltreated by the so-called civilised West."

CRLA had filed suits against the government for not granting appropriate help to Native Americans; the government officials were raging mad. Even the then Governor Ronald Reagan was so upset that he asked the federal government not to reauthorise funds to CRLA. However, he did not succeed because there was a lot of popular support for those services. By the way, CRLA was the first legal aid society in America for Native Americans.

Historically, before Christopher Columbus came to America, people were living in North America, who were later called American Indians or Native Americans. It is estimated that there were over 10 million natives living in their lands for thousands of years before Christ. Initially, the relationship between the natives and the Europeans was friendly, primarily out of curiosity for the new arrivals. Later on, Native Americans became victims of cruelty, diseases and other high-handedness of the 'intruders'. Native Americans were later kicked out of their lands. The promises made to them were not honoured and wars and massacres were rampant. The helpless natives didn't know what to do. They had no help, no recognition and no resources to depend on. Most of the other people were in agreement with the atrocities committed by non-Indians. A few sympathised with them and that was how they engineered the Legal Aid Society for the Native Americans. At that time, we had some people who had sympathy for the natives and stood by them and provided help. One of them was Marlon Brando; later on, Robert F. Kennedy also joined the team.

During my work at the office of CRLA, besides attending to legal cases, I had a few occasions to interact with the Indians at their social events. Once I visited a dance programme of the Native Americans. One professor from Harvard, Mr. André Rudy was attending our programme of CRLA. He wanted to go with me and so we went to the top of the hill of the reservation to participate in the evening dance programme. There were volunteers standing outside the hall and they stopped us, saying that we could not go in as the whites were not allowed. I said, "You cannot deny me entry. I am the real Indian. You inherited your name from me. The whites thought that you were all Indians. So, you cannot stop me." They discussed amongst themselves and then told me, "Okay, you come on in. This other man cannot join." Then I stopped and said, "Maybe I should tell you what Indian culture is and it should be your culture too. For Indians," I said, "guests come first." I also recited a Sanskrit verse on this. After consulting others again, they said, "Okay, we make an exception this time. You may join us." Rudy was very happy. I enjoyed the dance because their singing tone was close to the recital of Sanskrit verses from holy books. I liked the ceremonial way of singing and dancing.

Every time I observed Native Americans, I grieved for their plight. They had lost their territory, their moorings, their ambitions and their hopes. Professor Adam Crepelle of Southern University Law Center and I discussed the condition of native Americans. He sent me the following comments, which are worthy of reproduction: "The United States' American Indian citizens remain at the bottom of most socio-economic indicators. Life expectancy is less than 50 years old in some parts of Indian country[29] while the average reservation unemployment has remained over 50 per cent for years.[30] Hence, Indians have the highest poverty rate in the United States.[31] Despite constituting 1.7 per cent of the United States population in the 2010 Census,[32] seven of the eight poorest counties in the United States are majority American Indians.[33]Indians are also victims of violent crime at twice the rate of any other group[34] and have the highest rate of substance abuse.[35] The primary reason for the socio-economic malaise affecting American Indians is that American Indians still lack full rights under United States law;[36] indeed, the United Nations has described the United States American Indian policy as 'out of step with contemporary legal developments in indigenous rights.'"[37]

Although American Indians continue to endure hardships, there are many positive stories. Some of the 573 federally recognised tribes have managed to transform their economies and are actively engaged in preserving their language and revitalising their culture. Tribes have recently achieved major legislative success with the reaffirmation of their inherent sovereignty to prosecute non-Indian criminals who commit crimes on their land.[38] In 2014, the first American Indian was confirmed as a United States Ambassador[39] and the first American Indian woman was appointed as a federal judge.[40] The first two American Indian women were elected to Congress in November of 2018.[41] There is a new found pride in being American Indian. One hopes this will be a harbinger of a bright future for North America's first citizens.

□

6

Dr. Martin Luther King, Jr.—Southern University Law Center—Israel Peace Medal

When I was in India, we were inspired by the contribution of Dr. Martin Luther King, Jr. for social justice for all in America and elsewhere. It was akin to our regard for the standing of Mahatma Gandhi for freedom from tyranny of the British rulers. My dream was to meet Dr. Martin Luther King, Jr. The following short comments on the life of Dr. King are worth mentioning.

Dr. Martin Luther King dreamt that all inhabitants of the United States would be judged by their personal qualities and not by the colour of their skin. In April 1968 he was murdered by a white racist. Four years earlier, he had received the Peace Prize for his nonviolent campaign against racism.

King adhered to Gandhi's philosophy of nonviolence. In 1955 he began his struggle to persuade the US Government to declare the policy of racial discrimination in the southern states unlawful. The racists responded with violence to the black people's nonviolent initiatives.

In 1963, 250,000 demonstrators marched to the Lincoln Memorial in Washington, where King gave his famous "I have a dream" speech. The following year, President Johnson got a law passed prohibiting all racial discrimination.

But King had powerful opponents. The head of the FBI, John Edgar Hoover, had him placed under surveillance as a communist, and when King opposed the administration's policy in Vietnam, he fell into disfavour with the President. It has still not been ascertained whether King's murderer acted on his own or was part of a conspiracy."

While I was at Berkeley I had the opportunity to attend the program where Dr. King made a speech on the steps of Sproul Hall at the university. I was a member of the International Law Association of the law school and as such, got a seat. I was totally inspired by the powerful discourse of Dr. King. I still remember some of the words of his speech. Later that day, I had the opportunity to meet him. I introduced myself as a judge from India on leave to study at the law school and that I was also working for American Indians needing help to emerge from their miserable existence. I narrated my disgust with their treatment I remember he asked me, "Do you like America?" I said, "Yes, I do," and I explained why I liked this country and would like to live here. After a few more comments, he looked at me with a confident look and suggested that I should go to the South. If I wanted action, I would have ample opportunities to help people.

Southern University Law Center

I followed Dr. King's suggestion and moved to Baton Rouge, Louisiana, and joined Southern University Law School as a professor. At this at time, this school needed support and attention. Before joining, I had a meeting with the president of the university and he assured me that the Law School would be adequately supported for its growth. We developed the school beyond expectations of anybody in the state and the nation.

For lack of space and time, I do not intend to detail the historic development of the Law School as a national law school of great leadership and commitment. I was the longest serving head of an American law school. The statement contained in the resolution passed by the joint session of the Louisiana legislature on honouring me for getting the YWCA Racial Justice Award gives in a nutshell the present glory of Southern University Law Center's development. The following is the copy of the resolution:

Louisiana Senate

Regular Session, 2001

SENATE CONCURRENT RESOLUTION NO. 78

BY SENATORS C. JONES, BARMHAM, BEAN, BOISSIERE, CAIN, CAMBELL, CHAISSON, DARDENNE, DEAN, DUPRE, ELLINGTON, C. FIELDS, W. FIELDS, FONTENOT, GAUTREAUX, HAINKEN, HINES, HOLLIS, HOYT, IRONS, B. JONES, LAMBERT, LENTINI, MARIONNEAUX, MCPHERSON, MOUNT, SCHEDLER, SMITH, TARVER, THEUNISSEN, THOMAS AND ULLO

A CONCURRENT RESOLUTION

To commend and congratulate Chancellor B.K. Agnihotri of Southern University Law Center on being selected to receive the YWCA Racial Justice Award for his leadership in efforts "to eliminate racism in the struggle for peace, justice, freedom, and dignity for all people."

WHEREAS, it is with great pride that the citizens of Louisiana have learned of this great honor bestowed upon Chancellor B.K. Agnihotri; and

WHEREAS, the award was presented at the conclusion of "A Super Dialogue on Race" Friday, April 29, 2001 at the Living Faith Christian Center; and

WHEREAS, Agnihotri has been a professor and chief administrative officer within the law Center, he has provided exemplary teaching, leadership, and vision to the institution whose more than 12,300 alumni have entered the legal profession to "right the wrongs and create a better world for Equal rights and justice for all'; and

WHEREAS, Chancellor B.K. Agnihotri is the longest sitting head of a law school in the nation, and through his leadership the Southern University Law Center has received national and international recognition.

THEREFORE, BE IT RESOLVED that the Legislature of Louisiana does hereby Acknowledge the many outstanding accomplishments of B.K. Agnihotri and recognizes the prestigious honor he has received as the recipient of the YWCA Racial Justice award.

BE IT FURTHER RESOLVED that a copy of this Resolution be transmitted to Chancellor B.K. Agnihotri.

AMERICAN B/ ? ASSOCIATION

Section of Legal Education and Admissions to the Bar

Office of the Consultant on Legal Education to the American Bar Association

Indiana University
550 West North Street, Suite 349
Indianapolis, Indiana 46202-3162
(317) 264-8340
FAX (317) 264-8355
http://www.abanet.org/legaled

February 1, 2000

Chancellor B. K. Agnihotri
Southern University
Law Center
Baton Rouge, LA 70813

Dear Chancellor Agnihotri:

I am writing to inform you that our review of the records of deans of 182 J.D. granting law schools approved by the American Bar Association indicate that you are the senior serving deans among American law school deans. This is a rare accomplishment on your part. The Section and I congratulate you on your many years of service in improving legal education at Southern University School of Law, and your participation in the international legal activities of the Section.

Sincerely,

James P. White

James P. White
Consultant on Legal Education
To the American Bar Association

JPW/mb

Israel Peace Medal and Honorary Doctorate

During this time, I also received an honorary doctorate (LL.D.) from a university in Tennessee. I also received the Israeli Peace Medal in 1996 for helping in the Middle East peace process.

I was pleased to receive the following communication from President Bill Clinton regarding the Israel Peace Medal.

THE WHITE HOUSE

WASHINGTON

September 8, 1995

Dr. Bhishma K. Agnihotri
Chancellor
Southern University Law Center
Post Office Box 9294
Baton Rouge, Louisiana 70813

Dear BK:

Congratulations as you are awarded the Israel Peace Medal for your lifelong efforts to promote the ideals of liberty and justice.

Your courageous commitment to democracy and freedom in Israel and around the world has set the highest standards for others to follow, and your dedication to preserving and protecting human rights merits our deepest gratitude. Using your broad knowledge of diverse cultures, you have helped to create lasting bridges of cooperation and understanding that have fostered new international partnerships.

I salute you on behalf of all those who have benefited from your wisdom and energy. Your devotion to humanity has made the world a better, safer place.

Sincerely,

Bill Clinton

EDWIN W. EDWARDS
GOVERNOR

State of Louisiana
OFFICE OF THE GOVERNOR
Baton Rouge
70804-9004

POST OFFICE BOX 94004
(504) 342-7015

June 27, 1995

The Honorable William J. Clinton
President of the United States
The White House
1600 Pennsylvania Avenue NW
Washington, D.C. 20500

Dear Mr. President:

I am delighted to learn that you have agreed to appear at the convention of the Association of American Physicians of Indian Origin Friday in Chicago because the group's honorary legal advisor who will introduce you is a good friend of mine, Bhishma Agnihotri.

Dean Agnihotri came to Louisiana 25 years ago to teach at Southern University's Law Center and became its dean five years later. Largely through his leadership, the law center has become a modern, well-funded facility and a model of diversity in faculty and student body.

The Dean has been of great help to me and other political leaders not only in higher education planning but also in other areas, public and private, and has taken an active role in civic activities in Baton Rouge, as well. As a practitioner of international trade law in the Middle East, he made and today maintains ties with friends in the industrial and commercial sectors worldwide.

I know you will enjoy having the opportunity to get acquainted with Dean Agnihotri as I have.

Kindest regards and best wishes,

Edwin W. Edwards

EWE:sj

7

Serving Diaspora Organisations — H.S.S. - AAPI - VEDIC Cultural Society— World Fellowship of Religions—ISKCON

As mentioned above, I was totally committed and engrossed in the development of the Law Center and tried to make it a national Law Center of repute and commitment. However, in addition, my commitments to Indian diaspora and its concerns did not lack my attention. I was naturally engaged in helping the cause of the diaspora. The following few areas received greater attention from me.

Hindu Swayamsevak Sangh—President (U.S. Sanghchalak)

The USA has quite a number of individuals who have been members of R.S.S. As is natural for the dedication of those people, they wanted to get together as a group and follow R.S.S. regimen —"Shakha," games, discussion and prayers. As there was no formal R.S.S. in existence, the meetings were arranged without any formal name. Many of those were also participants in the activities of Vishwa Hindu Parishad of America, which has been active since the 1970s.

In the late 1980s/early 1990s, the group's leaders suggested that H.S.S. should be formally established. It could not be named "R.S.S." because that name pertains to India. Therefore, H.S.S. was formally organised and duly established under the laws of the USA.

Before H.S.S. was established, member of the group met at Sidhachalam, the Jain ashram. When all the members were in place, I was given a paper which contained a list of office bearers of the H.S.S. The top of the list was my name as President of H.S.S. I looked at Ramlal Ji, who gave me the paper, and I said that somebody else should be given that responsibility. He said that the senior members of the group made the decision, and I had no other choice but to accept the presidency of the organisation. After I kept on working as the head of that organisation until I became Ambassador.

AAPI (American Association of Physicians of Indian Origin)

I was approached by Dr. Roshan Lal, M.D. in 1986, to be Legal Advisor of AAPI. Dr. Lal was the third President of AAPI and it was the beginning of AAPI when I was requested to help them as an Advisor. I agreed with Dr. Lal that I would not charge any fees for my services. I would do it because I wanted to be part of the development of AAPI as a major organisation in America because it would help create a powerful base for the Indian community and give inspiration to the future generations. Being part of the Indian community myself, I considered it my contribution to AAPI. I was advisor to AAPI until I became Ambassador in 2001.

I did what lawyers normally do, except that I did not appear in court. For that, I advised the doctors needing legal help to appoint a local attorney and I would interact with both the attorney and the doctor concerned. I was a participant on a regular basis in the meetings of AAPI and helped them develop their legal documents, ensuring that AAPI followed its constitution and by-laws, including the other technical issues. I was greatly honoured to do this. I interacted with wonderful persons with great qualifications and compassion. There were occasions, of course, when there were some disputes regarding the leadership or prospective leadership. I intervened wherever I could and most of the time I succeeded to keep the organisation on track. My basic desire was to build AAPI into a major powerhouse in America. In my speeches, I used to say, "You are 30,000 millionaires, and you can accomplish anything in America if you stay united."

American Association of Physicians of Indian Origin

Executive Office: 17W300 22nd Street, Suite 300A, Oakbrook Terrace, IL 60181-4490
Telephone: (630) 530-2277, Fax: (630) 530-2475, Website: www.aapiusa.org
Legislative Office: 1818 N Street NW, Suite 700, Washington, DC 20036
Telephone: (202) 331-0343, Fax: (202) 331-9306

AMERICAN ASSOCIATION OF PHYSICIANS OF INDIAN ORIGIN — AAPI

President
S. 'Jay' Jayasankar, MD
jaymd@massmed.org
O:(781) 790-1007
F:(781) 790-1008

President Elect
Kiran Patel, MD
kpatel@wellcarehmo.com
O:(813) 290-6328
F:(813) 290-6306

Vice President
Sharad Lakhanpal, MD
slakhanpal@arthritis-dallas.com
O:(214) 879-6700
F:(214) 879-6741

Secretary
Jagan Ailinani, MD
ajagan@aol.com
O:(618) 549-0721
F:(618) 457-0444

Treasurer
Akshay Desai, MD
adesai2145@aol.com
O:(727) 321-0818
F:(727) 321-7832

Immediate Past President
Dayan Naik, MD
dnaik.md@att.net
O:(914) 723-3322
F:(914) 723-3592

Chair, Board of Trustees
Rajam Ramamurthy, MD
ramamurthyr@uthscsa.edu
O:(210) 567-5228
F:(210) 567-5169

YPS President
Ruchi Gupta, MD
ruchi@residentweb.com
H:(206) 352-6595

MS/R Section President
Majid Basit, MD
basitmajid@yahoo.com
H:(713) 796-8246

Regional Directors:
Elly Bhuyan, MD
Sudeep Kukreja, MD
Suresh Malhotra, MD
Birinder Marwah, MD
Hemant Patel, MD
Rachakonda Prabhu, MD
Sanku Rao, MD
Sampat Shivangi, MD
Ram Upadhyay, MD

Legal Advisor
Bhishma Agnihotri, JD
bkagni3@iamerica.net
O:(225) 771-2552
F:(225) 752-5240

Legislative Director
Anurag Varma, JD
av@cfpplaw.com

Executive Director
Lanny Hardy
lhardy@aapiusa.net

Dedicated to
EXCELLENCE · COMPASSION · COMMUNITY · ADVOCACY

September 13, 2001

Bhishma Agnihotri, JD
18110 North Mission Hills Avenue
Baton Rouge, LA 70810

Dear Agnihotriji:

First to congratulate on the phone, let me formally congratulate you on your appointment as the first Ambassador at large for the Indian Diaspora. Over the past 16 years you have done so much voluntary work for AAPI that I do not even know how to begin to thank you. This appointment shows how diverse your community involvement has been and continues to be.

You have been a great asset not only to the AAPI, but also to the Indian Community and the United States. Over the years I knew that we could always count on you when the times were demanding; you would always be there.

Prema's and my hearts are filled with joy and pride at this recognition. The Indian Government had many people to choose from and they chose the right person.

Please accept our congratulations and best wishes in this endeavor and for your wife and family.

Sincerely,

Jayasankar

S. 'Jay' Jayasankar, MD

SEP-24-2001 05:59P FROM:BK AGNIHOTRI 225 752 5240 TO:17167797254 P:1/1

In 1995, the leadership in AAPI sought my help to invite President Clinton to the AAPI convention in Chicago. My association with President Clinton was well known. I invited him to join AAPI on June 30, 1995, for its annual convention and he readily agreed. On May 5, 1995, I received a letter from William Webster IV, Director of Scheduling and Advance, that the President would be able to join on June 30 (*see* Appendix II). The President came to the meeting accompanied by his wife, Hillary Clinton. It was a great programme and very well attended.

President Clinton and Lata Mangeshkar

Something very unique happened. Some official of AAPI invited the famous Indian singer Lata Mangeshkar for the convention and told her that she would be honoured by the President. Somebody mentioned to me that Lataji was distressed because there was nothing scheduled for her presence, let alone any programme for honouring her. I went to see her because along with every other Indian, I grew up enjoying her songs. She is a unique person. I requested her to stay cool and would see what I could do. The President and Mrs. Clinton were in a holding area and I asked him to meet Lataji. I told him that Lataji is respected by everybody in India. Additionally, I said that seeing her would give him good luck for his coming election for the second term. He agreed. I brought Lataji and her companion singer to see President Clinton. He respectfully met her and a photograph was taken. She was pleased; their picture is in the book.

Vedic Cultural Society and World Hindu Conference

When we came to Baton Rouge, there were not too many families of Indian origin. Our kids were young, and the women were homesick. So I called all the families of Indian origin to meet every Sunday to stay in touch with the culture and the uplifting values and literature of India. Thereafter, the group began meeting every Sunday in different homes. I drafted and got approved 501(c)(3) document for tax exemption purposes, and it also reflected our organisation structure. We didn't have any president or any other office bearer. We gave the responsibility to a group of six people who would take yearly turns to run the operation of the society. The idea was not to serve any ambitious individual but to build a society dedicated to service. Later, I was told by the officials of the IRS that ours was perhaps the first community-based religious/cultural organisation of Indians in America to receive RS 501(c)(3) approval.

Vedic Cultural Society was a comparatively small organisation, but it hosted the World Hindu Conference in 1980 (*see* Appendix III). Vishwa Hindu Parishad was the main body to spearhead the conference. Its programme was held at the Centroplex in Baton Rouge, Louisiana. Interestingly, ours was the first programme held in the Centroplex. More than 30 countries sent representatives and close to 1,000 persons attended the programme. A great many thinkers representing different groups and sects made presentations and were appreciative of the gathering. A book of regular weekly recitation was prepared, which became a guide for many similar groups formed all over the country.

World Fellowship of Religions

In the 1970s, Muni Sushil Kumar visited Baton Rouge. He was the spiritual leader of Jainism in India. He addressed the community in Baton Rouge. Later we requested him to stay on in America to spread the message of peace and brotherhood of Jainism in this country. He agreed and we arranged for his permanent visa to stay in this country. He got the approval from the appropriate authority in a record two weeks' time. Muniji was a great scholar, a spiritualist and almost worshipped by the Jain community. Later we decided to form a World Fellowship of Religions with Muniji as the founder president. I was the secretary general of the organisation. There were more than 60 distinguished scholars and spiritual leaders from all over the world as active members (*see* Appendix III). Our office was in 777 United Nations Plaza in New York City. We organised many programmes on various occasions to spread the message of peace. One of the highlights of the group was the decision to establish a World Monotheism Centre, which was supported by the Shah of Iran. A comprehensive statement was prepared highlighting the oneness of world religions and naming the Centre as Temple of Understanding. The financial commitment was made for the Temple of Understanding. Unfortunately, the King of Iran was not well and had come to America for treatment. There was a revolution in Iran and the king was ousted from power. Khomeini had taken over.

ISKCON (International Society for Krishna Consciousness)

I had the opportunity to meet Swami Prabhupada in New York in 1972 while studying at New York University. At that time, his movement known as ISKCON was in the very initial stage. He was kind to me and asked me to stay in touch. It was unbelievable to see the way ISKCON grew up in America and all over the world. It was principally because of the scholarly and affectionate commitment of the followers. Its impact in the religious discourse of the American world was well known.

I was approached by the leadership of Hare Krishna movement to help them in their cases. I was not a member of ISKCON, but I had empathised with their commitment and sincerity. I was asked to help them in a case against the president of ISKCON temple in New York. As a co-chairman of World Fellowship of Religions, I made a presentation. One of the paragraphs, which has been quoted many times by ISKCON people, reads as follows:

'It appears, sometimes, some over-conscious parents get concerned about the changed dress style of their sons and daughters on their joining the society. Their apprehension is unfounded and misplaced. The authorities in the society cannot judge the quality of a faith on the superficial exterior. I think this country should thank the Hare Krishna movement and other such faiths who have taught the West to search for the real self in the human being, minus his possessions, his wealth and wardrobes.'

I also appeared as a lawyer in the Supreme Court of the United States in the case by International Society of Krishna Consciousness of California, *et al.* (petitioners) vs. Robin George and Marcia George (respondents) and we won that case.

I attended some of the programmes of ISKCON, but most of my time was consumed by other professional activities. However, they stayed in touch with me and were appreciative of my help (*see* Appendix III).

□

8

Moving to New York as Ambassador-at-Large After 9/11

International terrorism has a long history going back to the 18th century. Following the French Revolution, subdued by terror of the enemies of liberty, Maximilian Robespierre coined the word 'terror'. It is a long history, but it increased in intensity in the 1960s and 1970s. The latest movement was inspired by Al Qaeda. Suicide terrorism was inspired by extremist Islamic preaching wherein kids were brainwashed to resort to terrorism to reach heaven for virgins after death. America stayed safe and considered itself out of the reach of terrorists. They were shocked on September 9, 2001 when Islamic terrorists hijacked civilian airlines and used them to attack the World Trade Centre towers in New York City. In addition to causing harm to people in Washington D.C., other countries were subjected to terrorism in many ways. For example, in New Delhi, even the Parliament was attacked by terrorists; Bali was attacked by a car bomb; a train in Madrid was bombed; and many such instances can be added. One of the most heinous attacks was in Mumbai. People in the USA always felt safe from these kinds of attacks, but that secure feeling was nullified by the September 11, 2001, attack. Two prestigious towers were destroyed, 2,996 persons were killed, 7,000 were injured and the casualties covered almost all nationalities. It shook up New York, the home of people from all sections of the world. New York, which welcomes every outsider with love and grace, was horrified.

I got all the clearance immediately after the attack by terrorists. I resigned from my job at the Law Center and headed to New York, my new area of action, without any delay. It was a very sensitive time;

people were not travelling. Most of the people were scared of further terrorist attacks. My plane was almost empty. I reached New York and was anxious to work promptly to help the victims of the tragedy. The Consulate in New York, under the instructions of the MEA, provided me an assistant and a car and driver. We had to wait for more people to be assigned by the Government of India. It is interesting that the person who was provided to me as an assistant was known to be a difficult person in the Consulate. He himself told me that he would not get a promotion because he would speak the truth, and he would otherwise be considered difficult to work with. I had been an administrator all my life. I had run a law center for more than 28 years. I understood the adjustment problem of workers. I asked him to start working. I told the driver that though his job was driving, I would expect him to work on some papers, too, like bringing newspaper clippings and pasting them in proper form so that we could have a regular information collection and storage set-up.

I had to take blessings before I actually started my work. I visited the Swami Narayan temple in New Jersey. It is known as Baps temple. The temple was also engaged at that time in a prayer meeting for the victims of the World Trade Center. They were also involved in fundraising for the survivors and their families. This environment was conducive to start immediately to connect with families of the victims of the September 11th attack. I had lived in America for 30 years, so I had a high regard for the fairness and respect for their values. In India, of course, we have been used to acts of terrorism on a regular basis.

It was a shock in America – a country of freedom and liberty, a country of equal opportunity to all, a country which is open to all faiths, a country where a person can live without giving bribes. America was in pain and in pain were the families of the victims. I visited a few affected families; their pain stayed with me. One family I visited was in Yonkers, New York, and the victim was Mrs. Valsa Raju. When I was at their place, a prayer meeting was in progress. Mrs. Raju was from a devout Christian family, so the leaders of the community were present to express their sorrow. I met the husband, and he talked to me at length about his wife, her job and going to her office the morning of the attack. Many of the persons there were still in a state of shock. Some of them didn't believe that Mrs. Raju was gone; they thought she was still alive. When I went to the other part of the house, there were the kids playing, running, laughing and giggling, obviously unmindful of the situation. Their mother had just gone to work. She was not sick; she would be back. I offered the husband all the support we could give and to contact us at any time. I returned to my office, unable to digest this onslaught on humanity, which lives in New York. The whole world in terms of every nationality lives in New York. Hundreds of languages are spoken but all live as one united family.

I visited another family of late Shekhar Kumar. He had been married about nine months before the attack. His wife had recently joined him, just a few months before the attack. When I visited them, the lady was in a state of shock. Her brother had come to New York soon after the tragedy. His father also came along. The wife could not believe that her husband was dead. Friends were making all kinds of suggestions and somebody advised her to talk to an astrologer. She along with her brother met the astrologer who said that her husband was not dead; he was somewhere 30 miles southwest of New York. The wife and her brother should go in that direction and try to find Shekhar Kumar. Their theory was that the husband had escaped the attack and was running around in a state of shock. I also met many other sufferers in many different places and could see the tragedy, dismay and helplessness on their faces.

The External Affairs Minister, Shri Jaswant Singh, visited New York. I accompanied him to various places organised for the victims' families to provide information and other assistance. Later, we visited the action office for helping the victims' families. Mayor Giuliani was there to receive us. An awkward situation occurred when Mayor Rudy Giuliani started talking to me, ignoring our minister. I led him to meet the minister, who had brought a few things from India as a token of India joining America in their period of tragedy and grief. The minister presented a few items to the Mayor as a token of India's support. A programme was organised at the Union Square Park in Manhattan where we expressed our sympathy for the injury inflicted on the psyche and humanity of America.

□

9

Goals and Activities as NRI Ambassador

In order to perform my duties as an Ambassador, we had to establish some goals, markers and ideals followed by relevant action. On December 9, 2001, at the Crown Plaza Hotel in Milpitas, CA, I laid out an ambitious plan of action to advance several overriding and significant goals that I had established for myself as the Indian Ambassador-at-Large. These goals maybe summarised as follows:

First, I saw my role as encouraging building unity among the Indian diaspora, especially in the Indo-American associations through unanimous action. This would enable the Indian diaspora to exercise greater bargaining power in the arena of American politics and facilitate India to secure its legitimate status as a full member of the United Nations Security Council. National goals had to be tackled in unison at the national level.

Second, because the second-generation Indians seemed to be drifting away from the great heritage and culture of India, it was necessary to find a mechanism, whereby they would involve in projects that were dear to India and to the first generation of Indian diaspora. If the younger people of the diaspora were given the freedom of involvement, the results would be positive.

Third, Indians living in various countries across the globe needed to interact with the mainstream population and institutions. This could be accomplished by the Indian community working with social, cultural, economic and political organisations, while retaining and advancing the values of the Indian family and community.

Fourth, because Indians living in other countries could not live in isolation, it was essential to develop closer socio-economic and political ties with India. NRIs and PIOs had to strengthen their interactions with India, thus guaranteeing their continued connection and help for India's development.

Finally, the Indian diaspora is an international, nay a global, community. As I said at the time, 'the sun never sets on the global Indian community, 'hence, we should build global relationships among the diaspora with the intent of turning it into one family with common interests, common decisions and common sentiments.[42]

Unity

At the time of my appointment, the unity of the Indian-American community needed to be addressed. The non-resident Indians (NRIs) and the people of Indian origin (PIOs) needed to unite into one community. Whatever their respective background in India or whatever their professional or occupational associations be, these groups needed to speak with one voice. Region and religion, sects and creeds, cultures and traditions should not stand in the way of unity. Therefore, a minimum common programme was required around which the Indian diaspora could unify. I emphasised that only then would US policy-makers appreciate the role of the Indian diaspora in the wider American community.[43]

On various occasions, I noted that the organisations representing Indian Americans needed to overcome divisions and their trivial differences. I mentioned that there were approximately 300 Indian American organisations in Houston, 700 in New York City, and 80 in Chicago.[44] In many large metropolitan areas, there were between 30 and 100 Indian organisations to be found, each serving a relatively small group.[45] In such locations, I recommended that a core team of five volunteers be established in order to facilitate better co-operation among organisations.[46] One consequence of this fragmentation was that the extent of the relief for the victims of 9/11 had not been fully appreciated by the wider community because funds had been sent in by individual organisations. Such fragmentation of effort, I insisted, needed to be overcome. I suggested one way to proceed: establish an overarching organisation, a 'Council of Indian Americans', that embraced all non-resident Indians of whatever cultural or professional background they be.

Another element of a minimum common programme was to be for India American associations to urge their members to present their religious and cultural beliefs to their neighbours and co-professionals. In addition, the Indo-American community had not achieved its full potential but would do so once they began to make American policy-makers aware of their accomplishments and interests. For instance, I urged my audience at the Indian Cultural Center, in Houston, TX on October 12, 2001, to lobby with US policy-makers on how the recurrence of terrorism had 'hamstrung' India.[47]

Strengthening the Indian Diaspora

I was determined that the Indian diaspora needed to be strengthened. One critical challenge was bridging the gap between the first- and second-generation members of the Indian-American community. At one of my early press conferences, on October 3, 2001, I addressed my role in responding to this issue: "I will try to minimise differences and forge greater amity, friendship and togetherness. The second-generation is turning away from India as it finds the first generation engaged in constant infighting. I want to involve the second-generation Indians in a creative manner for the development of India."[48]

As the Indian Ambassador-at-Large, I travelled throughout India and the United States, Canada, England, Spain, France and Portugal to the island of Trinidad in the Caribbean Sea, and to Guyana and Surinam on the north-east coast of South America, and to the island of Mauritius in the Indian Ocean. There were over 20 million NRIs of which 1.9 million were to be found in the United States. I proposed a three-fold task. Beyond bridging the gap between the first generation and second-generation by getting them involved in projects related to India, I urged the youth to work for the motherland of their parents and grandparents by contributing to the economic development and infrastructure. Their contribution would, as I explained it, contribute to one global Indian family.

The 20 million plus Indians living overseas, if they acted as one united community, could 'give to all Indians abroad a strong sense of cohesion, unity and strength and also help India become a strong country'. It was (and remains) my firm opinion that Indians, no matter where they are from, should consider themselves to be members of one family. They must share their wealth, happiness, pain and sorrow within the family membership. If a member of the family needs help, everyone who can must help."[49]

Examples of how this might be achieved included offering the services of Indian-American doctors who would visit countries like Guyana for a month free of charge. I urged them that there should be better coordination among Indian-Americans and Indian-Guyanese. A second example of how an international family of Indians might cast a significant impact was with regard to raising the issue of human rights violations among the Indian-Fijians. A final possibility was that Indian-Americans and Indian-Canadians should connect at the local level with Americans and Canadians, respectively, in order to participate actively in the local, social, cultural and political life of their localities. In short, the youth of the Indian diaspora would become ambassadors of India to their places of residence.[50]

In seeking to bridge the gap between the first and second generations, I presented another approach during a public meeting held at Massachusetts Institute of Technology during my February 9-11, 2001, visit to Boston. Internships for the youth and retired individuals would be established so that both might work on projects related to India, held either in the United States or in India. One goal would be to foster emotional attachment to India and advance India's economic development.[51]

Finally, I helped to establish the *Pravasi Bharatiya Samman* (Overseas Indian Honour Award) and served on the first selection committee. First awarded on January 9, 2002, this honour recognised non-resident Indians and persons of Indian origin whose accomplishments were particularly meritorious. It also symbolised the contribution of all overseas Indians, wherever they resided, to the culture of India.

Fostering Ties Between the Indian Diaspora and India

In order to foster ties between the Indian diaspora and India, I, in my presentations to the community, specifically mentioned the outreach programmes for accomplishing that goal. In the address at the Mahatma Gandhi Community Centre in Houston, Texas, on

October 12, 2001, I said that I was interested in the constructive ideas and suggestions from retired NRIs in the US, especially those who could volunteer time for various projects to be introduced in India. I encouraged Indo-American college youth to spend their summers as interns in India.[52]

In a press conference at the Consulate General of India in New York City on October 3, 2001, I envisioned for myself a role to help the NRIs set up an education process to inform the natives about India and its culture. Citing the case of America, I said, the Indian doctors, engineers and other professionals should educate and inform their American counterparts, Congressmen and Senators about their country of origin.[53]

I said I was trying to get as many community associations as possible together and work out a common minimum programme to uplift India and to discuss India's issues. There are differences in different organisations. They had to develop something common so that they could count on the great reservoir of Indians in America for the sake of our motherland. The Indian government 'for the first time, has realised the strength, power and resources of NRIs'.[54]

In an address at the Crown Plaza Hotel in Milpitas, California, on December 9, 2001, I laid down more ways than one to strengthen the ties. The future of NRIs was closely linked with the future of India. "If India is great, you'll also be great. Your future is bright if the future of India is bright."[55]

"Give the community dreams. Make Indians best in the world. Learn from the Chinese expatriates, who have contributed a lot in China's progress," I said. Quoting Dr. I.G. Patel, former Governor, Reserve Bank of India, I said, "NRIs' heart is in India, but their money is somewhere else."[56]

I offered a five-point agenda for the Indian-American community – "Build bridges among Indian Americans. Chicago, I hear, has 80 Indian associations. We need to work together and find five issues on which we have no disagreement. If the community does this on a national level, imagine the clout we would have! We could then go to the White House and demand something for the community and our children, and our voice will be heard."[57]

I urged Indian-Americans to build a bridge with India: "Only 3 per cent of non-resident Indians invest in India, compared to 70 per cent of non-resident Chinese (in China). We talk of *Bharat Mata* all the time and complain of corruption and red tape in India. How can we remove these ills if we do not become active participants?"[58]

In an address at the Massachusetts Institute of Technology in Cambridge, Massachusetts in February 2002, I also saw a need for bridges amongst NRIs from different countries in order that all NRIs could become part of one community. Recent immigrants from India to the US, for example, should have better relations with Caribbean Indians in the US (whose forefathers had left India more than 150 years ago). Indians in difficult situations elsewhere in the world, like Fiji, should also be able to receive assistance from NRIs in the US.[59]

Elaborating my ideas of internships, in which the young and the retired would work on projects in the USA and in India, I said this would improve relations of USA with India, foster greater emotional attachment with India and of course, assist in development of India.[60]

I mentioned in the address on January 9, 2002, "NRIs helped India get her freedom, and the NRIs of today must help maintain that freedom and promote India's interests."[61]

It was laid down in the meeting that the topmost priority of my agenda was to establish unity among Indians settled abroad, and get coordination working between first- and second-generation Indians and those back home; and of course, keeping NRIs connected to their roots – socially, economically or culturally. "I also make sure that Indians in US maintain cordial relations with the Americans and are recognised for their varied contributions to the society."[62]

A larger international family of Indians, connecting NRIs and PIOs to India, unity in the Indian diaspora and involving second-generation Indians in projects back home were among the five major targets set by me.[63]I was quoted as saying, "Projection of India's image, creation of unity, addressing the concerns of NRIs and PIOs, development of an international Indian family or fraternity and harnessing the great potential NRIs and PIOs for the country."[64]

This being so, I was called upon to address many concerns, from the shabby-looking PIO card to furthering exchange programmes, to attracting foreign investment into India. My introduction to the audience, in fact, ended with the hope that I would 'ignite NRI-funds flow into the country'. Based in New York and with 20 million globally scattered people of Indian origin under my wing, I met various Indian groups, helped form councils in Washington, in New York and in Houston, and urged Indians to hire PR consultants abroad to prop up their image and to help them become more visible and vocal. I also organised a volunteer group of about 100 people who were close to retirement but could provide expert advice in various fields.[65]

Explaining my role as Ambassador-at-Large of India, I said this post was created solely to address the concerns of NRIs and PIOs all over the world. I stressed the need for NRIs to coordinate their political, economic and social efforts for the betterment of Indians and the Indian community everywhere. I emphasised the importance to develop a stronger voice in America and, thus, contribute to India's strength. "As NRIs, we have an obligation to stand up for ourselves as Indian-Americans and to support our homeland through financial and social contribution so that future generations will remain connected to India and their Indian heritage."[66]

In my speech, I said non-resident Indians should coordinate their political, economic and social efforts for the betterment of Indians everywhere. I said I had visited several countries where there were significant Indian populations, including Britain, the Caribbean and various parts of the US to listen to their concerns – all of which I had conveyed to Prime Minister Atal Bihari Vajpayee. I urged NRIs to be a stronger Indian voice in America.[67]

Facilitate the Connections between Indian-Americans and American Institutions

Speaking at India House banquet in Schaumburg in Chicago, Illinois, on October 28, 2001, I said my job involved building bridges between Indian and American institutions, between Indians and their children and between India and NRIs on various issues.[68] I said, "We have to be part of the American community life. I do not say give up your culture, but go to senior citizen homes; interact with Senators and Congressmen."[69]

Addressing the Mahatma Gandhi Community Center in Houston, Texas, on October 12, 2001, I said, "There is a definite need to educate Americans about India and its heritage so that there can be a better understanding between NRIs and mainstream Americans."[70] I cautioned that although Indian-Americans are educated and successful, energetic and zestful, the United States policy-makers ignored and did not give credit to the Indian-American community here in the US because NRIs/PIOs seldom worked together. I suggested that the different groups and associations in the community should come up with a common minimum programme.[71] I wanted to develop a better Indo-US relationship in which NRIs/PIOs could play a major role.[72]

At a press conference at the Consulate General of India in New York City on October 3, 2001, I said that if some Indians in a Caribbean island needed a doctor, I would persuade the Association of American Physicians of Indian origin to send their members there. At the same time, a corporate body or industry would be asked to fund the venture. Thus, I would help to bring a feeling of oneness among Indians all over the world. I envisioned for myself a role to help the NRIs set up an education process to inform the natives about India and its culture. I cited the case of Indian doctors, engineers and other professionals who should educate and inform their American counterparts, Congressmen and Senators about their country of origin.[73] About business and investments, I said, "We have to tell people what the government wants, what the government's policies are and how we can work better so that people are encouraged to invest in India."[74]

At a meeting at the Indian Consul-General Ringzin Wangi's residence in Houston, Texas, on October 13, 2001, I said, "I hope to be able to build bridges between the two countries." On the question of dual citizenship for NRIs, which has been desired for many years, I stated that yet another high-level committee was studying it and would report with specific recommendations soon.[75]

At a meeting of community leaders at Utsav in New York on December 15, 2001, I said there was "a good representation of the various Indian-American groups for the meetings at which the situation in India and a likely role for Indian-Americans was discussed." It was decided that short committees of five members each be formed to ensure that the Indian community was properly organised and garnered support from the mainstream community.[76] The committees would take steps to see that law-makers and politicians in the US were educated about the seriousness of the situation in India.[77]

In an address at the Indian Culture Centre in Tampa and Ocala, Florida, on January 26, 2002, I emphasised 'the need for unity' amongst all the Indian American Associations in order to achieve full, substantive and significant mainstream participation in USA, as also to achieve bigger and better things for all the NRIs there.[78]

In a speech at the Massachusetts Institute of Technology in Cambridge, Massachusetts, in February 2002, I implored the audience to strengthen bridges with India and urged the NRI community and the various representative organisations to stand united. I said, "Each large metropolitan area in the US has 30 to 100 or more Indian organisations, each serving a relatively small specific need." I appealed for more unity amongst all these organisations and NRIs. For this purpose, I recommended establishing a core team of five volunteers from these organisations for better coordination in their activities.[79] I also pointed out that their contributions to the society pooled together would appear far more significant than they did now.[80]

In an address in Houston, Texas, in March 2002, I said that Indians who had come to the US or gone to other countries to earn money were now in a position to play a major role in the political arena of the states they had adopted.[81] This was especially true of the US where they now are contributing substantial money to the political campaigns of candidates and parties, but did not have the clout which should come with that type of spending.[82] At present, even the political parties might not be aware of the total contributions Indians made. In this connection, I referred to the substantial contributions made by Indians to help families of the terrorist attacks in the US on September 11, but they did not get the recognition they deserved.[83] "Had they coordinated their activities and presented one check, it would have had much more impact. But now no one knows how much they have contributed."[84] I continued, "You cannot wipe out the differences, but what I am trying to do is to make you agree on a minimum common programme."[85]

Already at my suggestion, in some cities, including Houston, major Indian organisations were planning to constitute coordination committees. The committee's main agenda was to work in the political field to support India's causes and also to resolve problems that the community might be facing. The idea was ultimately to have a national committee.[86]

At a meeting in Chandigarh with Punjab and Haryana officials, during my first official visit to India as Ambassador-at-Large on March 17, 2002, I said, "A larger international family of Indians, connecting NRIs and PIOs to India, unity in the Indian diaspora and involving second-generation Indians in projects back home" are among the five major targets I had set for myself.[87] I took up this assignment seven days after the terrorist attack on the USA on September 11, 2001.[88]

A Punjabi by origin and an academician by profession, I set the ball rolling by not only travelling through the length and breadth of the USA, but also of the Caribbean.[89] There were 20 million NRIs of which 1.9 million were in the USA alone.[90] I maintain that creating unity among the Indian diaspora was my first and foremost task. Wherever I went, I told them that at least on a certain minimum programme, they must be united. Immediately after the December 13 attack on Indian Parliament, I had 50-60 opinion-makers of the Indian community in New York together and asked them to form councils of 5 to 10 representatives to give their opinion on such an important issue.[91] The third major task was to develop an expanded international family of Indians. When I went to the Caribbean, I met the President of Guyana, who was a PIO. There were three million Indian-Guyanese.[92] I offered him services of Indian-American doctors who would come and visit Guyana for a month or so free of cost. What I had been impressing upon them is that there should be better co-ordination and co-operation among Indian-Americans and Indian-Guyanese.

For example, Indian-Fijians could be helped. We now had political clout and could use this to help Indian-Fijians by raising the issue of human rights violations. So, we worked on creating an international family of Indians, which was close-knit and effective. At the same time, I also advocated that Indian-Americans or Indian-Canadians should get connected to local people, the Americans in America and the Canadians in Canada. They had to actively participate in social, cultural and political life of the area they resided in.[93]

At an address at MIT campus in Boston, Massachusetts, on February 9, 2002, I said that there were so many regional organisations in all the states that sometimes the major issues concerning everybody were not properly attended to.[94] Since we were so fragmented, we should have a common council of five or six people approved by all these organisations that would take up these common interests so that when they did come up, everybody would pool their resources.[95] One powerful voice would have a major impact on the people with whom they interacted. As an example, tons of money were collected for the WTC victims, but no one knew how much the Indians had contributed. So, no impact. Soon after the December 13th incident, I asked the tri-state area Indians to speak out in one voice and they did.[96] Once that process began, division would not occur and there would be more unity.

In a press conference at Utsav Restaurant in New York on June 3, 2002, I announced that I had set up nine groups of volunteers to look into issues of concern for the Indian-American community and India.[97] In a very bold initiative that started answering concerns and questions that were on the minds of most of the NRIs and PIOs, I announced the initiation of nine new projects for the NRIs to benefit their motherland and in doing so, benefit all NRIs/PIOs.[98] The main issues that the honorary volunteer groups were to look into included how to link the Indian diaspora; study successful diaspora models like the Jewish and Chinese; media bias against India; ways to promote NRI/PIO investments; NRI/PIO corporate executives' contribution to India's infrastructure development; NRI/PIO chambers of commerce and NRI/PIO involvement in India/US institutions.[99] I visited various parts of the USA, Canada, Caribbean and other countries since September 2001, and listened carefully to their concerns and complaints. I also met with various professional groups, like NetIps-NY, AAPI, Engineers' and Motel Owners Groups, etc, to see what they wanted to do and what type of volunteer help they could give me. And after holding a meeting, we came up with nine new projects.[100]

The projects included: 1) Global Indian Family Group; 2) Study of Diaspora Models (Chinese/Jewish groups); 3) Media Group; 4) NRIs/PIOs Investment Group; 5) NIRs/PIOs Corporate Executives Participation In India Infrastructure Development Group; 6) NRIs/PIOs Chamber of Commerce Group; 7) NRIs/PIOs Unity Group; 8) Web-Site and IT Group and 9) NRIs/PIOs involvement in India/USA Institutions Collaboration Group.[101] I explained that 54 volunteers were participating in these projects and then, described as to what each group would try to accomplish.[102]

At the 20th Annual Convention of AAPIO banquet held at the Sheraton Hotel in Chicago, Illinois, on June 28, 2002, alluding to the Kashmir issue, I said that we as Americans could help by educating our legislators and fellow Americans now that the US Government understood the issue better.[103]

Speaking at the 12th Biennial Convention of National Federation of Indian Association in Detroit on October 12, 2002, I said the Indian-American community needed to work to improve India's image, which was "getting a bad rap in the American mainstream media. Let's do something about it."[104] I praised the community for its role in strengthening India-US friendship and announced that I planned to sponsor workshops on public and media relations for Indian-Americans to help them enhance their efforts to promote stronger ties between the two countries.[105]

As the chief guest at the annual convocation of Bikram Choudhry's Yoga College of India in Los Angeles, California, on November 8, 2002, I spoke on the importance of a strong relationship between India and the U.S.[106]

Hosting 'India's Image in Western Media', the first media workshop in southern California on November 9, 2002, I proposed a rapid response team to immediately counter any negative image of India in the mainstream media.[107] At a round-table discussion to the academics, entrepreneurs and community leaders, I explained an 'organised' way of looking at the issue "so that we can have a ground-up approach and have the people say what should be done."[108] "Once the abundance of information has been collected, we will go national and create an awareness workshop, where we will discuss the recommendations from these five centres and put together the resources to implement them. Out of these discussions will emerge a national movement."[109]

Addressing the media workshop at the Lubin School of Business at Pace University in Pleasantville, New York, on November 17, 2002, I said, "There is a need to step up the media-awareness activity among the NRI/PIO community for a better reflection of India's image in Western media and of the Indian presence in the US."[110] Also, "I have heard these complaints all the time that foreign media are misrepresenting India. And, hence, I have decided to encourage the holding of several seminars all over the USA to know the feelings and chalk out a plan of action as to what we should do to see that India is represented accurately. I am just coming back from a seminar in California and now I am attending this second one in New York. I am glad that we have discussed many aspects of this problem in detail and now we are getting ready to do something."[111] I stated that there was a need to step up the media awareness activity among the NRI/PIO community for a better reflection of India's image in Western media and increase awareness of the correct media potential and of the image of Indian presence in the USA, and added that it was being proposed to organise a number of 'awareness and action workshops and seminars' related to the important issue of media awareness in the US and all over the world.[112] The major action points I made included Indians should learn from Jewish and Chinese diaspora as to how to project the media image of India and Indian community better and positively in the Western press and how to counter negative media campaign in a sustained manner. I asserted that greater interaction with the local political parties, national leadership and policy-makers was always helpful.[113]

Transnational Appreciation of Situation of Indian Diaspora Communities

In an address at the Mahatma Gandhi Community Center in Houston, Texas, on October 12, 2001, I said there was a definite need to educate Americans about India and its heritage so that there could be better understanding between NRIs and mainstream Americans.[114] Referring to the presence of NRIs/PIOs all over the world, I said the sun never sets on them.[115] It was time to network globally so that NRIs/PIOs of one country could help their brethren in other parts of the world, should a need arise.[116] For that to happen, I said, people without ego and selfishness should come forward to serve. However, being based in New York City, my domain would be every country in the world where approximately 20 million Indians or people of Indian origin lived.[117] In a press conference at the Consulate General of India in New York City on October 3, 2001, I said that Indians as far as Surinam or Trinidad or in Canada should feel that Indians belonged to 'an international co-operative family' and that was possible by helping each other.[118] I also discussed what I called the Indian global camp. "It's very important that

Indians living in Surinam, Trinidad, Canada, England or South Africa can feel that there is a universal Indian brotherhood... an international co-operative family atmosphere."[119]

Visiting Caribbean countries in Guyana around November 26-29, 2001, I spoke about the establishment of linkages between the Indo-Guyanese in Guyana and the NRIs in USA. I envisioned the visit of Indian doctors from USA to Guyana from time to time and spending a few weeks doing voluntary medical service. This suggestion was very much liked by the Indo-Guyanese community. I also spoke about the possible co-operation between IT experts in Silicon Valley and the industrialists in Guyana.[120]

At an address at the Gadar Memorial Library in San Francisco on December 8, 2001, I said to check this, "We have to have a connectivity with them", noting that high on my priority list was to develop 'friendship circles' between NRIs living in different parts of the world, something the President of Guyana, Bharrat Jagdeo, seemed enthusiastic about.[121] Perhaps mindful of the bickering and divisions among Indian-American organisations in California and elsewhere, I suggested that they bury their differences and help me in my plan to set up a 'Council of Indian Americans', an umbrella organisation that would embrace NRIs of every political, professional and cultural stripe.[122] I said that there were currently 300 Indian-American organisations in Houston alone, and 700 in New York. In the wake of the September 11 attacks, I said a number of Indian-American organisations raised a total of around $10 million for the World Trade Centre victims, but because the money was sent in fragments from each of those organisations, nobody realised just what a powerhouse the Indian-American community was.[123]

At a speech at the India Association Cultural and Education Center in Ocala, Florida, I said with a smile, "My goal is to unite all Indians from all over the globe to think and work as one. It's a mission I will not fail to accomplish."[124] I noted India's Prime Minister recently approved a measure – which must be ratified by the Indian Parliament – allowing Indians who were US citizens to hold dual citizenship. By the end of the year, I said the bill should become law. "It's the first step, in my view, that would unify us even more as Indians because most Indians who leave India are emotionally attached to their country. However, this is only the first step."[125]

In a speech at the Massachusetts Institute of Technology in Cambridge, Massachusetts, in February 2002, I discussed the need for building bridges amongst NRIs from different countries in order that all NRIs became a part of one community.[126] Immigrants from India to the US, for example, should have better relations with Caribbean Indians in US (whose forefathers had left India more than 150 years ago).[127] I said Indians in difficult situations elsewhere in the world, like Fiji, should also be able to receive assistance from NRIs in the US. I said I had plans of instituting internships, in which the young and the retired would work on projects in the US and in India. This would accomplish better relations between the US and India, more emotional attachment with India and faster development of India.[128]

At an address in Houston, Texas, in March 2002, I said that with Indians now occupying key positions in several countries, especially the US and Britain, it was of paramount importance that they started coordinating their efforts to collectively fight for the cause of the country and forcefully counteract any attempt to tarnish its image.[129] That, I said, would also help in organising an effective worldwide movement if Indians in a country found themselves in trouble.

At a conference at the Sheraton Music City Hotel in Nashville, Tennessee, on April 6, 2002, I urged AAPI members to be part of his global outreach programme for NRIs and PIOs.[130] I said that NRIs should coordinate their political, economic and social efforts for the betterment of Indians everywhere.[131] I said I had visited several countries where there were significant Indian populations, including Britain, the Caribbean, and various parts of the US to listen to their concerns – all of which I had conveyed to Prime Minister Atal Bihari Vajpayee.[132]

At the outset of a presentation at the India-America Chamber of Commerce (IACC) luncheon meeting at Harvard Club in New York City on May 29, 2002, I briefed the delegates on the purpose and function of this office, "the bridge-building vision of the office in the areas of culture, trade, investments, science and technology and all other aspects involving NRI/PIO diaspora."[133] I said, "The mandate of the office is global and the sphere of activity covers all such needs that afflict the 22 million members of the diaspora anywhere in the world."[134] I also urged the Indian-Americans to get themselves involved with NRIs in other countries and develop a global family, "for example, with Indians in the Caribbean. In Fiji, for instance, if the Indian-Americans had chipped in, we could have helped the country there especially after the recent crisis."[135]

In an address at Utsav Restaurant in New York on June 3, 2002, in a very bold initiative to answer concerns and questions playing on the minds of most of the NRIs and PIOs, I announced the initiation of nine new projects for the NRIs to benefit their motherland and, in doing so, benefit all NRIs/PIOs.[136] "I visited various parts of the USA, Canada, Caribbean and other countries since September 2001, and listened carefully to their concerns and complaints. I also met with various professional groups, like NetIps-NY, AAPI, Engineers' and Motel Owners Groups, etc. to see what they wanted to do and what type of volunteer help they can give me.[137] And after holding a meeting, we have come up with nine new projects." I detailed the projects as follows: 1) Global Indian Family Group; 2) Study of Diaspora Models (Chinese/Jewish groups); 3) Media Group; 4) NRIs/PIOs Investment Group; 5) NIRs/PIOs Corporate Executives Participation in India Infrastructure Development Group; 6) NRIs/PIOs Chamber of Commerce Group; 7) NRIs/PIOs Unity Group; 8) Web-Site and IT Group; and 9) NRIs/PIOs involvement in India/USA Institutions Collaboration Group.[138] I explained that 54 volunteers were participating in these projects and then described as to what each group would try to accomplish.[139] For example, Global Indian Family Group is where the selected group would research ways to link different diaspora communities as one global Indian family. The group would also research on the problems and issues that the Indo-Caribbeans, Indo-Canadians and Indian-Americans faced, as well as propose solutions for cultural preservation and linking these communities back to India.[140] NRI/PIO Chambers of Commerce Group would research on how to increase the NRI/PIO Chambers of Commerce in different countries, the goals they should pursue and how to align the different NRI/PIO Chambers of Commerce in a network.[141]

At a meeting with Honorary Project Associates (volunteers) at my office on May 23, 2002, I said, "To work out a model for utilising these offers, we had a meeting of young professionals and we established a network of contacts with more than 54 people throughout the US, and in some other countries like Trinidad and Canada."[142]

At a media conference on June 3, 2002, I said, "Volunteers will carry out research to link the Indian diaspora around the world so as to create a global Indian family."[143]

In an address at the Rathi Auditorium in the Community Center of the Lemont Temple in Chicago, Illinois, on June 30, 2002, reiterating my agenda of bringing global Indian immigrants under one umbrella with a single nerve centre to direct it, I announced that I had made a draft outline of the complete mega project with several sub-projects in it.[144] "My position is global, and issues are many," I said, stating that my job is to address NRI issues at the world level.[145] The main thrust of my entire interaction was more towards developing an international Indian family of immigrants. Citing the examples of the Indian diaspora in Trinidad, Ghana, and Surinam, I stated that their non-participation in the police and military professions was depriving them of power, forcing them to migrate. Twenty-two lakh Surinamis had left because they had no political clout.[146] I emphasised the need to research and develop a programme through which to handle the issues concerning migrant Indians at a global level. Stressing the need for keeping the upcoming generation in contact with India, I stated that parents must show concern about India, which would indirectly influence the children to remain connected to their country of origin. "You are an extension of India and your future generations are at stake here," I warned.[147]

At the 20th Annual Convention of AAPIO banquet held at the Sheraton Hotel in Chicago, Illinois, on June 28, 2002, I expounded on the various projects I had undertaken to bring the community together, especially, the 'Global Indian Family Group' that would research ways to link different diasporas into one global Indian family; 'Diaspora Models Group' to research other diaspora models like Chinese or Jewish and emulate their example and 'NRI Investment Group' to promote investments in India.[148] I said, "We can create wonders for India here," and emphasised the need to create a global family,[149]for which "I need your leadership."[150]

Addressing the 7th Annual Convention of the Vokkaligara Parishad of America at the Chesapeake Convention Center in Chesapeake, Virginia, on July 6, 2002, Ramachandra Gowda praised me for bringing together the global Indian community since I had taken charge of office.[151]

As a guest at the 30th Annual Celebrations of Gujarat Samachar in London, when it was suggested that the Indian government was reluctant to grant British Indians what they wanted – dual nationality– I shook my head.[152] "The PM has accepted the principle of dual nationality; we call it dual citizenship," I assured him.[153] I was hopeful that by the end of this year, the Cabinet would approve proposals for the amendment of Indian Citizenship Act of 1935 in order to grant Indians settled abroad, initially in the US, UK, Canada, Australia and New Zealand, the right to dual citizenship.[154] "The person with dual citizenship will have all rights minus political rights – he can't run for political office and he can't vote," I added, having retained my Indian nationality, though I had a green card for America.[155] I said that a final decision on granting dual citizenship to non-resident Indians and people of Indian origin in half-a-dozen countries, including in the UK and the US, would be taken before January 9.[156] I told reporters that the proposal, already accepted by Prime Minister Atal Bihari Vajpayee in principle, had been sent to various ministries for their opinion. "Once the review is done, it will go before the Cabinet," I said.[157] Stating that there was no need for any constitutional amendment, I said the changes could be effected under Section 12 of the Citizenship Act of 1955.[158] Noting that I had been visiting various countries to understand the 'concerns' of the 22 million Indians living abroad, I suggested that there should be 'unity among Indians wherever they are', so that they could take up issues concerning India and the Indians.[159]

Highlighting initiatives at the PIO Awards Ceremony organised by the PIO (Caribbean) on September 8, 2002,[160] and keeping in view the concerns of the PIOs, my office of Ambassador-at-Large took several initiatives to develop the concept of global Indian family, and protect and project the interests of NRIs and PIOs world over while, at the same time, helping them serve the cause of their domicile country and society in a highly functional manner. The one-million-strong Indian diaspora in the Caribbean had successfully continued to maintain the rich Indian heritage and cultural mores and tradition, I said.[161] The main countries were the former British colonies of Trinidad and Tobago, Guyana and the Dutch colony of Surinam, Trinidad and Tobago had 40 per cent of its total population of Indian origin, Guyana 51 per cent and Surinam 35 percent.[162]

I stated that after taking charge of the NRIs and PIOs world over, I had an opportunity to visit the Caribbean countries of Trinidad and Tobago, Surinam and Guyana. I interacted with the leadership of these countries, diverse Indian organisations and associations, various religious bodies and with the Indian Embassies and High Commissions. I had seen a number of mosques and temples during my visits and was proud that the PIOs had successfully continued to maintain the rich Indian heritage and cultural mores and tradition.[163] I said the Indian diaspora should be more united. While it was not possible on all issues, but the diaspora organisations could co-operate on common issues of universal interests. Benefits of the Indian origin population and safety and security of their person and property were such issues of common interest in the Caribbean countries. I met the Consul-General and other senior officers of CGI in Houston, Texas, on December 13, 2002, and, when asked about my impressions of Houston, said, "The community here in Houston is very effective, very cohesive and generally speaking, has different types of interests."[164] Speaking of the *Pravasi Bharatiya* Divas to be held in India during January 9-11, I said, "The significance of the day is that Mahatma Gandhi went back to India from South Africa as an NRI. In a way, this is a celebration of that event. I call it 'coming home emotionally'."[165] I said, "I see in this diaspora of 20-plus million people of Indian origin as a great Indian family. Though they come from different countries, in different stages, in different circumstances, still they have feelings for India and this is the common binding factor. This similarity brings them together and gives them the feeling of belonging to one Indian global family."[166]

Help Diaspora to Adjust to Host Country and become Active Contributors to Host Country

At a press conference at the Consulate General of India in New York, on October 3, 2001, I discussed how NRIs could help both their adopted homes and India.[167] "For example, if we have networking here, which we already have – doctors have networks all over the country – they can talk to colleges, schools, media, Congressmen about India's issues."[168]

At an address at the Gadar Memorial Library in San Francisco on December 8, 2001, I said that much to their credit, the NRIs there are maintaining their Indian culture and passing it on to their children.[169]They were, however, experiencing the kind of problems faced by those who are forced to live in a kind of vacuum and because of that, some are 'developing ties to other nations'.[170]

At an address at Indian Cultural Center in Tampa and Ocala, Florida, on January 26, 2002, I emphasised 'the need for unity' amongst all the Indian-American Associations in order to achieve full, substantive and significant mainstream participation in USA, as also to achieve bigger and better things for all the NRIs there.[171]

In an address at the Massachusetts Institute of Technology in Cambridge, Massachusetts, in February 2002, I urged the NRIs to be loyal to their adopted lands and build bridges with local communities by contributing in social, political and cultural arenas.[172] This would result in improving public relations for India in the eyes of foreigners. I said that NRIs should take a lead in projecting a positive image of India. Also, parents should involve the youth and children, well versed in the American ways and know how to get things done, in projects and activities aimed at promoting India so that their creative energies can be utilised, besides strengthening their bond with India.[173] Secondly, I said NRIs should be well connected with the land they live in.[174] For this, they should be socially and politically active and build bridges with the mainstream communities.[175]

At an award ceremony for Mark Massey at the Richardson Civic Center in Dallas, Texas, on March 30, 2002, I asked for active participation by Indians in civic life without which the community would not be integrated in the mainstream.[176] "The Indian community has to be American when in America," I said.[177]

At an address at the MIT campus in Boston, Massachusetts, on February 9, 2002, I also called upon all Indians to assimilate and enter into the mainstream of America, participate in the social and cultural process of this nation, volunteer in community programmes, provide support, service and aid to the aged and the elderly.[178] I also hoped that they would build effective public relations that would invite investment from companies abroad and help in boosting India's economy. Lastly, I hoped that in my role as Ambassador-at-Large, I would be able to build a global Indian family of NRIs all over the world and bring everybody together in a manner that it would be like a mini India away from India.[179]

In a conference at the Sheraton Music City Hotel in Nashville, Tennessee, on April 6, 2002, I urged NRIs to be a stronger Indian voice in America.[180] At a meeting with Indian High Commissioner Virendra Gupta at the commission's office on Victoria Avenue in Trinidad & Tobago, on May 17-20, 2002, I said, While we are Indians, we are also citizens of countries where we live and we must be devoted to nation-building and to our motherland," adding, "not forgetting to maintain the culture and tradition of India."[181]

In an address at Utsav Restaurant in New York, on June 3, 2002, in a very bold initiative that answered concerns and questions troubling the minds of most NRIs and PIOs, I announced the initiation of nine new projects for the NRIs to benefit their motherland and, in doing so, benefit all NRIs/PIOs.[182] "I have been visiting various parts of the USA, Canada, Caribbean and other countries since September 2001 and listened very carefully to their concerns and complaints. I also met with various professional groups, like NetIps-NY, AAPI, Engineers' and Motel Owners Groups, etc. to see what they wanted to do and what type of volunteer help they can give me. And after holding a meeting, we have come up with nine new projects."[183] I detailed the projects as follows: 1) Global Indian Family Group; 2) Study of Diaspora Models (Chinese/ Jewish groups); 3) Media Group; 4) NRIs/PIOs Investment Group; 5) NIRs/PIOs Corporate Executives Participation in India Infrastructure Development Group; 6) NRIs/PIOs Chamber of Commerce Group; 7) NRIs/PIOs Unity Group; 8) Web-Site and IT Group; and 9) NRIs/ PIOs involvement in India/USA Institutions Collaboration[184] Group.[185] I explained that 54 volunteers would be participating in these projects and went on to describe as to what each group would try to accomplish.[186] "I want all of you to be good citizens of the country you live in, but that should not preclude you to show your love and affinities to the country of your origin –India," I declared.[187]

In a presentation to the Indian-American Chamber of Commerce at the Harvard Club in New York City, on May 29, 2002, I explained my rationale that Indians, if they effectively involved themselves in community work in the US and elsewhere, could force governments all over the world to support India.[188] "Go and get involved in the community," I said last week.[189] "It is not enough to just go to a temple and feel that everything is okay. It is important to go and work in the community, in inner schools, at other places. And when you need help, you will find that they (the Americans) will help you."[190]

I urged the Indian-American community to model themselves on the lines of the Jewish community and integrate and involve themselves in American society while retaining their own culture, traditions and links with their mother country.[191] I said, "The NRIs should be comfortable in the country they live in. They should be loyal and a participating resident of the country. They should also involve themselves in the affairs of the community."[192] I clarified, "The Jewish community is a very good example of this participation and active involvement in local affairs, and yet, at the same time, they follow their traditions. They involve themselves, but also put their cap on."[193] Their third concern was how to involve themselves in community affairs, I said, and then cited the example of the Jewish community.[194]

Addressing the 7th Annual Convention of the Vokkaligara Parishad of America at the Chesapeake Convention Center in Chesapeake, Virginia, on July 6, 2002, I also stressed on the need for the Indians to actively participate in the socio-political and community activities of their adopted country.[195] This would lead to inculcation of discipline and moral character..[196] In this context, I cited the example of Dr. A.P.J. Abdul Kalam who, a good Muslim, a renowned scientist and a known musician, also was an epitome of a good Indian transcending the barriers of religion and caste.[197] Dr. Kalam was as proficient in the *Gita* as in the *Quran*, knows Sanskrit as well as Tamil and Malayalam.[198]

In an address at the 12th Biennial Convention of National Federation of Indian Association in Detroit, on October 12, 2002, I pointed out that it was vital for the community to participate in the American way of life. I said, "It will help the mainstream, which in turn will help us; create goodwill in the community and we can cash in on that goodwill when the time comes."[199] I covered issues of concern to the Indian-American community and issues of terrorism.[200] It was an exercise in enhancing relations among the community with mainstream America, especially in socio-political aspects.

□

10

Volunteer Groups, Workshops and Group Meetings in Different Cities

We were very anxious to involve the community in determining the projects we should undertake. At the same time, we were interested in the youth for their input and active participation in determining our goals and methods to reach those goals. On March 5, 2002, at NET-IP function in Manhattan, we met with young Indian professionals. I discussed with the group the importance of NRI/PIO unity and how they, as second-generation Indian-Americans, should be more involved in leadership roles within the Indian community and American society. The participants in the group were very enthusiastic about the opportunity, and many of them volunteered to work on the projects. On May 23, an Honorary Project Associates Event-2002 was held. Nine projects were initially chosen for the associates to work on. Mr. Stanley Berly, a young man from Houston who joined us as a volunteer, was made the Community Relations Director for the office of the Ambassador, in charge of coordinating activities. Fifty-plus volunteers met and discussed the various aspects of their involvement and came up with the following initial project groups.

Initial Project Groups

1. *Global Indian Family Group*
   This group will research ways to link different diaspora communities as one 'global Indian family'. The group will also research the problems and issues that Indian diaspora communities around the world face, as well as propose solutions for cultural preservation and linking these

communities with India.

2. *'Diaspora Models (Chinese/Jewish)' Group*
   This group will research other diaspora models, especially focussing on the Chinese and Jewish models. The success and failure of each model should be studied with emphasis on their applicability to the Indian diaspora.
3. *'Media' Group*
   This group will research the reasons for 'media bias' and propose ways by which the Indian community can work with different media sources to correct the misinformation.
4. *'NRI/PIO Investment' Group*
   This group will research the ways to promote NRI/PIO investment in India.
5. *'NRI/PIO Corporate Executives Participate in Indian Infrastructure Development' Group*
   This group will research the ways in which NRI/PIO corporate executives could utilise Indian infrastructure within the business models of their companies.
6. *'NRI/PIO Chamber of Commerce' Group*
   This group will research on how to increase the number of NRI/PIO chambers of commerce in different countries, the goals they should pursue, and how to network the different NRI/PIO Chambers of Commerce together.
7. *'NRI/PIO Unity' Group*
   This group will research ways to unite the NRI/PIO organisations, while maintaining their individual charter and unite various NRI/PIO communities around the world.
8. *'Website and it' Group*
   This group of students will help develop a website for the office of the Ambassador-at-Large for NRIs/PIOs and make suggestions for creating an 'integrated information flow' between the various departments.
9. *'NRI/PIO Involvement In Indian/US Institutions Collaboration' Group*
   This group will research ways in which NRIs/PIOs can facilitate collaborative interaction between Indian and American institutions and companies, so that there can be

a mutually beneficial transfer of knowledge, and research ways by which NRIs/PIOs can be resourced to Indian institutions and companies. The interests of students of various universities in the working of the projects was further reflected in the workshop for the 'Indo-American Students Workshop' mentioned later. One of the volunteers made recommendations as given below, which reflect deep thinking and sensitive concerns on the part of the youth.

Synergy between India and the Diaspora in the Context of Education – Some Thoughts

- If India were to emerge as a powerful nation whose competitiveness is sustainable, then access to good quality primary and secondary education is essential for all Indians
- Today the forces of globalisation and digital information dissemination are shifting the very paradigms on which societies are traditionally governed and people interact which each other locally, regionally and globally
- Globalisation depends on the theory of comparative advantage, whereby nations and communities focus on doing what they can do best with the resources they have. India, not only has natural resources, but also tremendous human resources
- Globalisation is inter-linking financial markets, environmental conditions, economic systems, information-sharing over wide geographies instantaneously. This is creating conditions where issues of global concern transcend action by individual nations and globalisation will rapidly interconnect civil societies around the world to take up causes of mutual and common interest. In these interactions, ideas will play a critical role and the influence of good, practical ideas will be widespread
- In the rapidly emerging marketplace for ideas (both within India as well as within the global community), it is imperative that all Indians (not just a few) participate
- Success in this marketplace of ideas hinges firstly on widespread literacy and, thereafter, on rational and contextual education. It is education that has to act as an essential

lubricant for all development in India in a very competitive world

- Let me first clarify that by literacy I do not mean solely the ability to read and write, but also the ability to develop the basic tools to discover information relevant to all aspects of day-to-day life, and then harness it to further our strengths and improve upon our weaknesses
- On the other hand, let me also clarify that by education, I do not mean rote learning; I do not mean reading about European history without first learning about India's own critical history written by eminent Indian scholars. I do not mean science education based just on textbooks, but where books supplement the real-life experiences of the common Indian; and maths education which does not derive exclusively from textbooks; rather one that derives its understanding and has application in the day-to-day life of the common Indian
- We have to recognise that all the wonderful strides that India has made in the field of Information Technology is expected to create five to 15 million jobs in the next five years. However, at the rate at which India's population is growing, we will have to create hundreds of millions of jobs just in order to reach the fruits of India's emerging economic prosperity to the common person in India who lives far from the technology centres of Hyderabad, Bangalore, Pune and other large metropolitan cities
- India needs educational infrastructure that is capable of creating such hundreds of millions of jobs. In other words, the educational system has to be structured in a way that it becomes a 'force multiplier' for widespread social entrepreneurship, economic development and healthcare at the local levels and empowers communities to harness their comparative advantages and assert their views in the formulation and implementation of policy that directly furthers their interests and welfare
- Above all, India's education system should be developed by Indians and the Indian diaspora for India
- Education is one area where the Indian diaspora can make a

tangible and immediate contribution to India's development and competitiveness.

- What can the diaspora do specifically ?
  - (a) Provide money for libraries and digital equipment.
  - (b) Help local organisations with capital and equipment.
  - (c) Adopt one primary school in and village in India and channel capital resources, tools for digital connectivity and teacher's education resources to those schools.
  - (d) Open channels for the diaspora, especially for retired and young people to come to India and teach for six months or more at a stretch.
  - (e) Link the resources available in their adopted countries with educational institutions at the state level in India.
  - (f) Initiate training programmes in India with the help of leading teaching/research institutions in their adopted countries.
  - (g) Develop centres for teaching excellence in India to help develop critical thinking abilities (from a very young age) rather than standard rote.
  - (h) Help develop leading Indian centres to be exporters of low-cost education technologies to other developing and developed countries.
  - (i) Develop educational test relevant to the Indian context.
  - (j) Create institutions of learning aimed at women, adults, healthcare delivery professionals and governance in India.
  - (k) Impart their own personal experience in developing suitable policy for India's benefit.
  - (l) Help to identify bottlenecks in the process by which NRIs make contributions in the educational sector and work with the government to eliminate them.
  - (m) Take upon ourselves the issue to digital divide and craft innovative and actionable solutions to reduce and eliminate the building divide.
  - (n) Help to develop insurance infrastructure for protecting schools from natural calamities, and unforeseen financial hardships, etc.

Other Suggestions by Group Associates

It was refreshing to find that honorary group associates were very active and creative in presenting proposals, which were very challenging and educational. Their commitment to the causes close to our mission was evident from the following proposals and suggestions made by them:

NRI/PIO Unity – Proposal

Mission

The NRI/PIO Unity Group will research ways to bring together Non-Resident Indians (NRIs) and People of Indian Origin (PIO) from various industries, professions, religious, cultural and ethnic backgrounds from all over the world to come together as one huge Indian family to network, support, share resources and enhance the lives of all Indians around the globe while maintaining their individuality and original charter.

Goals

Create a directory/database that will be managed by the office of the Ambassador-at-Large with all the relevant information as a resource guide that can be used by all NRIs/PIOs organisations. This is a very useful project that can directly bring NRI/PIO organisations into contact with the OAAL, which can act as a clearing house for information concerning NRIs/PIOs, thus increasing the awareness about the OAAL by the Indian community.

Acquire support from the office to facilitate more opportunities to network and communicate with other NRI/PIO groups to learn their goals and initiatives and how to establish synergies together. This is an important project, but will require someone who has worked with the Indian community before, has knowledge of various community issues and has leadership qualities so that a consensus can be reached. This project can further increase the image of the OAAL. The OAAL role as the representative of the NRI/PIO community falls in line with this project. The aim of that scope involves encouraging communities to come together to work on issues related to the Indian community in a united manner. Currently there is no one in the project group with the background to do this; we will have to look for capable individuals.

Create awareness about NRI/PIO events and resources through a newsletter dispatched to all organisations at least once or twice a year. This falls in line with the OAAL's bi-weekly/monthly newsletter. This can be done internally or by someone from the Unity Group. It will require time and resources.

Organise an NRI/PIO Unity Day in the US by working with various ethnic, professional, religious and cultural groups in the US. This is a project that was discussed before within the OAAL. It is critical for the OAAL to take the lead in bringing the Indians together. Events like this can highlight this role. The Unity Project Group can help in co-ordinating the function through mass correspondence and phone calls.

Task	Activity	Resources Required	Estimated Time/Assignments	Actual Completion
Gain NRI/PIO contact	Research website and gather lists of various ethnic, professional, religious and cultural groups in the US . Create a database that houses all contact information and have our directory as a central hub of connection with all NRI/PIO organisations. Initial research estimates 400,000 existing NRI/PIO organisations worldwide. Leverage the existing information that had already been created by others.	Single point of contact with organisations that collaborate with others. Single point of contact from office of Ambassador-at-Large.	Using existing information, this can take 2-3 months based on the number of resources that can work on this.	To be determined
Support from Ambassador-At-Large offices and Indian government.	Letter from Indian government to all organisations, thanking them for their work and encourage their support to India and other NRI/PIO organisations to establish synergies. Create awareness of the Ambassador-at-Large offices including our goals, initiatives and resources and how we can work together under one umbrella. Continue awareness in organisations with Obal.	Need to ensure that we have a robust contact database so we can contact all NRI/PIO organisations. Need to establish final mission statement from our ideas. Need support from Indian government to implement a global task that can be useful	Depends on the completion of data warehouse of contact information.	To be determined.

This falls in line with the unity projects at Houston, Tampa, and New York	NRI/PIO news and events. Develop a possible task/idea that all NRI/PIO organisations can implement and which will demonstrate the unity among us.	to all NRI/PIO groups.		
Developing relationships with NRI/PIO organisations	Align with large international NRI/PIO organisations, such as GOPIO, etc. Attend meetings of other organisations and gain knowledge on their mission/goals. Maintain contact via e-mail, in person, etc. to ensure awareness of all initiatives and determine if groups can work together to eliminate duplicate efforts. Share our group's resources with other groups to assist them in strengthening their individuality.	Letter from Indian government will establish our office and attract of NRI/PIO organisations to work with us. Developing and maintaining a data warehouse. Website that brings organisations together to share information and knowledge. Time commitment from both sides to share ideas and assist each other.	After completion of gaining contacts, this is achieved by resources participating in other organisations' meetings and events.	To be determined.

Events to attend to gain ideas for Unity Day I do not think that the individuals of the project group are ready to represent the office in this	Present our goals and plan other events and also learn about the processes of co-ordinating a Unity Day. Attend Network of Indian Professionals' (NET-IP) annual conference in Boston, MA, Attend GOPIO Networking of Entrepreneurs – Sept. 13-15, 2002 in NYC. Attend Indians Meet Indians event, Jan. 9-11, 2002 in New Delhi, India.	Individuals with time and commitment. Financial assistance to attend meetings, events, etc. Have a clear understanding of all the initiatives of the office of the Ambassador-at-Large.	This can be done all the year round.	Determined.
Manner, but we can find others who are capable.				
Summit Meeting and Unity Day. This is similar to the project we discussed before having an NRI/PIO conference in England/Canada/US.	Develop understanding of our mission and organise meetings to unite all organisations to work together and grow individually. Plan Unity Day in NYC for all NRI/PIO organisations based on learning from other events and combining efforts.	Individuals with time and commitment to take ownership of topics and preparation. Financial assistance to hold summit meetings and plan events. Time and material for planning and research.	Desired completion is Fall/Winter 2003.	

The 'Nri/Pio Chambers of Commerce' Group

This group will research on how to increase the amount of NRI/PIO Chambers of Commerce in different countries and how to bring the different NRI/PIO Chambers of Commerce together.

Honorary Project Associates

Mamta Sett, Initiator

Mahendra Ramgopal, Urmila Chandana

Objectives:

1. How to increase the amount of NRI/PIO CC in different countries.
2. How to bring the different CCs together.

I. Increase the NRI/PIO CC in different countries

Increasing awareness of the benefits of having a CC in a particular country so that individuals as well as groups get motivated to either join or create CCs in their work areas. This can be done by:

1. Creating and circulating a pamphlet along with national newspapers. Requisite (R): Printing of the pamphlets.

   Acquiring details of these CCs by speaking with heads of existing departments.

   Before circulating pamphlets, a database needs to be created, consisting of NRI/PIO organisations. Once this is done, we can target them with mailings and phone calls concerning the advantages of creating an Indian Chamber of Commerce.
2. Requesting the media to focus on CCs on certain days and allowing the existing Chambers of Commerce to run their advertisements in newspapers. (R): Contact point in the newspaper where it can be explained to them as to why the need to advertise is of primary importance.

   Here, the OAAL can get publicity in its attempt to foster Indian Chambers of Commerce throughout the world. I believe this to be an effective way of highlighting the importance of this office's role as a catalyst on NRI/PIO issues.

3 Televise shows wherein heads of such departments come in and talk about the progress that they have made or the ideas they propose to execute during their tenures.

   This is similar to the Community Councils we are currently

trying to implement. We need two to three test areas that can demonstrate the ability of the OAAL to facilitate the creation of Indian Chambers of Commerce.

4 Telephone assistance to PPI and those who wish to acquire details of either creating or joining a CC.(R): Dedicated individuals in the office to provide regular assistance to enthusiastic individuals.

II. Network the CCs

Unifying all the CCs will create a network that can be powerful as well as resourceful and eventually, extremely beneficial to the NRI/PIO community at large. This unification can be brought about by:

1. Create a directory wherein details of all the CCs is easily available.
   (R): Researching existing CCs and organising them into a directory.
   Time and web access from a team which can patiently research as well as create a directory.
2. Promote the idea that overall progress can be achieved by individual growth.
   (R): Meetings with SSs and acquiring knowledge on their goals and ambitions.
3. Assist in the maintenance of identities of different chambers and, at the same time, steering them jointly towards the progress of the community at large.
   (R): Motivate individuals who can attend meetings and provide assistance in matters.
4. Encourage exchange programmes with different CCs
   (R): Promote the general idea of exchanging PPI for a while in the same countries so that there is a free flow of ideas.
5. Award for the best performance.
   (R): The biannual award for the performance can be monitored by individuals on the basis of annual reports and progress in the regions.
6. Organise annual meetings of CC heads or representatives.
   (R): Space and ability to call a number of representatives from

different Chambers of Commerce and inform them on the progress being made in the different countries.

7. Create a grassroots organisation to resolve disputes as well as guide and motivate the various CCs.
   (R): Create a charter that contains rules and regulations of the organisation and individuals who can convince the existing sporadic CCs to unite and form inseparable branches of the grassroots tree.
8. Have a national Indian Chamber of Commerce to provide the same functions as AAPI or AI-IOA. Due to their larger size, they can have a greater impact concerning federal/state/provincial policies affecting NRI/PIOs and India. Eventually, an umbrella organisation of business, professional and community organisations can be created to represent the interest of Indians in the countries they are living in all aspects. This organisation can be of a size where they can fund projects in India and provide expertise to Indian organisations and projects. It should have a charitable wing, like AAPI fund projects in India and other NRI/PIO communities.

Proposals for Institutional Collaboration Project: Office of Ambassador of India for NRIs and PIOs

Mission Objectives

To establish, facilitate and deepen institutional-level co-operation between Indian and US institutions, both on a non-governmental as well as governmental level through leveraging existing institutional relationships of NRIs and PIOs, and their direct project-specific contributions.

To work with the Ambassador's office (which in itself is a nascent institution) to maximise its recognition and effectiveness amongst its target groups as well as to facilitate new ideas that are practical through this ambassadorial institution.

Recommended Initial Action Items

1. Set-up an Institutional Co-operation Co-ordination Group at the Ambassador's office to organise and co-ordinate:
   a. resources, b. ideas and c. implementation.

2. Set-up database/exchange that lists (and links) Indian institutions that seek assistance from NRIs and PIOs. The database would include a list of top three priority items per institution where assistance is required along with the nature of assistance required (e.g. financial, advisory, reference, etc).
3. The database may also include information about NRI and PIO volunteers, their professional accomplishments and their areas of volunteering interest [e.g. regional, technical, philanthropic, charity (adopt an institution), etc.]
4. Establish priorities to optimise resource allocation as well as monitor the implementation of priority projects, using a more evolved form of this sample matrix.
5. Identify selected and actionable projects for approval and resource allocation and select implementation team.
6. The co-ordinator of institutions' collaboration team should meet the Ambassador and with the coordinators of other groups at least once a month in order to cross-fertilise ideas and efforts.
7. Evolve a proposal for consideration of the Government of India to establish a high-profile 'Apravasi Awards' (e.g. Apravasi Bharat Ratna, Apravasi Bharat Bhushan and Apravasi Bharat Vibhushan) in recognition of their contributions to India or to the country of their domicile, the Indian community as well as for their personal achievements.

Investment Initiative
Proposals and Recommendations

Agenda/Primary Objectives

1. Identify reasons for NRIs investing in India.
2. Identify key growth areas/industries towards which investment energy should be directed.
3. Identify the key strategies that could enhance this effort.

Strategies

- Leverage India as an attractive investment destination.
- Target industries where India has global advantage/need for investment
- Information Technology

- Biotechnology/Biopharma
- Services
- Real Estate
- Infrastructure
- Build NRI/PIO investor confidence
- Identify what the problems have been in the past.
- Work on potential proposals to alleviate the problems.
- Identify ways to build the credibility of the government.
- Explore strategies on how to raise money in the international markets and ways in which NRIs can participate in this process.
- Direct philanthropic investments from NRIs into identifiable areas.
- Direct participation by NRIs in government's policy-making procedures.
- *Role of NRIs in financial education at all government levels*
- Open up finance/IAS services to allow NRI professionals to go back and serve for a few years.
- Budgetary allocation process is fundamentally flawed. Identify strategies to remove procedural hindrances and roadblocks.
- Identify ways in which NRIs can participate directly in local/regional development in India.
- Empower local/state governments to raise capital from NRIs to implement development at local levels.

Tasks

Conduct a survey with NRIs for ideas and suggestions. NRI feedback to be tabulated and kept confidential.

Organise educational/interactive discussion platforms/seminars.

Function as a market-making hub.

Workshops

In order to involve various segments of the Indian diaspora on major issues effecting NRIs and India, we held workshops in different cities of USA. The following major workshops were held: Workshop on *Women's Issues: A Diaspora Perspective* (New York, Atlanta, Baton Rouge), *Enhancing India's Image in the Western Media* (Los Angeles, New York, Houston and Atlanta), *Indo-Caribbean Leaders* (New York), *Meeting of the Inter-Religious Leaders* (New York), *Meeting of Leading*

Financial Institutions to Improve the Quality of Financial Services Aimed at NRIs and PIOs (New York), and Workshop for *Indo-American Students/Youth: Their Contributions & Concerns* (New York).

In order to justify the contribution and energy of the participants in various workshops, it would be better to refer to the details of each workshop in the reports prepared by the staff at the Ambassador's office. In view of the fact that reports are lengthy, it will be appropriate to place them in Appendix I. The pictures of the participants in the workshops are also given here and in the reports also.

□

11

Visit to the other Countries and Interactions with the Diaspora and the Concerned Officials

In furtherance of my assignment as a global Ambassador, I visited many countries, especially the countries with substantial Indian diaspora and these included Surinam, Guyana, Trinidad and Mauritius where the Indian diaspora has a long history. Other countries visited were Canada, United Kingdom, Japan (Osaka), Hong Kong, Thailand, Spain, Netherlands/Amsterdam, Portugal and France (Paris). All these trips were arranged with prior approval of the MEA and were duly suggested by appropriate officials of MEA. The reports of the visits were documented by the officials and others in the visiting countries. They are lengthy and, therefore, the following narration is sufficiently appropriate for those visits. Here we shall see that bonds of the global family, unity, togetherness and understanding are present everywhere.

Surinam Visit

The reports regarding my visit were prepared by the host staff in a very liberal manner. They gave a complete picture of my visit and interactions with various segments of the country. However, the following assessment report prepared by the Counsellor Ravi Thapar should suffice:

Visit to Surinam by Shri B.K. Agnihotri,

Ambassador-at-Large, Government of India
(November, 22-26, 2001)

Assessment

Shri B.K. Agnihotri, Ambassador-at-Large, for Government of India in New York, USA, accompanied by his wife visited Surinam from November 22-26, 2001. Although the visit was organised at very short notice, a fruitful and busy programme was organised for him by the Embassy of India in Surinam, as per the programme attached.

During his visit, Ambassador-at-Large (AAL) had intensive interactions with a wide cross-section of the Indo-Surinamese community and also with officials in the Surinam government. Among his important engagements were a luncheon meeting with senior functionaries of the Surinam Chamber of Commerce and Industry and with influential local businessmen; ITEC Day reception organised by the Embassy where he met several important Indo-Surinamese and Surinamese contacts; dinner meetings organised by the Embassy officials with leading members of the Indo-Surinamese community; dinner meeting with Hon'ble Vice President and his wife; meeting with Hon'ble Speaker, Government of Surinam; meeting with the Permanent Secretary in the Surinam Ministry of Foreign Affairs; luncheon meeting organised by GOPIO Surinam and meeting with leaders/representatives of various Indo-Surinamese religious and cultural organisations.

The visit was the first such tour undertaken by AAL after assuming charge in New York in September 2001. As such, it helped in informing the local Hindustani community about the extensive programmes planned by Government of India for involving NRIs and PIOs in India's future developmental activities and in its demarche for forging new linkages with other countries. The fact that NRIs and PIOs constitute a powerful constituency and can contribute tangibly to their country of origin through increased involvement in business, cultural, educational or other such developmental activities were fully explained to and understood by the Indo-Surinamese community.

Surinam is a developing country that is potentially rich-with huge natural resources of gold deposits, bauxite, oil and natural gas and abundant equatorial rain-forests, rivers and other such attributes.

However, the country has still not begun to scientifically exploit these resources or to manage its economy. Partly this is because of the weaknesses of its political system and over-dependence on its erstwhile colonial rulers, i.e. the Netherlands. In these circumstances, Ambassador Agnihotri's offer that NRIs abroad, who are leading professionals, e.g., senior Indo-American medical doctors and specialists, engineers and IT entrepreneurs, financial analysts, etc. would be willing to work for short-term assignments and projects in Surinam, often even on pro-bona or gratis basis was very well received. This was apparent both during his discussions with the Permanent Secretary in the Surinam Ministry of Foreign Affairs and also with the representatives of the Surinam Chamber of Commerce and Industry.

The possibility of stimulating business linkages between India and Surinam through the NRI and PIO channel has emerged as a distinct possibility. Mr. Bhagwan Ganga Ram Pandey, VP of the Surinam Chamber of Commerce and industry also had an individual one-to-one meeting with AAL during the visit and felt that Indo-American capital and technology coupled with professional expertise from India along with infrastructure support by the Indo-Surinamese and Surinamese community could go a long way in kick starting industrial and business ventures in Surinam. The fact that Surinam is now a full fledged member of the CARICOM and also hopes to become a fully integrated member of the FTAA market (Free Trade Area of the Americas) by 2005, opens up immense market possibilities for future economic/commercial interaction between India and Surinam.

The official dignitaries in Surinam were also very receptive to AAL's visit. Hon'ble Vice President, Shri Ajodhire iterated his country's willingness to promote closer linkages with India through such channels. Hon'ble Speaker, Ram Sardjoe also responded very positively to the idea of fostering closer links within the NRI and PIO community and through them, India and other countries. Permanent Secretary Limon expressed keenness in associating Indo-Americans and NRIs in development projects and suggested that this arrangement could be institutionalised in consultation with the Surinam Ministry of Education.

Involvement of NRIs in philanthropic and other such projects, however, need not be confined only to Indo-Americans and NRIs in developed countries. Rather, even in other countries, this process can be encouraged provided GoI feeds them with the required information and also keeps regularly in touch with them. This was apparent during the discussions that AAL held with Mr. J.T. Kirpalani, Managing Director of Messrs Kirpalanis in Paramaribo, Surinam. Institutions like the Kripalani Foundation have the potential of contributing tangibly to deserving NGOs and institutions in India and have in fact, been already contributing to various developmental and charitable projects in India. To continue doing this, such philanthropic institutions require constant feedback on the reliability and activities of potential recipient organisations and institutions in India.

In short, the AAL's office could collaborate usefully and effectively with the work of Indian missions in developed and Indian diaspora countries in forging closer links (cultural, people-to-people, business, economic and eventually, also political) between India and other countries. Building of close contacts with key and influential members of the NRI/PIO community and cultivating them or recognising them through establishment of some awards, etc. would seem to be important factors in the bridge-building process.

Ravi Thapar Counsellor
November 28, 2001
Ambassador of India in Surinam
Ambassador-at-Large

Guyana Visit

The following report has been prepared by the local embassy official regarding my visit. It gives a summary of my interaction with various officials and the community in the country.

1. Dr. Bhishma K. Agnihotri, Ambassador-at-Large based in New York, visited Georgetown from November 26-29, 2001. During this period, he met a large number of NRIs and prominent local citizens as well as ministers of the local government, including President and Prime Minister of Guyana. He was also interviewed by a number of TV channels. He was received enthusiastically everywhere and his visit would undoubtedly help to further strengthen the links between India and the people of Indian origin in this country as well as giving a boost

to bilateral relations between India and Guyana. Enclosed herewith are the particulars of various engagements and meetings organised for Dr. Agnihotri in Guyana.

2. Among the dignitaries on whom Dr. Agnihotri called were the following: President of Guyana, Mr. Bharrat Jagdeo, Prime Minister of Guyana, Mr. Samuel A. Hinds, Parliamentary Affairs Minister, Pandit Reepu Daman Persaud, Foreign Minister, Dr. Rudy Insanally and Minister of Fisheries, Crops and Livestock, Mr. Satyadeow Sawh. A reception was also organised by me for Dr. Agnihotri at my residence, which was attended by 50-60 leading personalities of Georgetown. He also addressed a press conference in the chancery on the last day of his visit.
3. Dr. Agnihotri's meetings with the ministers of the government, including Prime Minister and the President, were held in an extremely friendly and cordial atmosphere. Dr. Agnihotri explained at length the nature of his responsibilities and as to why the Government of India had deemed it necessary to appoint him as Ambassador-at-Large with jurisdiction over PIOs and NRIs spread all over the world. Dr. Agnihotri emphasised that his primary objective was to strengthen the links between people of Indian origin everywhere and foster a sense of Indianness among them. He also emphasised that while he would focus on people of Indian origin, he would be equally concerned with the interests of other communities.
4. During his meetings with the dignitaries in Guyana, Dr. Agnihotri put forth the following specific ideas. He said that it might be possible for him to arrange periodic visits of senior medical personnel of Indian origin from the USA to Guyana. These doctors would render their services, free of charge. Similarly, he also alluded to the possibility of establishing links between Indian professionals in the Silicon Valley and the IT sector in this country. Needless to say, both these proposals were warmly received by his interlocutors.
5. During his meeting with the President of Guyana, Dr. Agnihotri described him as a PIO. The President appreciated such a characterisation of him. The President, in turn, asserted that he was proud of his Indian ancestry. Dr. Agnihotri enquired

whether it would be possible for the President, during his forthcoming visit to New York, to address the annual session of physicians of Indian origin in the USA. The President welcomed the suggestion and said that he would be happy to do so.

6. The President clearly liked the concept of the deepening of bonds between people of Indian origin everywhere, including those in Guyana. The President expressed the hope that in the days to come, Guyana's relations with India would strengthen further, especially in the fields of technical co-operation, commerce, setting up of joint ventures, etc.
7. The President incidentally noted that though the member States of the CARICOM were small, each had one vote in the UN. He implied, in an oblique way, that he would be willing to work to promote India's interests in world for a, using his influence with CARICOM Heads of State.
8. Dr. Agnihotri's meetings with Pandit Reepu Daman Persaud, Minister for Parliamentary Affairs and Mr. Satyadeow Sawh, Minister for Fisheries, Crops and Livestock took place in a very cordial atmosphere. Both the ministers were thankful for the assistance being rendered by India to Guyana and expressed the hope that Indo-Guyanese relations will consolidate further in the days to come. They warmly welcomed the appointment of Dr. Agnihotri and wished that he would be able to play an important role in building bridges between people of Indian origin everywhere.
9. Dr. Agnihotri also met with Foreign Minister Dr. Rudy Insanally. The Foreign Minister appreciated the rationale behind Dr. Agnihotri's appointment and discussed how Indo-Guyanese relations could be further strengthened. Earlier, funds were collected in this country for the benefit of the victims of the Gujarat earthquake. A cheque for the amount so collected was presented during the meeting.
10. Dr. Agnihotri also met the Executive Members of the Guyana Chapter of Global Organisation of People of Indian Origin (GOPIO). They put forth certain concrete proposals to him seeking assistance from Government of India.

11. Dr. Agnihotri visited the Indian Cultural Centre and talked with the teachers and students there. He expressed great happiness over the manner in which the High Commission was engaged in propagating the Indian culture in Guyana.
12. To sum up, it can certainly be said that Dr. Agnihotri's visit to Guyana was a success and would help to further reinforce the links between India and the people of Indian origin here.

Trinidad Visit

The following communication from the official of the embassy explains, in short, my visit to Trinidad.

HIGH COMMISSION OF INDIA
P.O. BOX 530, PORT-OF-SPAIN TRINIDAD & TOBAGO, W.I.
Phone: 62-77480/81; 627-4027; *Telex No*:. 22514 HICOMIN WG
Fax No.: (868) 627-6985, *E-mail*: hcipos@tstt.net.tt

The Ambassador-at-Large Shri B.K. Agnihotri visited Port of Spain from May 17-20 this year to participate in the International Hindi Conference. Apart from participating in the conference, he met NRIs and PIOs. Friends of India organised a meeting where the Ambassador spoke about the importance of Indian diaspora. He also met Hindi Prachar Kendra chief, Mr. Ravindra Maharaj, popularly known as Raviji, who also organised a talk for the visiting Ambassador. Professor H.S. Adesh, Head of the Bharatiya Vidya Sansthan organised a luncheon meeting and invited various NRIs and PIOs.

The Ambassador addressed a press conference along with the High Commissioner and highlighted his responsibilities on the work allotted to him by the Prime Minister. He also mentioned that his main work pertains to developing relations with the 20 million-strong Indian diaspora spread worldwide. His interview appeared in the *Daily Newsday* of May 26 and weekly *Mirror* also, which are enclosed for the kind information of the Ambassador.

Although the visit was short, it was very successful. The Ambassador utilised this visit not only to participate in various functions connected with the International Hindi Conference but also met cross-sections of society of NRIs and PIOs based in Trinidad & Tobago. We strongly feel that he should visit Trinidad & Tobago along with Guyana, Surinam and Jamaica during October-November to see the religious activities of the Indian diaspora.

For your information please.
Mr. B.K. Agnihotri,
Ambassador-at-Large
C/o CGI New York

Mauritius Visit

My visit to Mauritius was very rewarding because it had a very dynamic PIO community substantially following the traditions of their ancestors. The following report prepared by an official regarding my visit appropriately covers my schedule.

Report

During his visit to Mauritius, Shri B.K. Agnihotri, Ambassador-at-Large for NRIs and PIOs, called on Abdool Raouff Bundhun, GOSK, Vice President, Republic of Mauritius on May 10, 2004. Shri Pripuran, Commissioner of India was also present on this occasion. The Vice President extended a warm welcome to AAL upon his first visit to Mauritius. He said that Mauritius was 'the great little India', as stated by Smt. Indira Gandhi during her visit to Mauritius. He said that the two countries shared a unique relationship and a common civilisational heritage. This dynamic relationship had been further strengthened in several key spheres of economy and commerce, science and technology, ICT, etc., in recent times. While giving a historical perspective, he recounted the arrival of Indians as indentured labour in Mauritius and their toil and sweat for centuries to build the country and bring it to its present status. He mentioned that the persons of Indian origin had maintained linkages with India, as manifest in their active participation in the Pravasi Bharatiya Divas (PBD) celebrations. The present President, Sir Anerood Jugnauth himself had led the delegation from Mauritius during the PBD in January 2003.

AAL thanked Vice President for receiving him and conveyed his pleasure to be in Mauritius. He said that he had always been looking forward to visit Mauritius and that the present visit had materialised after a long time. He said that the spectacular growth achieved by Mauritius in all fields was worth emulating and others could learn from it. He briefed Vice President upon the various activities undertaken by his office, such as organising workshops, reaching out to the youth and acting as a facilitator to connect the diaspora in different parts of the world with each other. He said that a major issue for the diaspora around the world was to make the younger generation aware of the values and the strength inherent in their civilisational heritage. The younger generation also needed to be made aware of the immense progress achieved by India in the fields of economy, education, science and technology. By making this happen, the diaspora in Mauritius could provide global leaders, and it was the objective of his office to work towards this goal. In the end, AAL thanked Vice President for giving him the opportunity to have a useful interaction with him.

Later, in the day, AAI and Mrs. Agnihotri visited the office of *Janvani,* the only Hindi weekly of Mauritius. *Janvani* has worked tirelessly for promotion of Hindi and has been the vehicle for disseminating the essence of Indian culture to its readers. *Janvani* is edited by Mrs. Sarita Boodhoo, a renowned journalist in Mauritius. She has also been associated with Mauritius-Bhojpuri Institute and the World Hindi Secretariat. During AAL's visit to *Janvani* premises, Mrs. Boodhoo also conducted an interview of AAL for its readers that would be carried in its next edition.

The Ambassador-at-Large also addressed a well-attended meeting of the leaders of around 20 PIO organisations on May 10, 2004. A rich variety of PIO representatives belonging to different cultural and religious affinities and different geographical and linguistic regions of India was present.

AAL stressed upon the unity in diversity of Indian diaspora. He said that the time had come for the 22-million-strong Indian diaspora to develop into a global Indian family, deeply rooted in culture and looking forward in the emerging areas of science and technology, trade and commerce. The networking of PIOs, transcending national boundaries, should result in mutual help and support. While welcoming the promotion of regional and religious identities, he urged that these varieties should be complementary to integrated Indian variety, like a bouquet of flowers with individual fragrance and colours but with a beauty of their own. Drawing attention towards the Indian ideal of *vasudha iva kutumbakum,* the Ambassador-at-Large appealed for a similar global feeling of togetherness among the Indian diaspora. He cited examples from his experiences in America of working together for groups like India Caucus, Friends of India, etc. to strive towards the diaspora's cause.

AAL showed his concern for the well-being of the younger generation and appealed for giving them more opportunities of expression, transferring the cultural heritage to them and also for striving for a better future. He said that our efforts of cultural promotion and preserving our identity would be fruitful only when we care for the aspirations of our youth power and synergising their aspirations and energy for the cause of world PIO family.

The Ambassador-at-Large urged PIO leaders that while retaining their group identity, they should have some common platform for interaction and united activities as Indian diaspora. India's national days like Independence and Republic Days would be ideal occasions for such interaction and show of harmony and solidarity.

The address was followed by a lively interactive session with PIO leaders. It reflected the keenness of PIO representatives to strive towards a global Indian family of Indian diaspora. They also showed their keenness for mutual support to move forward towards a bright future.

Shri Agnihotri praised Mauritius for preservation and promotion of cultural identity and also for making their presence felt in all walks of Mauritian life. He complimented Mauritius, not only as 'Mini India', but also as 'Real India'.

In May 2004, AAL visited Apravasi Ghat and Mahatma Gandhi Institute (MGI). Apravasi Ghat is the site where Indian indentured labourers, since 1834, touched the Mauritian soil for the first time. From here, they used to be sent to different sugar plantation fields. These labourers faced injustice, torture and penury, but never lost their hopes and cultural identity. With hard work and determination, they made a place for themselves and contributed towards building a modern Mauritius. Shri Agnihotri was given a warm welcome by the chairperson of Apravasi Ghat Trust Fund, Dr. Vijaylakshmi Teelock and her team of archaeologists. Shri Agnihotri was much impressed by the restoration work at the site, with the help of Indian archaeological experts, particularly Dr. Amitava Chowdhury. UNESCO is being requested to declare Apravasi Ghat as a World Heritage Site.

At MGI, Shri Agnihotri was welcomed by the chairman, director general and senior faculty members. MGI is the apex institute of oriental languages, arts, music and culture. It was established with Indian support in 1970, jointly inaugurated by the then Prime Ministers of both the countries, Sir Seewoosagar Ramgoolam and Smt. Indira Gandhi. Shri Agnihotri was deeply impressed by the upkeep of the Museum of Indian diaspora; archives with well-maintained records of the arrival of Indian indentured labourers; and overall ambience of Indian arts and culture.

AAL also interacted with the Heads of Indian public sector undertakings, [namely, LIC, Indian Oil Ltd., Bank of Baroda, TCIL, SBI (Mauritius) Ltd., New India Assurance Company]. He also interacted with the representatives of Mauritius Chamber of Commerce and Industry. Shri Agnihotri shared the vision of resurgent India with these representatives.

I had an extensive programme in Mauritius. I felt like going back to history myself because 70 per cent of people in Mauritius are of Indian origin and they still follow the ancient traditions and cultural values.

U.K. Visit

Pursuing my mission to other parts of the world, I visited the United Kingdom and interacted with the Indian diaspora in London, Manchester, Leicester-Birmingham and with various other officials and leaders. It was a rewarding experience in discussing issues of NRI/PIO community. The Indian diaspora there was very alert and desirous of connection with India. My visit was very well organised and I was invited to various programmes in different parts of England.

Canada Visit

I visited Canada on April 11-17, 2002. It was a real fun and positive experience. A large number of NRIs/PIOs are in Canada from Punjab. So, it is very interesting to meet the people, whom I have known principally in childhood. I visited Toronto, Montreal, Quebec and some other cities. Wherever I visited, people were full of joy and felt very close to my background. A publication by the name of *Ghadar* was published in Quebec and it was rich with information about the Indian diaspora. I also visited Nanaksar Gurudwara. Warmth was all over and

Indian communities in different locations gave me the opportunity to interact with them. I also visited Saifre mosque.

Spain Visit

I had the opportunity to meet the Indian community in Spain. Spain has a vibrant Indian community. The report regarding my visit covers my visit substantially. It is as given below.

Report by Office of Ambassador-At-Large

Dr. Bhishma K. Agnihotri, Ambassador-at-Large for Non-Resident Indians (NRIs) and Persons of Indian Origin (PIOs), paid an official visit to Portugal for two days from April 24-25, 2003. During the visit, he met leaders/representatives of various sects of the Indian community residing in Portugal. These included representatives of (Sikh) Gurudwara Committees, social workers, leaders of the Hindu community, the Ismailis, the Sunni Muslims and the Goan community. In these meetings, Dr. Bhishma K. Agnihotri stressed the importance of Indians from all walks of life living together as 'a global family'.

Dr. Bhishma K. Agnihotri took note of the grievances expressed by the Sikh community and these included the inordinate delay in receipt of passport clearances from the local passport offices in India as also the verification reports/authentication reports in respect of birth and marriage certificates from the concerned district authorities in the state of Punjab. He was also apprised of the lack of institutional support for the repatriation of the mortal remains of deceased Indians, who died in harness. Representatives of the Guru Ravidas Committee also highlighted the need for opening a branch of an Indian bank in Portugal and the introduction of direct flights between Lisbon and New Delhi. In his response, Dr. Bhishma K. Agnihotri assured that he would take up these matters with the concerned authorities in India.

Mr. Kantilal Jamnadas, president of the Hindu community, stressed the need for improving the investment climate in India with particular reference to labour laws. Dr. Bhishma K. Agnihotri informed Mr. Kantilal Jamnadas of the changes made in the recent past and the ongoing second-generation economic reforms. He also explained the constraints in making such changes at a rapid pace in a democratic set-up, as contrasted with the changes made in China.

Dr. Bhishma K. Agnihotri expressed his admiration at the architectural excellence of the Ismaili Centre and said he was overwhelmed at the breadth and depth of the social welfare activities being undertaken by the Aga Khan Foundation. While reiterating his emphasis on *vasudha iva kutumbakam*, he underlined the importance of explaining to the people of the West, Islam in its right perspective, to ally distortions brought about the events of September 11.

Dr. Abdool Vakil, president of the Sunni community briefed Dr. Agnihotri on his bank's (Banco Effisa)'s involvement in a major hydroelectric project in the state of Madhya Pradesh. During his visit to the Casa De Goa in Lisbon, the Goan community made a presentation of their objectives and future plans. They also enquired about the status of dual nationality. Dr. Bhishma K. Agnihotri informed that a bill for the purpose is likely to be introduced in the Parliament in its current session.

Japan, Hong Kong and Thailand Visit

In my efforts to promote first Pravasi Bharatiya Diwas and also to interact with a very vibrant diaspora of Hong Kong and Thailand, I visited Japan, Hong Kong and Thailand on my way to India. I met the leadership and other prominent persons of Indian origin in Japan, Hong Kong and Thailand, and impressed upon them the goals and ideals of being promoted by me as Ambassador. Most of them were very kind. I also visited places of worship, that is, the Gurudwari temple and a mosque.

Netherlands Visit

I visited the Netherlands on October 8, 2003, and stayed there for a day. I interacted with the Ambassador of India, Syamala B. Cowsik, to discuss various issues concerning the Indian community. I also had a meeting with the Indian community in addition to meeting the chairman of GOPIO. It was a short, but very fruitful visit.

Paris Visit

I visited Paris from October 10-12, 2003. The report of my visit summarised by my office is given below and substantially covers the particulars of my visit. I was pleased with the meetings with leaders of the diaspora and other influential persons. A report was prepared covering my visit.

Report

Dr. B.K. Agnihotri, Ambassador-at-Large for NRIs and PIOs, visited France officially from October 10-12, 2003. The visit, which included wide-ranging interactions with the Indian community and community leaders in France, was organised by the Embassy of India, Paris in co-operation with more than 30 Indo-French organisations.

The Ambassador-at-Large visited the prestigious educational Fontainebleau Institute, INSEAD and interacted with the Indian-origin faculty members and students of the prestigious institute. While addressing the institute, Ambassador-at-Large highlighted the role of diaspora, perception of growing socio-political and economic role of the diaspora envisaged by the Government of India and various policy measures being implemented by the Government of India to network with the Indian diaspora worldwide and increase the two-way interaction process.

Dr. Agnihotri held a meeting with more than 30 Indian community leaders in the chancery of the Embassy of India, Paris on October 1, 2003. He briefed the community leaders on the dual nationality issue, invited them to participate in large numbers in the Pravasi Bharatiya Divas celebrations in January 2004 and advised them to maintain a continuous link with suggestions and proposals with his office. Dr. Agnihotri also briefed the community leaders on the highlights of the recent visit of the Prime Minister to New York.

In the same evening, a community meeting was held at India Centre of the local university. The Ambassador-at-Large addressed the meeting, which was followed by a question-answer session. The programme was organised by the local Gujarati Samaj. The Ambassador-at-Large also visited the ISKCON temple.

□

12

PM's Programme in New York Presenting United Diaspora

The Prime Minister of India visited New York in late September 2003. I received a communication from his office in New Delhi on August 1, 2003, informing me that he would be visiting New York, and our office was assigned the task of organising a public meeting on September 21. That was the first time the office of Ambassador-at-Large had the opportunity to organise the Prime Minister's programme. The time was short and a lot of preparations had to be made. Public leaders of different organisations were informed and were invited to a meeting in our office to plan the programme. We formed several committees, and one was charged with finding the proper venue for the programme. It looked into several possible locations, and ultimately, recommended the Jacob K. Javits Centre, which could accommodate 4,000 persons. One of the committee members was hesitant about the location because according to him, it was too huge for the audience normally attending former programmes of the Prime Minister. The community leaders from the various organisations met regularly in our office for the preparation and management aspects of the programme. We decided that we would not collect any funds or raise any money through tickets, food or snacks, etc. No refreshments were served to the people attending. Our office made entry passes and announced that attendees could pick up the tickets at my office or other designated places. The purpose was to ensure that the passes did not go into wrong hands. An interesting thing happened – one or two individuals, who were leaders of a group were not happy with our handling of the programme, and it was reported by my office that they were taking passes for their group and throwing them in the garbage, and later coming back for more passes. We had an idea about these individuals, but I told the officer in charge of distribution to print more and not to bother about people who were reportedly trying to sabotage, and give them passes even if they wanted more. Their strategy did not work because more than 4,000 people were in the Jacob K. Javits Centre to listen to the Prime Minister. There was no empty seat.

So far as I was concerned, I wanted to highlight the occasion in presenting the goals, missions and accomplishments of our organisation by offering programmes highlighting our work. In order to involve the major organisations, we invited their leaders to participate in the decision-making process. We decided that no leader of any group would sit on the stage, and this was quite unusual. Incidentally, one person who wanted to sit on the stage very cleverly asked me if he could give a million-dollar donation for the programme in exchange for a seat on the stage. I declined his offer and told him that we were not taking any donations for the programme. The decision was made that the leaders of the organisations would come on the stage as a group, one by one and greet the Prime Minister and stand in a queue with other invited leaders. These leaders numbered 34 and represented the main non-religious NRI organisations in the USA. A plaque was presented to the Prime Minister signed by all leaders carrying commitments as given hereunder.

Charter of Solidarity and Commitment

The following national Indian-American organisations serving diverse causes and interests of the Indian diaspora in the USA welcome your presence in the USA. We are very proud of India's rich heritage and resurgent India's future as a world leader. Indian-American community of over 2 million people in the US has been making enormous contribution to their motherland. In the future also, India's interests including Indo-US relations shall be vigorously promoted. In doing so, we hereby affirm to work in unison to:

- Promote harmony and brotherhood among Indian diaspora
- Strengthen cordial relationship between the United States and India
- Help to improve India's image in the Western media

- Encourage the new generation to learn about Indian values and heritage
- Help India become developed country by 2020

The following persons presented the plaque representing the national organisations:

1. American Association of Physicians of Indian Origin (AAPI): Dr. Sharad Lakhanpal/president
2. Asian-American Hotel Owners Association (AAHOA): Hitesh Bhakta/chairman
3. Association of Indians in America (AIA): Dr. Piyush Agrawal/president
4. American Society of Engineers of Indian Origin (ASEI): Ravi Rout/chairman
5. Association of Kannada Kootas of America (AKKA): H.S. Jayaswamy/first president
6. Alliances of Sindhi Association: Lal Motwani/executive director
7. Association of Jats in America (AJA): R.S. Arya/president
8. American Telugu Association (ATA): A.V.N. Reddy/president
9. Telugu Association of North America (TANA): Dr. Navneeta Krish Gorrepati/president
10. Bihar Association of North America (BANA): Pankaj Kumar/president
11. Brihan Maharashtra Mandal: Shri Thanedar/president
12. Cultural Association of Bengal: Pranab Das/president
13. Federation of Tamil Sangams of North America (FeTNA): K. Sivaraman/president
14. Federation of Kerala Associations in North America (FOKANA): George Koshy/president
15. Non-Resident Keralite Affairs in North America (NORKANA): Zach Thomas/president
16. Global Organisation of People of Indian Origin (GOPIO): Thomas Abraham/president
17. Global Punjabi Diaspora: Inder Singh/president
18. International Punjabi Association: Sant Singh Chatwal/president
19. Gujarati Samaj: Bharti Desai/president

20. Indian-American Forum for Political Education: Sudhir M. Parikh/president
21. Indian-American Friendship Council: Dr. Krishna M. Reddy/president
22. Indian National Overseas Congress: Dr. S.S. Malhotra/president
23. Indo-Caribbean Association: Ramesh Kalicharan/president
24. Kashmiri Overseas Association, Inc.: Sanjay Kaul/president
25. North American Federation of Indian Associations (NAFIA): Anna Prasad/president and Ramesh Patel/chairman
26. Network of Indian Professionals (NEtIP): Amit Saraff/Philadelphia Chapter
27. National Federation of Indian-American Associations (NFIA): Dr. Rajen Anand/president-elect
28. Overseas Friends of BJP: S. Vemuri/president
29. Orissa Society of the Americas (OSA): Prof. Durgamadhab Misra/secretary and treasurer
30. Rajasthan Association of North America (RANA): Chandra Mehta/member
31. Society of Indian Academics in America: Dr. Rishi S. Raj/president
32. The Indus Entrepreneurs (TiE): Parag Saxena/president, TiE Tri-State
33. Uttar Pradesh Association of Mid-Atlantic (UPAMA): Rama Shankar Singh/president
34. Uttaranchal Association of North America (UANA): Ajay Rawat/president

As part of the program, a group of children recited some of the Prime Minister's poems. The Prime Minister's address was very timely and pleasing. He also recited one of his poems. I purposely decided not to speak, except for conducting the programme. I then invited the Prime Minister to speak without any introduction, except for saying, "I now request the Prime Minister of India to address us." The beauty of the whole programme was that it was the first time such an event was translated on the huge screen in English. It was beautifully arranged by Mr. Dinesh Agrawal and Manish Srivastava, who co-ordinated the immediate translation.

Obviously, the Prime Minister was very pleased. On his return, he sent a very nice letter to us on the success of the programme. Newspaper articles about the event were generally favourable and complimentary, praising the great success of the event. One newspaper was unhappy that there was no Muslim representation on the leadership parade. Our office prepared a report on that matter, which clarified the matter.

Subject: Prime Minister's Public Meeting and Participation by Muslim Community: A Fact-Sheet

1. The office of Ambassador-at-Large for Non-Resident Indians and Persons of Indian Origin received a formal communication from the Prime Minister's office on August 1, 2003, assigning this office to organise the public meeting of the Prime Minister on September 21, 2003, in New York.
2. Following this, a series of meetings involving a large number of community leaders and office-bearers of Indo-American organisations and associations to exchange ideas on various aspects leading to organise the Prime Minister's public meeting were convened. Such meetings continued till middle of September 2003.
3. The very first meeting organised on August 6 was attended by the following Muslim community leaders:

1. Dr. Shakir Mukhi, vice president, Islamic Circle of NA
2. Shk. Tayeb Poonawala, Bohri Jamaat
3. Mr. Amin, managing director, All for Food and member ICNA

4. Based on these, the very first announcement published by the ethnic media included the name of Islamic Circle of North America. The leaders who attended the meeting were members of ICNA.
5. However, immediately on publication of the advertisement, the vice president of Islamic Circle of New York protested inclusion of their names among the other national organisations welcoming the Prime Minister and telephonically informed Shri Amarendra Khatua, minister that they were not willing to be a part of the group of the national bodies to welcome the Prime Minister and organise the public meeting. Due to this protest, the name of the

Islamic Circle of North America was dropped from other such advertisements welcoming Prime Minister.

6. Based on such reaction from a national body, we decided not to give recognition to religious, sectoral and regional organisations on the dais, so that the little time this office had to organise the meeting could be fully devoted for the public meeting and not to discuss issues of political, regional or religious nature.
7. Shri Poonawala was inducted as a member of the Brochure Committee. Bohri Jamaat of New York collected passes for distribution among the community members to participate in the public meeting.
8. It may be mentioned that all the 34 organisations that were recognised in the public meeting through their leadership have a large number of Muslim members. However, none of these organisations are headed by a Muslim.
9. Several Muslim members of Indo-American community participated in the public meeting on September 21, 2003.

Many newspapers carried positive narrations. They were complimentary on the number of people attending, the clear message by the involvement of the leadership of major organisations in USA, and, of course, the Prime Minister's message. Additionally, the precision of the programme was appreciated. Some comments from some of the well-known journalists are representative of the coverage by the press.

The Times of India reported on September 22, 2003:

"But Vajpayee, vintage and vigorous, disarmed the gathering and won a warm applause by declaring 'we are not just eyeing your money (for developing India), we are also after your hearts and minds'. He hardly needed to make the pitch. Rallied together by India's Ambassador-at-Large, Bhisham [sic] Agnihotri, 34 Indian and Indian-American organisations representing a wide spectrum of India's regional and professional diversity, were introduced to the Prime Minister and together they pledged to help India become a developed country by 2020.

"It was a stirring display of Indian pluralism and unity by groups often seen as divisive and scrappy. In fact, the entire event, which lasted just over an hour, was organised with clockwork precision and was probably shortest Prime Ministerial NRI engagement in the five visits he has made here in six years."[201]

Jyoti Malhotra of *Indian Express*, who had been proverbially anti-Agnihotri since my appointment as Ambassador, also ended up writing a quasi-complimentary comment. In addition to general coverage of the programme, the following comments were enjoyable coming from her:[202]

Ringleader Agnihotri

"Love him or hate him, you certainly can't dismiss Agnihotri anymore. The function to felicitate the PM was intended to display the 34 Indian-American Associations (Jat Association of America, Uttaranchal Association of America, the Overseas Friends of the BJP, the very powerful Association of American Physicians of Indian Origin, etc.), along with the subliminal message that the ringleader of them all was Agnihotri. You had to give it to him last night. He had ensured that the Jacob K. Javits Centre became the Boat Club of New York for one evening. The hall was jam packed with throaty supporters of the BJP from all the ethnic communities as well as key businessmen, who could now nicely come to the aid of the party back home. Indian ambassador Lalit Mansingh, also sitting on stage, was forced to grimly watch the proceedings. Agnihotri had neatly slipped the carpet from under his feet and he hadn't even known. It was a classic display of power and the IFS, once again, had refused to stoop to the occasion just in case it got its hands dirty. The rumour after the function that Agnihotri was a serious contender for the job of India's ambassador to the US –once Mansingh gives over in February – almost became a credible one."

K.P. Nayar of *The Telegraph* covered the programme quite extensively and neatly.[203]

"Prime Minister Atal Bihari Vajpayee may not have his way with the Vishwa Hindu Parishad (VHP) and its clones in India, but in New York, it is a different story. When representative of 34 Indian-American organisations in the US queued up yesterday to greet Vajpayee here, missing from the line-up were leaders of the Vajpayee-baiting hardline outfit along with the equally hardline Hindu Swayamsevak Sangh (HSS). Bhishma K. Agnihotri, India's Ambassador-at-Large for overseas Indians and the host of a largely-attended reception for the Prime Minister, excluded the VHP and the HSS from the reception committee, sources which helped organise the event said.

"To Vajpayee's surprise, the line-up of 34 leaders, included S.S. Malhotra, president of the Indian Overseas Congress, who is widely tipped to take Agnihotri's place if Sonia Gandhi ever became the Prime Minister.

"The Congress Party outfit and the Overseas Friends of the BJP were the only non-ethnic, non-professional bodies represented among the organisers."

On October 3, 2003, Shibi Alex Chandy wrote in *News India-Times:*

"The event, according to those familiar with the activities of Indian-American organisations, was unprecedented. Never before, said one observer, had 134 such groups come together on one platform.

"The credit," he said, "must surely go Ambassador-at-Large Agnihotri, who had apparently been working hard for some six months now to get as many groups on board."[204]

On September 22, 2003, *The Times of India* wrote:

"Anticipation was high at the event organised by Bhishma Agnihotri, Ambassador-at-Large for NRIs and PIOs, as well as some 134 Indian-American organisations – 34 of which presented the Prime Minister with a plaque inscribed with a 'Charter of Solidarity and Commitment' to help India become a developed country by 2020."

"The event, according to those familiar with the activities of Indian-American organisations, was unprecedented. Never before, said one observer, had 134 such organisations come together on one platform. 'The credit,' he said, 'must surely go to Ambassador-at-Large Agnihotri,' who had apparently been working hard for some six months now to get as many organisations on board as possible."[205]

In an article-titled 'Show of Unity, First for Community', *The Indian Express*, which generally had a problem with our office, published a very positive story on October 3, 2003.

"The theme *Unity in Diversity* blossomed last week at the Jacob Javits Centre in Manhattan. In a collective show of strength – the kind that has never before been seen – all major Indian-American organisations came together under one roof to listen to Prime Minister Atal Behari Vajpayee's speech and felicitate him with a plaque that affirmed the NRIs' commitment to their roots, the desire to inculcate the same ideals in successive generations and promote India-US ties.

"Said Dr. Rishi Raj, president, The Indian Academics in America: 'I have been 30 years in the US and have never seen anything close to the organisation and planning and the collective response that was generated.' This sentiment was echoed by most of the heads of the 34 organisations, which were present at the meet and many of whom later spoke to *The Indian Express*."[206]

□

13

Memorable Events Having Historical Impact

Problems of a Section of Sikhs in Vancouver/Canada

In one of the meetings, a reporter asked me a question as to what were my special contributions in my tenure as an Ambassador. I replied that one of my most satisfying achievements was my interaction with the Sikh groups in Canada. I was contacted by the leaders of the South Asian Human Rights Group of Canada. Before that meeting, I had arranged for the group to meet with the Deputy Prime Minister of India, Shri L.K. Advani, on June 13, 2003, in New York. It was a very good meeting. Thereafter, I was invited by the Canadian group to meet their leaders in Vancouver. Sikhs in Vancouver area were not interacting with the Indian consulate officials in Vancouver. After the movement for Khalistan and following the Operation Bluestar, there was resentment among the Sikhs, which developed into anti-India activities. As a consequence of that, many Sikhs involved in or thought to be involved in anti-India activities were denied the visas to visit India.There was a sort of standstill, at the minimum an unfriendly relationship, between the Sikhs of the area and the Government of India.

A meeting was arranged on the night of August 27, 2003, with the distinguished leaders of the communities representing all the Sikh groups in the hotel where I was staying. It lasted for three hours, and we discussed a number of issues beginning with the assassination of Prime Minister Indira Gandhi, the killing and torture of Sikhs in 1984, emergence of terrorism and demands of Khalistan. Our interaction was very emotional and passionate. As I happened to be from Punjab,

I related with them with openness and warmth. Most of them were almost crying at the end of the very long meeting. In order to wipe out the enmity and anger, the participants suggested and requested that persons who were barred from visiting India should be issued visas so that they could visit their families, as they had not visited for many years. After our discussions, I told them that I had been in touch with the Prime Minister of India and there might be some relief for some Sikhs on the blacklist.

A public programme was scheduled for the following day where all of the Sikh leaders and others interested would be present. I told those in the group, which was very warm by the end of the meeting, that I would see what I could do by the next day. I immediately got in touch with Mr. K.P. Singh (I.G. Police), the Prime Minister of India's contact person. All night, I kept on working on the list supplied to me by the group of the people desperately in need of visas. Mr. K.P. Singh had been working on the list before that evening and he had cleared some names before the meeting. The rest of the list of 22 was cleared at midnight. However, I kept that to myself to be announced publicly after we received appropriate statements from the affected persons.

The next day was the public reception/get-together. It was a full house; every chair was taken. The leaders of the Sikh community came one by one on the stage and made very positive statements. There were some members of the Canadian legislature and government also present, and they also expressed their feelings about the situation. Then the affected individuals who were seeking visa entries to India also came, one by one, on the stage and declared their love, affection and loyalty to India. After all the speeches, I addressed the group. My presentation was summarised by a reporter, R. Paul Dhillon, in the following words: "Yesterday (Wednesday) it was as a big family meeting and we were all talking and discussing – if I can be very honest – it was very emotional because so many of these people have not been able to visit India and, in the meantime they lost loved ones – parents, brothers and sisters – and they couldn't attend their funerals," Agnihotri said. "Whatever has happened in the past is the past. We cannot change that. But we can affect the future and I hope this is a starting point for improved relations between India and its Sikh family abroad."

For those critical of these developments and wanting to categorise these efforts as political, Agnihotri had a clear response. He said the Indian Prime Minister Atal Behari Vajpayee has never played politics with the Sikh community.

"For Vajpayee, this is not a matter of politics or strategy –in fact – this is he felt in 1984 and he feels the same way today," Agnihotri said, "We will welcome these people when they come home."

Agnihotri said India belongs to the Sikhs because they have made great contribution to its history, from Guru Gobind Singh and Guru Teg Bahadur to Kookas, who began India's freedom struggle in 1857 and to the Ghadhri Babas who took the freedom struggle from the North American shores to India and were later followed by great freedom fighters, like Kartar Singh Sarabha, Udham Singh and Bhagat Singh.

"We can't underestimate the contributions the Sikhs have made to India and its struggle to win independence," he said. "If we look at the past century – there is no doubting the great role they have played in India's defence forces. Even today, they are of Indian society."

Agnihotri was impressed with the people he met in Vancouver and said the interaction was emotional and affectionate and very real.

After I finished my address, I made the announcement that the Government of India has removed the 22 persons from the blacklist following our discussion of the previous night. This followed a great, joyful atmosphere throughout the audience. It really started a new chapter in the history of concerned Sikhs' relationship with India.

Bangladesh

In a few days after I assumed office, there was news about the upheaval in Bangladesh. The Hindus, especially women, were attacked and there were incidents of rapes and other tortuous acts. Some temples were also violated. People from Bangladesh, accompanied by a group of Hindus from other countries, approached my office and they brought a big, thick folder containing all the items in the newspapers regarding the incidents against Hindus in Bangladesh. In fact, one young Bangladeshi man almost cried when they were making the presentation. They submitted to me the memorandum and also gave me a copy of the big folder depicting the atrocities committed by Muslim terrorists. I was also moved by the facts presented to me. I called the

Prime Minister of India. He came on the telephone, and I was almost rude in asking him what the Government of India was doing about the conditions in Bangladesh. They must have all the reports. I told him also that I was sending the complete documentation submitted to me by diplomatic pouch so that quick action could be taken. I also told him that the massacre of Hindus in Bangladesh was our problem, too. India got freedom by partitioning India, and we represented the Hindus to get what we got as part of new India. The Prime Minister was very receptive and assured me that he would look into this. The following morning, he sent his Chief of Staff and National Security Advisor, Mr. Brijesh Mishra to Bangladesh and apparently, he carried a firm message from the Prime Minister. Historically, Bangladesh was created because India helped save the people of East Bengal, now Bangladesh, from the torture of Pakistani outfits and helped the Bangladeshi movement establish an independent country. I talked to the delegation of Bangladeshis and explained to them that hopefully the Prime Minister of Bangladesh would take the appropriate steps to stop the situation.

Ghadar Movement in North America

I had the privilege of participating in and addressing the 90th anniversary programme of the *ghadar* (revolution) movement by early immigrants from India. That movement started in 1913. This was a very inspiring occasion. My presentation on the occasion covered the importance of the occasion; so, it is given below.

Ambassador Bhishma K. Agnihotri's Inaugural Address to the Historic 90th Anniversary Celebrations to Commemorate Founding of the Ghadar Movement in North America

Delivered in San Francisco, USA on June l, 2003.

Today's historic celebration brings to life the memory of one of the finest chapters in the history of India's freedom struggle from colonial rule. It would not be an exaggeration to say that while India's First War of Independence was fought in 1857, its Second War of Independence started with the Ghadar Movement in 1913 here in North America. The selfless and innumerable sacrifices made by the activists, leaders and martyrs of the *ghadar* movement in order to achieve their aim of bringing liberty, freedom and independence to India and its people continues to inspire us here in North America, in India and around the world. Every Indian, who enjoys the fruits of freedom and dignity, shall forever remain obliged to the participants of the *ghadar* movement. Those Indians who are still struggling to secure their rights continue to be inspired by the *ghadar* movement.

The sacrifices of the activists, leaders and martyrs of this movement shall remain an integral part of the collective memory of the Indian nation. Their historic contributions to the cause of India will continue to inform the current and future generations of Indians everywhere of their patriotism and dedication to India and which transcended the boundaries of time, distance and faiths. The ideals, vision and wisdom of the leaders of the *ghadar* movement remain as relevant today as they were when the movement was formally initiated in 1913.

We have come a long way since 1913. Today, the eminence and size of the already 22-million strong Indian diaspora is rapidly increasing, both here in America as well as throughout the world. Through our hard work, perseverance and ingenuity, we Indians are becoming financially prosperous and are rapidly increasing our political clout. Many amongst us are being recognised for some exceptional achievements in various academic and applied fields, as well as for our unique professional expertise, excellence and contributions. As a result of the path of dedication and service shown by early generations of Indian immigrants to North America, the second and third generations are well positioned and able to build their own capital and clout. This new generation is also making tremendous value-added contributions in all spheres, to benefit the countries of their birth. The *ghadar* movement also remains an integral and a very valuable part of the collective history and identity of this new generation.

It is important to remember that in the very early part of the 20th century, America and Canada were in the grip of racism and segregation. Early Indian immigrants to North America faced intense discrimination and insult at all levels. They had to struggle against discriminatory laws that trampled on even their fundamental rights which our generation takes for granted. In 1907, a bill was passed in Canada which denied voting rights to Indians. At the time, Indian immigrants were barred from running for public offices and were prohibited from practicing lucrative and respectable professions. When, as a result of this discrimination, Indians began to migrate southward to America, anti-Indian riots broke out in Bellingham, Washington. By 1908, the discriminatory restraints on Indians were expanded to firmly close all channels of immigration to North America. Those Indians, who were already in America, were neither allowed to own land (except for religious buildings) nor permitted to independently own any business.

The plight of these Indian immigrants was exaggerated by a complete indifference and even active collusion of the British government in India to curb their rights throughout the world. While the interests of the Japanese and Chinese immigrants were protected by their respective governments, Indian immigrants received no such protection from the British. Indian immigrants recognised that their treatment in their adopted countries would not change as long as India remained enslaved to colonial rule. They also realised that their destinies in their adopted countries were intricately linked to the politico-economic conditions back in India. As a result of this realisation, in 1908, a small group led by Tarakanath Das, started a monthly publication called *Free Hindustan* in Seattle, Washington. Another publication *Swadesh Sewak* was also started in Punjabi, Gurudutt Kumar.

In the background of this rising patriotic activism amongst Indian immigrants, intellectuals such as Lala Hardayal (a visiting professor at Stanford University who was inspired by Vir Savarkar) and Bhai Parmanand, activist-intellectual Kartar Singh Sarabha and community activists like Sohan Singh Bhakna and several others organised a meeting of Indians in Astoria, Oregon in 1913. The Hindi Association of the Pacific Coast was formed at this meeting. Its membership reflected the unity in diversity of India's demographics and representative faiths. The defining aim of this Association was to end the British rule in India through violent means and armed rebellion and to establish a republic based on freedom and equality. This association also began publishing a weekly paper called *The Ghadar* to keep the memory of the 1857 revolution alive in the hearts and minds of Indians everywhere. The first issue of *The Ghadar* declared 'Our Name, Our Work – *Ghadar*.' Within a short period of time, *The Ghadar* became a highly prominent voice within Indian communities throughout the world and established itself as a leading forum for exchange of ideas on how India could achieve freedom from colonial rule and economic oppression. With the success of its publication, the Hindi Association of the Pacific Coast itself came to be recognised as the Ghadar Party and its activism came to be known as the *ghadar* movement. As a result of effectively igniting the patriotic passions of Indians worldwide, the *ghadar* movement rapidly mushroomed into an international movement for securing India's independence.

The forum for intellectual debate offered by *The Ghadar* ignited the hearts and minds of all Indians, irrespective of where they lived. It inspired Indians to re-capture the spirit of 1857 revolutionaries, whose valiant actions had fundamentally shaken the conditions under which the British had operated in India.

The Ghadar Party was also truly representative of peoples' aspirations. Besides publishing articles by Vir Savarkar on the history of India's First War of Independence of 1857, *The Ghadar* also published songs and patriotic poems. It called upon Indians to go back to India and launch a revolution. It inspired Indians to infiltrate the British army in India and convince Indians in that army 'to fight the British' rather than 'for the British' in the first Western World War. It also forcefully argued for attacking British military personnel, freeing political prisoners, seizing British government treasuries in India, disrupting communications and transportation, and above all, for training young Indians to organise the revolution on their own terms. The movement organised several rallies in America and forged alliances with Irish activists and German diplomats. The rapidly growing influence of the *ghadar* movement in North America sent shivers through the spine of British establishment in India and forced them to use significant resources to infiltrate and damage the movement.

The power of the *ghadar* movement was such that in response to its call, many Indians left their universities, resigned from academia, gave up their comfortable lifestyles, collected funds and organised dissent in order to wage a war for India's freedom. The movement's impact was far reaching. It inspired Shaheed Bhagat Singh, Ras Behari Bose, Sachindra Sanyal and their colleagues, in their revolutionary pursuits within India. The leaders of the *ghadar* movement planned a large uprising in India in February 1915. About eight thousand activists of the *ghadar* movement returned to India to participate in this project. Unfortunately, the British government received advanced information of their plans. Upon their arrival in India, several of these freedom fighters were arrested, some shot dead, some 45 were hung to death and many were sent to the Cellular Jail in *KalaPani*, where they were tortured. On November 16, 1915, in Lahore Central Jail, seven heroes of the *ghadar* movement, including Kartar Singh Sarabha (who was only 19-years old) and Vishnu Pingle (who was only 23-years old) were hung to death by the British. On July 31, 1940, another hero of the *ghadar* movement, Udham Singh, was hung to death for assassinating General O'Dweyer who was responsible for the Jalianwala Bagh massacre of Indians, in Amritsar.

Those involved in the *ghadar* movement were a unique and extraordinary people who have left an equally extraordinary benchmark of commitment towards India, for us and our future generations to emulate. Their sacrifices, patriotism, visionary convictions, and above all, their belief in the capacity of Indian people to create a resurgent and powerful nation continue to guide India, its leaders and Indians everywhere.

As before, the need to continue the spirit of *ghadar* remains highly relevant today. Like the founders of the *ghadar* movement, all of us need to realise and accept the fact that our destinies in our adopted countries are intricately linked to three factors. Firstly, our shared destinies depend on the positive contributions we continue to make to benefit our adopted societies and countries. Secondly, it will depend on the quality of politico-economic conditions prevalent in India. Thirdly, it will depend on how India is represented (and, therefore, perceived) in media and academic discourses throughout the world.

With respect to the first factor, the vision of the founders of the *ghadar* movement is captured in their foresight as expressed in item number 9 of the Ghadar Party Manifesto.

This manifesto states: "Every member is duty-bound to participate in the liberation struggle of that country in which they were resident."

Another Ghadar Party statement published in 1917 demonstrates the vision, wisdom and Indianness of its leaders. It states:

"The Ghadar Party is not national but international in the sense that its ultimate object is to bring harmony in the world by respecting and guaranteeing the diverse interests of the different nations; it aims not at competition, but at co-operation between the different nations and states, and in this respect, it follows the footsteps of the great Indian *rishis*...good for humanity is no vain and an empty word for Indian revolutionaries."

These statements reinforce that Indianness which stands for the ideals of *vishwashanti* (world peace) and *vasudhaivakutumbakam* (one world, one family) manifested itself in the very foundation of the *ghadar* movement. Therefore, as inheritors of their legacy, members of our contemporary Indian community should not hesitate to leverage our Indianness in order to fight for the improvement of the overall human condition in the countries where we live.

The second important factor which is intricately linked to the destiny of our Indian diaspora is the status of India and the conditions prevalent there. India has over centuries been a continually renewing civilisation which has witnessed several inflection points that have altered the course of its history. Today, once again, India stands at the crossroads of another historical transformation. After years of colonial rule and almost five-and-a-half decades of work by Indians to restore its foundations as a nation, India today is a redeveloping nation ready to take-off on the trajectory of rapid economic growth. From our standpoint, accelerating this redevelopment process is the true continuation of the spirit of *ghadar*.

In the contemporary context, *ghadar* continues to symbolise a 'struggle' to positively support measures being currently undertaken to improve conditions in India. This spirit of *ghadar* implies supporting efforts to build an India which is free of poverty, corruption, red tape, injustices, illiteracy and nepotism. It also implies building diplomatic and moral capital to fight against the export of terror to India, and to convincingly reject any attempt by others to create disunity within India and amongst Indians. Equally important to the continuation of this spirit of *ghadar* is the task of aggressively and positively harnessing the collective desires and talents of the Indian diaspora to participate in India's overall redevelopment so that India can, once again, become an economically prosperous and developed society.

Today, India is a redeveloping nation and is in the process of consolidating its position amongst world's great powers. To fully realise these objectives, India needs the sustained commitment and unyielding participation of its global diaspora. In the spirit of *ghadar*, I urge the Indian diaspora to further enhance their contributions to India. Let us all respond to the clarion call for the Ghadar Army which is still relevant. It urged: "Come brothers, you have earned plenty of dollars! Come, let us go back to our motherland and raise the banner of *ghadar*! . . .Do not delay! Only he is a brave fighter who fights for his country even if he is cut into pieces, he does not leave the battlefield!"

In the context of our commitment to the redevelopment of our India, the words and actions of Shaheed Kartar Singh Sarabha will always continue to strengthen our resolve. As brave Kartar Singh had pledged:

"Our struggle will continue as long as a handful of men, be they foreign or native, or both in collaboration with each other, continue to exploit the labour and resources of our people. Nothing shall deter us from this path."

Soon many non-residents and non-citizens amongst our Indian diaspora will have the opportunity to re-establish Indian citizenship. In the light of this, their commitment to India becomes all the more important and relevant. Let us further solidify our resolve to significantly enhance our efforts to ensure that India, once again, becomes a developed nation by the year 2020. Let us immediately step up our work towards establishing the required framework to make this possible even earlier.

The third important factor which is intricately linked to the destiny of our Indian diaspora is the quality and accuracy of India's representation in media and in academic discourses around the world. There is an urgent need for a cooperative and a multi-dimensional effort on the part of our diaspora to highlight any inaccuracies that may be prevalent in the representation of India and, therefore, in the knowledge of India. History has taught us that knowledge is a critical instrument of power. Destinies of nations and people are shaped by the way they are represented. This effort is especially significant when the construction of knowledge on India is, at least partly, being shaped by those within and without India whose motivation to power may lead to an intellectual marginalisation of India, its history, geography, culture, technology, resources and other interests.

Therefore, I urge you to utilise your intellectual capital and goodwill to ensure that any such misrepresentations are corrected. This will ensure that a more accurate repository of knowledge of India is established for our next generations to learn from. An accurate representation of India will go a long way in helping our coming generations to develop a positive image of their heritage and, consequently, a solid self-esteem and identity as Indians. It will also create for people around the world, a correct and positive image of India and help India to secure its rightful place in the emerging mosaic of global powers.

It is critical to emphasise that only through our commitment to these three critical objectives, our diaspora can offer their richest tribute to the memory of the brave martyrs of the *ghadar*.

Finally, on behalf of our office, I would like to offer our services and assistance to catalyse and streamline the participation of the diaspora in the cause of India's redevelopment. We encourage you to actively participate in the media project already being facilitated by our office to improve India's image in the Western media. There are several other projects which have also been initiated by our office and in which you can actively participate. We promise a prompt response from our office, to any request or queries, from all well wishers of India.

The programme was covered extensively by the media.

Indo-Caribbean Academicians Forum

Our Indo-Caribbean leaders' forum was held on May 28, 2003. The report of that was filed earlier with the workshops. In order to further our plan to work with the Indo-Caribbean community, a workshop on Indo-Caribbean academicians in New York was held on March 27, 2004. My office prepared the following report:

Report

A workshop on 'Indo-Caribbean Academicians: a Diaspora Perspective' was organised by the office of Ambassador-at-Large for Non-Resident Indians and Persons of Indian Origin on March 27, 2004 in New York. The workshop was based on the three themes –'Experiences of Academicians of Indo-Caribbean Origin in the United States of America's Educational System'; 'Problem and Perspectives of the Indo-Caribbean Academic Diaspora in the United States of America' and "Expectation of the Academic Diaspora from the Indo-Caribbean Community, if any'. The workshop was chaired by Dr. B.K. Agnihotri, Ambassador-at-Large for non-resident Indians and Persons of Indian origin.

The three main theme discussions were presented respectively by Mr. Frankie Ramadhar, Mrs. Chan Jamoona, Mrs. Sue Ann Commissioning and Dr. Mahin Gosine. The workshop was attended by a large number of Indo-Caribbean teachers, educators, writers and academicians. The highlights of the workshop included a number of observations that reflects on the problem of social integration and assimilations by the small Indo-Caribbean population within the American academic system. There are discriminatory practices confronted by the Indo-Caribbean entrants; the clash of value systems also sometimes hinder clear growth process and intimidates the Indo-Caribbean students/ academicians. The text and curriculum in a large number of cases have not been culturally conducive and sociologically appropriate. Most of the time, there is no imparting of education including that of the social anthropology and the history of the Indo-Caribbean diaspora by the US education system to these groups. This leads to creating generational gap among the diaspora community. Non-availability of books, bookshops and academic material on the history of Indo-Caribbean diaspora also do not help in ameliorating this situation further.

A number of suggestions for greater interaction, adopting integrated approach and creation of special studies and facilities, etc. were made by the participants. Dr. B.K. Agnihotri expressed his thanks to Mrs. Bhanu Dwarika for her assistance in organising the workshop and added that his office would continue to establish greater interaction with the Indo-Caribbean community on such issues of social and political importance. He mentioned that a report incorporating of the suggestions and recommendations will be formulated and circulated among policy-makers and community organisations.

Outreach Programme specially for a Muslim Group

At the request of the Houston Chapter of the American Federation of Muslims of Indian Origin, I attended their meeting in Houston. It was a breakfast meeting and there was a large attendance. Many women also joined. I spoke briefly and asked them to ask any questions so that we can have a proper dialogue and clear up any misunderstandings. Unfortunately, the first question they asked was about Modi, who was the Chief Minister of Gujarat. Obviously, it was February 2003, and it was right on top in their minds as to what was happening in Gujarat. There was a lot of propaganda about the events in Gujarat, and their apprehensions were well placed. In my response, I declared that I was very unhappy about the happenings in Gujarat. I was equally unhappy about burning of thc people in the train in Godhra. Then I asked the question, "Have you been equally depressed about that, too?" They kept quiet. Then I made an announcement that before I came for the meeting, I watched the news that perhaps they had not watched. The news stated that Modi has been re-elected as the Chief Minister of Gujarat with an overwhelming majority.

Then I said, "Look, we have to be equally pained for all, especially for people of India, irrespective of their religions. That is the beauty of our culture." They asked many other questions and I responded to them, but I also told them that as Indian origin persons, they should always get out and support Indian causes in America and join with other Indian groups in support of Indian causes that will develop close relationship with all people of Indian origin. Of course, I mentioned the greatness of Indians from all walks of life in America and other things.

It was a long meeting, but everybody was pleased and happy about the meeting and my role as Ambassador of all NRIs and PIOs. The report of this event was published in the newspapers.[194]

□

14

BJP Lost the Election

I was travelling from Mauritius to New Delhi. When I arrived, I saw the news that Prime Minister Vajpayee was trailing in the parliamentary election. I called the Prime Minister, and his secretary immediately connected me to him. I asked what had happened, and he said he lost the election and that he was ready to submit his resignation to the President. I asked him to wait because I was on my way to meet him. On arrival, I went to his office and submitted my resignation to him. I told the Prime Minister that I wanted to be the first to resign. He mentioned that I could not resign then and there. I had to go back to my station and resign from there. I returned to the USA and resigned from my job. Then, I returned to Louisiana and joined a law firm.

I stayed engaged in my activities with the community, law practice and teaching law. I am not giving the details which are not relevant for our main subject matter for the book.

Bharat Swabhiman Overseas – Anti-corruption Movement

Baba Ramdev, a well-known yoga exponent, asked me to head Bharat Swabhiman Overseas as chairman. I respectfully agreed and worked with him and various other members of the group initially in the anti-corruption movement. Various rallies and programmes were held to highlight the problems of corruption, especially in India. One of the initial programmes was held in Washington, D.C., where Baba Ramdev addressed the audience on the forum held under the auspices of the Bharat Swabhiman Overseas and Friends of India Society International. Work is still continuing in other spheres.

Interaction with His Highness Dalai Lama

I had the opportunity to interact with His Highness the Dalai Lama regarding the suggestion made by various leaders in India to suggest to him to become an Indian citizen. Despite my efforts and his initial positive feelings for the suggestion, he ultimately decided not to accept Indian citizenship.

Friends of India Society International

The Society held many seminars in America, Canada, England and other places, on various concerns. Prominent amongst them was on the issue of Tibet and the glory of India, the contribution of Sardar Patel, Dr. Ambedkar and others.

Global Law Seminars

As Chancellor Emeritus of the Southern University Law Center, I offer two seminars to the graduating lawyers. One covers global law and practice reflecting among others the relevance of the United Nation and its impact in development of international norms.

The second seminar focuses on trade issues effecting the world especially in the current environment. The programme has been very successful and innovative. Books prepared by me are prescribed to all the students without any costs.

Practising Law

Senior Special Counsel to a law firm.

□

15

Some Interesting Personal Memories of Atal Ji

Since my meeting with Atalji at the programme for Dr. Syama Prasad Mookerjee mentioned earlier, I had been in contact with Atalji on a regular basis. Here-are a few of my memories of his visit to the USA. In 1984, Atalji visited Louisiana. He-stayed at our house at Baton Rouge. It was just before lunch that I asked Atalji, "Would you like to address the Louisiana legislature?" He agreed without much ado. I contacted the Speaker of the House and informed him about Atalji and requested him to organise a joint session, if possible, that afternoon. It was immediately agreed upon for Shri Atalji to address the joint session of the legislature. I accompanied him. At that time, Atalji had just lost the election in Parliament and BJP had only two legislators in the Parliament. The Speaker asked me to introduce Atalji to the session. I introduced him, mentioning his contributions to Indian polity, etc. Then I ended the speech by saying, "I have the pleasure of presenting to you the future Prime Minister of India." Atalji looked at me, visibly showing his displeasure. After his speech was over and we started walking down the stage, he asked me in Hindi, "Were you making fun of me?" I told him, "I was not saying that you are going to be the next Prime Minister of India. I only said that you would be the future Prime Minister of India and then, who knows the future?"

Later on, in 1996, when Atalji became the Prime Minister of India for the first time, I phoned him and congratulated him. In his usual style, he replied in Hindi, "I have become the Prime Minister for a few days only to honour your statement in the Louisiana legislature." It was a typical Atalji's response to the situation. As is well known, he had to resign after 13 days.

Another incident worth mentioning is when President Clinton visited India in the year 2000. A luncheon programme was arranged in his honour. Attendees had lined up before lunch. One by one, they were moving in a queue to shake hands with the President Clinton and Prime Minister Vajpayee. I too stood in the queue. When I got to them, President Clinton took the initiative and said to the Prime Minister, "Please meet my good friend, B.K. Agnihotri from Louisiana." The Prime Minister promptly responded, "I was going to say the same thing!" Then I remarked, "How lucky am I to be a friend of two world leaders," and then moved on to my table for lunch.

□

Endnotes

1. https://thediplomat.com/2015/05/indias-soft-power-potential
2. https://thediplomat.com/2014/09/indias-soft-power-advantage/
3. http://www.indiafoundation.in/indias-soft-power-and-cultural-diplomacy the-role-of-yoga-and-dharmic-traditions/
4. https://www.outlookindia.com/website/story/indias-soft-power-strategy/295206
5. https://qrius.com/indias-soft-power-public-diplomacy/
6. Shakuntala Rao and Navjit Singh Johal, 'Ethics and News Making in the Changing Indian Mediascape,' *Journal of Mass Media Ethics*, Vol. 21, No. 4 (2006), p. 287.
7. Vandana Aggarwal quoted by Shakuntala Rao and Seow Ting Lee, 'Globalising Media Ethics? An Assessment of Universal Ethics Among International Political Journalists',*Journal of Mass Media Ethics*, Vol. 20, Nos. 2 & 3 (2005), p. 107.
8. *Ibid,* 115.
9. A. Kumar, Trends in Modern Journalism (New Delhi: Swarup, 2002) quoted by Rao and Johal, *Ethics and News Making*, p. 290.
10. Rao and Johal, *Ethics and News Making*, pp. 292-301.
11. J. N. Dixit, *Hindustan Times*, New Delhi, August 30, 2001, p. 12.
12. *The Times of India*, New Delhi, September 3, 2001, p. 10.
13. *India Today*, September 10, 2001, pp. 38-9.
14. S. K. Singh, *Hindustan Times*, October 10, 2001.
15. Praful Bidwai, 'All in the Family: Vajpayee's Credibility as a 'Liberal' is Badly Eroded by his Own Actions,' *Hindustan Times* August 31, 2001, p. 12.

16. *The Hindu*, August 30, 2001, p. 11.
17. Dr. Surinder S. Malhotra to President of India, Mr. K. R. Narayanan, n.d. as quoted in *The Hindu,* August 30, 2001, p. 11.
18. Seema Guha, *Times News Network,* 'Oppn [Opposition] terms appointment of ambassador-at-large 'illegal': Agnihotri entry irks ministry mandarins,' *The Times of India*, Pune, August 31, 2001, p. 1.
19. 'Walk out in Lok Sabha over appointment of Agnihotri,' *Hindustan Times*, August 31, 2001, p. 10.
20. Opposition walks out over Agnihotri's US appointment, *The Asian Age*, August 31, 2001, p. 3.
21. 'RSS grounds BJP's overseas wing, PM fed up with feuds,' *Indian Express*, January 6, 2003.
22. J. N. Dixit, 'All the PM's Men: The Appointment of an Ambassador-at-Large in Washington will lead Us into a Diplomatic Black-Hole,' *Hindustan Times*, August 30, 2001, p. 12.
23. S.K. Singh, 'Super Ambassador: Will this New Envoy become A Fifth Wheel of our Diplomatic Cart in Washington?' *Hindustan Times*, September 10, 2001. .
24. Dixit, *All the PM's Men*.
25. Singh, *Super Ambassador*.
26. Singh, *Super Ambassador*.
27. Dixit, *All the PM's Men*.
28. Aziz Haniffa, Agnihotri's Appointment aimed at Boosting US Ties, India Abroad, August 31, 2001, p. 1. As Raj Chengappa reported in *India Today*, I stated regarding my relationship with Ambassador Mansingh, 'We will complement and supplement each other. There won't be any turf battles. I am a team player.' Raj Changappa, 'Privilege Posting,' *India Today*, September 10, 2001, p. 39.
29. https://www.nytimes.com/2012/02/03/us/wind-river-indian-reservation-where-brutality-is-banal.html
30. https://www.indian.senate.gov/sites/default/files/upload/files/January2820102.pdf
31. https://www.census.gov/newsroom/facts-for-features/2015/cb15-ff22.html
32. Tina Norris et al., The American Indian and Alaska Native

Population:2010, US Census Bureau, C2010BR-10, 4 (2012) http://www.census.gov/prod/cen2010/briefs/c2010br10.pdf.

33. S. REP. NO. 111-118, at 2 (2010), https://www.indian.senate.gov/sites/default/files/upload/files/January2820102.pdf.
34. https://www.bjs.gov/content/pub/pdf/cv13.pdf at 6
35. https://www.samhsa.gov/sites/default/files/topics/tribal_affairs/ai-an-data-handout.pdfat3
36. https://digitalcommons.law.utulsa.edu/cgi/viewcontentcgi?article=2441& context=tlr at 358 ("Judges, attorneys and scholars often describe the trust duty of protection as a principle deriving from a guardian-ward relationship between the federal government and tribes. This paternalistic characterisation has its origin in an analogy made by Chief Justice Marshall in Cherokee Nation v. Georgia, where he commented that the tribes were 'domestic dependent nations', whose 'relation to the United States resembles that of a ward to his guardian'.")
37. Committee on the Elimination of Racial Discrimination 59th Session Summary of the 1475thmeeting, CERD/C/SR/1475 p. 9, para. 33 (Aug. 22, 2001).
38. https://www.justice.gov/sites/default/files/tribal/legacy/2014/02/06/vawa-2013-tribal-jurisdiction-overnon-indian-perpetrators-domesticviolence.pdf
39. https://www.huffingtonpost.com/2014/06/04/keith-harper-ambassador_n_5446900.html
40. https://newsmaven.io/indiancountrytoday/archive/diane-humetewa-confirmed-to-federal-bench-makes-history-yq9JQViqdEGhOxS_adBLXQ/
41. http://time.com/5446593/sharice-davids-deb-haaland-first-native-american-woman-congress/
42. Jagdish Seth, 'Sun Never sets on Indian Diaspora: Dr. Agnihotri,' *India Post*, December 14, 2001, p. 18.
43. Gitesh Desai, 'Agnihotri calls for unity,' *India Post News Service,* nd (?), held at the India Cultural Centre, Houston, Texas, October 12, 2001.
44. Viji Sundaram, 'Envoy-at-large urges NRIs to get united,' India-West, December 14, 2001, pp. A? and A 32; Ashok Easwaran,

'Be proactive in fighting negative image of India: Agnihotri,' *India Abroad*, November 9, 2001 (Address to the Indian House Banquet, Schaumburg, Chicago, October 28, 2001).

45. "Ambassador Agnihotri calls for unity among NRIs,' *India Post News* Service, nd (?), pp 12-13. (A public meeting held at the Massachusetts Institute of Technology, Feb. 9-10, 2002).
46. Prakeash M. Swamy, 'One-stop window to woo NRI Investments,' no title, no date, no pages??? (MIT event).
47. First Name?,Gadgil, 'Agnihotri stresses Indian American unity,' *India Herald* (?), October 19, 2001, p. 1. Another article on presentation at the India Cultural Centre, Houston, Texas, October 12, 2001.
48. Prashanth Lakhihal, 'Agnihotri lays out his agenda,' *India Post News Service,* October 12, 2001 (A Press Conference, New York, October 3, 2001).
49. "January 26, 2002 ... India's Republic Day Celebrations in Tampa, Florida,' *We Indians*, Jan/Feb 2002, p.3. (Emphasis in the original; Republic Day presentation to five hundred Indians gathered in the Indian Cultural Centre, Tampa, FL, January 26, 2002).
50. Prashjot Singh, 'His aim is one global Indian family,' *Tribune, News Service,* March 18, 2002, p. 13.
51. Abraham Thariath, 'India declares January 9 as NRI Day,' *India Abroad*, February 22, 2002, no page?. ((A public meeting held at the Massachusetts Institute of Technology, Feb. 9-10, 2002).
52. Sindwani, Dr. K. L. 'At Long Last, an NRI's Ambassador', source/ date/page unknown.
53. 'Agnihotri lays out his agenda' *India Post,* October 12, 2001, p. 6.
54. Adhikari, Ravi. 'B.K. Agnihotri outlines his plans for the global NRI', *Desi Talk,* October 26, 2001, p. 6.
55. Seth, Jagdish. 'Sun never sets on Indian Diaspora: Dr. Agnihotri', *India Post,* December 28, 2001, p. 26.
56. Seth, Jagdish. 'Sun never sets on Indian Diaspora: Dr. Agnihotri', *India Post,* December 28, 2001, p. 26.
57. Easwaran, Ashok. 'Be proactive in fighting negative image of India: Agnihotri', *India Abroad,* November 9, 2001.
58. Easwaran, Ashok. 'Be proactive in fighting negative image of

India: Agnihotri', *India Abroad*, November 9, 2001.

59. *India Post News Service.* 'Ambassador Agnihotri calls for unity among NRIs', p. 12-13.
60. *India Post News Service*, 'Ambassador Agnihotri calls for unity among NRIs', p. 12-13.
61. Thariath, Abraham. 'India declares January 9 as NRI Day', *India Abroad*, February 22, 2002.
62. Singh, Preet Onkar. 'Our Guardian (angel) in US'.
63. Singh, Prabhjot. 'His aim is one global Indian family', *The Tribune*, March 17, 2002, p.13.
64. "Persons of Indian Origin – A peeved lot', *The Hindu Business Line* (http://www.blonnet.com/2002/03/21/stories/2002032102810300.htm).
65. "Persons of Indian Origin – A peeved lot', *The Hindu Business Line* (http://www.blonnet.com/2002/03/21/stories/2002032102810300.htm).
66. "Support India financially, Agnihotri tells NRIs', *Indian Express*, May 3, 2002, page unknown.
67. Author unknown. 'Agnihotri attends AAPI's Tennessee Spring conference', *India Abroad*, May 24, 2002, p. 50.
68. "NFIA organises fund-raiser, welcomes Agnihotri', source/date/page unknown.
69. Easwaran, Ashok. 'Be proactive in fighting negative image of India: Agnihotri', *India Abroad*, November 9, 2001, p. unknown.
70. Sindwani, Dr. K. L. 'At Long Last, an NRI's Ambassador', source/date/page unknown.
71. Desai, Gitesh. 'Agnihotri calls for unity', source/date/page unknown.
72. Desai, Gitesh. 'Agnihotri calls for unity', source/date/page unknown.
73. Lakhihal, Prashanth. 'Agnihotri lays out his agenda', *India Post*, October 12, 2001, p.6.
74. Adhikari, Ravi. 'B.K. Agnihotri outlines his plans for the global NRI', *Desi Talk*, October 26, 2001, p. 6.
75. Malhotra, Jawahar. 'Coalesce Ideas into Workable Profacts for India,' *Indo-American News*, ? 19, 2001, p. C?.
76. Srirekha, N.C. 'NY group to support India's action', *India Post*, date/page unknown.

77. Srirekha, N.C. ‘NY group to support India’s action’, *India Post*, date/page unknown.
78. Soparawala, Ramesh. ‘Tampa Bay Indians celebrate Republic Day’, *India Post,* date/page unknown.
79. “Ambassador Agnihotri calls for unity among NRIs’, source/date unknown, p. 12-13.
80. “Ambassador Agnihotri calls for unity among NRIs’, source/date unknown, p. 12-13.
81. “Fight for causes of India”: Agnihotri, source/date/page unknown.
82. “Fight for causes of India”: Agnihotri, source/date/page unknown.
83. “Fight for causes of India”: Agnihotri, source/date/page unknown.
84. “Fight for causes of India”: Agnihotri, source/date/page unknown.
85. “Fight for causes of India”: Agnihotri, source/date/page unknown.
86. “‘Fight for causes of India’: Agnihotri’, source/date/page unknown.
87. Singh, Prabhjot. ‘His aim is one global Indian family’, *The Tribune*, March 17, 2002, p.13.
88. Singh, Prabhjot. ‘His aim is one global Indian family’, *The Tribune*, March 17, 2002, p.13.
89. Singh, Prabhjot. ‘His aim is one global Indian family’, *The Tribune*, March 17, 2002, p.13.
90. Singh, Prabhjot. ‘His aim is one global Indian family’, *The Tribune*, March 17, 2002, p.13.
91. Singh, Prabhjot. ‘His aim is one global Indian family’, *The Tribune*, March 17, 2002, p.13.
92. Singh, Prabhjot. ‘His aim is one global Indian family’, *The Tribune*, March 17, 2002, p.13.
93. Singh, Prabhjot. ‘His aim is one global Indian family’, *The Tribune*, March 17, 2002, p.13.
94. Garimella, Nirmala. ‘B.K. Agnihotri, Advisor and Ambassador-at-Large visits Boston’, http://www.lokvani.com/lokvani/article.php?article_id=79.
95. Garimella, Nirmala. ‘B.K. Agnihotri, Advisor and Ambassador-at-Large visits Boston’, http://www.lokvani.com/lokvani/article.php?article_id=79.
96. Garimella, Nirmala. ‘B.K. Agnihotri, Advisor and Ambassador-at-Large visits Boston’, http://www.lokvani.com/lokvani/article.php?article_id=79.

97. Lakhihal, Prashanth. 'Agnihotri appoints nine study groups,' *India Tribune,* June 15, 2002, p. unknown.
98. Pancholi, Chandrakant. 'Agnihotri Announces Nine Projects to Benefit India, NRIs and PIOs', *India Weekly*-USA, June 9, 2002, p. 3.
99. Lakhihal, Prashanth. 'Agnihotri appoints nine study groups,' *India Tribune,* June 15, 2002, p. unknown.
100. Pancholi, Chandrakant. 'Agnihotri Announces Nine Projects To Benefit India, NRIs and PIOs', *India Weekly*-USA, June 9, 2002, p. 3.
101. Pancholi, Chandrakant. 'Agnihotri Announces Nine Projects To Benefit India, NRIs and PIOs', *India Weekly-USA,* June 9, 2002, p. 3.
102. Pancholi, Chandrakant. 'Agnihotri Announces Nine Projects To Benefit India, NRIs and PIOs', *India Weekly-USA,* June 9, 2002, p. 3.
103. Ullal, Surendra. 'Dual Citizenship next year: Agnihotri', *India Post,* July 12, 2002, p. 12.
104. Haniffa, Aziz. 'VIP no-shows take gloss off NFIA convention,' *India Abroad,* October 25, 2002, p. unknown.
105. "Remarkable display of unity at conference,' *News India Times,* date/p. unknown.
106. "Agnihotri charms Yoga teachers,' *Voice of Asia,* November 29, 2002, p. unknown.
107. Potts, Michel W. 'Workshop Offers Ways to Improve India's Media Image', *India West,* November 15, 2002, p. unknown.
108. Potts, Michel W. 'Workshop Offers Ways to Improve India's Media Image', *India West,* November 15, 2002, p. unknown.
109. Potts, Michel W. 'Workshop Offers Ways to Improve India's Media Image', *India West,* November 15, 2002, p. unknown.
110. "Agnihotri sets out to improve India's image in the media', *India Abroad,* December 13, 2002, p. C4.
111. Pancholi, Chandrakant. 'Agnihotri Moves Against Western Media Belying India,' *India Weekly USA,* November 24, 2002, pp. 16.
112. "Agnihotri for raising media awareness among NRIs', *India Post,* November 29, 2002, p. 14, 22.

113. "Agnihotri for raising media awareness among NRIs', *India Post,* November 29, 2002, p. 14, 22.
114. Sindwani, K. L. 'At Long Last, an NRI's Ambassador', source/date/p. unknown.
115. Desai, Gitesh. 'Agnihotri calls for unity', *India Post,* date/p. unknown.
116. Desai, Gitesh. 'Agnihotri calls for unity', India Post, date/p. unknown.
117. Desai, Gitesh. 'Agnihotri calls for unity', India Post, date/p. unknown.
118. Lakhihal, Prashanth. 'Agnihotri lays out his agenda,' *India Post,* October 12, 2001, p. 6.
119. Adhikari, Ravi. 'B.K. Agnihotri outlines his plans for the global NRI', *Desi Talk,* October 26, 2001, p. 6.
120. Author unknown. 'Dr. Bhishma Agnihotri Visits Caribbeans', source/date/p. unknown.
121. Sundaram, Viji. 'Envoy-at-Large Urges NRIs to Get United', *India - West,* December 14, 2001, A1, A32.
122. Sundaram, Viji. 'Envoy-at-Large Urges NRIs to Get United', *India - West,* December 14, 2001, A1, A32.
123. Sundaram, Viji. 'Envoy-at-Large Urges NRIs to Get United', *India - West,* December 14, 2001, A1, A32.
124. Miller, Austin L. 'Indian ambassador aims for global unity', *Star-Banner,* Sunday, January 27, 2002, 1B-2B.
125. Miller, Austin L. 'Indian ambassador aims for global unity', *Star-Banner,* Sunday, January 27, 2002, 1B-2B.
126. Author unknown. 'Ambassador Agnihotri calls for unity among NRIs,' *India Post,* date unknown, p. 12-13.
127. Author unknown. 'Ambassador Agnihotri calls for unity among NRIs,' *India Post,* date unknown, p. 12-13.
128. Swamy, Prakash M. 'One-stop Window To Woo NRI Investments,' source/date/p. unknown.
129. Author unknown. 'Fight for causes of India': Agnihotri', source/date/p. unknown.
130. Author unknown. 'Support India financially, Agnihotri tells NRIs', *Indian Express,* May 3, 2002, p. unknown.
131. Author unknown. 'Agnihotri attends AAPI's Tennessee Spring conference', *India Abroad,* May 24, 2002, p. 50.

132. Author unknown. 'Agnihotri attends AAPI's Tennessee Spring conference', *India Abroad,* May 24, 2002, p. 50.
133. A.G. 'Bhishma K. Agnihotri addresses India-America Chamber of Commerce', *Indian Reporter,* June 7, 2002, p. unknown.
134. Author unknown. 'Agnihotri urges diaspora to invest in India', *India Post,* June 7, 2002, p. 7.
135. Lakshman, Ganesh S. 'NRIs must get involved in American society', *News India Times,* June 7, 2002, p. unknown.
136. Pancholi, Chandrakant. 'Agnihotri Announces Nine Projects To Benefit India, NRIs and PIOs', *India Weekly*-USA, June 9, 2002, p. 3.
137. Pancholi, Chandrakant. 'Agnihotri Announces Nine Projects To Benefit India, NRIs and PIOs', *India Weekly*-USA, June 9, 2002, p. 3.
138. Pancholi, Chandrakant. 'Agnihotri Announces Nine Projects To Benefit India, NRIs and PIOs', *India Weekly*-USA, June 9, 2002, p. 3.
139. Pancholi, Chandrakant. 'Agnihotri Announces Nine Projects To Benefit India, NRIs and PIOs', India Weekly-USA, June 9, 2002, p. 3.
140. Rajan, Sujeet. 'Agnihotri Proposals', *Indian Express,* June 14, 2002, p. unknown.
141. Rajan, Sujeet. 'Agnihotri Proposals', *Indian Express,* June 14, 2002, p. unknown.
142. Mozumder, Suman Guha. 'Agnihotri announces nine projects to help diaspora', *India Abroad,* June 14, 2002, p. 1.
142. Suhasini, Gloria. 'Agnihotri announces projects for diaspora', *News India Times?,*June 7, 2002? p. unknown.
144. Author unknown. 'Agnihotri updates community', *Indian Reporter,* July 5, 2002, p. 29.
145. Author unknown. 'Agnihotri updates community', *Indian Reporter,* July 5, 2002, p. 29.
146. Author unknown. 'Agnihotri updates community', *Indian Reporter,* July 5, 2002, p. 29.
147. Author unknown. 'Agnihotri updates community', *Indian Reporter,* July 5, 2002, p. 29.
148. Ullal, Surendra. 'Dual citizenship next year: Agnihotri', *India Post,* July 12, 2002, p. 12.

149. Dutt, Ela. 'India's Kashmir position better understood now', *News India Times,* July 12, 2002, p. unknown.
150. Dutt, Ela. 'India's Kashmir position better understood now', *News India Times,* July 12, 2002, p. unknown.
151. Thariath, Abraham. 'six hundred attend Vokkaliga convention,' *India Abroad,* August 2, 2002, p. unknown.
152. Roy, Amit. 'Eye on England,' www.telegraphindia.com/archive/1020714/editoria.htm.
153. Roy, Amit. 'Eye on England,' www.telegraphindia.com/archive/1020714/editoria.htm.
154. Roy, Amit. 'Eye on England,' www.telegraphindia.com/archive/1020714/editoria.htm.
155. Roy, Amit. 'Eye on England,' www.telegraphindia.com/archive/1020714/editoria.htm.
156. Author unknown. 'Final decision on dual citizenship is expected before January,' www.rediff.com/us/2002/jul/12uk.htm.
157. Author unknown. 'Final decision on dual citizenship is expected before January,' www.rediff.com/us/2002/jul/12uk.htm.
158. Author unknown. 'Final decision on dual citizenship is expected before January,' www.rediff.com/us/2002/jul/12uk.htm.
159. Author unknown. 'Final decision on dual citizenship is expected before January,' www.rediff.com/us/2002/jul/12uk.htm.
160. Author unknown. 'Ambassador-at-Large taking initiatives to develop global Indian family,' *India Post,* September 20, 2002, p. 8.
161. Author unknown. 'Ambassador-at-Large taking initiatives to develop global Indian family,' *India Post,* September 20, 2002, p. 8.
162. Author unknown. 'Ambassador-at-Large taking initiatives to develop global Indian family,' *India Post,* September 20, 2002, p. 8.
163. Author unknown. 'Ambassador-at-Large taking initiatives to develop global Indian family,' *India Post,* September 20, 2002, p. 8.
164. Author unknown. 'Reception in honour Ambassador-at-Large for NRIs and PIOs,' source/date/p. unknown.
165. Author unknown. 'Reception in honour Ambassador-at-Large for NRIs and PIOs,' source/date/p. unknown.

166. Author unknown. 'Reception in honour Ambassador-at-Large for NRIs and PIOs,' source/date/p. unknown.
167. Adhikari, Ravi. 'B.K. Agnihotri outlines his plans for the global NRI', *Desi Talk,* October 26, 2001, page 6.
168. Adhikari, Ravi. 'B.K. Agnihotri outlines his plans for the global NRI', *Desi Talk,* October 26, 2001, page 6.
169. Sundaram, Viji. 'Envoy-at-Large Urges NRIs to Get United', *India-West,* December 14, 2001, A1, A32.
170. Sundaram, Viji. 'Envoy-at-large Urges NRIs to Get United', *India-West,* December 14, 2001, A1, A32.
171. Soparawala, Ramesh. 'Tampa Bay Indians celebrate Republic Day', *India Post,* date/p. unknown.
172. Swamy, Prakash M. 'One-stop Window To Woo NRI Investments,' source/date/p.unknown.
173. Swamy, Prakash M. 'One-stop Window To Woo NRI Investments,' source/date/p.unknown.
174. Thariath, Abraham. 'India declares January 9 as NRI Day', *India Abroad,* February 22, 2002.
175. Thariath, Abraham. 'India declares January 9 as NRI Day', *India Abroad,* February 22, 2002.
176. Joseph, George. 'Mark Massey honoured for rescuing Tulsa Company workers', *India Abroad,* April 26, 2002, p. 8.
177. Joseph, George. 'Mark Massey honoured for rescuing Tulsa Company workers', *India Abroad,* April 26, 2002, p. 8.
178. Garimella, Nirmala. 'B.K. Agnihotri, Advisor and Ambassador-at-Large visits Boston', http://www.lokvani.com/lokvani/article.php?article_id=79.
179. Garimella, Nirmala. 'B.K. Agnihotri, Advisor and Ambassador-at-Large visits Boston', http://www.lokvani.com/lokvani/article.php?article_id=79.
180. Author unknown. 'Agnihotri attends AAPI's Tennessee Spring conference', *India Abroad,* May 24, 2002, p. 50.
181. Author unknown. 'Indian envoy: Love your country first', source/date/p. unknown.
182. Pancholi, Chandrakant. 'Agnihotri Announces Nine Projects To Benefit India, NRIs and PIOs', *India Weekly*-USA, June 9, 2002, p. 3.

183. Pancholi, Chandrakant. 'Agnihotri Announces Nine Projects To Benefit India, NRIs and PIOs', *India Weekly*-USA, June 9, 2002, p. 3.
184. Pancholi, Chandrakant. 'Agnihotri Announces Nine Projects To Benefit India, NRIs and PIOs', *India Weekly*-USA, June 9, 2002, p. 3.
185. Pancholi, Chandrakant. 'Agnihotri Announces Nine Projects To Benefit India, NRIs and PIOs', *India Weekly*-USA, June 9, 2002, p. 3.
186. Pancholi, Chandrakant. 'Agnihotri Announces Nine Projects To Benefit India, NRIs and PIOs', *India Weekly*-USA, June 9, 2002, p. 3.
187. Rajan, Sujeet. 'India calling', *Indian Express*, June 7, 2002, p. unknown.
188. Rajan, Sujeet. 'India calling', *Indian Express*, June 7, 2002, p. unknown.
189. Rajan, Sujeet. 'India calling', *Indian Express*, June 7, 2002, p. unknown.
190. Lakshman, Ganesh S. 'NRIs must get involved in American society', *News India Times,* June 7, 2002, p. unknown.
191. Lakshman, Ganesh S. 'NRIs must get involved in American society', *News India Times,* June 7, 2002, p. unknown.
192. Lakshman, Ganesh S. 'NRIs must get involved in American society', *News India Times,* June 7, 2002, p. unknown.
193. Lakshman, Ganesh S. 'NRIs must get involved in American society', *News India Times,* June 7, 2002, p. unknown.
194. Author unknown. 'Agnihotri lauds role of Karnataka community', *Indian Express,* July 19, 2002, p. unknown.
195. Ghosh, Ajay. 'Vokkaligara Parishad of America holds annual convention', *Indian Reporter,* July 19, 2002, p. unknown.
196. Ghosh, Ajay. 'Vokkaligara Parishad of America holds annual convention', *Indian Reporter,* July 19, 2002, p. unknown.
197. Ghosh, Ajay. 'Vokkaligara Parishad of America holds annual convention', *Indian Reporter,* July 19, 2002, p. unknown.
198. Haniffa, Aziz. 'VIP no-shows take gloss off NFIA convention,' *India Abroad,* October 25, 2002, p. unknown.
199. Balachandar, Punithalakshmi. 'Talking ties and terrorism', *Indian Express,* October 25, 2002, p. unknown.

200. Chidan and Rajghatta. 'Vajpayee serves old wine in new bottle', *The Times of India,* September 22, 2003, p. unknown.
201. Jyoti Malhotra. 'PM mixes poetry with unity call', *Indian Express,* September 23, 2003, p. unknown.
202. K.P. Nayar. 'Baiters barred, 'poet' PM blooms', *The Telegraph,* Tuesday, September 23, 2003, p. unknown.
203. Chandy, Shibi Alex. 'Four thousand at Jacob Javits Center public meeting', Desi Talk, September 26, 2003, p. 10.
204. Author unknown. 'If there are computers, there will be Indians: PM', The *Times of India,* September 22, 2003, p. unknown.
205. Sujeet Rajan. 'Show of unity, first for community', *The Indian Express,* October 3, 2003, p. 18.
206. Dispatches: 'Agnihotri meets Muslim community in Houston', *India Abroad,* February 14, 2003, p. C1.

□

Appendix

Ambassador-at-Large, Bhishma Kumar Agnihotri
with Former Prime Minister Shri Atal Bihari Vajpayee.

Shri L.K. Advani and Dr. B.K. Agnihotri in Washington DC.

Dr. Bhishma Agnihotri with Prime Minister Shri Narendra Modi.

President Clinton and Mrs. Clinton with Dr. Agnihotri & Ms. Lata Mangeshkar.

Ambassador Agnihotri with Mayor Giuliani after 9/11–in N.Y.

Acharya Sushil Muni with Dr. B.K. Agnihotri and others.

Ambassador Agnihotri at Mahatma Gandhi Institute,
Aapravasi Museum, Mauritius.

Ambassador Agnihotri visiting Nanaksar Gurudwara,
in Toronto, Canada.

Ambassador Agnihotri with Minister of Education of Trinidad,
Hon'ble Hazel Manning.

Ambassador Agnihotri with Prime Minister of Trinidad and Tobago,
Hon'ble Patrick Manning and the Indian High Commissioner.

Ambassador Agnihotri with Governor Edwards of LA and Ambassador of ISRAEL.

Dr. Agnihotri with H.H. Dalai Lama.

Baba Ramdev speaking at a FISI programme.

Former MP Shri Shanta Kumar addressing FISI.

Gadar Memorial Presentation in San Francisco.

President Clinton, Mrs. Clinton, Mrs. Kim, wife of President Kim of South Korea and Dr. Agnihotri at a State Dinner in Washington D.C.

U.S. Vice President Gore with Dr. B.K. Agnihotri.

Ambassasor Agnihotri with Pandit Reepu Daman Persaud, Parliamentary Affairs Minister of Guyana and High Commissioner of India to Guyana Dr. P.V. Joshi.

Ambassador Agnihotri visiting Gandhi statue in Atlanta, Georgia.

Ambassador Agnihotri with major organisations in Vancouver, Canada.

Ambassador Agnihotri in a community programme at the Indian Cultural Centre in Paramaribo, Suriname.

Ambassador Agnihotri in a community programme at the Indian Cultural Centre in Paramaribo, Suriname.

Dr. Agnihotri with the leaders of the Caribbean community in New York.

Dr. Agnihotri with community leaders from Ohio.

Media workshop in Los Angeles.

Ambassador Agnihotri visiting Al Masjid us
Saifee Mosque in Toronto, Canada.

Ambassador Agnihotri with business leaders workshop in New York.

Dr. Agnihotri with leaders of Indian community
in a workshop in his office.

Dr. Agnihotri with some of the participants of the workshop on students and youth.

Dr. Agnihotri with the participants at Baton Rouge workshop on women's issue.

Dr. Agnihotri at Kawdiar Palace, Trivandrum visit H.H. Uthradam Thirunal Marthanda Varma, Maharaja of Travancore, Royal Princess Gowri Parvathi Bhayi & Special Officer IID

Shri Ashok Gehlot, Chief Minister of Rajasthan, with Ambassador Agnihotri in New York in 2003.

Appendix-I

Enhancing India's Image in the Western Media Executive Report

April 2003

Los Angeles

New York

Houston

Atlanta

Historical Overview

During the visits of Dr. B.K. Agnihotri, Ambassador-at-Large (AAL) for NRIs/PIOs to various places in the US and to countries including Canada, UK and the Caribbean and his wide-ranging interaction with the diaspora, the NRI and PIO community has been voicing their concern about the wrong, narrow and one-sided media perception and image of India being presented by Western media.

The office of the Ambassador-at-Large had, as part of its on-going work, established nine Project Groups consisting of Indian professionals and intellectuals throughout the US, Canada and the Caribbean who had offered their enthusiastic support and assistance to the AAL during the interaction. One of these groups includes Media Project Group which had been assigned the project of studying the reasons and proposing ways by which the Indian community could work with different media sources to correct the misinformation and media imbalances. This group had submitted a draft proposal for further consideration and follow-up.

The office of the Ambassador-at-Large is facilitating the project in formulating long-term policies and suggestions which would help improve media coverage and the image of India therein. It was decided to hold workshops in various regions of the USA to create broader awareness and to receive more input from a large number of community members for formulating action plans. Workshops were held in Los Angeles, New York, Houston and Atlanta.

These workshops were organised at area universities with participation from academicians, media personnel, eminent NRIs/PIOs and interested local Indian populace from the region. Each workshop put forward suggestions and action points which were to be further studied for formulating proposals for implementation.

There was active involvement by the audience in discussing the relevant issues. The workshops were designed to encourage audience participation, so that a constructive dialogue could be developed between the speakers and the audience. Audience members also made recommendations for the various groups discussed at the workshop. Based on the interest indicated by the communities all over, awareness workshops may be conducted in other states in the future.

Part of the process of creating the final report has included a draft summary of the media workshops created by Mr. Vivek Menon and Mr. Sanjay Ramabhadran (Houston, Texas). The draft summary was forwarded to the media committee of the office of the Ambassador-at-Large for NRIs/PIOs (Honorary Associates - Mr. Amit Sarkar, Mr. Udayan Chattopadhyay and Mr. Sanjay Acharya) for further action. In addition to this, the draft summary was sent to the panelists of all the media workshops for review and comment. Their comments and the comments of the media committee were sent back to Mr. Vivek Menon and Mr. Sanjay Ramabhadran to be incorporated as needed in order to create the final report.

Executive Summary

The 1.7-million strong Indo-American community has seen an unprecedented growth in the last decade. Having established its professional and economic credibility, the community has matured over the years and has lately focused on the image of India and Indo-Americans in the media. Recognising this heightened level of concern within the diaspora, the office of the Ambassador-at-Large initiated an effort to enhance India's image in the western media. A series of workshops were initiated to understand the perception of India in the Western media, analyse the present level of coverage and recommend initiatives to enhance India's image. The first workshop at the University of California, Los Angeles (UCLA) set the stage for the series of workshops that followed at Pace University in New York, the University of Houston, and Atlanta. Each workshop drew on the success of the previous and attracted panelists and audience from the length and breadth of the United States.

It is critical to understand that the Western media operates like a business with its coverage being dictated by ratings. This in turn means the media must reflect the interests, values and prejudices of the general audience and the interest of its business. Consequently, foreign news coverage often tends to be limited to sensational news items, such as coups, catastrophes and corruption. The stability of India's democracy has resulted in recent coverage focusing on the undesirable adverse news items. India has to be 'different' in important ways to the western world. A well thought out, clear and feasible strategy followed by a nation-wide concerted effort is critical to enhance the image of India.

There is a dire need to convey the message of the Government of India and Indian-Americans in a clear, concise, compelling, credible, captivating and timely manner to appeal both to the media and its audience. Recognising that the messenger is as important as the message, spokespersons for the community need to be chosen, presentable, knowledgeable and articulate. Improving India's image gets a significant boost with the individual participation of Indian-Americans.

This report broadly classifies recommendations as those to be undertaken by the Government of India and those undertaken by Indian-Americans. The focus needs to be on measurable goals leading *to* a nationwide movement to enhance India's image in the Western media. Understanding the existence of an inter-relationship between the media and governmental policy, the services of a public relations/ lobby firm would greatly benefit the cause. There is a need to continually and effectively monitor the media and foster relationships with media personalities at the local, state and national level.

Having recognised the need to influence the Western media as a business, the Indo-American community has to orchestrate a co-ordinated effort. The complete solution involves the role of Indo-Americans not merely as ambassadors of India but as volunteers in a concerted effort to cultivate, nurture and develop long-term relationships with the media. This effort is within the control of the local communities all across the country and needs to be co-ordinated nationwide. The synergy of a collaborative effort between the Government of India and Indian-Americans would greatly accelerate attaining the goal of enhancing the image of India in the Western media.

Background

The Indo-American community has seen an unprecedented growth in the last decade as evidenced by the 2000 US census. Known for its professional and economic achievements and contributions, the community has matured over the years and has lately focused on the image of India and Indo-Americans in the media. The majority of the1.7-million strong community feel that the Western media focuses more on the negatives than on the positives of India's image. The recent adverse coverage and seeming non-recognition of key events in the sub-continent have been a cause for concern amongst the diaspora. While the Indo-American community is a force to reckon with at the local level in terms of its contributions, there is a need for a concerted national effort to address India's image.

Introduction

Recognising the heightened level of concern within the diaspora, the office of the Ambassador-at-Large has initiated an effort to understand, evaluate and enhance India's image in the Western media. Deeply concerned with India's insignificant coverage in the Western media, a series of workshops were initiated, devoted to understanding the perception of India in the Western media, analysing the present level of coverage and recommending initiatives to enhance India's image.

The Media Workshop Series

The first workshop at the University of California, Los Angeles (UCLA) set the stage for the series of workshops that followed. Second in the series was a workshop held at Pace University in New York. Third in a series of four, the Houston workshop built on the success of the earlier two workshops with participation from the University of Houston's Department of Communications. The final workshop was held in Atlanta. The workshop series saw both panelists and participants from the length and breadth of the United States.

The Panels

The illustrious panels consisted of experts from the media, academicians, corporate executives, doctors, attorneys, political activists and those intimately involved with the activities of the Indo-American community. The panelists included:

1.	Mr. Rajiv Malhotra	19	Mr. Harish Dhruv	37	Dr. P.V. Pathak
2.	Attorney Madvi Verma	20	Mr. Sanjay Acharya	38	Mr. Vivek Menon
3.	Dr. Sudhir Parikh	21	Dr. Chandrakant Panse	39	Mr. Sockalingam (Sam) Kannappan
4.	Dr. Rajesh Shukla	22	Mrs. Usha Chopra	40	Mr. Amit Kataria
5.	Dr. Surendra Kaushik	23	Mr. Amit Sarkar	41	Mr. Subash Razdan
6.	Mr. Ram Narayanan	24	Prof. Rishi Raj	42	Mr. Basant Tariyal
7.	Dr. Krishna Reddy	25	Mr. Devinder Singh Sawhney	43	Mr. Bhu Dev Sharma
8.	Ms. Anna Prasad	26	Mr. Udayan Chottopadhyay	44	Mr. Ram Sidhaye
9.	Mr. Narpat Bhandari	27	Mr. Narayan D. Kesawan	45	Mr. Srikanth Konda
10.	Dr. Kumar Patel	28	Mr. Chandrakanth Pancholi	46	Mr. Shyam Tiwari
11.	Dr. Satinder Swaroop	29	Dr. Garth Jowett	47	Mr. Amit Shah
12.	Dr. Lakshman Koka Pancholi	30	Dr. Stephen Klineberg	48	Mr. Bikhu Patel
13.	Mr. Indra Gandhi	31	Dr. Alok Bhargava	49	Mr. K. K. Vijai
14.	Mr. Jaydev Rao	32	Dr. T.R.N. Rao	50	Mr. Amitabh Sharma
15.	Mr. Ravi Tilak	33	Mr. J.V. Lakshmana Rao	51	Mr. Girish Patel
16.	Dr. R. Anand	34	Mr. Bernard J. Shapiro	52	Mr. Ashwin Patel
17.	Mr. Mahinder Singh	35	Mr. Pramod Kulkarni		
18.	Mr. Navin Doshi	36	Mr. Pradeep Anand		

Understanding the American Media

Dr. Garth Jowett, from the University of Houston, said it best when he noted that the American media tends to focus on the three C's, namely, Coup, Corruption and Catastrophe in relation to foreign news.

As media companies grow and a shrinking number of them shape what we view and read, it becomes paramount for us as a community to put forth a message that is clear, concise and captivating. The Western media is a business, which, like any other business is run primarily to make money. This means that the media must continually attract readers, listeners and viewers, keep their interest and also attract advertisers that are their prime source of revenues. This in turn means that the media must reflect the interests, values and prejudices of its general audience and also the interest of its business. It's probably cliche to say that it's all about ratings and that the media tends to focus on that which is sensational.

Normally, the media should not be expected to develop a strong and sustained bias against any nation or group of nations or any religion, but under controlled circumstances media bias can manifest itself. The media is said to often times reflect the political message, which is often populist and often self-serving, but it results in the censorship of the press. That being said, the media is obliged to maintain a measure of credibility. The media has to address human beings who have a need to feel that what they are being told is trustworthy. The journalists themselves are human beings with some feelings and moral conscience and therefore for most of them there are limits to which they can go in hiding or distorting facts. Competition within the media business also induces objectivity, and hence when a newspaper or television station is consistently hiding or distorting a particular set of facts, another newspaper or station can publish those facts or present them in a more plausible light and thus discredit the competitor. For reasons such as these, the media is under some pressure to be objective and balanced in its reporting.

The age of the internet and e-mail has heralded a new era in mass communication. With an information overload, people are selective about what they watch, hear or read. The message has to hence be concise, palatable and interesting. Thomas Friedman of the *New York Times* recently said, "In the last 15 years, we've gone from walls to Webs referring to the fall of communism and the advent of the World Wide Web. In the era of globalisation, we are increasingly connected but no one is in charge... It should come as no surprise to learn that half the terrorists responsible for the September 11 attacks made their reservations on Travelocity.com ...When you take away the walls, individuals can act on the world stage without state sponsorship."

There can be no question about the important role media plays in shaping public opinion and image, which in turn affect official policy. However, India does not seem to appreciate this enough. India's spokespersons, when they have appeared, have not always conveyed their message convincingly. Lack of sufficient familiarity on the part of Indian officials with the West in general and the media in particular, are partly to blame for our diminished coverage.

Reasons for the Current Level of Coverage

India's image in the Western media has not been as sharp as it should be due to several reasons. Firstly, India as a democratic political power is extremely stable and there is hardly any threat of a coup or collapse. Here its strength becomes its weakness. Another reason for India's short scripted coverage is the fact that Americans in general have a limited appetite for foreign news and as a whole, have a short history with India.

India, in the opinion of some experts, had missed the industrial revolution and colonialism has taken its toll on the people. Indians and Indian Americans still look to the West for recognition. India would have to do more in its own public policies, many of which need to be revitalised. India's indifference to the impoverished has not only precipitated the problem but has also brought it on to the centre stage among developing countries. A· complete failure of the healthcare system has gone un-addressed. In this case the adverse publicity has hurt India's image and the great contributions it has made to the world.

India has to be 'different' in important ways to the Western world. In the business world, companies spend billions of dollars to be different in important ways and it is called differentiation. Indian Americans however do not have a problem being different. We look different, speak in different accents, have a very different cuisine, produce different movies, and share a significantly different cultural heritage. But the question that persists in the minds of many is, does this uniqueness make a difference?

In order to address this, there are some truisms about the media including the newspapers, television, radio, cinema, and even the Internet. The media has many masters – most importantly the shareholders, customers and advertisers. As Yogi Berra once said, "You can observe a lot by just watching." Watching the local news, reading the local newspapers or even going to the movies reveals a media that is focused on war, violence, safety, threats, corruption, money, victory, loss, tragedy, health, weather and charity. When Indian Americans do get coverage, it is when we affect Western civilisation in dramatic ways. It follows that the threat of nuclear war, religious violence, tragedies and catastrophes attract the media's focus. However, the question that persists is do we really want this kind of coverage. The emphatic answer is no.

Moving up from the individual to the state brings to light another important point. States have to be a significant economic, military and cultural partner sharing obvious dependencies between them to draw media attention. A case in point is reflected in our local print media such as *The Houston Chronicle* or for that matter *The New York Times, The Washington Post, The LA Times* and *The Wall Street Journal.* In a typical 100-odd page newspaper, about four pages are dedicated to world news or editorials and it's a matter of coincidence if India is mentioned once, and that too in a positive light. The obvious reason is because we are culturally, economically, and militarily distant from the United States, and there are other countries ahead of us. We hence have to stand in line for media attention.

Today, what grabs the headlines are all dramatic threats namely Iraq, Al-Qaeda, North Korea, Israel and Palestine, the petroleum industry strike in Venezuela and even Catholic priests in Boston. Then comes news about major partner countries. In that pecking order Europe comes first, and amongst the Europeans, the British are on top of the list. After the Europeans, Latin Americans come next followed by Canada. Partners with mutual dependencies, such as Japan, China, and the OPEC countries, follow this.

However, closer Indo-US relations have brought about a radical change in the thinking. Businesses worldwide are recognising India as an important economic partner and as a source of low-cost intellectual capital. Several Fortune 100 companies are in the process of changing business models to take advantage of the Indian work force. Information technology was the harbinger but now US and European firms are setting up wholly owned subsidiaries in India. GE has over 17,000 employees and not a day goes by without some major firm committing to an outsourcing or opening a subsidiary in India. So far, India has not been perceived to be a strong economic, military, and cultural partner. But that will change during the next decade and with that will change the Western media's perception of India.

Media magic happens when it is managed and hence has to be orchestrated. Yogi Berra once said, "You've got to be very careful if you don't know where you're going, because you might not get there." The same is true of media management. It needs goals and strategies. Unfortunately, as a country we are yet to see a well articulated strategy with clear objectives to manage media relations.

Spokespersons for the country have to be articulate and polished, and appeal to Western sensibilities. Artful use of the English language and a pleasant personality are of prime importance for effective communication with the media, which passes through to their audiences. If we have to influence the Western media, we have to play by their rules. Reporters and writers are very insightful people with great integrity, but most important of all, they are neither omniscient nor omnipotent. They cannot be everywhere and see everything and that too objectively, and in the 'right' light. People in the media have to be nurtured, cultivated and provided with information that gives them better insight to report objectively. What is evident in the media is the result of a 'fumble and tumble' strategy or an accidental one. We, as a community and country are dependent on the good sense of individual reporters and influential writers, such as Thomas Friedman of the *New York Times*, and Francois Gautier, who see India as a balancing force, with bright, luminous examples of successes, in a world of turmoil. Media has to be managed and influential champions have to be nurtured and supported to promote the best interests of the country. India has not had a master at managing media since Mahatma Gandhi.

Word-of-mouth is the most powerful of all methods of promoting products and services in the business world. In *every* business, the ultimate goal is to promote strong word-of-mouth dissemination of information for favourable perceptions. People buy products when their friends and colleagues give unbiased references. We can learn a thing or two from Hollywood and Bollywood who rely completely on word-of-mouth references to create box-office hits. Word-of-mouth propagation is the ultimate strategy in good references, and creating great perceptions. That puts the responsibility of a favourable image of India on each and every Indian-American. Every Indian by birth or by choice has a role to play in enhancing the image of India. As Indian-Americans we carry on our shoulders a *very* heavy responsibility of representing India in *every* thought, word, and deed, as we go through our daily life at work and at play. We collectively have to be the influencers in this world. Each and every one of us has the responsibility to be articulate representatives of India in all walks of life, from the corridors of power to our colleagues at work and within our neighbourhoods. The need for Indian-Americans to be knowledgeable on India-US relations, Indo-Pak situation and the rationale behind traditions and customs, thus becomes of paramount importance.

Without our individual participation there is little chance of improving India's image in the Western media. Most importantly each one of us is an ambassador for India. Without this vital link, the rest of the chain is meaningless. At the end of the day, each and every one of us is responsible for how the media and its audience see us and our country of origin.

Indian-Americans are all citizens of the world, with deep, strong roots in India, and there can be no better representation of the country than all of us together. While the Government of India could retain the services of a public relations (PR) firm. it is time for us to take to heart in John F. Kennedy's words, "Ask not what the country can do for you but what you can do for your country". However, there is no doubt that the American press needs to do more since India is extremely important to the US both in terms of maintaining global stability and in its partnership in the global marketplace.

Conclusions and Recommendations

The mood at the workshops reflected the enthusiasm that had been generated within the Indian diaspora as a result of the media workshops arranged under the auspices of the Ambassador-at-Large. India's open arm welcome to the diaspora being celebrated as Pravasi Bharatiya Divas was seen as the first right step in that direction.

More than 90 per cent of the attendees were strongly disturbed by the fact that India had been consistently portrayed as a caste-ridden, poverty-stricken society where women played a stereotypical role of being subjugated. More than 80 per cent of the attendees felt that the Western media has been misinformed on issues related to Indo-Pak territorial disputes, Indo-US bilateral relationships, economic growth, defence capabilities, and human rights issues. Majority of the participants blamed Indian popular mainstream media for providing improper, subjective, biased coverage that was often contradictory in nature. They also expressed concern that the PR work by the government of India was not doing enough to project India's image in a positive way.

More than 99 per cent of the attendees agreed that there was a need for political education of NRIs and PIOs through local or national political education forums, awareness seminars, newspapers and magazines. Development of first-generation immigrant Indians had to be looked into differently from the needs of, and approach to, the second and third-generation Indian-Americans. The Indian-American media could play a very important role in addressing the issues of second- and third-generation Indian-Americans.

Broadly classified as those initiated by the Government of India and those undertaken by Indian Americans, the following recommendations focus on measurable goals leading to a nationwide movement to enhance India's image in the western media.. The Government of India should recognise the need to engage not only the American media and political persona but also the masses and understand their role in shaping media and policy. It is to our advantage to use the high degree of accountability and responsibility that the American public expects of its media and polity. The role of the Government of India is summarised below. Several short-term initiatives, which are of high priority, are listed as follows.

Messages from the Government of India need to be clear, concise and captivating to appeal to the media and its audience.

"The Government of India is in dire need of a PR firm to project the 'right' image of India and its people. Understanding the existence of an inter-relationship between the media and governmental policy, the services of a public relations/lobby firm employed by the Government of India would greatly benefit the cause of improving the image of India in the Western media.

The Government of India has to take pains to see that media is given all relevant information in a timely manner. Timing is everything when it comes to media coverage. India has to seize every opportunity to let the world know that we are a very mature democracy. The importance of India having been able to sustain continuously the democratic form of government is lost on the Western media.

The Indian government has to be ever vigilant to identify the reporters in the Western media who are prejudiced and do the reporting without paying attention to facts or just knowingly ignore the facts and intentionally try to depict India in poor light. This has not been pursued vigorously. When the reporting is not supported by facts or when the facts are turned on their head, the Indian government should immediately contact the responsible media and set the record straight. This has to be pursued right away, not months later.

The success of these short-term initiatives is contingent on an ongoing effort focusing on definite long-term goals discussed below:

To gain credibility with the world press and American polity, the Indian government needs to take several concrete steps in the right direction. Corruption, lawlessness, indifference to poverty, an inefficient and inadequate healthcare system, a neglected education system, and fundamentalist actions have all contributed to the negative image of India in the Western media. Corrective action in these and other areas needs to be initiated and the success of legislation needs to be given due coverage.

The Western media has not seen any other country of one billion people going to the polls and electing a new government every five years. They have, therefore, no idea of what a monumental task it is to conduct polls in the country where many areas have no concrete roads, many villagers are not literate, and there are no means of communication for many voters other than just some candidate or their volunteers talking to them for a short time. There are no televised debates and even if they were, majority of households have no television sets like here in the United States. Once the Western media understands not only the tremendous effort but also the commitment of India and its people to sustain the democratic form of government, they will pay more attention to properly cover India. The Western media will then realise how close the Indian government and its ideology are to the United

States. The point that India is the world's largest democracy needs to be emphasised time and again in every possible forum.

As much as media influences politics, public policy and politicians influence media. The Indian government has not, to our understanding developed a comprehensive strategy to educate as many Senators and Congressmen as possible about India. When these legislators speak positively about India or speak out against someone bashing India relying on unsubstantiated facts, the media does take notice. The more legislators speak about India, the more coverage the media will give. A campaign to brief the legislators on India is essential so that they may speak out in India's favour. When the Indian government engages the legislators, and ideally, it should be one hundred percent of the members of the Senate and the House, the NRls can supplement these efforts and thus solidify the positive images about India conveyed to them by the Indian government. This will encourage the members of Congress to take informed decisions about matters relating to India and they will speak about those matters often and at length. The media will then have no choice; they cannot afford to ignore the views of the members of Congress.

Closer economic ties between India and the US will go a long way in moving India-related news up the hierarchy. The need to be different in an important way to the US can be accomplished by making India a choice destination for American business. While the IT boom has made India the destination of choice, the Government of India needs to take a business-like approach in 'selling' India to the world media. The greatest democracy in the world runs its governance in tune with the established practices of 'corporate management'. The key to achieving success in the Western world is that India should project its presence as 'India, Inc.' The media package must bring out a resolute decision that India means business. The implementation has to be on several fronts including projecting India's strength as a 'quality vendor' to the world, showing amenable business policies and a very friendly business atmosphere, and projecting that India cares for preservation of business value, business ethics and loyalty. This has to be a show, hand in hand, of India's tangible and not so apparent strengths...the opinion of India's English print media is the source of many news articles in the Western media. It is the opinion of many outside India that in an attempt to appear unbiased, India's English print media at times starts the process of portraying India negatively. While censorship of the press is definitely not the solution, it is important for the government to keep an eye on how Indian media portrays India as well and treat reporters within India with the same level of importance. A positive image has to also start from within India.

The use of tourism as a vehicle to impact public opinion on India is an area that has not been tapped to its fullest potential. Entities within the public and private sector tourism and hospitality industry need to work hand-in-hand in promoting an image of India that reflects its grandeur, history, and wealth of tradition and culture. This message provided through the American mass media via advertising campaigns will go a long way in fostering a positive image of India while generating revenue and facilitating a personal understanding of India and its people.

Having recognised the need to influence the Western media as a business, the Indo-American community has to orchestrate a co-ordinated effort. Addressing the image of India cannot be solved by focusing on the media misrepresentation or bias alone. The involvement of media, society, polity and academia is necessary to bring about holistic change. This section summarises key actions to be taken by Indian-Americans at the local level that could then feed to a national effort. While short-term initiatives bringing about 'quick wins' are necessary, the Indian-American community needs to be committed to sustaining the effort in the longterm.

Projecting a positive image of India in the United States and strengthening the political, economic, social and cultural links between the world's two largest democracies requires a strategy that is varied, immense and as multi-pronged as the channels of connectivity between the two peoples. The overall strategy should also address the mechanism and structure by which core groups in various cities can achieve this goal. Once defined, the efforts need to be coordinated by a central group interfacing with core groups in major cities. Groups of individuals, who enjoy high credibility with the US media and who can count on the support of everyone involved, should contribute to and present a unified message. To be effective, this effort should be managed by a private entity, rather than one employed by the Government of India.

Targeting the Efforts

This requires that the team or individual handling the project be extremely well versed with how the media operates in the United States. To a large extent, this would require cultivating influential columnists in the print media as well as commentators in the broadcast media. It would require meetings with editorial boards and producers of print and broadcast media. The opinion pages and the 'talk shows' on TV should be leveraged to put forth the Indian-American view on the merits and demerits of news coverage.

Story ideas that emphasise a positive image of India while maintaining the interest of the audience should be developed to increase the likelihood media acceptance. In this context, the name of Mahatma Gandhi provides access and entry to not just the media but also activist circles in the United States. It can also serve as a crucial link between India, Indian-Americans and African-Americans. In addition, close links with the African-American, Latin American and Jewish American constituencies can help buttress the support among mainstream Americans for positive links with India.

Foster relationships with journalists or writers who are dedicated to the promotion and defence of India. It is up to the community to monitor the manner in which India is reported, discuss counter measures with established media professionals and intervene when they believe India is maligned. Recently, Francois Gautier and Rajeev Srinivasan founded one such association with the charter of the association referring it asaAn Association of Journalists and Writers friendly to India.

Indians in America can take a leaf from the pages of the Israeli and Taiwanese lobbies on how to impact on public opinion and Washington's policy-making apparatus. Both the Israeli and Taiwanese lobbies rely on grass-roots efforts – established by members of their respective communities – to get their viewpoints across. Contrast this with the failure of Japan to gets its viewpoints accepted in the United States, despite the fact that the Japanese have poured billions of dollars into this effort. Or consider how Saudi Arabia's hiring of a PR firm in New York to state its case has backfired. So, the key is to identify leaders of the Indian-American community throughout the country, and help them organise such grass-roots efforts. They will be the ones talking to the local media, sending in the letters to the editor or submitting opinion-page essays for publication. This 'going local' effort will also help ensure that the Indian perspective gets across in the media throughout the country, rather than being restricted solely to the New York-Washington media axis.

Indian-Americans need to interface with American electronic, radio and print media. This interface should comprise of chosen, presentable, knowledgeable and articulate spokespersons from the community. A single compelling, credible and concise message needs to be forged and disseminated at all times. While the phrase 'dealing with the media' sounds grandiloquent, many times all this requires is cultivating individuals. While there may be some individual journalists with set agendas and who are determined to report with malice about India, they are the exception. Most times, it is not an 'agenda' that journalists come with, but a 'mind-set'. And dealing with this 'mind-set' requires understanding how that worldview came to be shaped. Once this is understood, the next step often is less difficult. It is using the paradigms of that worldview to re-shape the mind-set of the journalists and get the point across.

The community should take extensive help from professional PR firms, cultivate people in the mainstream media and develop closer relations with prominent political figures at the local, state and national level. The need and importance of spreading the message through word of mouth and independently contributing in this effort cannot be overemphasised. The goal is to promote this effort as a national movement across the United States. Funding for this effort should come not from the government, but from private sources like wealthy members of the Indian diaspora in the United States, private corporations and others with a vested interest.

Public and media relations firms have the capability of providing a wide range of services including,

- Pitching local, national and international members of the press
- Preparing press kits, writing releases and letters-to-editors
- Creating and maintaining press lists
- Tracking issues
- Managing press conferences
- Providing media training

- Preparing our spokespersons and political aspirants for debate

Indian Americans need to come to terms with what sells in American media. While most Indo-Americans would like the western media to focus on and portray India's glorious contributions to the world and how India is on the right side of the Kashmir issue; the media is 'buying' a completely different set of stories that are sensational. Recognising this, Indo-Americans need to adapt their message to a form that is appealing to the media and its audience. Just as in any business, the packaging is critical for the product to sell and the message to get across.

The media loves personalities, rather than issues. The key is to identify personalities in the United States and in India who can present the arguments and project the image of India. These personalities should have the eloquence and dexterity to present their views in a manner palatable to the journalists. Putting a face to the issue can attract media attention more easily than just debating the merits of the case through written analyses. It is here that the film industry can play a role in portraying the impressive aspects of India and Indian history and culture rather than only the mythical and mystical aspects.

Outreach various inter-faith groups interacting with media to promote a true perspective of Hinduism.

In times of crisis, crisis communication and management becomes the key. A proactive approach, as against reactive, would help the community mobilise instantaneously to provide strategic and focused initiatives. Areas identified for key consideration include creation of crisis plans, crisis audits and risk analysis, developing crisis communication strategies, providing experienced spokespersons, creating a quick response media team, managing the media, identifying critical audiences, media monitoring, review and evaluation and conducting crisis simulation drills and media training.

Promote the idea of 'India' rather than 'South Asia'. The South Asian concept dilutes the Indian identity and adversely affects the image of India as a progressive, democratic society. While a positive relationship with other South Asian communities is essential, the emphasis should be on selling the definite, tangible 'brand image' of India.

The American mainstream has a profound influence on what the media presents. Indian-Americans, as ambassadors of India, need to initiate an individual, parallel effort to interact with and influence the mainstream community. Their active participation in mainstream civic and professional organisations will provide a forum to discuss India and issues of common interest with Americans.

It is a well known fact that the messenger is as important if not more important than the message. Supporting elected representatives with a pro-India focus at the local, state and federal level through contributions and volunteer efforts will serve the community well in making our voices heard. This is especially important in areas with significant Indian-American population and for those representatives who hold key positions in influencing legislative and business policy. Public figures speaking positively about India are critical in shaping public opinion. The community should encourage these public figures to hold press conferences to speak in favour of India in times of need.

A think tank to develop strategies to promote India will also assist in developing relationships with leaders of opinion-shaping organisations and other think tanks and can serve as a link between India and Indian organisations across the globe. Events such as the Pravasi Bharathiya Divas present an ideal opportunity for exchange of ideas and experiences in promoting India.

Indian-Americans should reach out to potential mentors in the media, learn from the experiences of established media personnel and leverage individuals who have influence in political and media circles.

Recognising that enhancing the image of India requires a grassroots effort, the community should assist educational agencies in developing school curricula that is truly reflective. Current school and university curriculum should be monitored and meetings with responsible entities need to be initiated to address bias or misconceptions.

Monitoring the media on a consistent basis to counter media bias that currently exists – daily newspapers that cover foreign policy issues, TV and radio news, talk shows and articles in political magazines.

This programme would need dedicated and committed volunteers from all across the United States to regularly monitor the daily newspapers published in their respective areas and the local, regional and national TV and radio news and related programs. About 190 such newspapers are listed, state-wise, on the US-India Friendship website (http://www.usindiafriendship.net/media/lettertoeditor/

lettertoeditor.html and click: 'list of newspaper links'). In today's age, practically all these newspapers are accessible via the internet. While there are individuals and groups of people monitoring these in various parts of the country, there is a need for a coordinated effort that can effectively monitor and react to adverse coverage.

Create a Writers' Databank

There are many Indian-Americans who have special capability to write concise acceptable letters or articles that have a high probability of being published. We need to identify as many such people as possible throughout the United States and make use of their talents. It is critical to nurture and further develop these skills as some of them may well grow into op-ed writers in due course.

While the ideal situation is to have proactive pro-India articles and TV and radio coverage, the ability to quickly react to both adverse and complimentary coverage is essential to counter adverse coverage and fortify pro-India coverage.

Cultivate relationships with media persona by forming dedicated groups in cities around the US

The need for a trusted source is of incredible importance in the media world. Indo-Americans need to position themselves as the 'go-to' resource for local and national op-ed writers, columnists and reporters specialising in foreign policy and international business issues, as well as editors responsible for international news and articles. There is a critical need for individuals that are not only knowledgeable and interested in personally cultivating these relationships. In addition to their commitment, these individuals need to have the ability to present their viewpoint in a clear, concise and captivating manner. The idea is to gradually bring them around, where necessary, as better-informed media professionals and staunch friends of India. While this is not a short-term effort, it is an ideal solution to the question of really winning friends and influencing the media. This effort, if begun now, can in a period of three years or so, bring about a sea of change in the quality and quantity of coverage on India and US-India relations in the American media. Would you like to volunteer or would you be able to inform your friends/relations living in any part of the United

States who may be willing to volunteer – those who are prepared to cultivate their local editor/reporter/columnist/syndicated writer/ news producer/talk show producer/anchor or whoever, that is those involved in writing or reporting or editing pieces relating to foreign policy issues, including international business?

Identify experts willing to appear on TV and radio talk shows and interviews

TV and radio talk shows – we need to identify as many experts as possible living in the United States who are friends of India and can talk with authority on India and US-India relations, who are effective on such shows. We need to collect the bios of such people, and after getting them, suggest their names, in a suitable manner, to TV and radio talk show producers and hosts.

There would also arise a need for volunteers who can help develop and maintain the database once the five-point action programme starts moving ahead.

Educate Indo-Americans, the ambassadors of India, on Indo-US relationship, Indo-Pak situation and the influence of media on policy and vice-versa

As the frontline ambassadors of India, what Indo-Americans say about India very often will have far reaching implications. That being the case, the need for Indo-Americans to be educated and knowledgeable on basic issues such as Indian traditions and customs and hot issues such as the Indo-Pak situation, the Kashmir issue and Indo-US relations cannot be overemphasised. A web-based data bank maintaining facts relating to India and Indo-US relationship and media kits can assist Indian-Americans in targeting the media. Indo-American news media can assist by targeting some of its programming towards engaging Indian-Americans in current issues and facts about India. Local communities need to work with Indo-American news media to promote ideological similarities between India and the US.

While it is important for Indo-Americans to be passionate about India's democracy, rule of law, secularism and pluralistic society; *it* is equally important to avoid manipulating adverse events in India in an attempt to justify them. Condemning these acts is critical to establish and maintain credibility both with the media and people that they interact with daily. It is important to realise that the only good source of information is a 'credible' source.

Encourage young Indo-Americans to take up journalism

The younger Indo-Americans will be our most valuable asset in conveying the message to the media and its audience. Our investment in engaging the younger generation is critical to maintain their link with India and enhancing India's image in the Western media. Second- and third-generation Indian-Americans with an interest in journalism, media management or public life should be encouraged and supported to pursue their dreams. Increasing our representation within the media will go a long way in improving India's image.

A two-pronged approach is essential to tackling the image of India in the Western media. The complete solution involves the role of Indo-Americans not merely as ambassadors of India but as volunteers in a concerted effort to cultivate, nurture and develop long-term relationships with the media. This effort is within the control of the local communities all across the country and needs to be co-ordinated nationwide.

The synergy of a collaborative effort between the Government of India and Indian-Americans would greatly accelerate attaining the goal of enhancing the image of India in the Western media.

This paper is a co-operative effort with input from the workshops on media relations held in Los Angeles, New York, Houston &Atlanta, the panelists and audience, community leaders, participating organisations and friends of the community.

Indo-Caribbean Leaders' Forum

Held May 28, 2003

Executive Summary

I. Context

Part of an ongoing series of initiatives undertaken by the office of India's Ambassador-at-Large to foster dialogue with Indian communities around the world.

II. Community Representation

Topmost community leaders including one Padma Shri and several Indians who participated in freedom struggles of Caribbean countries.

III. Themes Discussed

1. Global Indian family
2. Exposing the youth to Indian culture and India
3. Economic ties between the diaspora and India
4. Ensuring human rights in diaspora countries
5. Creating linkages between diaspora communities
6. Representation of India in Western media

IV. Key Recommendations

1. Develop scholarship programmes for diaspora youth to study in or visit India.
2. Have a co-ordinate effort to stamp out human rights violations against the diaspora.
3. The Government of India should take a more assertive role in protecting the rights of the diaspora.
4. Recognise the contributions and achievements of people of Indo-Caribbean community in all spheres.
5. Create programmes designed to promote knowledge about India amongst the diaspora.
6. Craft mechanisms to substantially increase sustained exchanges within the Indo-Caribbean community with other first generation non-resident Indian communities.

V. Next Steps

1. Continue leadership meetings
2 Work actively with the office of India's Ambassador-at-Large
3. Have interactive sessions with other diaspora communities
4. Get more involved in youth initiatives

Indo-Caribbean Leaders Forum Schedule (May 28, 2003)

> Invocation: Pandit Ramlall, Imam Hazi Zakir, Reverend Seupaul Singh
> Welcome and Occasion: Dr. Bhishma K. Agnihotri, Ambassador
> Self-introductions: Attendees

> Initial Themes: proposed for by leaders	1	Building bridges amongst India, NRIs, and the Indo-Caribbean community.
	2	Commemorating the contributions of the PIO community to the Indian independence movement.
	3.	Promoting Indian cultural awareness and values amongst the Diaspora.
	4.	Setting up a PIO Trust Fund.
	5.	Difficulties for Indo-Caribbeans in obtaining PIO cards.
	6.	Any other concerns.
> Brief Comments:	1.	Mr. Ramesh D. Kalicharran (Moderator)
By Discussion	2.	Pandit R. D. Upadhyaya
Initiators	3.	Dr. Tara Singh
	4.	Ashook Ramsarran
	5.	Professor Roopnarine Persaud
	6.	Mr. Pritha Singh
	7.	Dr. Dhanpaul Narine
	8.	Pandita Indranee Rampersad
> Discussion		
Closing Remarks:		Ambassador Agnihotri

Historical Overview

The Office of India's Ambassador-at-Large for NRIs/PIOs has undertaken, as part of its mission, the project of promoting the idea of a global Indian family. At 22 million people, India has one of the largest diaspora communities in existence. Despite being large in number, the Indian diaspora has yet to frame a process of regular dialogue with each other and with India. Some communities have been able to maintain linkages with India, while others, due to historical circumstances, have lost that connection with their ancestral homeland. This office seeks to assist in the restoration of that connection.

Of the global Indian diaspora communities spread throughout the world, the Indo-Caribbean community is one of the oldest and largest. Many families have been in the Caribbean region since the mid-19th century. Most came as indentured labourers to work in the sugar-cane plantations. Despite the great distance from India, the Indo-Caribbean diaspora managed to maintain their tradition and culture. In fact, their distinct tradition heavily influenced the culture of the Caribbean countries that they were a part of. For example, many of the foods that we know today as 'Caribbean' have their roots in the early cuisine of the Indo-Caribbean community.

Perhaps the strongest example of the Indo-Caribbean diaspora's ability to maintain Indian culture has been in the area of the family. Similar to India, the Caribbean-Indian community has been able to maintain strong family and social networks. This can be contrasted with the challenges facing the Indian- American and the Indo-Canadian diasporas. The strong social networks and time have also allowed many of the regional Indian traditions to melt, creating a broader sense of Indian cultural identity.

It is for these reasons that the office of India's Ambassador-at-Large for NRIs/PIOs views it as a priority to increase its interaction with the Indo-Caribbean community. In 2002, Ambassador-at-Large, Dr. Bhishma K. Agnihotri visited the Caribbean countries of Surinam, Guyana and Trinidad & Tobago to meet with and listen to the needs and concerns of these three Indo-Caribbean communities. As an ongoing part of this effort, the office of the Ambassador-at-Large for NRIs/PIOs has contacted the Indo-Caribbean community in the United States. It is through this effort that the meeting of the Indo-Caribbean leaders with Ambassador Agnihotri has developed. The Government of India places critical importance to this dialogue and desires to solidify and expand this relationship.

Highlights of the Indo-Caribbean Leaders Forum (Meeting)

Inauguration and Welcome

Ambassador-at-Large Bhishma K. Agnihotri initiated and chaired the first Indo-Caribbean Leaders' Forum at his office in New York. This event was a continuation of Ambassador Agnihotri's series of efforts to interact and listen to the needs of the Indian community around the world. At the forum, the Indo-Caribbean community was represented by eminent leaders from Guyana, Trinidad & Tobago, Surinam, North America and other parts of West Indies. In addition, several prominent representatives from the Indian and Caribbean media were also present.

Reflecting the true spirit of Indianness as manifested in the diversity of its faiths, the programme started with spiritual invocations of three faiths. The first invocation was presented by Pandit Ramlall (spiritual leader of the Arya Spiritual Centre), the second by Imam Hazi Zakir (founder of the United Muslim Organisation) and the third by Reverend Seupaul Singh (leader of the International Gospel Assembly and Fellowship of the Assembly of God in Cypress Hills).

Ambassador Agnihotri welcomed the leaders of the Indo-Caribbean community and said that he was pleased to see the intense desire on their part to remain connected with India and to further deepen that connection. He also stated that Indian culture has retained its vibrancy and richness in the Indian communities of the Caribbean. Citing the examples of (i) the ritual of *Ganga nahan* that is prevalent amongst the Indian community in Surinam, and (ii) the celebration of Deepawali by Indians in Trinidad, he stated that by celebrating their Indian identities in their adopted countries, the Indian diaspora has continued to demonstrate their undiminished love for India. The Ambassador also stated that Indianness transcends diversity of faiths and reflects in the intense desire of the Indo-Caribbean communities to remain united. The Ambassador also mentioned that during his last visit to the Caribbean countries and his recent visits to Portugal and Spain, he had the opportunity to go to a mosque, a temple and a church. He expressed his great satisfaction that PIOs of all backgrounds and faiths were present and were working as one signifying togetherness and Indianness.

The Ambassador highlighted that the Indo-Caribbean community is an embodiment of the uniquely powerful Indian idea of *vasudhaiwakutumbakam* (one world, one family) because it has transcended region(s), religion(s) and even their distance from India as measured in terms of time (forefathers of the community departed from India more than 165 years ago). He also said that the leaders of this community are the true ambassadors of Indianness and agreed with one of the leaders who poignantly pointed out that it was the Indo-Caribbean community which first exposed the West to India's spiritualism.

The Indo-Caribbean community leaders enthusiastically introduced themselves and thanked the Ambassador for his pioneering initiative in organising the forum. They stated that they have been truly touched by the Ambassador's commitment to their cause and for organising the forum. In response, Ambassador Agnihotri stated that his contribution reflected the commitment of the Government of India and especially of the Prime Minister in furthering the cause of Indians throughout the world. The Ambassador urged continued proactive engagement of the community with his office and promised that the office will promptly respond to their suggestions.

Terming the forum as a 'truly historic' occasion, Ambassador Agnihotri stated that the forum was personally a rewarding experience for him. He enjoyed the remarkable ability of the leaders of the Indo-Caribbean community to articulate their thoughts constructively. He thanked the community leaders for their enthusiastic participation and for their contributions in expanding Indianness around the world. Appreciating the spectrum of views expressed and the diversity of background of the participating leaders, he stated that the pluralism and diversity reflected in such a forum was healthy and contributed to the richness of discussion and facilitated a vibrant exchange of ideas in the forum.

Moderator and Discussion Leaders

The forum discussion was moderated by Mr. Ramesh Kalicharran (a leading Indo-Caribbean community activist). The initiators of the discussion included Pandit R.D. Upadhyaya, Dr. Tara Singh, Mr. Ashook Ramsarran, Professor Roopnarine Persaud, Dr. Dhanpaul Narine, Smt. Bhagmani Pooran, Mr. Vishnu Bisram and Panditalndranee Rampersad.

Some other participants in the discussion were Mr. Deo Gosine, Ms. Barbara Lemoine, Mr. Ramdular Singh and Pandit Krishna Tiwari.

Commitment by the Government of India to the diaspora Ambassador Agnihotri stressed that the Government of India is committed to the cause of Indian diaspora around the world. He stated that in light of (a) the extensive distractions of multiple and immediate material choices, (b) peer pressure imposed upon them to 'fit in,' and (c) the lack of adequate infrastructure to facilitate sustained exposure and interactions with things that are Indian, the second-generation Indians often find it difficult to maintain their links to India and its culture. He also stated that a resurgent Indian nation has initiated steps to address this important issue.

Closing

Citing the interest expressed to him by people interested in expanding the interactions of Indian civil society groups throughout the world, Ambassador Agnihotri stated that it may be possible to channel philanthropic contributions to facilitate some of the specific objectives highlighted in the forum, including but not limited to increasing the availability of Hindi teachers to teach the language to second-generation Indians.

Regarding the interest expressed by the leaders to have access to *Ramayana*, *Mahabharata*, *Vedas* and *Upanishads* from India, the Ambassador stated that these texts belong to the entire humanity and to the world and transcend all the narrow definitions of religion. He stressed that these texts promote inclusiveness and encourage pluralism that forms the basic fabric of India's civilisation.

Ambassador Agnihotri urged the Indo-Caribbean community leaders to continue to assert their Indianness and educate the world about the open, tolerant and accepting nature of India's great civilisation. He stated that India has always stood for peace and brotherhood and the community leaders should continue to take pride in their heritage and work together to strengthen it.

Finally, Ambassador Agnihotri stressed that this gathering of Indo-Caribbean leaders is the first in a series of interactions between his office and this community.

Recommendations Developed at the Forum

The following are some suggestions that were provided by the

Indo-Caribbean community leaders in the discussions:

1. Develop creative mechanisms to encourage the new generations to be more involved with their Indian roots by creating targeted scholarship programmes, which could be funded at least partly by the Indian government;
2. Strengthen bonds with India by creating more opportunities for youth to learn Indian classical dance(s), music, literature, classical texts (*Ramayana, Mahabharata, Upanishads, Vedas,* etc.), language(s) and drama, etc.;
3. Increase business and trading relationship between Indian businesses and those countries in the Caribbean that have large Indian population;
4. Pursue sustained and collective actions to (i) prevent the violation of the rights of Indians and Indian communities; and (ii) to prevent any methodological marginalisation of their culture throughout the world;
5. Re-establish and address the psyche of the Indo-Caribbean community (which was displaced from India some 165 years ago) by facilitating the formation of their 'body-politic' and by undertaking a project to re-construct the knowledge of history of these communities;
6. Craft mechanisms to substantially increase sustained exchanges within the Indo-Caribbean community with other first-generation non-resident Indian communities;
7. Recognise the contributions and achievements of people of Indo-Caribbean community in all spheres;
8. Urge the Government of India to be more vigorous and assertive in protecting the interests of the Indian communities in Caribbean countries and elsewhere; and
9. Rectify the fallacies and biases that seem to be omnipresent in the representation of India (and its culture) in Western media as well as in the educational/intellectual discourses of the West.

Invitees

The invitees consisted of community leaders, activists, academicians, corporate executives, doctors, attorneys and those intimately involved with the activities of the Indo-Caribbean community. The invitees included:

1.	Pandit Chandrica Persaud	22	Pandit Chunelall Narine	43	Dr. Taj Rajkumar
2.	Mr. Bhoj Dindiyal	23	Mrs. Bhagmanee Pooran	44	Imam "Abdul" Azeem Khan
3.	Mr. Mohan Singh	24	Pandit Ramlall	45	Mr. L. Harrycharran
4.	Pandit Prakash Gossai	25	Mrs. Kamla Ramkissoon-Sahabir	46	Mr. Churaumanie Bissundyal
5.	Pandit Gunananda	26	Mr. Bisram Rajkumar	47	Prof. Roopnarine Persaud
6.	Pandit Krishna Tiwari	27	Dr. Tara Singh	48	Mr. Sham Boodram
7.	Srimati Urmilla	28	Dr. Dhanpaul Narine	49	Mr. Ashook Ramsarran
8.	Pandit Oumadatt Maharaj	29	Mr. Tony Yasin	50	Mrs. Janet Maragh
9.	Pandit R. D. Upadhyaya	30	Mr. Vishnu Bisram	51	Mr. Pritha Singh
10.	Mr. Latchman Budhai	31	Mr. Vishhnu Mahadeo	52	Professor Balkrishna Naipul
11.	Pandit Jito Misir	32	Mr. Rudy Samaroe	53	Dr. Shaan Sharma
12.	Mr. Gorden Puran	33	Mr. Ed Ahmad	54	Mr. Satya Narayana Mourya
13.	Mr. Deo Gosine	34	Imam Hazi Zakir	55	Pandita lndranee Rampersad
14.	Pandit Loknath Sukul	35	Mr. lsardat Ramdehol	56	Reverand Seupaul Singh
15.	Pandit Satish Prakash, Phd.	36	Mr. Dhanraj Singh	57	Mr. Balakrisha Naipaul
16.	Pandit Roop Sukhram	37	Pandit Parsueram lndrajit	58	Mr. Ramond Bacchus
17.	Pandit Vishnu Sukul	38	Pandit Jai Misir	59	Mr. Ramesh Kalicharan
18.	Pandit Tilack Seeratan	39	Mrs. Barbara Lenaoine	60	Ms. Janet Maragh
19.	Pujari Basdeo Mangal	40	Mr. Krishna Subrian	61	Mr. Yassim Sattar
20.	Pandit Ramesh Maharaj	41	Mr. Bhanu Dwarka	62	Imam Zameer Sattaur
21.	Pandit Rohit Deocharan	42	Pandit Motiram		

Profile of Some of the Invitees

The office had requested all of the invitees to provide a brief background of themselves. The following is a list of individuals who sent the requested information about themselves:

Mr. Ramesh Kalicharran

Mr. Ramesh Kalicharran is from Essequibo Coast, Guyana. He migrated to the United States in 1970. He is the head of the Kali Group of companies, a conglomerate. Since his arrival to the United States, Mr. Kalicharran has worked vigorously to promote unity within the Indo-Caribbean community. He has been involved in a venture to enable Caribbean Mandir associations to visit India. In 2000, Mr. Kalicharran helped put together an educational and cultural mission of the Guyana Youth Corp to India. He has donated his time and resources to charitable and humanitarian causes. He is a founding member of the Indo-Caribbean Federation of North America in 1984, of GOPIO in 1989, of USA Pandit's Parishad, of 'Sangeet Mala' programme, Gyaan Bhakti Satsang in 1984, and the annual Phagwa Parade started in 1990. He has been a member of the American Federation of Police since 1972, co-ordinated the Asian pavilion at the Queens Festival, served as Director of India Festival Committee, and has been an organiser of Miss India NY USA & Worldwide Pageant.

Professor Dhanpaul Narine

Professor Dhanpaul Narine was born in Guyana. He studied at the University of Guyana, Cambridge University and the London School of Economics and Political Science where he obtained his Ph.D, was president of the Third World Society and taught at the Department of Social Sciences from 1983-1987. In New York, Professor Narine has actively been involved in the Indo-Caribbean community. He was one of the founders of the Federation of Hindu Mandirs, the Mahatma Gandhi Peace March, Youth Conventions, and the Joyti Satsangh programme on ITV(77); he is also the host of this programme. He is currently president of the Shri Trimurti Bhavan. Professor Narine has worked with many groups and organisations to promote peace, understanding and tolerance in NYC and beyond. He along, with Dr. Tara Singh founded Guyana Watch Inc., which makes annual medical missions to Guyana. He is author of *Children of the Ganges* and co-author of *Sojourners to Settlers*.

Dr. Tara Singh

Dr. Tara Singh was born in West Bank Demerara, Guyana. He attended the universities of

Guyana, Wales, London and Montclair State College. He has written several scholarly articles in journals and newspapers, as well as policy-oriented manuscripts. He is a former Commonwealth Senior Fellow and a Fulbright Scholar. Dr. Singh has been in the US since the mid-1980s and has been actively involved in community/humanitarian work. He, along with Professor Dhanpaul Narine, founded Guyana Watch Inc., which makes annual medical missions to Guyana. Dr. Singh has also founded the Guyana Youth Corp, which arranges dialogue and cultural exchanges between the youth of various Indo-Caribbean countries. He was founder of the individuals who facilitated in taking a group of Indo-Caribbean youth to India. He has received several citations for service, including from the Indo-Caribbean youth.

Professor Roopnaraine Persaud

Professor Rooopnarain Pesaudwas born in Guyana. He finished his B.A. at the University of Guyana, his M.A. in Management/Planning, Urban & Regional Studies, Makato, Minnesota, and G.C.E and C.P. from the University of London. His professional focus is in teaching and management. He is currently co-ordinator at Goodwill Industries Family Learning Centre in Brooklyn, New York, a real estate licence instructor and an accident prevention and defensive driving instructor. Professor Persaud is owner of RDS Multi-- services, a management and consulting firm engaged in real estate planned unit development in Florida. He is general secretary/founder of the World Union of Guyanese for Democracy and a poet. Professor Persaud has also participated in the return of democracy/free and fair elections to Guyana.

Ms. Pritha Singh

Ms. Pritha Singh was born in Guyana. She is a multi-disciplinary artiste– actor, dancer, choreographer, poet, playwright and storyteller and her work as a producer combines tradition with modern theatre techniques. Ms Singh studied at the American Academy of Dramatic Arts, the Herbert Berghof/Uta Hagen Studios and Playwrights Foundation, Pace University in New York (majoring in English theatre) and the Royal Academy of Dramatic Arts in London. She studied the Mariammen Theatre of Guyana. Ms Singh is particularly interested in preserving and presenting neglected heritage art forms, many of which are unique variations of originals, evolved from the diaspora experience in Guyana, Surinam and the Caribbean islands, like Trinidad. In 2001, she was awarded a grant for playwriting *Women of the Mahabharata* by the Queens Council on the Arts, the NYC Department of Cultural Affairs and the New York State Council on the Arts. Ms Singh is also a founder of Rajkumari Cultural Centre, which promotes the cultural and artistic life of the Indo-Caribbean community.

Pandit RadhaRaman Upadhyaya

Pandit Upadhyaya was born in Guyana. He is past president of the University of Guyana Hindu Society, Shri Krishna Campbellville Jawaan Sangh, Guyana, and USA Pandits' Parishad. Pandit Upadhaya is a science educator and a Guidance Counsellor with the Department of Education, New York. He is working president of the New York Chapter of the Vishwa Hindu Parishad of America, New York Chapter and Karyawah of Hindu Swayamsevak Sangh, New York City Chapter.

Mr. Ashook K. Ramsaran

Mr. Ashook Ramsaran was born in Guyana. He came to the US in 1968. He received his B.A and M.S. from Polytechnic University (Brooklyn, New York). He served in management positions at engineering firms. In 1988, Mr. Ramsaran founded Ramex, Inc., an engineering and manufacturing company. He is secretary general of the Global Organisation of People of Indian Origin (GOPIO) and director of the East Indian Civic Association (GEICA). Mr. Ramsaran is also a board member of the Fresh Meadows Homeowners Civic Association (FMHCA) and Elder of Session at First Presbyterian Church of Flushing.

Pandita lndranee Rampersad

Pandita lndranee Rampersad is the foremost and most well-recognised female Hindu priest from the Caribbean. She is an accomplished journalist, and has travelled several times to India. Pandita Rampersad is currently teaching with the Board of Education and is in the process of finishing her Ph.D.

Pandit Ramlall

Pandit Ramlall was born in Guyana. He played a prominent role in the Guyanese independence movement and taught at Corentyne, Guyana. Pandit Ramlall was one of the first Guyanese scholars to be awarded a scholarship by the Government of India to study in India. In

1984, he founded the Arya Spiritual Centre and is a practicing priest of the Arya Samaj. He is a founding member of the Phagwah Parade in New York and has published the *Vedavandana*, a spiritual book. He is a senior member of the Vishwa Sanskriti Sanstan, India, commissioner of Deeds, New York, member of the Interfaith Council of NYC, secretary of Queens Clergy Council, Voluntary Chaplin for NYC Transit, and patron of Arya Pratinidhi Sabha, America.

Reverand Seopaul Singh

Reverand Seopaul Singh was born in Guyana. He worked as a teacher in Annandale ECO, Guyana for 10 years and for the Government of Guyana for 22 years. In 1992, he was recruited by the International Association of Emergency Managers and concurrently by the United Nations Geneva UNV HRU. He was ordained a Christian minister both in the US in 1977 and in Guyana in 1979. Reverend Singh writes regularly for the Guyana journal, *Caribbean Indian Times* and occasionally in the *Caribbean New Yorker* and *Kaiteur News*. He is a founding member and the public relations officer of the Association of Artists and Writers and has published poetry through the American Poets Society.

Imam Hazi Zakir

Imam Hazi Zakir was born in Guyana. He is the founder of the United Muslim Organisation. He has worked to promote unity within the Indo-Caribbean community.

Ms. Janet Maragh

Ms. Janet Maragh was born in Jamaica. She was the driving force in re-establishing the Sanatan Dharma Maha Sabha of Jamaica, and has laid a strong foundation for the revitalisation of Hinduism in Jamaica. Ms. Maragh is a registered nurse and is director of Patient Services in New York City. She devotes a considerable amount of time for volunteer activities and promoting Indian arts and culture in New York City.

Mr. Balkrishna Naipaul

Mr. Balkrishna Naipaul was born in Trinidad. He studied history, economics, and international relations in London. He has served as the permanent representative of Development Educators for World Peace at the United Nations. In 1992, together with Mr. Ramesh Kalicharran and Prof. Ved Nanda of Colorado, he petitioned the Government of India to erect either a statue, or a publicly displayed monument bearing a plaque that would recognise the contributions of the people of Indian origin to the cause of Indian independence. Mr. Naipaul is also the founder of *Global Times*. He is one of the founding members of GOPIO. He is also a writer of such books as *Arc on the Horizon* and *Legends of the Emperor's Ring*.

Imam 'Abdul' Azeem Khan

Imam 'Abdul' Azeem Khan was born in Guyana. He earned a B.A and M.S. in Computer Science from NYU. Imam Khan is founder of MasjidOmar Ben Abdel-Aziz in Queens, NY. He is affiliated with Majlis Ashura and the American Society of Muslims. Imam Khan is also an entrepreneur and owns a Halal Meat Market and Grocery Store. He has worked extensively with community organisations to promote unity and understanding.

Pandit Krishna Tiwari

Pandit Krishna Tiwari was born in Guyana. He is a founder of Cypress Hill Joyti Mandir in New York, which was established to promote and practice Indian culture. He has worked to promote peace and unity in the community.

Mr. Deo Gosine

Mr. Deo Gosine was born in Trinidad. He is an engineer by profession and is currently president of Amatech Corp. Mr. Gosine is a founder trustee of Sanatan Dharma Maha Sabha, Queens, NY. He has served on the Advisory Committee to the NYC comptroller and the Elemhurst Economic Development Committee. Mr. Gosine is currently president of Lions International, Elmhurst, New York. He is active in promoting Indo-Caribbean interests.

Imam ZameerSattaur

Imam ZameerSattaur is the resident Imam of Masjid Al-Abidin, which is the largest Indo-Guyanese Muslim mosque in New York. He is a registered marriage officer for the tri- state area and D.C., a family counsellor and a police clergy liaison with the NYPD.

Mr. Raymond Bacchus

Mr. Raymond Baccus is the general secretary of the MasjidOmar Ben Abdel-Aziz in Queens, NY.

Ms. Bhagwatie Bhanu Dwarika

Ms. Bhagwatie Bhanu Dwarika is a GOPIO board member for the Caribbean, Co-chair Asian Heritage Committee, District Council 137, and Executive Director of Shandana Resource Centre. Ms Dwarika is currently a programme co-ordinator for the District Council 137 Education Fund. She was a founding member and VP of the Indo-Caribbean Federation of North America.

Pandit RoopSukhram

Pandit RoopSukhram was born in Georgetown, Guyana. He has served as secretary for USA's Pandit Parishad and served as senior vice president for the Federation of Hindu Mandirs. He founded the Sri Ram Mandir in Brooklyn, NY in 1991. He has published two books, *Bhakti Joyti–Light of Devotion* and *Atma Joyti–Light of the Soul.*

Mr. Yassim Sattar

Mr. Yassim Sattar is assistant secretary/treasurer and general maintenance officer for building of MasjidOmar Ben Abdel-Aziz in Queens, NY.

Pandit Edward Motiram

Pandit Motiram was born in Guyana. He helped found the International Cultural Society in Brooklyn New York, the first Indo-Caribbean Mandir in the US. He is currently senior priest at Bhavanee Maa Mandir in Brooklyn, NY. He is founder/director of the Federation of Hindu Mandirs and Mahatma Gandhi Peace March.

Mr. Annan Boodram

Mr. Annan Boodram was born in Guyana. MrBoodram is founder and editor-in-chief of the *Caribbean Voice Newspaper*, Inc. and a leading Caribbean journalist. He has served in the US Army Reserve and is also a teacher in New York City.

Pandit Rohit Deocharan

Pandit Rohit Deocharan was born in Guyana. He is the officiating priest of the Bhavani Mandir.

Mr. Vishnu Bisram

Mr. Vishnu Bisram was born in Guyana. He is a pollster, political commentator, journalist and educator in New York City. He has served as director of the North American Caribbean Teachers Association. Mr. Bisram has been a founder of the Indo-Caribbean Federation and the World Union of Guyanese.

Mr. Satya Narayan Mourya

Mr. Satya Narayana Mourya is an accomplished artist from India. He made a significant contribution at the Diwali Nagar in Trinidad by making over 108 paintings.

Mr. Rohan Narine

Mr. Rohan Narine graduated from Queens College (CUNY) with a B.A. in accounts and economics. He is a ranked chess player and is a Hindu priest-in-training.

Comments on the Forum by Some Invitees

Professor DhanpaulNarine

"My impression of our recent meeting with the Indian Ambassador-at-Large has been positive. It was good of the Ambassador to reach out to our community. Once the follow-up arrangements are planned efficiently, many good things will flow out of our discussions, including the practical policy decisions. A structure should emerge on future meetings. The Ambassador-at-Large will be the head and will bring us together, as well as representatives drawn from his office as well as from our community. In future, the Indo-Caribbean Federation would like to set-up a high level meeting with the Government in India, which will also involve the young Indo-Caribbeans.

Pandit Radha Raman Upadhaya

The efforts of Dr. Bhishma Agnihotriji and his staff of proactively involving all Indians in the diaspora are very commendable. It is the first time that leaders of various Caribbean Indian organisations in New York City were requested to have an interactive session with such high-level representatives of India. This meeting was not only a historic one, but it laid a firm foundation for greater benefits for all Indians.

"The immediate benefits include the warm acceptance by Bharat of her children from the Caribbean. For too long, especially during the Congress government, the Indians in the Caribbean have experienced abandonment, neglect and non-inclusion into the global Indian family. With this new shared trust, Indians can now work together to realise their unique spiritual role in the new world order."

Pandit Krishna Tiwari

"This historical and momentous meeting with the Indian government and the Indo-Caribbean community has been long overdue. It will definitely bridge the gap of time and distance that separated us over the years."

Observations about the Indo-Caribbean Diaspora by Some Invitees

Imam 'Abdul' Azeem Khan

"The communities must work together in order to bring unity among the Indo-Caribbean brothers and sisters; not only being involved in their place of worship, but also support each other in other areas that would benefit all."

Professor DhanpaulNarine

"The Indo-Caribbean community has India close to its heart. On a daily basis, India is invoked in our presence through worship, movies, songs, etc. There is no doubt that India has a lot to offer to its many children abroad. As a mother, it needs to embrace its kin in its bosom and rekindle the fire of love, hope and oneness."

Pandit RadhaRaman Upadhaya

"The bridges that were erected between Hindustan and the Caribbean bring with it responsibilities from both sides. We are aware of what will happen if we construct bridges where one or both ends have weak supports. It is imperative that we vehemently work together to strengthen Bharat as well as the Caribbean. However, we must not lose sight of the need to expand our involvement in our new home–the United States of America for the sake of this and future generations of Indians. As inheritors of the same glorious heritage of Bharat, we owe it to our *rishis* and our children to advance and disseminate Vedic wisdoms among all people.

"Finally, while we seek ways of meaningful interactions, involvements and joint projects; we must give opportunities to Indians in every country to excel in every field of human endeavours. By adopting and promoting such collaborations, our greater achievements will be realised in a much shorter time."

Pandit Krishna Tiwari

"It is my firm opinion that most Indians (PIOs) outside of India do not properly represent their people and culture due to an inferiority complex. I also express my concern at Bharat's unwillingness to accept and represent the PIOs. Bharat has a lot to learn from us and our way of life. This family reunion will tremendously enhance the flow of East-West integration of culture, trade and commerce. A parent body should be established to help facilitate the process.

"Pandit Edward Motiram would like to see a student exchange programme between our community and that of India.

"This would go a long way towards cementing the bonds of friendship and understanding between India and the diaspora."

Pandit Rohit Deocharan

"With this new bond that we have made among the Indian diaspora, as one global family, one of my priority goals is to incorporate Hindi as part of the language curriculum at all levels of school. I also envision an Indian Cultural Centre established to teach all aspects of Hindu culture including music, philosophy, art, language, scriptures, etc."

Professor Balkrishna Naipaul

"A. Strike a committee comprising of prominently involved PIOs and NRIs who have shown a visible interest in the need to break down the barriers between these two groups outside India. But in doing so, ensure that the persons involved are not in it for some personal interest, or to get a chance to enhance their already inflated egos.

"B. Look into the possibilities of setting up a trust fund, something like India Trust for the purpose of enhancing a set of immediate goals and objectives that would immediately go to the issue of building the global Indian family.

"C. Along with the above two objectives, start working on initiatives to secure NGO status with the United Nations. This would give a certain degree of credibility to the idea of the global Indian family as well as drawing strength from like-minded organisations, whose interest is at once culturally universal and kinetically linked to the spirit of kinship in a particularly cultural and spiritual matrix.

"D. Create a business network among PIOs and NRIs that could be advantageous to both India and the areas where PIOs live. There could be strong interests here on joint ventures in important sectoral trade where the movement of capital, goods and services, and technology transfer would enhance both the image of PIOs, as well as lending assistance to the development of regional economies. Indeed, involvement like this can go a long way to breaking down cultural divides and serve to advance the best attributes of cultural mixes that are at times not only volatile, but easily erupt as dysfunctional societies. A case in point is the fragile nature of both Trinidad's and Guyana's pluralistic societies that are sometimes classified as 'racially charged' or the misapprehensions that are sometimes met between PIOs and NRI who often see each other more as strangers, rather than belonging to the same family.

"E. Make a determined effort to get youth involvement. After all, it is here where the future of our family will meet some of the greatest challenges in the future. Everything must be done to get their views about the need to enhance the cultural and spiritual matrix of the global Indian family, especially among newer transplants in places like New York, London, Toronto. In many ways the Indian youth of North America and Europe is at a greater disadvantage than say, the youth from Fiji, South Africa or the Caribbean. It is an area that needs urgent attention and I think this is one area where the idea of a trust fund can be of greatest assistance."

Background of the Indo-Caribbean Community

The famous Indian leader, Jawaharlal Nehru, once said that "wherever Indians go, they take a little piece of India with them." Today, East Indians live in many parts of the world, making outstanding contributions to their respective societies.

There are about 1.2 million East Indians (primarily, descendants of East Indian immigrants) who inhabit various parts of the Caribbean(perhaps, another 600,000 now reside in Europe and North America!) Of all the Caribbean countries, Trinidad & Tobago have the highest number (500,000) of East Indians living there; followed by Guyana with 400,000; about 175,00 for Surinam (East Indians now constitute the largest ethnic group in all three countries); and 25,000 for Jamaica (this represents less than 2 per cent of Jamaica's population). Figures are not available for Martinique, Guadeloupe and other smaller Caribbean islands. However, out-migration and declining fertility levels may continue to reduce the East Indian proportion of population in these countries.

In Guyana (formerly British Guiana), East Indian indentureship began in 1838; in Trinidad and Tobago it commenced five years later in 1843, and in Jamaica it started in 1845, following the abolition of slavery in the British colonial empire in 1833. Emigration continued with minor interruptions until 1917, when that iniquitous system was terminated by the British government. During this time, of the 37,000Indians imported to Jamaica, about 38 per cent were repatriated. In Guyana over 238,000 Indians were imported, of which less than 30 per cent returned to India. In Trinidad & Tobago, less than 30 per cent of all Indians imported were repatriated. In Guadeloupe, less than 21 per cent (or 10,000) of the 42,000 Indians were imported and just about 20 per cent (or 4,000) of the 20,000 who went to Martinique, ever returned to India. From transient labourers, they eventually took on the status of permanent settlers.

East Indian indentured (five-year period) labourers were brought into the Caribbean to replace the ex-African slaves who had withdrawn their labour from the plantations following emancipation in 1833. Experiments with free labour to fill the labour vacuum between 1833 and the 1840's from other parts of the Caribbean, North America, North Africa, China and Europe, did not prove to be productive. Planters were, therefore, forced to seek alternative sources of labour that was reliable and industrious, and who could also withstand the rigours of the harsh tropical climate. East Indians were thought to fit nicely into that type of environment. Thus, began the flow of Indian immigration mainly from north India; the Uttar Pradesh region in particular. Over seven in every 10 Indian immigrants to the Caribbean came from Uttar Pradesh.

They arrived on various ships, including the '*Whitby*', and the '*Hesperus*'. Conditions aboard these ships were dehumanising, as they were during African slavery. When the indentured labourers reached the Caribbean, some of them thought that they were still in India because they were tricked into thinking that they were going only on a short distance. Uncertain, confused and apprehensive, indentured labourers took solace in their religious text, such as the *Gita*, *Ramayana*, and the *Qur'an*.

Originally, they were bonded to plantations for a period of five years, after which they could return to India. However the majority of Indians, as we have indicated before, stayed on in Trinidad & Tobago, Guyana, Jamaica, Surinam, Martinique and Guadeloupe on the promise of grants of small sums of money and land. Repatriation policies and practices did not promote, but rather, inhibit repatriation.

Although Indian labourers did not earn much in the Caribbean plantation system, they were still able to send money to India. In 1911, East Indians from Guyana, for example, remitted (US) $90,645 to India. Their counterparts in Trinidad did even better by remitting U.S. $425,000. These sums were sent mainly to relatives in India. As East Indians were catapulted into the hegemony of the plantation system, ex-slaves had an earlier start in civil society. By 1900, Afro-Caribbeans (ex-slaves and descendants) had begun to climb the occupational ladder in significant ways. They used education as the principal mechanism for mobility and social status. East Indians were not encouraged to pursue a Western education, which would have made them equally mobile, and thus drift them away from plantation labour. They had to provide a ready labour pool for the sugar plantations.

In 1933, the colonial office in London sent a team of experts to investigate social and economic issues affecting the Caribbean. This mission was known as the Moyne Commission, which duly proceeded to discuss such issues as East Indian education, among other things, but there was no East Indian present to give testimony. The head of the Commission, Sir Walter Citrine, expressed disbelief that out of a total number of 1,086 teachers in Guyana, only 67 East Indians (55 men and 12 women) were in that profession. One had to be a Christian to become a teacher then and since most Indian immigrants were not Christians, they were not employed, despite their qualifications.

Even though their contributions to economic development in their new countries have not always been acknowledged (for example, this history of the Caribbean is often referred to as the history of Afro-Caribbeans), East Indians have been responsible for the development of the sugar, rice, lumber, small manufacturing, and other industries. During the latter half of the twentieth century, East Indians had firmly established themselves as business entrepreneurs, and had also been entering the ranks of the professional groups. With independence for these countries came not only the perception of 'freedom from the plantation system', but also a resurgence of Indian ethnic pride, which has been buttressed over the past decades by such stalwarts, as Mr. Jagai of Jamaica, Mr. Bhadase S. Maraj of Trinidad & Tobago, and Dr. Balwant Singh of Guyana. The Indian church (*mandirs* and mosques) and socio-cultural organisations also played a significant role in promoting traditional cultural and religious revival.

In 1995, Jamaican Indians celebrated 150 years of Indian immigration to that island. Noted film actress and former Miss World, Aishwarya Rai, was their chief guest-of-honour and to further mark the occasion, the Jamaican government issued a special commemorative postal stamp. In Guyana, Trinidad & Tobago and Surinam several activities were held to commemorate the 150th anniversary of Indian immigration. Conferences and cultural events were also held in New York, Toronto and elsewhere.

Increasing political awareness, combined with the formation of trade unions and political parties, had enabled East Indians to increase their participation in the teaching profession as well as in other sectors of the economy. However, these advances were to be later undone by constant political uncertainty and deteriorating economic conditions, which led to several waves of East Indian immigration to the United Kingdom in the 1950s and 1960s and then to Canada in the 1960s to the present, and from the 1960s to the present in the United States. Not even the election of Indian leaders, like Cheddi Jagan of Guyana and Basdeo Panday of Trinidad & Tobago to head the government in Guyana and Trinidad &Tobago respectively could stop the flow of outward migration. Over the last 20 years, migration to North America has increased to such a degree that there are probably more East Indians from the Caribbean living in North America than East Indians living in the Caribbean.

The Ind0-Caribbeans' (East Indians of the Caribbean) contribution to neighbourhood revitalisation in New York and elsewhere is well established. Indo-Caribbeans occupy key slots in all sectors of the economy. They are yet, however, to stake a claim to political office in New York. Economic advance was achieved to some extent at huge social costs, such as family instability, alcoholism, school dropouts and truancy. Community groups are trying to grapple with these issues, which are however, not peculiar to the Indo-Caribbean, but also, to the wider community.

As they did, a 165 years ago, when they landed in the Caribbean for the first time, East Indians have stuck to their culture which provided them with a strong sense of ethnic pride. While they had become ambivalent towards India, they never wholly accepted Guyana either, as their home. The 'transient settler' mentality which was developed during the plantation system, continued to shape their attitudes in this regard. However, for the second journey of immigration to Europe and North America from the Caribbean, there has been less ambivalence. Our youth in particular see themselves as Americans, and while tempted to discard their Indian heritage, are still able to recognise and experience the glory of Indian culture. But the situation is not stable; its tenuous. We have to spend more time with them and help them to better understand the significance of our rich cultural heritage. This is one of the Indo-Caribbeans' biggest challenges. Preserving traditional culture from the onslaught of the dominant Western value system has often led to ongoing clashes (which is largely inter-generational in character). It would take clever social engineering and a re-defined vision to ease these culture-based tensions.

With proper cultural guidance, our youth will understand as we do, that science and logic cannot answer or solve all our problems/ mysteries. Strength also comes from the things that we can comfortably lean on, such as our religion, our culture and our history.

Financial Institutions to Improve the Quality of Financial Services Aimed at NRIs and PIOs

June 17, 2003

Executive Summary

I. Background

The meeting of leading financial institutions to improve the quality of financial services for NRIs and PIOs was organised as part of an ongoing series of initiatives undertaken by the office of India's Ambassador-at-Large to foster dialogue with Indian communities around the world.

II. Representation

Executives and senior managers of various banking organisations.

III. Themes Discussed

1. India as an attractive investment location.
2. The global Indian family.
3. Increasing the impact of Diaspora on India's development.

IV. Key Recommendations

1. The need to offer custom, country-specific financial services programmes.
2. Creating a database to facilitate the meeting of buyers and sellers.
3. Implementation of an effective communication platform to link NRls to investment opportunities in India.
4. Implementation of a stronger public relations campaign, as well as more articulate programmes and strategies, by the Government of India and Indian companies to more effectively promote India's interests

V. Next Steps

1. Increase interaction and networking between diaspora bankers.
2. Continued dialogue with the office of the Ambassador-at-Large.
3. Develop actionable strategies that can be quickly implemented.

Enhancing the Quality of Financial Services for the Indian Diaspora
June 17, 2003 (Programme)

)- Welcome and Occasion: Dr. Bhishma K. Agnihotri, Ambassador-at-Large for NRls and & PIOs

)- Self-introductions: Attendees

)- Suggested Framework For Discussion: 1. Nature and level of participating financial institution(s) with the Indian diaspora I community.

2. What can be done to expand and qualitatively improve this interaction in ways that could benefit the diaspora in their personal, business, investment, and philanthropic activities.

3. Mechanisms by which information on policy and regulatory changes (in India and in the countries where they reside) is currently disseminated to the Indian diaspora;

4. Possible ways to improve the information flow as well as underlying products/services;

5. Ways in which this office can work to facilitate this process as well as any process improvements.

6. Other issues and next steps.

)- Closing Remarks: Ambassador Agnihotri

Overview

The office of India's Ambassador-at-Large for NRls/PIOs, as part of its mission, has been evolving programmes that connect the NRI/PIO community to India in many ways. Besides community and culture-based initiatives, the office has focussed on investment-oriented initiatives to connect NRls/PIOs to India. India is embarking on an economic revolution that is changing the lives of Indians in India and throughout the world.

The world is becoming aware of the potential and size of India's market. This economic revolution is aimed at making India into a world economic leader and project its humanistic values onto the world stage. A benefit of this will be to improve the image of Indians in all other countries. As part of the process, the NRI/PIO community has an important role to play. They can contribute in many ways to India's development. Besides working with the governments of the countries they reside in, the NRI/PIO community can also directly invest in India's development.

The office of India's Ambassador-at-Large for NRls/PIOs has set a priority to increase its interaction with members of the NRI/PIO community in the banking/financial services sector. Many of these individuals are experts in their fields, have considerable experience and expertise relating to international finance, investments, import/export banking and other related fields, and have worked on investment initiatives in India for their respective companies. It is for this reason that a meeting was organised between NRI/PIO representatives of leading financial institutions and Ambassador Agnihotri.

The goal of this meeting was to develop a working template on how to encourage the NRI/PIO community to get more actively involved in India's economic development, promote greater savings and develop ways of increasing investment into India. This was at first in a series of meetings between Ambassador Agnihotri and NRI/PIO representatives of leading financial institutions

Highlights

Ambassador Bhishma Agnihotri initiated and chaired the first meeting of representatives of various global and Indian financial institutions. The aim of the meeting was to initiate a process of finding and implementing ways to improve the quality of financial services being offered to the Indian diaspora and to increase NRI-investments into India. The meeting was part of a series of such initiatives undertaken by Ambassador Agnihotri's office to promote the interests of the Indians throughout the world.

Top-ranking executives and representatives from all major financial institutions that offer financial services to the Indian diaspora participated in the meeting. Some of the participants were: Mr. Ravi

Lochan Pola and Mr. Hemand Mundra (Kotak Mahindra), Mr. Shesh Iyengar and Mr. Dhananjay Tambe (State Bank of India), Ms. Shanta Lall (Citigroup), Ms. Jyoti Chopra (Merrill Lynch), Mr. M. Balachandran (Bank of Baroda), Mr. R. Madhavan (American Express), Mr. Anil Bhalla (J.P. Morgan Chase), Mr. Rakesh Bhargava (Wachovia Securities), Mr. David Rasquinha (Export-Import Bank of India), Mr. Madhav Kalyan and Mr. Amit Dhawan (ICICI Bank), Mr. Sanjiv Patni (ICICI Securities), Mr. M. B. Battliwala (ICICI Infotech), Mr. R. S. Reddy (Bank of India), Mr. Vipp Jaswal (HSBC), and Mr. R. S. Reddy (Bank of India).

Initiating the discussions, Ambassador Agnihotri stated that financial services form the essential lubricant by which the Indian diaspora could (a) enhance their own prosperity while maintaining their unique culture and life-style choices, (b) increase their contribution to India's overall economic development, and (c) provide informational feedback to help in the evolution of policy frameworks to make India a far more attractive investment destination and responsive towards the diaspora's investment needs. He mentioned that through his travels around the world, he had been impressed by the eagerness of the Indian diaspora to contribute and leverage for India, their material, financial and intellectual resources and skills. He also asked the participants to freely express their views and provide suggestions for future interactions.

While introducing themselves and their financial institutions, the participants congratulated the Ambassador for his tireless efforts to organise such forums and offered their full support to implement his vision of establishing a 'global Indian family' connected to an 'India that cares'. The participants also contributed to a rich and stimulating discussion and offered an expansive range of ideas. Some of the thoughts presented by the participants were as follows:

Mr. M. Balachandran, CEO of Bank of Baroda, stated that the office of Ambassador-at-Large offers a unique value-added leadership to bring together the various Indian communities around the world. He also mentioned that his organisation actively works with the Indo-Caribbean diaspora and congratulated Ambassador Agnihotri for establishing, through his personal initiative, a forum of dialogue for leaders of that community with the Indian government. Mr. Balachandran also emphasised the need to offer localised treatment –

from a financial services and information standpoint, to each country where Indians live.

Mr. Shesh Iyengar, CEO of the State Bank of India, stressed the need for stepping up the quality of financial services and product offerings for the diaspora. He also stated that there remains a need for an effective database to facilitate the meeting of buyers and sellers and therefore increased transaction activity.

Ms Jyoti Chopra, Director and Head of South Asian Business Development at Merrill Lynch stated that the dynamics of the Indian community in the United States are unique. Indians are hard working and wealth preservation continues to be their topmost priority, especially in the current economic environment. She stressed the importance of the implementation of an effective communication platform to link these priorities of NRIs with investment unities in India. She also mentioned that in her view the diversity of financial service institutions represented in the meeting offers unique opportunities for inter-company linkages to address the objectives set by Ambassador Agnihotri.

Ms Shanta Lall, Head of NRI Banking at Citigroup, Inc., mentioned that based on her 16 years of experience working with the Indian diaspora, there was an urgent need to have a more effective public relations management strategy by India's government and companies.

Along similar lines, Mr. Madhav Kalyan stated that India is investment hub effective communication is required to manage the views of rating agencies which do not consider India to be investment grade yet.

Mr. David Rasquinha, resident representative of the Export-Import Bank of India, provided his insights into the nature of ties that NRIs have with India and emphasised the need for marketing India in a better way through well-articulated programmes and strategies. Mr. Sanjiv Patni stated that there is a lack of adequate communication of changes and developments taking place in India for the NRIs.

Mr. Anil Bhalla, Managing Director of J.P. Morgan Chase, also provided detailed and insightful feedback on the financial service needs of the Indian diaspora.

Ambassador Agnihotri thanked the participants for their enthusiasm and concluded the meeting by stating that he was highly encouraged by the level of participation and the desire on part of the banking community to support his efforts. He stated that as a next step, a framework would be established to have frequent meetings in future on specific issues. Finally, he thanked the participants for honestly communicating their views and promised that inputs provided in the meeting will be conveyed to the Government of India and that their views would be utilised in the formulation of future policies in India.

Recommendations of the Meeting

Some suggestions developed during the meeting centred on:

1. The need to offer custom, country-specific financial services programmes.
2. Create a database to facilitate the meeting of buyers and sellers.
3. Implement an effective communication platform to link NRIs to investment opportunities in India.
4. Implement a stronger public relations campaign, as well as more articulate programmes and strategies by the Government of India and Indian companies to more effectively promote India's interests.

Recommendations from Invitees

Ms Joyti Chopra

Director, Multicultural & Diversified Business Development
Merrill Lynch

1. Form an advisory council to your office of key representatives from a cross-section of the participants (i.e. retail brokerage, commercial banks, asset management, institutional firms, etc.)
2. Identify the top four or five financial services needs of your various constituents (i.e. Indians in the US/Indians overseas/ Indians in India/Indian government) and develop a roadmap/ work plan to support these needs.
3. Conduct a financial services survey/assessment among your constituents
4. Put together a financial services products team/working group to support integration of appropriate Indian organisations/

non-profits in US distributed products (e.g. donor-directed mutual funds).

Mr. Anil Bhalla

Managing Director, JP Morgan Chase

New York

In response to your request, here are some observations and suggestions from the JP Morgan Chase team:

1. The financial needs and objectives of the Indian diaspora should be evaluated with two distinct arguments in mind:; (a) the first generation immigrants who are now professionally and financially mature with many approaching their retirement age, and (b) the second generation NRI's/PIO's comprising the children of the first generation, now adults, and the young, more recent arrivals into the US, such as the IT professionals. The distinctive characteristics of the two groups also stem from the fact that the first generation of NRI/PIO migrants to the US comprised mainly of professionals - doctors, engineers, bankers, etc., whereas their children and the more recent arrivals pursue a mix of entrepreneurial and professional careers.
2. The financial demands and the investment objectives of these two groups are different from each other insofar as the first, quite naturally, is now biased more towards wealth preservation and lifestyle maintenance, whereas the latter is focused largely on wealth creation and asset building. The provision of the right financial services to both groups should therefore recognise and target their individual needs and objectives.
3. The first category would most likely prefer investments, both in the US and in India, that generate a good current income but also create little or no risk to capital/principal. They would look to financial institutions for professional and objective advice to do this. Government and investment-grade corporate bonds, high-quality asset-backed securities and shares in blue chip corporates with a stable dividend history, for example, would fall into the category of the likely investments that might be suitable for them. The first generation NRIs/PIOs

is also more likely to remit funds to their extended family in India or towards buying/building a house there for part-time use during their retirement.

4. The latter category, the second generation and young NRIs/PIOs, would for the most part, have a stronger need for help in establishing themselves in the US and a greater tolerance for risk in their quest for creating wealth and building assets. They would also therefore, require a greater array and sophistication of financial services and products. If they are in business, they might look to financial institutions in the US to help them with private equity capital, or bank funding for expansion, or to introduce them to suitable joint venture opportunities for growth. Being in the asset building stage, and whether they are entrepreneurs or professionals, they would look to the financial institution to offer them personal services and products, such as credit cards, mortgages, auto loans and help with setting up 401 K's and other saving avenues, including for their children's education in the future. They are less likely to remit money to India for family reasons bur once successful, would be more drawn to undertake and support charitable causes.
5. It would follow from the above that for either category of NRIs/PIOs, the decision to invest in India is increasingly a question of whether or not it fits into their specific financial and economic objectives, rather than simply an emotional desire to do so. Put another way, if faced with two or more opportunities for investment and one of them came from India, they might give India a preferential treatment but only if their risk to return matrix is not worse in making that choice. The only exception might be in times of severe crisis or calamity in India (such as the dire forex shortage in 1991) when NRIs/PIOs might make an 'uneconomic' decision to help the country. Such situations hopefully, will be rare in the future.

   This has therefore, significant bearing on how 'investing in India' is sold to the NRIs/PIOs in future and it stands to reason that the marketing would have to be focused heavily on products and services that are tailored towards their 'risk tolerance relative to expected return' objectives and 'wealth creation' goals, and only secondarily and softly on emotion.

6. As we discussed yesterday, JP Morgan Chase is uniquely positioned to serve all the needs of the Indian diaspora through our branch network, our consumer lending products (credit cards, mortgages, auto finance, others), our industry leading small business and middle market platforms, our wholesale bank capabilities and the JP Morgan Private Bank. For individual clients we can provide wealth accumulation, preservation and/or wealth transfer for first generation NRls/PIOs or the more fundamental banking, investment and/or insurance products needed by immigrants, who are new to the US. With a great many people of Indian origin employed at JPMorgan, we have a strong understanding of the culture and financial needs of the community.
7. Lastly, we also wanted to reiterate our belief that the office of Ambassador-at-Large could make a significant contribution to the Indian NRI/PIO community by acting as a resource to help people of Indian descent build wealth through access to financial services for both personal and business needs. This role could also be extended by actively working with individual Indian companies to assist them in setting up relationships with US banks, securing access to the financial markets. The natural by-product of the overall financial and economic well-being of the Indian diaspora would of course be to encourage greater investment into India. We would like very much to work with you and your team in this regard and to help you meet your goals.

Mr. David Rasquinha

Resident Representative

EXIM Bank of India

NRls and PIOs (used interchangeably from now on) have two kinds of ties to India:

a. Familial and cultural.

b. Economic.

As regards familial and cultural ties, these are inculcated at home and create a certain amount of affinity for and empathy with India and things Indian. This is, however, merely a basis. Ultimately, no matter how great the emotional tie to India is, when it comes to economics, we are basically rational animals. In order to invest funds in India or return to India to set up business, an NRI needs to be convinced that the investment makes economic sense (in terms of opportunity, risk-reward and future growth).

Undoubtedly, there are numerous problems (of infrastructure, of corruption, etc.) that India presents and we are all aware of them. However, to my mind, there is a key opportunity that India offers which is not so well realised. If we look at the world around us, two factors of key importance emerge:

a. Economic.

b. Demographic.

What does this mean? Today, India and China are the only economies of any significant size (I am ignoring tiny cases) that are growing consistently at a rate of over5 per cent p.a.

Japan is in a deflationary spiral; Europe's common monetary policies and common currency are reducing all members to the lowest common denominator (Germany, the main engine, is already faltering); the USA is (in my inexpert opinion) headed for economic troubles (growing unemployment, deflationary tendencies, unsustainable public finances).

A demographic time bomb in the form of aging population combined with unfounded pension obligations looms large over most of the developed world, which will impact manufacturing industries as well as further exacerbate public finances.

In short, over the next decade, the best (in some cases the only!) opportunities for economic growth and market acquisition lie in India and China (given our continuing growth, huge market, skill base). It is therefore, in the rational self-interest of any investor (NRI or otherwise) to look to India (and China of course; we can separately look at why India will in the long run be superior) if he wants his business to grow.

We need to market this. Large American businesses have realised this a long time back; witness the huge investments in China (even if no profits are accruing now, they are beachheads for the future). Many Fortune companies are in India as well (GE, IBM, Microsoft, Oracle, Motorola, Ford); yet as regards NRls, there is just a trickle (investment as well as returning Indians setting up businesses). Should we not be alerting them that they are missing the bus? I believe a marketing thrust, focusing on the above, would be useful.

Mr. M. Balachandran
CEO
Bank of Baroda

It is necessary for creating a proper information-dissemination mechanism within the financial and banking institutions to provide timely service and inputs to the NRI/PIO community. The need of the diaspora from different countries and different professional strata varies; hence, the information package to be provided to the community must be specialised and comprehensive.

Mr. Vipp Jaswal
Senior Vice President
HSBC Bank

1. Creation of data base of the NRI/PIO community will help in reaching out to them with specialised services and packages. The office of the Ambassador-at-Large could utilise services of the banks and financial institutions to upgrade and prepare such a data base.
2. As there are a large number of NRI/PIO bodies and each of them requires specialised need- and project-based services, the banks and financial institutions will require assistance of the office of the Government of India's missions and posts to reach out to these bodies in a structured manner.
3. Financial institutions and banks working in the areas to promote NRI and PIO investment and interest need to co-operate closely and interact with each other on regular intervals.

Profile of Firms and Executives

Kotak Mahindra

Kotak Mahindra is one of India's leading financial institutions, offering complete financial solutions that encompass every sphere of life. From banking, to stock broking, to mutual funds, to life insurance, to investment banking, the company caters to the financial needs of individuals and corporates.

Kotak has a group net worth of around Rs1,400 crore and currently employs over 2,000 dedicated employees in its various businesses. With a presence in about 50 locations in India and offices in New York, London, Dubai and Mauritius, the group currently services a customer base of over 5,00,000.

The group has international partnerships with Goldman Sachs (one of the world's largest investment banks and brokerage firms), Ford Credit (one of the world's largest dedicated automobile financiers) and Old Mutual (a large insurance, banking and asset management conglomerate).

Mr. Ravi Lochan Pola

President & CEO

Mr. Hemand Muna

Manager

Citigroup

Citigroup Inc. is a diversified global financial services holding company whose businesses provide a broad range of financial services to consumer and corporate customers with some 200 million customer accounts in over 100 countries and territories. The company's activities are conducted through the global consumer, Global Corporate and Investment Bank (GCIB), private client services, Global Investment Management (GIM) and proprietary investment activities business segments.

For financial reporting and internal operational purposes, Citigroup is largely organised into five groups: Citigroup Global Consumer Group, Citigroup's global corporate and investment bank, Citigroup Global Investment Management, Citigroup International and Smith Barney.

Citigroup Global Consumer Group

The Citigroup Global Consumer Group businesses comprise the financial service sector's most diverse consumer product offerings – banking services, credit cards, loans and insurance.

Our businesses also offer industry-leading advanced technology, a strong worldwide presence and a powerful global franchise in Citibank.

Global Corporate and Investment Bank

Citigroup's Global Corporate and Investment Bank has emerged as the premier organisation for meeting all the financial services of corporations, governments and institutional and individual investors around the globe.

Smith Barney

Smith Barney is the global private wealth management and equity research unit of Citigroup. It is a leading provider of comprehensive financial planning and advisory services to high net worth investors, institutions, corporations and private businesses, governments and foundations. With more than 300 research analysts around the globe and nearly 12,400 financial consultants in some 500 offices, Smith Barney offers a full suite of investment services, including asset allocation, private investments and lending services, hedge funds, cash and portfolio management, as well as retirement, education and estate planning. A division of Citigroup Global Markets, Smith Barney currently serves more than 7.5 million client accounts, representing nearly $900 billion in client assets.

Citigroup Global Investment Management

Citigroup Asset Management provides investment management and related services to a broad spectrum of clients around the world, from the beginner investors to wealthy individuals to large institutions, both public and private. It boasts of one of the most impressive research teams on Wall Street and some of the most well-known brands in money management –Smith Barney, Brothers and Citibank. The Citigroup Private Bank offers boutique services to its clientele while, at the same time, being backed by the full power of Citigroup. With offices in 59 cities around the world, it is one of the world's most global private banks. Global Retirement Services provides for the retirement and pension needs of clients around the world.

Citigroup International

Citigroup, principally through Citibank, has a long and unrivalled history as a provider of financial services throughout the world. Our global footprint includes more than 100 countries in North and South America, Asia and the Pacific, western, central and eastern Europe, the Middle East and Africa.

Ms. Shanta Lall

Vice President of NRI Services

Mr. Masroor Satin, Assistant Vice President, NRI Services

J.P. Morgan/Chase

J.P. Morgan Chase & Co. is a leading global financial services firm with operations in more than 50 countries. The firm has five business segments:

Investment Bank

Investment Management & Private banking

Treasury & Securities Services

JP Morgan Partners

Chase Financial Services

A component of the Dow Jones Industrial Average, JP Morgan Chase headquartered in New York, serves more than 30 million consumer customers and the world's most prominent corporate, institutional and government clients.

At the centre of the investment bank's franchise are financial institutions, extensive relationships with corporations, governments and institutional investors worldwide. The firm provides a full range of investment banking and commercial banking products and services, including advising on corporate strategy and structure, capital raising in equity and debt markets, sophisticated risk management and market-making in cash securities and derivative instruments in all major capital markets. The firm also commits its own capital to proprietary investing and trading activities to capture market opportunities.

JP Morgan's research underpins that the business that is being done is available to all clients. The firm's research is split into three groups: Equity, Economics and Global Markets, which cover Fixed Income, Credit, Derivatives, Emerging Markets, FX, Structured Finance, Technical and Bond Index research. JP Morgan Partners (JPMP) is a global private equity organisation, which provides equity and mezzanine capital financing primarily to private companies. JP Morgan is one of the world's largest providers of custody- and investor-related services, with $6 trillion in assets under custody, of which approximately $2 trillion are global custody assets. JP Morgan provides investor services to mutual funds, investment managers, pension funds, insurance companies and banks throughout the world.

The consumer, small business and middle market financial services franchise of J.P. Morgan Chase & Co-operates falls under the Chase brand. Chase delivers financial products, services, advice and planning to more than 30 million individuals, small businesses and middle market customers across the United States.

Mr. Anil Bhalla

Managing Director

Mr. Julian D'Ambrosi

Ms. Michelle Kim

Private Client Group

State Bank of India

State Bank of India is the largest bank in India and has been operating for over 190 years. Today, State Bank of India's assets exceed US$59 billion and ranks among the top 25 commercial banks in Asia. The bank functions worldwide through a most extensive network ever owned by a commercial bank. With over 8,998 branches in India and 52 foreign offices in 31 countries, the bank's total deposits exceed US $45 billion.

State Bank of India , through branches worldwide, is best placed to serve Non-Resident Indians with a wide range of deposits and investment banking services and to enable one to earn interest rates amongst the highest offered anywhere in the world. The bank has services in personal banking, gold banking, NRI banking, international banking, corporate banking, small-scale industries, small business finance, rural banking, and government business.

Mr. Sheshadn lyengar

CEO, New York Operations

Mr. D.A. Tambe

Vice President New York Operations

Merrill Lynch

Merrill Lynch is a leading global underwriter of equity and deposit securities. Merrill Lynch serves as an essential and strategic advisor to governments, corporations, institutions and individuals around the world. Merrill Lynch has offices in 36 countries and total client assets of approximately 1. 3 trillion.

Merrill Lynch is coordinated in the following three interrelated businesses:

The *Global Markets & Investment* banking group, (GMI) is one of these three global businesses of Merrill Lynch & Co. GMI offers equity, debt and investment banking services to financial institutions, corporations, agencies and governments around the world. Global Private Client Group, (GPC), the second of the global businesses, provides advice-based wealth management products and services through 13,600 financial advisors in 650 offices around the world. Merrill Lynch Investment Managers, (MLIM) is one of the largest investment managers in the world, with approximately $442 billion of client assets under management. The third business and division offers a wide range of investment capabilities including fixed income, equity, cash management, indexed and enhanced index products to individual and institutional investors.

South Asian Business Development Programme

The South Asian programme focusses on generating business opportunities and building new client relationships for Merrill Lynch Global Private Client among individuals legally residing in the US of South Asian origin or heritage. These include individuals from the Indian sub-continent including India, Pakistan, Nepal, Bangladesh and Sri Lanka. Merrill Lynch's South Asian programme focusses on the following population segments: Physicians & Health Care Providers; Technology Entrepreneurs; Business Owners, Corporate Executives and Art Patrons and Affiliates. Key markets for Global Private Client programmes and activities in 2003 were: Boston, Chicago, Dallas, Edison, Houston, Los Angeles, New Brunswick, New York City, Orlando, San Francisco, San Jose and Washington DC.

Ms. Joyti Chopra

Director, Multicultural & Diversified Business Development

Ms Jyoti Chopra, director, is head of South Asian business in Merrill Lynch Global Private Client's Multicultural and Diversified Business Development group. In this role, she is responsible for strategic planning, new business origination, community leadership and client relationship development for the South Asian market, in particular the wealth management of Indian investors around the world. Previously, Jyoti was director of Client Acquisition for Merrill Lynch Direct and responsible for new account acquisition and marketing for Merrill Lynch's and online trading platform (www.mldirect.ml.com). In addition, she managed investor education and content for the Merrill Lynch Direct website.

From 1999 until July 2000, Jyoti was director of eMedia communications for the digital business development group at Merrill Lynch. She managed and directed the marketing, communications and media strategies for the firm's technology initiatives, including investments and strategic alliances.

Jyoti joined Merrill Lynch in 1998 as vice president and manager of education services and developed diversified financial educational and marketing programmes targeted at women, families, domestic partners and multi-cultural groups. These efforts included providing financial education materials, sales promotion literature and support for Merrill Lynch offices and financial advisors. This group managed Merrill Lynch's annual International Savings Month campaign, a global educational programme promoting financial literacy. She served as the firm's representative to the Investor Education Committee for the Securities Industry Association from 1998-2000 and is currently Merrill Lynch's representative to the SIA diversity committee.

Before joining Merrill Lynch, Jyoti was a writer and media consultant who covered human development and issues affecting women and children at the United Nations. Between 1993 and 1997, she developed a global broadcasting campaign at the United Nations Children's Fund

(UNICEF). From 1984 until 1993, Jyoti worked in the office of Human Resources

Management at the United Nations Secretariat. Jyoti was born and raised in London, England. She studied economics, English literature and law at London University and holds a Bachelor of Arts Honours degree in journalism from New York University. She completed the Securities Industry Institute at the Wharton School, University of Pennsylvania in 2002. She is also a director of the Princeton YWCA.

Wachovia Securities

Wachovia Corporation is registered as a financial holding company and a bank holding company, providing a range of commercial and retail banking and trust services through full-service banking offices in Connecticut, Delaware, Florida, Georgia, Maryland, New Jersey, New York, North Carolina, Pennsylvania, South Carolina, Virginia and Washington, D.C. Wachovia Bank, National Association operates those banking offices, except those in Delaware, which are operated by Wachovia Bank of Delaware, National Association. The company also provides various other financial services, including mortgage banking, credit card, investment banking, investment advisory, home equity lending, asset-based lending, leasing, insurance and international and securities brokerage services, through other subsidiaries.

Mr. Rakesh Bhargava

Managing Director

Ms. Aradhana Bhargava

Financial Consultant

Ms. Ardhana Bhargava was a former trader trainee at Spear, Leeds and Kellogg (SLK), a division of Goldman Sachs. She participated in SLK's Rotational Trading Programme, with the rotations including NYSE, AMEX (Derivatives, Options and Equities), Fixed Income and Proprietary Trading. Ms Bhargava worked summers under Sameer Arora, Manager Asia Fund, Alliance Capital in Singapore. Roy Niederhoffer of Neiderhoffer Capital Management (CTA), Ranjan Tandon of Libra Advisors (Hedge Fund) and at CIBC Oppenheimer, South Asia Group.

She holds a licence for Securities Sales, Series 63 as a registered investment advisor (Series 65), Futures Sales (Series 3), Equity Trading (Series 55) and Life, Accident and Health Insurance. Ms Bhargava earned a BBA from the University of Michigan Business School with concentration in finance. She had done a study abroad programme in Germany and played on University of Michigan's Women's Tennis Team in 1997-1998.

HSBC

Headquartered in London, HSBC holdings' pie is one of the largest banking and financial services organisations in the world. HSBC's international network comprises over 9,500 offices in 80 countries and territories in Europe, the Asia-Pacific region, the Americas, the Middle East and Africa.

HSBC has listings on the London, Paris, Hong Kong, and New York markets. Shares in HSBC Holdings pie are held by around 190,000 shareholders in some 100 countries and territories. The shares are traded on the New York Stock Exchange in the form of American depositary receipts.

Through an international network linked by advanced technology, including a rapidly growing e-commerce capability, HSBC provides a comprehensive range of financial services: personal financial services; commercial banking; corporate, investment banking and markets; private banking; and other activities.

Mr. Yakub P. Mathew

Senior Vice President

Mr. Vipp Jaswal

First Vice President

American Express

American Express Company is primarily engaged in the business of providing travel-related services, financial advisory services and international banking services worldwide. Through American Express Travel Related Services Company, Inc. (TRS), the company offers travel-related products and services including charge cards, card member lending products, travellers' cheques and corporate and consumer travel services. Financial advisory services and products include financial planning and advice, investment advisory services and various products, including insurance and annuities, investment certificates and mutual funds. Through American Express Bank, the company provides private, financial institution and corporate banking, as well as personal financial services and global trading.

Mr. R. Madhavan

Senior Director

ICICI Bank

ICICI Bank is India's second-largest bank with total assets of about Rs. one trillion and a network of about 540 branches and offices and over 1,000 ATMs. ICICI Bank offers a wide range of banking products and financial services to corporate and retail customers through a variety of delivery channels and through its specialised subsidiaries and affiliates in the areas of investment banking, life and non-life insurance, venture capital, asset management and information technology. JCICI Bank's equity shares are listed in India on stock exchanges at Chennai, Delhi, Kolkata and Vadodara, the Stock Exchange, Mumbai and the National Stock Exchange of India Limited and its American Depository Receipts (ADRs) are listed on the New York Stock Exchange (NYSE).

ICICI Bank was originally promoted in 1994 by ICICI Limited, an Indian financial institution, and was its wholly-owned subsidiary. ICICI's shareholding in ICICI Bank was reduced to 46 per cent through a public offering of shares in India in fiscal 1998, an equity offering in the form of ADRs listed on the NYSE in fiscal 2000, ICICI Bank's acquisition of Bank of Madura Limited in an all-stock amalgamation in fiscal 2001, and secondary market sales by ICICI to institutional investors in fiscal 2001 and fiscal 2002. ICICI was formed in 1955 at the initiative of the World Bank, the Government of India and representatives of Indian industry. The principal objective was to create a development financial institution for providing medium-term and long-term project financing to Indian businesses. In the 1990s, ICICI transformed its business from a development financial institution to offer only project finance to a diversified financial services group offering a wide variety of products and services, both directly and through a number of subsidiaries and affiliates, like ICICI Bank. In 1999, ICICI become the first Indian company and the first bank or financial institution from non-Japan Asia to be listed on the NYSE.

Mr. Madhav Kalyan

Chief Representative & Country Manager

Mr. Amit Dhawan

Regional Manager

ICICI Securities

ICICI Securities is a strongly positioned investment bank in India and provides products and services in fixed income, equities and corporate finance. In the fixed income business, ICICI Securities is a leading market participant in the country. ICICI Securities fixed income activities include interest rate trading, derivatives trading, research and issue management.

The Corporate Finance business focusses on industry consolidation. ICICI Securities has been involved in a number of mergers, cross-border acquisition, equity and bidding for a number of reputed companies. The equity business offers research, sales and execution services to institutional investors in the secondary market and capital market-related services, such as execution of public offerings, structuring and regulatory and legal documentation services.

In order to assist/provide corporate clients and institutional investors with investment banking services in the United States of America, ICICI Securities has set up two subsidiaries, namely, ICICI Securities Holdings Inc and ICICI Securities Inc. ICICI Securities Inc has become the registered broker dealer with the National Association of Securities Dealers Inc, empowering it to engage in a variety of securities transactions in the US market.

ICICI Brokerage Services Limited, a member of the National Stock Exchange of India Limited, is the domestic broking subsidiary of ICICI Securities.

Mr. Sripat Pandey

President

Mr. Sanjiv Patni

Senior Vice President

ICICI Infotech

ICICI Infotech Inc. is a global technology solution company operating in the US, Europe and Asia. ICICI addresses the critical challenges of today's business community with innovation and initiative. The goal of the company is to deliver quality services and products that integrate and optimise technology.

ICICI Infotech's solutions enable companies to manage relationships with their customers, suppliers, partners and employees. ICICI Infotech has successfully deployed numerous applications for state and local government agencies. Because so many of these projects involve accessing data and applications that reside of legacy systems, ICICI Infotech is also making legacy systems available through the Web.

ICICI Infotech was promoted in 1999 by ICICI Bank, India's largest private sector bank and the country's first company to be listed on the New York Stock Exchange. The company expanded rapidly and in a span of four years it has grown to a US$ 50 million company, with offices in eight countries across four continents. It currently has over 1,300 employees.

A range of software products and services form the company's core offerings, spanning across industries like banking, insurance, manufacturing, distribution and contracting. In addition, the company also offers managed IT services, security and other consulting services and solutions for state and local governments.

In USA ICICI Infotech has a staff of around 150 persons at its offices in Edison, NJ and

Farmington, CT.

Mr. M.B. Battliwala

General Manager

M.B. Battliwala, general manager, is in charge of global public relations of ICICI Infotech Ltd. (part of the US$ 22 Billion, NYSE listed ICICI Bank Group, India's largest private sector bank.)

He joined ICICI Limited in 1992 and has held several senior positions in the company and its group companies since then. During 2000-01 he was executive vice president and regional head of Tricolour Infotech (a joint venture between the Emirates Bank Group of Dubai, UAE and ICICI Infotech) in the Middle East, based out of Dubai Internet City. He was instrumental in setting up ICICI Infotech's operations in Dubai. Earlier in April 2000, as executive vice president, he started the operations of ICICI Infotech Inc. in USA. Prior to that, he was head of Marketing and Business Development, and earlier head of Transaction Processing Operations in ICICI Infotech. He was also instrumental in setting up the UK operations of the company. Mr. Battliwala had a long stint of 20 years from 1972 to 1992 with State Bank of India, during which he held several positions in the credit and computer areas, and rose to the position of chief manager (Systems), before he joined ICICI.

Mr. Battliwala has done his Masters in Science (Physics) and Masters in Financial Management from the University of Bombay. He is also a certified associate of Indian Institute of Bankers (CAIIB), and holds diplomas in computer management and systems management from the University of Bombay.

EXIM Bank of India

Bank provides export of Indian machinery, manufactured goods, consultancy and technology services on deferred payment terms. Lines of credit/buyer's credits are extended to overseas entities, i.e. governments, central banks, commercial banks, development finance institutions, regional development banks for financing export of goods and services from India-Project and Trade finance.

In addition to finance, the bank provides a range of information and advisory services to Indian companies to supplement their efforts aimed at globalisation of Indian business.

Mr. David Rasquinha

Resident Representative

Bank of India

Bank of India is a premier and one of the oldest commercial banks in India with a presence all over India as also in all time zones of the world. The bank has a glorious history dating back to the early years of this century. The bank was founded in September 1906 and has all along maintained a position of pride among the top five commercial banks in the country. In July 1969, the Bank of India was nationalised along with 13 other large Indian commercial banks. Since then, the bank has made an enormous contribution to India's efforts towards agricultural and rural development, industrial diversification and modernisation and export development. Keeping pace with financial sector reforms in India, the bank has ventured into merchant banking, mutual funds, housing finance, custodial &depository through its subsidiaries.

Mr. R.S. Reddy

General Manager & CEO, US Operations

Bank of Baroda

International network and today it is a leading international bank from India having significant international presence with a network of 61 branches (including of subsidiaries/ joint ventures) in 16 countries spread all over the world. The Bank of Baroda is the second largest bank in India with the maximum number of branches abroad among the Indian banks. BOB is well positioned to offer a variety of services, products and financial solutions to a cross-section of clients, suiting to their banking requirements through one of the best banking relationship networks, both in terms of strength and spread among the Indian financial entities.

The banking services at the International Business Branches (188), Non-resident Indian branches, 116 authorised branches as well as 2,500 other branches are provided for the benefit of Indian customers, corporates, NRIs, overseas corporate bodies, foreign companies/

individuals as well as foreign banks, etc. BOB provides a wide range of products/services to its customers for their international business requirements. Brief details of services provided are as under:

The following are a few services that BOB provide:

1. All general banking services including corporate/retail lending.
2. NRI banking.
3. Foreign currency credits to the Indian corporate.
4. Arranging/participating in the syndicated loans of Indian corporates as well as rated multinational corporates.
5. Correspondent banking services to the Indian banks/ corporate.
6. Trade Finance (bills discounting)..
7. International treasury services.

Mr. M. Balachandran

CEO, US Operations

Mr. Jayant Vyas, Bank of Baroda, Chief Manager

Meeting of the Inter-religious Leaders

June I 5, 2003

Executive Summary

I. Context

The meeting of the NRI/PIO inter-religious leaders was organised as a part of an ongoing series of initiatives undertaken by the office of India's Ambassador-at-Large to foster dialogue with Indian communities around the world.

II. Themes Discussed

1. The global Indian family.
2. Ways in which religious leaders can help the Indian diaspora connect with India and Indian culture.
3. How Indianness can be preserved and strengthened amongst the second/third-generation in the United Sates.
4. Ways in which the office of the Ambassador-at-Large for NRIs/PIOs can be helpful.

III. Key Recommendations

1. Develop an ongoing process of inter-religious dialogue and interaction between the various religious communities from India.
2. The inter-religious leaders should have a continued dialogue with the office of the Ambassador-at-Large for NRIs/PIOs with the goal of developing actionable plans that will foster unity and understanding among the diaspora communities and offer second/third-generation Indians exposure to Indian religious faiths and their rich philosophy.
3. Ambassador Agnihotri should be invited to visit the various Indian religious institutions in America to meet with congregations in order to listen to their needs and concerns and assist them in finding solutions.

Meeting of the Inter-religious Leaders
June 15, 2003
The Programme
Invocation: Reverend Gurudev Chitra Bhanu
Welcome and Occasion: Dr. Bhishma K. Agnihotri, Ambassador
Self-introductions: Attendees
Initial Themes: Proposed for by leaders

1. How religious orders can help the Indian diaspora bond among themselves and with India.
2. How Indianness can be preserved and strengthened amongst the second/third-generation of the diaspora.
3. How the office of the Ambassador-at-Large/Government of India can be helpful.

Discussion
Closing Remarks: Ambassador Agnihotri

Overview

The office of India's Ambassador-at-Large for NRls/PIOs has undertaken, as part of its mission, the project of promoting the idea of a global Indian family. Religion is an important contributor to promoting and inculcating this idea in the lives of Indians everywhere. It serves a vital role in the life of the Indian diaspora community by imparting culture, values, tradition and a sense of spirituality.

Religious institutions have historically served as havens for newly-arrived immigrants from India. They have helped the immigrants to get settled in their new surroundings and have served as a familiar place where they can always turn to for assistance. Religious institutions, through their support networks, have also been educational for children interested in the Indian culture. Children often attend cultural classes at religious institutions throughout the diaspora communities.

The office of India's Ambassador-at-Large for NRls/PIOs has initiated an interactive dialogue with all religious institutions and organisations throughout the diaspora communities. On his travels to various diaspora communities throughout the world, Ambassador Agnihotri made it a point to visit all religious organisations in an effort to promote the concept of a global Indian family. He believes that religion is an important component in maintaining culture and traditions, especially in projecting a positive Indian identity to the second/third generations.

It is for this reason that the office of India's Ambassador-at-Large for NRIs/PIOs organised the 'Meeting of the Inter Religious Leaders'. The goal of this meeting was to (i) foster a dialogue between the different faiths, (ii) promote the concept of global Indian family, and (iii) find solutions to the challenges facing the Indian American community. Some of these challenges are the submergence of Indian identity and value systems in the mainstream culture, especially among the second/third generations, lack of familiarity of the richness of Indian culture within the mainstream American community and how best to care for the rising senior citizen population in the truest of Indian tradition.

Highlights of the Meeting of the Inter Religious Leaders

Ambassador Agnihotri chaired a meeting of representatives of various religious organisations at his office in New York. This meeting was one in a series of initiatives undertaken by his office to promote the interests of the Indian diaspora, including one significant initiative undertaken by Ambassador Agnihotri to rehabilitate those Indian Sikhs who had participated in the Khalistan movement.

The meeting started with an invocation by Gurudev Shree Chitrabhanu, a Jain religious leader who had been invited to the US House of Representatives to inaugurate their session. In his invocation, Gurudev stressed the need amongst all Indians to understand the common spiritual dimension underlying all religious beliefs in order to alleviate ignorance and social fractures around the world.

Some of the other representative religious leaders who participated in this meeting included: His Grace, Dr. Thomas Mar Makarios and Very Reverend Father Cherian Neelankal (American Diocese of Indian Orthodox Church), Kaulacharya Rajendra Teerth (Neelkantha Dhaam), Leela Maret (Indian Catholic Association}, Subash Arora (Arya Samaj Samiti), Shive Prabhat (Hindu Temple Society of North America), Father Jose Kandathikudy and Jose Mullakkary (St. Thomas Catholic Church), Devender Singh Sawhney (Deshmesh Sikh Centre), Ashok Wahi (Sant Nirankari Mission), Uday Gosalia, Pankaj Patel and Darpesh Patel (International Swaminarayan Satsang Organisation), Arun Ahluwalia (S.N. Mission), Most Reverend Bishop, Dr. Isaac Mar Cleemis

(Malankara Catholic Church), Philip John, Reverend A.C. George (India Pentecostal Church), and Swami Sitae.

Welcoming the religious representatives, Ambassador Agnihotri stressed that the religious leaders have a great role to play in guiding the destiny of humankind, especially in uncertain contemporary times. He reminded the gathering that secularism in the Indian sense does not imply a denial of one's religiousness; rather Indianness fosters equality of religions, a dialogue amongst faiths, tolerance and an undiminished commitment to the path of non-violence in the resolution of differences. Ambassador Agnihotri also mentioned that the 22 million members of the Indian diaspora should understand their rich Indian heritage, celebrate their Indianness and spread the message of peace, togetherness, oneness and universal brotherhood. This celebration of commonality is an important way to solve some of the world's problems.

Ambassador Agnihotri also requested the participants to give their suggestions on what should be done further to improve India's image in the United States. He explained that since religious institutions play a key role in the Indian diaspora communities, they can also play an important role in helping improve the image of India in the US. He praised the tremendous work Christian churches have done in the United States to promote a sense of community. He explained that Indian religious institutions should create a working dialogue with their American counterparts to foster understanding and co-operation.

During the discussions that followed, several ideas were floated to help the process of bonding the Indian diaspora with India. Thoughts were also shared regarding how Indianness could be preserved and strengthened amongst second- and third-generation members of the Indian diaspora. Finally, there was a discussion on how the institution of the office of Ambassador-at-Large and the Government of India could help the representatives of various faiths representing India in their effort to promote dialogue and foster commonality of Indianness amongst the Indian diaspora.

In his concluding remarks, Ambassador Agnihotri emphasised that all religious or spiritual streams in the world should shun acts of terror (both in thought and action), promote tolerance through shared dialogue and foster an openness of mind to understand each others' views and philosophical differences on specific issues.

Recommendations Developed at the Meeting

Some suggestions developed during the meeting centered on:

1. Continuing an ongoing process of inter religious dialogue and interaction between the various religious communities from India.
2. The need of frequent dialogue between inter religious leaders and the office of the Ambassador-at-Large for NRls/PIOs with the goal of developing practical plans that will foster unity and understanding among the diaspora communities and offer second/third- generation Indians exposure to Indian religious faiths and their rich philosophy.
3. More visits be undertaken by Ambassador Agnihotri to different Indian religious institutions in America to meet the congregations and listen to their needs and concerns and assist them in finding solutions.

Invitees

Invited religious leaders from various communities included:

1.	Gurudev Sree Chitrabhanu	16.	Most Reverend Bishop, Dr. Isaac Mar Cleemis	31.	Mr. Arvinder Singh
2.	Mr. Akbar Himani	17.	Reverend A.C. George	32.	Mr. Swaran Singh
3.	His Grace, Dr. Thomas Mar Makarios, Senior Metropolitan	18.	Dr. K Bapineedu	33.	Mr. Abdul Jaffar
4.	Mrs. Leela Maret	19.	Swami Jyotishraj Neelkanth Dham	34.	Reverand Jose Kandathikudy
5.	Guru Ma Jyotishanand	20.	Mr. Bhaktibhai Patel	35.	Mr. Harpreet Singh Toor
6.	Swaraswati Pandit Kaulacharya Rajendranand Teerth	21.	Mr. Shiv Kumar Prabhat	36.	Mr. Anand Singh
7.	Mr. Baljeet Singh	22.	Dr. Hemant Patel	37.	Mr. Pritpal Singh Khandhari
8.	Reverand Simon Palliparambil	23.	Swami Jagdish	38.	Mr. Arun Ahluwalia

9.	Mr. Devender Singh Sawhney	24.	Swami H Puri	39.	Mr. Ashok Wahi
10.	Mr. Joseph Kalapurakal	25.	Mr. Shiv Shakti Peeth	40.	Dr. V. Subbarao
11.	Mr. Inderjit Singh	26.	Mr. G. Chhabra	41.	Dr. Shakir Mukhi
12.	Metropolitan Mathews Mar Barnabas	27.	Mr. Nari Lakhani	42.	Mr. Subhash Arora
13.	Very Reverand, Father Cherian Neelankal	28.	Mr. Sajat Dirmani	42.	HH Sitae Swami
14.	Mr. Bhairva Murthy	29.	Mr. Amir Khalfan	43.	Mr. Satwant Singh
15.	Mrs. Harpreed Kaur	30.	Bishop, Dr. Euyakim Mar Coorilos Episcopa		

Profile of Some of the Invitees

"(The office had requested all of the invitees to provide a brief background on themselves. The following is a list of individuals who sent the requested information about themselves.)

His Grace, Dr. Thomas Mar Makarios, Senior Metropolitan

His Grace, Dr. Thomas Mar Makarios is Senior Metropolitan of the American Diocese (Malankar Orthodox Church of India) and Metropolitan of the Diocese of Canada, UK, and Europe. He is also a Professor in the department of philosophy and religion at Alma College, Alma, Michigan. His Grace, Mar Makarios has also served as a Vicar at Orthodox Parish, New Delhi and Ecumenical Officer of the World Council of Churches, Geneva, Switzerland. He completed his Bachelor of Divinity at the Orthodox Theological Seminary in Kerala and at Nashotah House in Nashotah, Wisconsin and Bachelor of Arts at Punjab University, New Delhi. His Grace, Mar Makarios completed his M.A. at Virginia Theological Seminary, Alexandria, Virginia and his PHO at Union Theological Seminary, Richmond, Virginia. He also holds an honorary doctorate from Alma College, Alma, Michigan.

Pandit Kaulacharya Rajendrand Teerth

Pandit Kaulacharya Rajendrand Teerth is the founder and head priest at the Neelkanth Dham Temple in Queens, New York. He has a B.A. in Ayurvedic Medical Sciences from Rajkiya Ayurvedic and Unani Chikitsa Parishad. He has received the title of 'Kaulacharya' from Maithali Vishwa Vidyalaya. Kaulacharya Teerth also holds the titles of Dharmacharya, Vedangacharya, Vaidya Visharad, Jyotish Ratna, Jyotish Samrat and Jyotishacharya. He is expert in *vastu shastra, reki, mantra* healing, *paravigyan*, and *darshan shastra*. Kaulacharya Teerth is presently working with Spiritual Sciences Research Institute in New Delhi.

Mrs. Leela Maret

Mrs. Leela Maret is the current secretary of the Indian Catholic Association of America. She is a committee member and past vice president of the Kerala Samajam of Greater New York. Mrs. Maret is the current vice chairperson of the World Malayalee Council and of South Asian Heritage. She holds a master's degree in chemistry and works as a scientist at the NYC Department of Environmental Protection. Mrs. Maret is also a part-time lecturer at Bronx Community College. She is treasurer of South Asian Indo-Caribbean organisations for political programmes and executive board member of Eastern Queens Democratic Club.

Very Reverend, Father Cherian Neelankal, Cor-Episcopa

Very Reverend, Father Cherian Neelankal, Cor-Episcopa has been the parish priest of St. Thomas Orthodox Church in Yonkers, New York for the past 25 years. He has a M.A. degree in theology and a M.A. degree in clinical psychology. He has worked as staff psychologist in New York State O.M.R.D.D. for the last 30 years and is now working full-time at the parish level. He has been very focussed on increasing church activities and is working with the second generation on Church-oriented activities and passing on India's cultural heritage to them.

Mr. Shivakumar Prabhat

Mr. Shiva Kumar Prabhat has been a member of the Board of Trustees and treasurer of The Hindu Temple Society of North America, Queens, NY since 1993. He is currently the chief financial officer and administrative officer of North American Operations for DCA Advertising in New York, New York. Mr. Prabhat completed a B.A. in economics and history from the University of Utaki, a B.L. in law from the University of Bangalore, and an M.B.A in finance and accounting from New York University, New York.

Mr. Bhaktibhai Patel

Mr. Bhaktibhai Patel is president of the Weehawken, New Jersey, temple of the International Swaminarayan Satsang Organisation (I.S.S.0).

Most Reverend Bishop, Dr. Isaac Mar Cleemis

Most Reverend Bishop, Dr. Isaac Mar Cleemis is the apostolic visitor and administrator for the Indian Malankara Catholic Church in North America and Europe. He studied philosophy at St. Joseph's Seminary in Kerala, theology at Papal Seminary in Poona. He received his M.A. in theology from Dharmaram College in Bangalore and doctorate in ecumenism from St. Thomas University in Rome. He has been a St. Thomas Cathedral parish priest and St. Thomas Minor Seminary Rector. He has also served as chancellor and Vicar General for the Diocese of Bathery. He was appointed Bishop by Pope John Paul II in June, 2001.

Mr. Arun Ahluwalia

Mr. Arun Aluwalia is head of the New York metropolitan branch of the Sant Nirankari Mission. He is an executive with a large international re-Insurance company. He completed his B.E. in civil engineering from the University of Bombay.

Father Jos Kandathikudy

Father Jos Kandathikudy has been vicar and pastor of the SyroMalabar Catholic Church since March, 2002. He completed his seminary studies in Kerala and went to Rome to finish his masters in theology from the Urban University. He has founded several parishes in India and in the US. In the US, he was appointed director of the Syro Malabar Catholic Mission at Bellwood, Chicago. Father Kandathikudy was instrumental in petitioning Pope John Paul to create a Syro Malabar Catholic Diocese in the United States.

Reverend A.C. George

Reverend A.C. George studied theology for three years in a Bible College. He arrived in the US 34 years ago. He came as a missionary later on to help the newly-arriving immigrants from India. He founded India Pentecostal Church, Inc. in 1974. Reverend George helped the jobless in the 1970s, establishing them in various places. He founded the Indian Pentecostal churches of the eastern region. He is also a police clergy, engaged in community relations with the 105 Precinct of the New York Police Department.

Mr. Pankaj Patel

Mr. Pankaj Patel is a senior representative of I.S.S.O.'s youth group, the NarNarayan Dev Yuvak Manda! (NNDYM), Weehawken, NJ chapter.

Mr. Uday Gosalia

Mr. Uday Gosalia is a senior representative of I.S.S.O.'s youth group, the Nar Narayan Dev Yuvak Mandal (NNDYM), New York chapter.

Mr. Darpesh Patel

Mr. Darpesh Patel is a senior representative of I.S.S.O.'s youth group, the Nar Narayan Dev Yuvak Mandal (NNDYM), Weehawken, NJ chapter.

Comments from Invitees

His Grace, Dr. Thomas Mar Makarios, Senior Metropolitan:

'God bless you for initiating such a historic meeting of religious leaders to enhance the image of our Mother country in the Western society. Every reasonable person would admire your vision and support your goal. As a leader of the Christian community in the United States, I pledge my support for your efforts to create unity, understanding, and harmony between our communities which was the glorious tradition of India for thousands of years.'

Pandit Kaulacharya Rajendrand Teerth:

'This is a great step to improve the image of Indians and India in the world. This is a very great step. We need to have a religious forum to begin the process to educate the youth about Indian culture. We should also have a secondary meeting of religious figures, who are directly serving the public to get their input.'

Mr. Shivakumar Prabhat

'I was honoured to be at the meeting on the 15th. All of us, if united, can do a lot for our country.'

Workshop for Indo-American Students and Youth (NEW YORK)

November 1, 2003
New York

Executive Summary

I. Context

The workshop titled 'Indo-American Youth/Students: Their Contributions & Concerns' is a part of an ongoing series of projects undertaken by the office of Ambassador-at-Large to accomplish its vision to network and study the issues concerning the Indian diaspora. It is an effort which would help address the needs, concerns and tap the potential of the global Indian community in the United States and the world.

II. Themes Discussed

The workshop's objective was to study the following:

1. The concerns & challenges of Indo-American students/youth.
2. The contributions of Indian American students/youth.
3. The role Ind0-American youths/students can play in educating other Americans and American media about India.

III. Participants:

Representative groups of local youth populace and students from universities in the north-east region participated in the workshop. The workshop put forward suggestions and action points which were used for formulating suggestions and recommendations assimilated in this report.

IV. Key Recommendations

1. Centres for Indian studies should be established in some of the top US universities.
2. Indian government, Indian embassies, consulates and NRI/PIO bodies should have facilities for providing resources/information about India.
3. Promote universally accepted ancient Indian disciplines, such as yoga and ayurveda.
4. Recognise the contributions and achievements of people of

Indo-American community.

5. Develop student exchange programme with top Indian institutions, such as Indian Institute of Management (IIMs) and Indian Institute of Technology (IITs).
6. Create resources and funds for providing India-promotion events in institutions and communities.
7. Leadership role may be extended to contact and convince all major American corporations having large Indian professional staff to organise Indo-centric events.

V. Next Steps

1. Continue such meetings and workshops with participation from student community/youth.
2. Involve students/youth in initiatives, projects and events undertaken by the office of Ambassador-at-Large.

Highlights of the Workshop

1. Ambassador-at-Large for NRIs and PIOs, Dr. B. K. Agnihotri chaired the workshop on 'Indo-American Youth/Students: Their Concerns and Contribution' on November I, 2003. The event was in continuation to the efforts of the office of Ambassador-at-Large for NROs and PIOs to interact with diverse segments of the diaspora populace and articulate their demands, suggestions, proposals and recommendations in a thorough and positive manner so that these could be relayed to policy makers in India. The workshop was attended by a large number of students and youth leaders from American universities consisting of Cornell University, Rutgers University, Wharton Business School, University of Pennsylvania, Stem Business School NYU, Columbia Medical School, Pace University, University of Toronto, Stony Brook University SUNY, Polytechnic University and young professionals from IBM, JP Morgan, etc. Two eminent Indo-American academicians also participated as academic advisors.
2. Initiating the meeting, Dr. Agnihotri informed that the projects being undertaken by his office are geared towards identifying issues of global and national concern to the

NRIs and PIOs. The present project of youth and students is basically a starting point from which his office intends to adopt a national approach and organise such workshops in various, select universities countrywide. These workshops will be projected in a programmed manner to identify problems and concerns being confronted by the second- and third-generation youth, Indo-American students' community and Indian students coming to America for the first time for further study purposes. The proceedings of these workshops will then be compiled into recommendations, which will be submitted to policy makers for consideration.

3. The workshop discussion was on the basis of three specific themes initiated by Dr. S.K. Kaushik, Mr. Sanjay Sanghoee, Mr. Nikesh Shah and Mr. Nikunj Trivedi. These themes were:

(a) The concerns and challenges of Indo-American students/youth.

(b) The contributions of Indian-American students/youth. The role Indo-American youths/students can play in educating other Americans and American media about India.

(c) What can the office of Ambassador-at-Large do to help Indo-American community in understanding concerns of India and Indo-Americans?

The presentations were followed by full-fledged discussions on various aspects of the mentioned topics among the participants.

4. On the theme of concerns and challenges of Indo-American youth/students, the presentation highlighted that growing up as Indian-American youth in USA involved reconciling conflicting identities. Assimilation of values creates challenges for the youth. Easy information sources are not available. In this context, maintaining a proper balance between Indian and American identity becomes difficult. There are a large number of students coming from India to study in American universities every year. India has become the number one country by sending about 72,000 students during this academic year to USA for study purposes, thus surpassing the number of students coming from China. There are also a large

number of Indo-American students born and brought up in USA and studying in various universities. The dimension and level of challenges being confronted by these students and youth are directly related to the future growth potential of the diaspora..

5. To address some of these concerns and challenges, the presentation and subsequent deliberations stressed on the requirement of making efforts to enhance India's image in the media as well as in the society as a whole. Both the Indian government as well as NRI/PIO bodies need to increase their efforts at propagation of correct ideas. Study materials of universities and colleges and school textbooks need to incorporate the right and adequate information on India. Changing the mindset is also an important factor. By projecting prototypes, Indian youth fail to avail the advantages of Indian achievements in the fields of technology, trade, financial and scientific sectors.
6. For the purpose of comprehensive discussion, the presentations on the contributions of Indo-American youth and students and the role of Indo-American youth and students can play in educating other Americans and American media about India were made together. The presentations highlighted the existing gaps of perception of the recipient society experienced by the second- and third-generation Indian youth and the growing community of Indian students. The moderators stated that continuous projection of poverty, cultural stereotypes and pure traditional aspects has its own limitations. In American society, India's image must be propagated as a developing society with solid economic achievements, strong democracy, effective scientific and economic strength and its intellectual contribution to those countries and societies where the diaspora members are residing or active socially and economically. Dr. Kaushik added that nobody could run away from his identity. Therefore, the interaction process needs to be strengthened to promote a strong identity. Promoting institutional linkage between universities and encouraging non-Indians and Americans to

participate and increase their awareness of India will help substantially. The interaction process must not be limited and could cover such interactions between fellow students and teachers, educational institutions, educational media in schools and colleges, with the community outside the campus as well as with the Indian community in America.

7. There are a large number of Indians working in major American corporations and conglomerates. However, these mega organisations, while organising community and participatory events, do not promote India-specific events. India is mostly bracketed with other Asian heritage events. There is a need to talk to the top echelons of decision makers of these corporations and convince them on the need to organise Indo-centric events. Promotion of setting up of Indian diversity groups within these corporations will also help in germination of greater awareness on India among other workers in the corporation, for example, recently GE celebrated India Day on its corporate township and broadcasted useful packages, Indo-centric programmes and speeches of various invitees, including the Ambassador-at-Large globally to all GE offices. Similar events could be planned in all major American corporations where a large numbers of Indian professionals are working. This will help in increasing awareness about India, enhancing India's image and providing smooth interaction to Indians with their non-Indian colleagues.
8. There are a large number of Indian student bodies in all American colleges and universities. These bodies can play a very constructive role in enhancing India's image in American media. Through their annual events and interactive programmes, they can create greater awareness of India. However, these bodies think in terms of setting up a national association or apex body to unify their efforts and for greater interaction and exchange of ideas. Most of these bodies also have problems of generating funds. Indian government, Indian embassies, consulates and NRI/PIO bodies may consider the issue of providing some resources to these bodies on

continuing basis and help them to propagate the cause of India.

Recommendations

Based on the above discussions, the following broad suggestions and recommendations were made by the moderator and participants and are annexed to this report. These broad recommendations are:

(a) Indian youth and students must increase their interaction among fellow students and teachers, with their educational institutions, with educational media in schools and colleges, with community outside the campus and Indian community in America. Such an interaction process as a whole or sectionally will help in increasing awareness and developing community strength.

(b) In order to project and communicate effectively with the American society and media, Indian youth and students must convey Indian viewpoints in their cultural context. Efforts to do away with stereotypes need to be stepped up.

(c) Active participation in American life will help in raising awareness of our heritage and establish direct and effective contact with mainstream America and media.

(d) Leadership role may be extended to contact and convince all major American corporations having large Indian professional staff to organise India-centric events.

(e) The public relations efforts of the Indian government and NRI/PIO bodies to enhance India's image in the American media and society are limited and must be broadened with focus and involvement of Indo-American youth and students.

(f) While there are more socio-cultural acceptance of ancient Indian disciplines, such as yoga, ayurveda, etc. in American society, India does not promote this as originating from India. A number of eastern traditions are exclusively promoted by China and Japan which helps them in the cultural context.

(g) The Indo-American youth and students' organisations lack resources and funds for organising India-promotion events in their institutions and communities. Some efforts may be made by government bodies and NRI/PIO organisations to assist them.

(h) The Indo-American youth and students, which could actively participate in American social, political and cultural scene, must enhance their learning and awareness of Indian culture and values to maintain their Indianness. Identity does not go away. This needs to be inculcated in the minds of Indian youth and students. For this, the role of parents and peer groups and NRI/PIO institutions is invaluable.

(i) Centre for Indian studies are different from such centres covering Asian studies as a whole, may be established in top US universities, both with the help of the Indian government as well as philanthropists and NRI/PIO bodies.

(j) Student exchange programmes with Indian universities for short-term period may be institutionalised. This could be done through institutional arrangements between universities of the two countries and could form part of the established course programme for the concerned educational institutions.

Theme : Concerns and Challenges of Indo-American Students/Youth

Report submitted by: Mr. Nikunj Trivedi, Discussion Leader

Introduction

Growing up as Indians in USA, our generation has always had to bear the burden of reconciling belief systems and cultures of two societies. Our generation is constantly challenged on issues regarding identity and heritage. The workshop focused as a platform to highlight these issues and chart out a long term plan to address them.

Specifically, the participants during this session outlined the following concerns about India:

1. India still portrayed as a land of snake charmers, cows on the street, people suffering from poverty and over population, in both the academia and media. Thus, the 'average American' discounts India as yet another backward country lacking any richness in culture or lifestyle.
2. Lack of sufficient PR from the Indian government to improve its image in the Western media. Compared to governments

of Japan, China, Pakistan, and other countries, the Indian government does not invest sufficient resources in portraying India in a positive light.

3. The continuing lack of proper infrastructure system in India. The recent Goldman Sachs report on India economic expansion highlighted the potential of Indian economy. However, progress in India will only take place if India provides its citizens with basic needs, such as proper highways, proper means of transportation and communication, reduction in corruption at all levels, etc.

   1: Currently assistant vice president at JP Morgan Chase; graduated from Rutgers University

4. Insufficient support for promoting ancient disciplines as yoga, ayurveda, etc. Yoga and ayurveda have grown rapidly as ways for enhancing efficiency, health and living a holistic life. Most Hollywood actors/actresses, executives and managers of every major corporation, medical experts, etc. practice and/or recommend them. These ancient disciplines are Indian in origin, yet only a fraction of Indians all over the world practice them. In addition, these disciplines are not seen as originating from India, but rather China, Japan or some Eastern tradition.

The negative portrayal of India and Indian culture not only impacts the perception about India, but also impacts the formation of a strong Indian-American identity, particularly amongst the second-generation and third-generation Indian-Americans.

The participants outlined the following concerns about Indo-American identity:

1. Indians are always lumped into the South Asian identity and never given self-recognition (unlike the Chinese, Japanese, Malaysians, etc.). This creates an obstacle in developing an Indian-American identity because one does not use the term in daily conversations and does not ponder upon the meaning/significance of the meaning of the term Indian-American.
2. Indian government is not providing enough resources inside and outside of US universities, for students to learn about

Indian heritage and culture. Many teachers/schools/books portray India in a negative light. Much of the information on India is 'half-truth' and many books are outdated. As a result, the average Indian-American student develops an inferiority complex about Indian culture and has nowhere to turn to for an alternative (and more positive) source to challenge such depictions.

3. Traditionally, the Indian embassies and consulates have shown only modest interest in Indian-Americans. Appointment of the Ambassador-at-Large for PIOs and NRIs has been a positive step in remedying such a shortcoming. However, more efforts should be made by this office to support, morally and financially, the good work that Indian-Americans, and in particular, the Indian-American youth are doing to improve India's image in the United States.
4. Indian-Americans have a personal interest in promoting a positive image of India in America as it has a direct effect on their image in American society. India must work more closely with Indian-American organisations to achieve this.
5. India has demonstrated its interest in the NRI/PIO community, especially through such events as Pravasi Bharatiya Divas. However, more work needs to be done on the ground where NRIs and PIOs reside.
6. There are a few challenges to Indian-Americans assimilating and Americanising. The greatest challenge comes from integrating American culture and values while maintaining Indian culture and values.

Recommendations

The participants offered various recommendations for enhancing India's image and to help second- and third-generation Indian-Americans maintain a strong Indo-American identity:

1. 'Centres for Indo-Centric Studies' should be established in some of the top US universities with the help of Indian government. Traditionally, education on Indian culture has been pushed under Asian Studies or South Asian Studies. Even within these area studies, the focus on India is rather

small when compared to the size of India as a country (and its rich and ancient culture). Centres for Indic Studies will focus on India, its culture and issues, and will allow students, professors and researchers to hone in on India.

2. Indian embassies should have some sort of school/community centre that provides resources to learn about Indian culture. Often, students (both Indian-American and non-Indian-American) look for alternate sources to find information on India and its culture for their papers, projects, etc. The Indian embassies can serve as a central point to provide these resources and work with students to get what they need.
3. Indian-Americans should be equipped with the right resources/education about India (via books, speakers at various universities, funds provided by Indian government, etc.). Many times, college-based Indo-American organisations (and university departments) hold debates/discussions/workshops about India. Indian students often struggle to find talented speakers to present the Indian perspective (due to lack of funds, contacts, etc.) and are left with inviting fellow students or professors with a different area of expertise, to represent the Indian voice. Hence, the debate/discussion/workshop is not as effective as it should be.
4. The office of the Ambassador should work with Indian organisations in the US to promote a positive image of India and Indian culture. There are many Indian organisations, both on and off-campus that are working on promoting Indian culture. The office of the Ambassador can initiate effort to bring such organisations on to a common platform and work with them to enhance the image of India. These Indian organisations can provide the needed volunteers and propagation channels.
5. Have conferences, seminars, lecture series, etc. open to public about India throughout various universities. Many organisations and university departments will be quite willing to host such conferences, seminars, etc. These initiatives can be ongoing.
6. Establish an initiative to promote Indian-American identity

and culture to third-generation Indian Americans. Support needs to be given to parents and community leaders of Indian-American youth to help the upcoming generations maintain Indian values. Initiatives, such as video series, stories on Indian epics, heroes, etc. and books for children can immensely help Indian parents entice their kids into learning about Indian culture and values.

Theme: Role Indo-American Students/Youth can Play in Educating Fellow Americans and American Media about India

Report Submitted by Dr. Surendra K. Kaushik and Mr. Sanjay Sanghoee,

Discussion Leaders

Indian-American students representing intellectual and cultural resources of India in large numbers in American schools, colleges and universities can play a very significant role in educating and informing fellow-Americans directly and through American media. Some of the ways in which they can bring India's past to America and create a bright future for themselves, for India, for America and indeed for the world, are through the following channels:

Interaction of Indian youth and students with fellow students and teachers

- High academic achievements (12 Rhodes scholars from 1998 to 2002).
- Student associations.
- Lectures/presentations.

1. Professor of finance, associate director, Centre for Applied Research, Lubin School of Business, Pace University, New York; Founder-Chairman. Mrs. Helena Kaushik, Women's College, Malsisar, Jhunjbunu, Rajasthan, India (www.helenakausbik.org); Oiainnan, Resources & Environment Group, Inc. (a non-profit international research organisation, www.reginc.org).
2. An investment banker from Lazard & Wasserstein; author of a novel due to be published by St. Martin's Press; Worked with Fortune 500 companies in publishing, movies and new media, and is currently consultant with media companies for

Mergers & Acquisitions and Fundraising.

- Guest lectures from the US and India.
- Organising and participating in academic, cultural, and social events, like fairs, movies, holidays, thematic conferences and discussion groups.
- Travels to India.
- Student and faculty exchanges between the US and India.

Educational institution/s

Institutional linkages among American and between Americans and Indians.

- Contact with administration, trustees, faculty and staff.
- Helping build library resources.
- Helping bring/create exhibits on India.
- Special institution-wide lectures by invited academics, diplomats, artists, musicians, industrialists, politicians and others.
- Helping create new courses, programmes, centres of study and research, and other labs and units on or related to India.
- Establishment of scholarships.
- Establishment of professorships.

Educational media in schools and colleges

- Student newspapers.
- Serving as reporters, contributors, production staff and editors.
- Feeding stories, news, events.
- Contributions to and participation in other college/university publications, like catalogues, flyers, magazines, journals for community outside the campus.
- Visiting local friends and their families.
- Participation in community events.
- Contacting local, regional and national, political and industrial leaders interested and knowledgeable about India, and those who should be community leaders.
- Establishing working relationships with media regarding coverage of India-related items and events..

Indian community in America

- Indian-American associations

- Interact with academic, artistic, cultural, social, scientific, entrepreneurial, industrial and political associations for mutual programmes and ties for resources, support and strength.
- Create and implement programmes linked with 1,200 or so Indian-American associations involved in charitable, community, political, business, cultural and social activities. For example, Association of Indians in America (AIA) initiatives in education, health and political leadership through their India awareness in school programmes, Education Council, youth leadership programmes and similar programmes of AAPI, and other organisations. These associations may also be sources of financial support and networking for a variety of resources to student associations.
- Community activity in education, health, women's issues, the elderly, and the youth.
- Learning from Indian elders and being role models to younger Indian-Americans.
- Presenting special talents to the community.
- Sharing cultural specialties and heritage from different parts of India.

Mr. Sanjay Sanghoee, co-discussion leader on the topic of Indo-American students/youths, author and investment banker, spoke about the perception of Indo-Americans in the media and practical ways to raise the profile of Indians in the US. The role of Indo-American students in raising the awareness of Indian issues and culture in the media is paramount, since most Americans develop their attitudes and impressions about Indians during the high school and college years. In order to communicate effectively with Americans, it is necessary to convey Indian viewpoints in their cultural context.

One essential component of this is the need for more Indo-American students to enter the field of media and the arts. By gaining access to media platforms in this manner, Indians will be better positioned to communicate their message and viewpoints to a wider and a mainstream audience. Moreover, it is important for Indians to not just focus on those issues that concern the Indian community, but to involve themselves in all aspects of American political and cultural life. We are Indians, but also Americans, and only by participating actively in all aspects of American life will we truly be able to raise awareness for our heritage and establish an effective line of contact with mainstream America.

In addition, it is necessary for Indians to shift the focus of the media away from solely cultural aspects of Indian life (such as arranged marriages and religious rituals) towards the considerable professional achievements of Indo-Americans in all fields, including medicine, law, engineering and finance.

The trends that are taking shape in the media world bode well for Indo-Americans. These include the entry of Indians into the world of mainstream television (the Indian actress on ER) and movies (the Indian director M. Shyamlayan). By mastering the fields that have traditionally been occupied by non-ethnic people, these Indians have positioned themselves ideally to enhance India's image in the eyes of all Americans. Indo-American youth must strive to achieve similar laurels for the Indian community in the US.

Questionnaire

1. Are you aware of India's current economic, commercial, industrial and educational achievements? In your view where can the Indian policy improve?

I am aware of India's current economic situation as well as the future potential it holds. However, there must be a major policy shift. Expatriates should be looked upon for direct investment in India and the laws should accommodate this as is done in China. This infusion of capital can be the best source of development. Also, new health care and education policies are needed to lower the mortality rate and further increase the schooling of lower income students. Granted that India has made major strides in increasing the literacy (10 per cent in 10 years), there is no harm in further increasing this number. Another policy shift must be made in the way business is viewed in India. Banks and local governments need to encourage entrepreneurs by offering interest loans to help achieve local businesses. Most importantly, Indian policy should not focus on a hierarchical structure, enabling the wealthy and NRI to have more privileges than the poor. A system should be in place which accords all citizens the same basic rights. This can be obtained through the much talked about uniform civil code in which all citizens have the same known rights. This would help minimise corruption. However, I feel that the government should focus on attaining more capital and formulate policies that can achieve this. They should not view Western business and NRI money as harmful and this change is evident.

2. What are the bottlenecks that impinge on India becoming a developed country?

Despite the amazing advancements, there are some major stumbling blocks which I feel the current administration must overcome in order to make India a truly developed nation by 2020 (as it envisions). First of all, there must be labour law reforms as the current laws are far too archaic. India's policy, that a company with more than 100 employees cannot lay off employees without the consent of the government, impedes on the profitability of corporate India and deters foreign enterprises from entering. More so, the privatisation drive must move further and faster in order to achieve the open economy which India needs. Not only do the IPO's from the privatisation enable the government to increase its revenue, but it also helps Indian industries become competitive. It is possible for private companies to be major players in the international community as can be seen with Wipro and Infosys; however, government enterprises must be liberalised and be able to function with private investors, not bureaucrats. In addition, India has to focus on its image as an FDI destination. This can be achieved by the Finance Ministry relaxing the foreign investment caps in certain sectors. Telecom is clearly a sensitive sector; however, cell phone companies should be allowed to flourish simply for the purpose of expanding the reach of telecom throughout India. More so, other areas must also have an easing of restrictions, such as the stock markets and other major industries. This will help Western companies to open up their bases in India, infusing the much-needed capital to help the nation develop. Even though the scientific community has advanced greatly so far, more must be done in the fields of biotechnology development and space exploration. This can only be achieved by retaining the brightest Indian's (instead of having them move West) through lucrative positions and treatment. India has clearly focussed its attention towards infrastructure development which I feel is a good sign. The plan to develop and advance highway system and metro system in many cities will help develop India. It will facilitate the transportation of goods and provide employment; however, more must be done here as well. The current airports in India ranked last in a global survey and should not have been so, considering it is the first sight of India that tourists notice. Not only are airports important as a symbolic piece of property, they help advance nations by lowering the cost of travel. In essence, the government has to minimise its role in the daily lives of citizens and allow entrepreneurs to be born. The role that the government should play is to provide extensive infrastructure and economic reforms. That is the only way India will be able to achieve the necessary 8-I 0 per cent GDP growth in order to become a developed nation.

3. Your view on Indo-US relations. What more can India do to improve bilateral relations? What role can the Indian diaspora in the US play in this regard?

I feel that the best way for Indo-US relations to further improve is through a strong lobby. Many other nations have developed lobbies and special interest groups, which have produced great results. With such a large number of Indians and such great wealth, this lobby group can be easily created; however, the Indian diaspora must be willing to donate to politicians. Pressure from these individuals, especially those with very strong business connections in this country, can help reform the relations between these two nations. Indo-US relations should focus more on technology in the fields of biotech and IT. This will help increase India's economic potential if more Americans were to view India as a strategic business ally. Also, the media is a very important arena to re-organise the relations. Media coverage is known to sway public opinion, which can affect U.S. policy makers when they revise Indo-US relations. Again, the diaspora must become involved with the media by correcting all irregularities or biases originating there. India has to be promoted in a positive light and as a wealthy nation with great potential. The greatest problem is that there is lack of education in America in respect to India and this can be blamed on the media. Whenever there are reports on India in the US media, it is always in a negative light. More so, there is no flow of information on India through the US media. However, this is changing. The media has for the past few years portrayed China as a major player in global business, but has not treated India the same way. This is changing as we see more articles and news broadcasts about India. Very few people know anything about the nation, what it has done, what it can do. India's achievements must be promoted. In essence, the Indian diaspora must become very closely connected with US policy makers in order to bring about a shift in the relationship. This group must join together to achieve the same goal, instead of being disjointed. Even then, there has been a tremendous amount done to date and it is evident that there have been major strides since over a decade ago.

4. What problems do Indo-American students face in the American universities? Any suggestions to improve upon them?

There are no major problems which students face. However, some Indo-American students face a loss of identity and placement in US universities. 'This is in part due racism felt in parts of this nation, which makes some individuals ashamed of their background. Whether they are educated about their country or culture is not necessarily the main issue; the cause of concern is the lack of cohesion among students. Of course, there are on-campus clubs which help to promote unity and culture, which are very effective. However, many campuses do not have Indian study programmes whereas they do have Chinese study programmes. Indian students should not be made to feel inferior to other Asian nations; there should be more programmes on campus devoted to promoting India and Indian thoughts. Programmes should be meant to help Indians feel more united and powerful as they can, not only help Indian students, but educate others about the achievements made by India. Such programmes would help prompt Indian students to do more and play an active role in helping India.

5. As an Indo-American student, what do you expect the Indian government to do for you?

As a US citizen, I do not expect the Indian government to focus directly on me; however, I do expect the Indian government to engage the Indian community in India as well as the US policymakers. As I mentioned earlier, colleges need more programmes to unite the Indians. For example, at my school (New York University) there are study programmes and research departments devoted to Israel, Japan's economy, Spain; however, India is not on this list. I have been trying for three years to have NYU develop such a programme, bit it requires donations. Acquiring such donations is very difficult and there must be a starting step. This starting step can be facilitated by the government by having guest speakers come to our school, by having Indian officials engage with college administration members to develop courses and departments intended to further advance India's image. The government should play an active role in this since colleges help promote intellectual thought processes. Many already know about India's IITs and amazing business, but everyone should be knowledgeable about these topics. If an education division or research departments is created, not only will Indian students attend and learn more about their country and how to help it economically, but others will too. I feel that the Indian government should make its case at colleges since the main audience will be in a position to give back in the coming years. The next generation is in a position to be wealthier than the first and can provide the much needed FDI for India. China is viewed as a major economic powerhouse because its government promotes it as such; India can do the same. I personally would not want the Indian government to do anything for me, but I would like it to become involved in campuses by promoting India and creating groups aimed to help India.

6. What kind of educational co-operation you expect between India and the USA? What role can you play to enhance it?

I think that exchange programmes can best help the education co-operation process. NYU currently has a study aboard programme in which students can spend a semester in a European city and I think India should be added to this. A lot of people regard India as a country of top-notch education, this should play to India advantage. More so, as I mentioned earlier, if India funds and creates research departments and study programmes focussing on India, the education co-operation can expand further. This can also be obtained through scholarships as was done recently by Turkey.

7. Suggest some projects, proposals, ideas involving specific areas (for e.g. enhancing India's image in the Western media or transfer of technology at university/research institute level/ or creation of an apex Indo-American Students Co-ordinating Committee on common minimum issues).

India's image can be advanced if more Indian officials visit the US, speak with the media, meet college students and help promote India. Again, the diaspora has an important role as well by helping to sway the media and creating lobby groups. As I mentioned earlier, research and study programmes are crucial to help college campuses better understand what India is. One project should be to create a lobby group and hold more nationwide functions for Indians to unite themselves as a major force in this nation. If untied, more can be achieved and would help facilitate lobbying as well as influencing the media to portray India in a positive light. A co-ordinating committee to spearhead these concepts would facilitate this and help arrive at a common goal, instead of every campus attempting to achieve their own agenda. It should not be about individual campuses getting more money; it should be about India's image gaining popularity in America.

8. Any other Suggestions

I do not have any additional suggestions to make at this time, but I would like to re-emphasise the importance the media has in promoting India properly. This can help make changes in India's economy. More so, a united diaspora is equally important in order to implement the necessary changes on this side of the hemisphere. Also, the government should engage colleges to educate and promote India. Finally, I look forward to meeting you on November 1st and hopefully a great deal can be achieved. I am proud to see the monumental changes that have taken place in India in the past IO years as well the changes amongst Indians in America and the Indo-US relationship. I hope to help these causes further and look forward to speaking with you.

Questionnaire

1. Are you aware of India's current economic, commercial, industrial and educational achievements? In your view where can Indian policy improve?

I feel that I am aware of most of India's current achievements in the economic and educational sectors. I think Indian policy has neglected the infrastructure of the country for far too long, both on the Centre and state levels. Though the current national government has taken large steps to reverse this trend, I think that there needs to be even more investments in infrastructure, which alone can help spur economic growth.

2. What are the bottlenecks that impinge on India becoming a developed country?

I think there are two major bottlenecks – the first, as I described above, is the fact that the national infrastructure (power, water, roads, etc.) needs to be improved significantly; the second is that the educational system is not fully developed yet in large parts of the country, along with other governmental services. Investment in that will help India gain worldwide acceptance as a developed country.

3. Your view on Indo-US relations. What more can India do to improve bilateral relations? What role can the Indian diaspora in the US play in this regard?

My view is that India and the US have much more in common than is realised. Not only are we both democracies, but we have similar national security concerns and complementary economies. The synergies from these need to be highlighted more in the American media. While India does a good job in diplomacy, what it needs to do is court American public opinion. A full-out PR blitz, with support from the Indian diaspora, will provide a positive image of India to the media and strengthen the power of the Indian lobby in Washington.

4. What problems do Indo-American students face in the US universities? Any suggestions to improve upon them?

I think the major problem that Indo-American students face in US universities (and the school system in general) is a mis-portrayal of India as a backward, undeveloped country where the majority of people follow a crazy and insensible religion and culture. (The sad part is, some students start believing this to be true!) I think the Ambassador's office can help spearhead an effort to provide more truthful material to universities and schools in order to counteract this trend. (I know the German government does this with the Goethe Institute).

5. As an Indo-American student, what do you expect the Indian government to do for you?

I don't expect much from the Indian government as a student. Funding exchange programmes or fellowships like Indicorps would be a great thing though. As an Indo-American student, however, I expect to be helping India more for it providing something to me.

6. What kind of educational co-operation do you expect between India and the USA? What role can you play to enhance it?

The fostering of educational links at many levels would be great, along with the exchange of information. I think students here can help spearhead that effort.

7. Suggest some projects, proposals, ideas involving specific areas(for e.g. enhancing India's image in the Western media or transfer of technology at university/research institute level/ or creation of an apex Indo-American Students Co-ordinating Committee on common minimum issues).

I think enhancing India's image in the Western media is extremely important and that the Indian government should undertake significant investment in that area.

Questionnaire

1. Are you aware of India's economic, commercial, industrial and educational achievements? In your view, where can Indian policy improve?

India has made clear strides towards progress in the past two decades; however, there is much room for improvement and economic growth and modernisation. India must continue its trend of economic deregulation, privatisation, and liberalisation. The past few decades have shown the potential of such policies. The next round of policies should include the reduction of trade barriers in India's relatively closed economy. India should also focus on investing much more in education and investment on human capital as well. These policies can lead to an export growth strategy that marked the growth and development of Japan, Germany, and now China.

2. What are the bottlenecks that impinge on India becoming a developed country?

One element which prevents India from developing rapidly is its government. Indian government has historically kept its economy underachieving with over regulation and corruption. These policies have also led to India being short changed in foreign investment, which it will need in an increasingly larger part to become an international player.

3. Your view on Indo-US relations. What more can India do to improve bilateral relations? What role has the Indian diaspora in the US to play in this regard?

Both India and Indo-Americans can play their role in improving Indo-US relations. Indo-Americans can lobby their government to grant India more defence and trade concessions; however, the role of US business and the US tech industry will play a much larger role in this regard. (Microsoft's lobbying efforts can outdo the entire Indo-American community's efforts.) India has to play a much larger role in improving these relations. India must not play on the domestic-political hatred among some Indian nationalists toward the United States, but rather work co-operatively with the US.

Unfortunately, recent examples have shown the wrong trends. In Iraq, India refused to send Indian troops at the Bush Administration's request. In the last round of global trade talks, India tried to oppose Western efforts at avoiding talks on global agricultural trade by leading the Group of 21 developing States in an effort stop the talks without the talks addressing the issue. In both cases, India seems to be getting ahead of itself. It is behaving as a world power before it has established itself as one, both politically and economically. India needs to behave more co-operatively with the US and not pander to the political bloc of blind anti-American nationalism, if it wishes to form strong ties with the US.

4. What problems do Indo-American students face in the US universities? Any suggestions to improve upon them?

Lndo-American students as a group, in my opinion, face few problems in US universities. US universities are very open-minded and accepting to minorities and cultural diversity. The only problem may be that because Indian culture is so readily accepted, Indo-Americans tend to segregate themselves into an exclusive social entity and fail to experience all facets of university life. However, this is not something the government or even the school should do anything about; it is a de facto social development.

5. As an Indo-American student, what do you expect the Indian government to do for you?

Possibly for Indian citizens, but not at all to US citizens of Indian origin.

6. What kind of educational co-operation do you expect between India and the USA? What role can you play to enhance it?

India and the US can play a great role in co-operative education. Undoubtedly, many Indians have an interest in coming to US schools for undergraduate and graduate studies. There is a newer and larger demand among American social activists and internationalists studying political science or sociology planning to do work for international institutions seeking to fight global poverty, to spend time in the US. Their increased acceptance in India can enhance educational co-operation.

7. Suggest some projects, proposals, ideas involving specific areas (for e.g. enhancing India's image in the Western media or transfer of technology at university/research institute level/

or creation of an apex Indo-American Students Co-ordinating Committee on common minimum issues).

This question offers the idea that there are specific, non-policy-based solutions to increase US-India relations. The answers lie in the actions of the Indian government.

8. Any other suggestions.

Strengthening US-Indo relations is incumbent on India. It needs to move towards economic liberalisation and a pro-US. foreign policy. These initiatives will force the coalition in power to make tough political decisions and thus requires strong political leadership, the likes of Margaret Thatcher and Ronald Reagan.

Questionnaire

A workshop for Indo-American youth has been something Indians have needed for the past couple of years. Being a native-born American myself, I have seen a steady dilution of the Indian culture among the youth in our generation. Many of today's Indian parents came to America in the 70s and 80s for a chance to accomplish something in the 'land of opportunity', but I feel in the midst of this ambition, our generation has slowly lost the desire and necessity to be and remain Indian. I see Indians my age not performing the most common Indian cultural acts in their day-to-day life. Unfortunately, there are very few Indians I know who speak Hindi fluently, respect their elders the way Indians traditionally do so, or even have any Indian culture embedded in them at all. To me, there is no concrete distinction between Indian kids today and Americans, other than the way they look. Of course, America is known as the biggest melting pot in the world and yes there is pride in that because this is a place where people of different origins can connect. However, that does not mean that people have to completely reduce their culture to a gross conglomeration of one culture, a so-called American culture. This is not only the case with Indian culture, because there are many other cultures dealing with the same identity or cultural crisis themselves. So I propose that before moving on and trying to make all of America aware of Indians and India, a more important and beneficial mission can be to make Indians in America more Indian than they are.

Although the Indo-American Youth Workshop revolves around educating America more about India, why not work more on educating

Indians about India and its culture first? When our own people seem to be getting detached from our culture, then what would be the use of educating non-Indians about India? It would be better to have a stronger force of Indians in America, who feel so strongly about being Indian that they would be devoted towards making their voices heard clearly in America. By having a much bigger group of people work to make Indians more influential in America, I feel that the process of making America more aware of Indians would go much faster and be much more successful. Another reason for turning towards educating Indians about being Indian is to give purpose to our workshop. What would be the use of making such a workshop for America's Indian youth, if no Indians will make any use of it? Also, for whom would this workshop be made, if no Indians from our generation or the next would ever want to use the opportunity of having a more India-aware America?

My suggestion would be to come up with a solid plan to systematically educate Indian kids about being Indian. There are many Indians living in America who, for geographic or socio-economic reasons, are unable to be a part of the Indian community. Of course, we cannot go around picking out these people and placing them in an Indian community, but we can try to make Indian communities across America make an effort to extend their arms out to other Indians who are not a part of their community. By actively enforcing Indians to take part in a community, there can be a sense of unity among all Indians across America. Also, as we make these Indian communities, we can start to connect all of them together, so there would be a single thread uniting all Indians in America and thus making our efforts to make America more aware of India and Indians much easier.

Since the culture embedded in children is a direct result of what parents or other authoritative figures impose on them, I feel that having seminars for parents would be an effective tool to help get this Indian culture run across America. These informative seminars can directly address the issue of how Indian kids are really not Indian anymore. Perhaps these seminars may cause parents to realise how big the cultural gap has grown between them and our generation. If these seminars prove to be effective, then the results would steadily trickle down to our generation and that distinct change in 'Indianness' will be visible not only to the parents, but also the whole Indian community taking part in this effort.

However, the problem would remain that everyone in our generation has a mind of his or her own. Of course there are a few who would listen to their parents and the seminars would truly help them. But what about those independent Indian teenagers, who do not wish to do anything unless they feel they should do it? For this situation, I would suggest that our workshop should come up with a variety of ways to persuade the Indian-American towards being more Indian. Everyone has his or her own personal interests; some are influenced by music, others by environment, others through religion, and still others through politics. By giving these Indian-Americans a chance to explore India and its culture themselves, it may prove more effective than by forcing the Indian culture on them. Indian communities can bring religious speakers to talk to our generation, or political figures may try to involve our youth to take an active stand in the government. The only thing to keep in mind would be to have speakers come every couple of months, instead of once every year. The effect of having such influential people needs to be felt by the Indian communities constantly and by having speakers come every couple of months, the Indian youth may build a desire to learn more and do more. Whatever method is employed, it can be a potential way to help our workshop reach out to the Indian-Americans in America.

Although this is a very rough sketch of a possible plan to help educate Indians, it is a proposal with an approximate solution to a very serious problem. I feel that our workshop needs to first take a step towards Indians and then towards Americans. By visiting Indian communities, we can extract ways for Indians to uphold our Indian culture. And by sending speakers and teachers to communities, a desire to learn something Indian can be sparked in many of the youth in every Indian community. The last point I would want to leave you with would be the fact that before going to every single Indian community, there needs to be some experimentation done for this proposal to work. It will only be through trial and error that this plan can be solidified and made to work on most Indian communities. If this proposal works for one community, we can easily go from one community to another, helping their youth learn more about their true identities of being true Indians.

Questionnaire

1. Are you aware of India's current economic, commercial, industrial and educational achievements? In your view, where can Indian policy improve?

Yes, Indian foreign policy needs to take greater cognisance of the present international realities. India must depart from its still largely insular foreign policy and engage strategic countries, such as the United States by demonstrating more substantive co-operation. The NAM should be recognised as irrelevant in today's international political environment.

Primary education in India still needs much improvement. Access to education in rural areas needs to be expanded and ultimately made universally accessible.

Economic liberalisation should continue with greater liberalisations in other sectors beyond technology. The government has done well in resisting pressures from *swadeshi* groups, but needs to move forward with liberalisation with even stronger resolve. Stock Exchanges should be amalgamated into a small number (four or five) exchanges to provide for greater efficiency.

2. What are the bottlenecks that impinge upon India becoming a developed country?

Population needs to be controlled. Corruption among government officials and civil servants must be eradicated. The legal system needs to be improved to provide for greater efficiency. The implementation of Lok Aadalats is a positive step towards improvement in the administration of the judicial system but greater steps are necessary. Infrastructure in India needs substantial improvement, especially with regards to transportation and telecommunications.

3. Your view on Indo-US relations. What more can India do to improve bilateral relations? What role can the Indian diaspora in the US play in this regard?

India needs to extend greater co-operation with the United States. India squandered an opportunity to improve Indo-US relations with its condemnation of the war in Iraq. This error in judgement can still be rectified by India sending peacekeepers/security forces to Iraq. India needs to expand its lobbying budget in the United States, though such need not be allocated only to law firms and lobbying firms. Rather, the GoI should also provide financial assistance to Indian-American organisations that make valuable contributions in the US in improving India's image and America's relations with India.

4. What problems do Indo-American students face in the US universities? Any suggestions to improve upon them?

The greatest problem faced by Indian-American students is curricular in nature. Indian subject matter is either not taught in US universities or is taught inaccurately and insensitively. Few scholars of India and Indian philosophy are of Indian origin and thus their academic understanding of things related to India is often far different from the real and practical understanding.

5. As an Indo-American student, what do you expect the Indian government to do for you?

By affirmatively taking steps to gain American goodwill, the treatment and acceptance of Indo-American students will improve dramatically.

6. What kind of educational co-operation do you expect between India and the USA? What role can you play to enhance it?

India should extend greater resources to enable US educational institutions to expand and improve Indian study programmes in the US. In exchange, the US can provide professional assistance in further improving Indian technical and management programmes at the post-secondary school-level and in structuring primary education programmes to improve primary education in India.

7. Suggest some projects, proposals, ideas involving specific areas (for e.g. enhancing India's image in the Western media or transfer of technology at university/research institute level/ or creation of an apex Indo-American Students Co-ordinating Committee on common minimum issues).

Several valuable organisations are already active in trying to improve India's image in the Western media, in the US government and on US campuses. The Indian government/office of the Ambassador-at-Large should provide material support to such organisations

8. Any other suggestions.

Questionnaire

1. Are you aware of India's current economic, commercial, industrial and educational achievements? In your view, where can Indian policy improve?

Yes, I am well aware of some of the recent economic, commercial, industrial and educational developments. There are several challenges currently facing Indian policy makers. It is important that as a nation, India has favourable policies to foster innovation and research, simultaneously opening up the market for globalisation and creating new jobs, and positively affecting the labour market. Another area where policy could have a great impact is a tighter regulation of the industrial sector.

2. What are the bottlenecks that impinge on India becoming a developed country?

At the tip of the iceberg are corruption, lack of good opportunities and lack of uniformity in the different states. However, the critical underlying problem is the ever-growing population making it difficult for the government to provide sufficient resources to individuals. This indirectly results in increasing illiteracy and unemployment.

3. Your view on Indo-US relations. What more can India do to improve bilateral relations? What role can the Indian diaspora in the US play in this regard?

The last couple of decades have witnessed considerable growth in Indo-US trade improving bilateral relationship. There have been several collaborations in the industrial sector and the Indian diaspora has made some great strides. India should continue the exchange of knowledge and expertise by way of intellectual property in terms of bright Indian students that come to work for the US as well as in terms of bilateral trade. The Indian diaspora can complement this effort and make a huge impact on Indo-US relations. The Indian diaspora should actively support growth in India (intellectually and financially) as well as be politically active in the US to communicate our interests.

4. What problems do Indo-American students face in the US universities? Any suggestions to improve upon them?

With the growth of the Indian-American community, Indo-American students in the US do not face many challenges as far as adapting to the culture and learning environment is concerned. However, they still appear to be conservative which restricts their overall growth. We should try to encourage them to realise their true potential and make optimum use of available resources. Their immediate family and peers would be a major influence in this regard.

5. As an Indo-American student, what do you expect the Indian government to do for you?

The Indian government should encourage and support Indian-American students to contribute to the growth of the nation in any way, shape or form. Fostering interest in the Indian economic and political scene can attract students to be involved with the dynamics of the country and the challenges faced by the nation.

The Indian media can definitely play a major role by recognising some of the achievements of Indian-Americans and promoting further involvement.

6. What kind of educational co-operation you expect between India and the USA? What role can you play to enhance it?

The government should continue to encourage US education but at the same time avoid brain drain and provide incentives to students to come back. They also need to improve and strengthen the educational system to provide world-class education to students. They could organise exchange programmes for Indian-Americans to come to India and share diverse experiences and cultures.

With globalisation of businesses, efforts should be taken to encourage corporate giants to provide financial support to bright students to pursue their academic goals. At the same time, the Indian diaspora can actively support both Indian and the Indian-American student community in the US, both financially and in terms of access to resources.

7. Suggest some projects, proposals, ideas involving specific areas (for e.g. enhancing India's image in the Western media or transfer of technology at university/research institute level/ or creation of an apex Indo-American Students Co-ordinating Committee on common minimum issues).

a. The Indo-American community needs support and encouragement to be unconventional and explore a broad range of academic and professional career options. Majority of second-generation Indian-Americans look at medicine as their first choice. This needs to be changed.

b. The Indo-American community needs to take special efforts to recognise achievements of second-generation Indians and attract media attention, especially where there are pockets of large Indian communities, involvement in local community organisations, school boards and other such institutions can be a good place to start.

c. Indian government must ensure that Indian students that come to the US to study and develop their academic careers actively contribute back to the growth of India. Majority of Indians who leave the country do not return and this leaves an unfinished agenda for the Indian government. One way could be to sign a bond for a few years of service in exchange for limited financial support.

Questionnaire

1. Are you aware of India's current economic, commercial, industrial and educational achievements? In your view, where can Indian policy improve?

No, I am not aware of many of India's achievements.

2. What are the bottlenecks that impinge on India becoming a developed country?

The simplest largest problem is the corruption. Indian government has got to sit back and clear itself of the people who are holding the country back with their personal agendas.

3. Your view on Indo-US relations. What more can India do to improve bilateral relations? What role can the Indian diaspora in the US play in this regard?

Our relations are strained because of the US closeness with Pakistan and our inability to work with that country, and with Pakistanis in the US. I cannot speak for what India should do as the emotional barriers seem great, but such co-operation should be emphasised and encouraged in America, if only for the sake of being properly noticed as a minority and given the benefits that minorities should be given. The diaspora of the US should be lobbying and more politically active and aware. Although we are a small minority, voting as a block, keeping the Indians who are taxi-drivers and the Indians who are doctors, etc. together is extremely important.

4. What problems do Indo-American students face in the US universities? Any suggestions to improve upon them?

Indo-American students as a group, in my opinion, face few problems in US. universities. US universities are very open-minded and accepting to minorities and cultural diversity. The only problem may be that because Indian culture is so readily accepted, Indo-Americans tend to segregate themselves into an exclusive social entity and fail to experience all facets of university life. However, this is not something the government or even the school should do anything about; it is a de facto social development.

5. As an Indo- American student, what do you expect the Indian government to do for you?

I expect the Indian government to help with keeping track of immigrants in this country and their political representation, their financial position, their social condition as far as discrimination, etc. Is concerned. We are in the 'first world' and part of one of the most powerful countries in the world. Thus our diaspora has a great need of representation, not only for Indians, but for the rest of the diaspora.

6. What kind of educational co-operation do you expect between India and the USA?

What role can you play to enhance it?

We should have more programmes for kids to study abroad, get degrees abroad and not be hindered when transferring to an American school. Indian schools should rise in quality and be competitive as well with their research opportunities. This can only happen when charity money, and other funds are not being diverted by political radicals or religious radicals, who are only out for their own agenda. We should also make sure that Hindu and islamic faiths are properly represented and our culture is something that is widespread and understood

7. Suggest some projects, proposals, ideas involving specific areas(for e.g, enhancing India's image in the Western media or transfer of technology at university/research institute level/ or creation of an apex Indo-American Students Co-ordinating Committee on common minimum issues).

Workshop on Women's Issues: A Diaspora Perspective

February 7, 2004
Atlanta, Georgia

Executive Summary

I. Context

The workshop titled 'Women's Issues: A Diaspora Perspective' is a part of an ongoing series of many projects undertaken by the office of the Ambassador-at-Large to accomplish its vision to network and study the issues concerning the Indian diaspora. The workshops already undertaken by this office include 'Enhancing India's Image in the Western Media', 'Indo-Caribbean Leader's Forum', 'Indo-American Youth/Students: Their Contributions & Concerns', 'Meeting of the Inter-Religious Leaders', Improving the Quality of Financial services aimed at NRIs& PIOs'. etc. The first workshop on women's issues was organised on February 1, 2004 in New York.

The workshop highlighted the common needs, concerns and recommendations of the Indo-American diaspora women in professions and as homemakers. This workshop was an effort by women to highlight the common concerns as immigrants.

II. Themes Discussed

The workshop's objective was to study the following:

1. Challenges and problems, if any, faced by Indo-American women: their perspective & experiences in American society.
2. How Ind0-American women can be instrumental in helping India preserve the Indian value system in America and guide the new generation.
3. Role that Indo-American women can play in educating Americans about India and Indian heritage.

III. Participants

Representative groups of leading women academicians, doctors, lawyers, accountants, social workers etc. in the greater Atlanta region participated in the workshop. The workshop made suggestions, recommendations and action plan for addressing issues on the national agenda.

IV. Key Recommendations

1. Sincere community support is required by women, whether single, divorced or senior citizens going through or facing a crisis.
2. To overcome the paucity of information that new immigrants and non- immigrants face on arrival in America, a welcome wagon with information/literature about their city and availability of various services is required.
3. Assisted living projects which cater to the ethnic needs of the aging Indo-American population need to be undertaken by hoteliers in conjunction with the medical professionals.
4. Using the regional language or mother tongue in the home is important. Bal Vihars also play a valuable role in the process of learning about Indian culture and for socialisation.
5. Teach children, especially young girls, the value of financial independence and foster independent thinking and survival skills.
6. Invite Americans to Indian social, religious and community programmes to help educate them.
7. Volunteer at local libraries and projects; contact public libraries to get material, books, tapes from India added to their collection.
8. Contact school boards to get India properly represented in school curriculum.
9. Take action to get media misrepresentation corrected; provide requisite material so that media can report on positive developments too.
10. Get involved politically in any capacity to gain community visibility.

V. Next Steps

1. Continue such meetings, workshops with broader participation.
2. Involve office of Ambassador-at-Large in seeing some of the recommendations come to fruition.
3. Form self-help groups in local areas to address some of the needs outlined at the workshop.

Programme Schedule

- Welcome - Mr. Amitabh Sharma, vice president, Regional, NFIA
- Opening - Ambassador Bhishma K. Agnihotri
- Moderator - Mrs. Rachna Gupta
- Discussion on the following issues:

Theme 1: Challenges & Problems, if any, Faced by Indo-American Women: Their Perspective & Experiences in American Society - Discussion Leader: Mrs. Aparna Bhattacharya

Theme 2: How Indo-American women can be instrumental in helping India preserve Indian Value System in America and Guiding the New Generation - Discussion Leader: Mrs. Indu Dey

Theme 3: Role Indo-American Women can Play in Educating Americans about India and Indian Heritage - Discussion Leader: Mrs. Preeti Sharma

- *Summation*- Mrs. Rachna Gupta
- *Closing* - Ambassador Agnihotri
- *Vote of Thanks*- Mr. Amitabh Sharma

Highlights of the Workshop

Introduction

The workshop titled 'Women's Issues: A Diaspora Perspective' in Atlanta, Georgia was chaired by the Ambassador-at-Large for NRIs and PIOs Dr. Bhishma K. Agnihotri on February 7, 2004. This workshop was a continuation of such workshops organised by the office of Ambassador-at-Large to accomplish its vision to network, study the issues and highlight the common needs, concerns and recommendations of the Indo-American diaspora women and to relay the same to policy makers in India for further action.

1. The workshop was attended by women from a diverse background: physicians, therapists, religious, social and community activists, law graduates, legal researchers, freelance writers, librarians, school teachers, professors, accountants, businesswomen, home-makers and retirees.
2. Initiating the meeting, Dr. Bhishma K. Agnihotri said that the workshops were being organised to discuss issues of great concern for the Indian diaspora. He said that often male ego

hindered examination of issues that were of great concern to women and ultimately to the family; therefore it was the woman who has to rise to the occasion to identify problems and help in finding solutions. The office of the Ambassador-at-Large would use these workshops to develop a national agenda and submit the same to policy makers for consideration.

3. The workshop discussed three specific themes initiated by Ms. Aparna Bhattacharya, Ms. Indu Dey and Ms. Preeti Sharma. After their brief presentations, all participants made their valuable contributions to the discussion on following themes:

Themes Discussed

(a) Challenges & Problems, if any, Faced by Indo-American Women: Their Perspective &Experiences in American Society.

(b) How Indo-American Women can be Instrumental in Helping India Preserve Indian Value System in America and Guiding the New Generation.

(c) Role Indo-American Women can Play in Educating Americans about India and Indian Heritage.

4. On the first theme, one of the participants, who spoke from her everyday experience as Director of 'Raksha', a community support group, highlighted the common issues, identifying women of various age groups and then addressing their specific problems or concerns. Young Indo-American women needed to deal with assimilation, acculturation, self-identity, bridging of two cultures, academic pressure, peer pressure on drinking, taking drugs, becoming sexually active, dealing with taboos surrounding reporting incidents of incest/child molestation/date rape, lack of communication with parents, pressure to get married and struggle between marriage and career.

5. The challenges faced by married women or mothers related to acclimatisation to a totally new environment and to new roles at the same time. They ended up juggling the traditional role of homemaker with the new role of working woman single-handedly (9 to 5 and then 5 to 9) with very little assistance from their partners and oftentimes did not know where to turn to get answers. The participants pointed instances

where the problems were compounded due to the existence of domestic violence, abusive in-laws, dowry issues, lack of transportation, lack of access to education, isolation, limited support networks, lack of access to medical or health care, jobs without benefits, denial of access to services based on immigration status, lack of knowledge about the working of criminal justice, civil legal systems, lack of leadership opportunities, pressure to be perfect, raising children with two sets of values and cultural preservation with children.

6. The participants also noted that the elderly women often lacked access to affordable healthcare and insurance, lacked knowledge of benefits, SSI and social security and suffered from isolation, depression, non-availability of long-term healthcare options, social activities, emotional and self-sufficiency support and help with estate issues when a partner or spouse died.
7. To address some of these concerns, the presentations and deliberations stressed the need for sincere community support when women were going through a crisis or recovering from one, availability of forums or workshops composed of professionals who understood the dynamics of the Indo-American community for counselling and resolving interpersonal conflicts, formation of more self-help groups, need to overcome the paucity of information by having a welcome wagon or package with information/literature about the city, services availability, specific needs and requirements, one-stop non-profit centre manned by Indians to give information or answer questions as and when there were changes in laws or regulations.
8. To ameliorate the problems of the aging Indian community in this country, it was suggested that assisted living projects which catered to the ethnic cultural, spiritual and dietary needs of the aging Inda-American population could be undertaken by hoteliers in conjunction with the medical professionals. Further, government could be asked, under Title VI, to provide interpreters in hospitals and Hindu priests and Muslim *imams*to help community members get through

difficult times. In essence, community needed to get involved to address the challenges faced by their senior citizens.

9. On the second theme, the participants felt that the Indian value system could be preserved through structured religious and cultural classes/meetings wherein the broad general features should be explained to the participants and not imposed and an access to the regional or national language should be provided. But on the issue of what values are to be imparted to the new generation, the group was divided and questioned whether the values that the present generation grew up with in India were the same now or had they changed even in India? The group felt that to guide the new generation, parents needed to educate themselves to form a better understanding of the challenges that the new generation faced here. Open and free communication was the biggest key and parents needed to talk to youth about smoking, drugs, dating, sex and alcohol in a non-judgmental and age-appropriate manner.
10. On the theme of the role that Indo-American women can play in educating Americans about India and Indian heritage, it was felt that there were negative stereotypes as Americans lacked knowledge on the subject and if the Indo-Americans volunteered more and became a part of the larger American community, they could not only teach them but also learn from them and from other ethnic minorities. The interaction could be used to dispel myths about India or Indians.
11. Some concrete suggestions were that of volunteering at school libraries, interacting positively with Americans at every level in schools, clubs and workplace, inviting American friends to Indian functions, arranging trips to India, getting involved in children's sports and homeowners' associations and request public libraries to collect more material relevant to Indo-Americans.
12. Based on the above discussions, the following broad suggestions and recommendations were made by the discussion leaders, moderators and participants:

Recommendations & Suggestions

(a) Use of regional language or mother tongue in the home is important. Bal Vihars are valuable for learning about Indian culture and for socialisation.

(b) Regular communication between parents and children is very essential – not as imposition but in a natural, non-judgmental, rational way.

(c) Meeting the children's peer group; offering to coach, volunteer and chaperone to games; field trips assists for experiencing their interaction.

(d) Need to create forums where children can intermix with other Indo-Americans and also forums where young Indo-American adults looking for life partners can socialise.

(e) Teach children, especially young girls, the value of financial independence and foster independent thinking and survival skills.

(f) Learn from other immigrant communities about the programmes that they have implemented to make the process of acculturation easier for new groups; include women of colour in the sharing of ideas.

(g) Invite Americans to Indian social, religious and community programmes to help educate them.

(h) Organise tours to India or to local Indian centres; exchange homemade Indian crafts, food, etc.

(i) Know your community; take an active role in homeowners' association, PTA and professional organisations.

(j) Volunteer at local libraries and projects; contact public libraries to get material, books and tapes from India added to the collection.

(k) Contact school boards to get India properly represented in the curriculum.

(l) Take action to get media misrepresentation corrected; provide material so that the media can report positives too.

(m) Get involved politically in any capacity to gain community visibility.

Theme I: Challenges & Problems, if any, Faced by Indo-American Women: Their Perspective and Experiences in American Society

Introduction

General observations on issues facing the South Asian community:

Children

- Assimilation, acculturation
- Bridging the two cultures
- Unlearning violent behaviours if they grew up in a violent home
- Hate crimes, especially after 9/11
- Academic pressure
- Grief
- Incest and child molestation (lack of conversations around it)

Youth /College/ Age Issues

- Identity themes
- Eating disorders
- Peer pressure– to drink, take drugs, engage in permissive sexual behaviours/practices.

1. Mrs. Aparna Bhattacharya, Raksba, Inc. Executive Director -over the last eight years, she bas trained law enforcement, victim advocates, social workers, community members, refugee/immigrant women, and healthcare providers on the dynamics of family violence and the needs of refugee and immigrant families. She was awarded with the Indian Professionals Network (JPN) award in 1997 and 1998 for her service to the community; Member of the Georgia Advisory Committee for the US Commission on Civil Rights; a board member for International Women's House; board secretary for Tapestri, Inc. and a board member for the Dekalb County Domestic Violence Task Force.

- Gang Violence - joining gangs
- Parents talking directly to them about issues they may face
- Suicide
- Communication with their parents
- Parents providing youth with tools to protect themselves
- Pressure to get married
- Struggles between marriage and career

- Non-traditional careers
- Sexual assault and rape - date rape

Women

- Juggling household duties and careers/jobs (9 to 5 and 5 to 9)
- Lack of access to medical or health care
- Domestic violence
- Lack of leadership opportunities
- Raising children with two sets of values
- Cultural preservation with children
- Abusive in-laws/dowry issues
- Lack of transportation
- Lack of access to education
- Isolation
- Limited support networks
- Pressure to be perfect
- Knowledge of how the systems work (criminal justice, civil, legal)
- Classism
- Jobs that do not have benefits
- Access to services based on immigration status
- Gender roles and sexuality
- Homosexuality- lack of support from community when coming out

Elderly

- Access to affordable healthcare and insurance
- Knowledge of benefits, SSI, social security
- Isolation, especially when they are in an area with limited transportation and people
- Depression
- Long-term healthcare options (especially for terminally ill, those with Alzheimer's)
- Activities
- Emotional support when a partner or spouse dies; help with estate issues
- Self-sufficiency support when a spouse dies
- Grief

One participant talked about how we should look at the woman as the centre of a series of concentric circles. She stated we should look at woman as an individual, so that she can be strong. The family represented the next circle; the society is the outer circle.

Recommendations & Suggestions

Support Systems for Women

- The women discussed the need for creating support networks when they are sick and mourning or going through divorce. Many a time, divorced women are isolated from the community and are treated as pariahs.
- There is a lack of adequate public transportation. This plays a role in isolation, not just for women, but also the elderly.
- Our community/Indian friends are not always there when they are needed. Many of the women have had experiences where their American friends or friends from other religious communities are there for them more than their own religious community or Indian community.
- There was a discussion about how there is more prejudice/ workplace discrimination against women in the United States than in India, especially at the workplace. Some women stated that they even did not experience this in the workplace back home (this also depended on the class, religion, education and privilege of the woman).

Elderly Needs and Access to Health Care

- There is a need for nursing homes that are culturally appropriate and cater to specific dietary needs. One participant stated, "We have a right to die feeling loved."
- As women were also becoming parents to their grandchildren, this brings challenges on how they compare notes with their children. The women asked: How are we revisiting parenthood. ?This turns many of the women's roles into parenting vs. grand parenting role in America.
- It is important to get Indian doctors, therapists and businesses to come up with nursing homes that meet the needs of Indian community.
- There are also income inequalities and health disparities. Language is a problem in getting healthcare. Title VI does

provide some protections and rights as far as hospitals having to provide interpreters or at least a plan is concerned.

- There is a need for the presence of Hindu priests and *imams* at hospitals so that the community members can obtain help from them through difficult times. There is also the challenge that many of the priests may not speak English, so it may be difficult for them to work with the hospitals.
- Community members cannot in each case personally get involved and dictate how people care for their elders. Each family will have their own individual needs, limits and resources.
- There is a need for more support in providing opportunities and activities for elderly programming. for example, there were only eight volunteers with senior citizen programmes.
- There is a need for support networks in regard to heart-related healthcare.
- There is a need for medicine, medical help and resources.
- Individuals need to know about Cobra– how to access when they lose jobs.
- Elderly parents often become the babysitters for their children.

Raising Children

- It is important not to impose religion on children but to teach and explain it to them.
- There is a need for classes on religion.
- Provide structure for the classes (religious and cultural classes)
- School systems need to have correct information on Hinduism, access to language classes.
- Bal Vihar offers classes for individuals of all ages– children, teens and college students.
- There was a question about "What are our values?"
- Are the values we grew up with in India the same now? Or have they changed back home. There were some that still believed nothing had changed and some that recognised that the values had undergone a change.

Additional Feedback given after the Workshop, either by Conversations or E-emails

- There were discussions about how women need support groups and additional workshops. There was also a need for marriage counselling, family communication workshops and help with parenting. Some participants talked about their own experiences and how challenging it was for them to find the support they needed.
- Some suggestions on the topics to be covered when organising workshops for new immigrants were received;
- There was a need for one-stop information centres manned by Indians to explain on regulatory changes introduced by the American government (for example, last year H4 visa holders were not allowed a driver's licence. Individuals had to run from pillar to post to just find out the procedural changes).
- Details regarding the education system m the USA must be disseminated as the same is different from the education system in India.
- Parental guidance on dealing with young children exposed to new environment.
- How can parents take part in school activities?

Theme 2: How Indo-American Women can be Instrumental in Helping India Preserve Indian value System in America and guide the New Generation

Introduction

As a discussion leader, Mrs. Indu Dey emphasised that we, women and now parents must understand and follow the Indian value system ourselves before expecting it to be preserved and emulated by the next generation.

I would like to pose a question as: What are we trying to present to the two generations, namely the one born and brought up in America and the other, the young new immigrants? Are we trying to impart traditional or modern Indian value system and what is the relevance and role of Indian values in modem multicultural American society?

The present-day truth is that the new generation is forward looking, in search of its identity and anxious to learn more and more about real values, character, and meaning of life than ever before, if only, their elders have answers, resources and approaches to explain these to them and make them part of the community organisation's agenda.

The group at Atlanta, though small (30 women), was very active in their participation and open exchanges of thoughts and ideas on this subject.

In my view, some of the challenges were:

- Parents trying to control the lives of their children
- Children having to live a double standard of life
- One to convince their parents and the other to be acceptable to their peer group
- Feeling of isolation
- Loneliness and confusion
- Identity crisis
- Lack of sense of security and belonging among the new generation immigrants
- Confusion in regard to social ethics

Almost all the participants agreed that these were indeed challenges and problems that Indo-American parents face when dealing with the new generation. The question of 'dating' was discussed at length.

Monica Gupta, who is a second-generation, 28-year old single Indo-American said that parents thought that by not discussing the issues, the issues as well as the situation would disappear. Also, after making dating a taboo subject for the entire school and college life, suddenly parents wanted their children to get married and settle down (which goes without saying that the parents will themselves consider suitability of boys from their own regional, ethnic community) more acceptable. Youth here are not inclined to marry without seeing and knowing the prospective partner closely and this causes a certain amount of strain in the parent-child relationship.

Aparna Bhattacharya, director of 'Raksha', a second-generation Indo-American herself, said, "Reality is never explained; value of religion is never explained to children and they are just forced to visit temples and congregate at Indian gatherings." What children do not understand, they do not imbibe. Sandhya Bhagat said our narrow mindedness, preventing our children from mingling with American society and our division into regional groups rather than a consolidated group, also pose challenges.

Suggestions

The following suggestions were made on the above discussion:

- Creation of parent education groups
- Renewed approach and representation in media
- Establishing youth sections in all Indo-American organisations, national-level youth conferences and debates, new role of religious centres to impart universal value system relevant to the global human family
- Building youth cultural, recreational and art of living support system

Monica Gupta said that there was a need for parents to communicate openly and discuss all issues without making it sound like a taboo or using body language by which it is seen as such by the children. Her mother Madhur Gupta, who also attended, felt that sometimes the new mothers just did not know how to raise the children in a new setting as the support and knowledge of an extended family and elders were missing. It was basically a trial-and-error method on the new soil. She and Manju Tiwari felt that teaching Indian national language or regional languages, celebrating Indian festivals and storytelling from rich Indian literature could make the new generation aware of the Indian culture.

Dr. Indrani Dutta-Gupta said that we need to inculcate strong moral qualities and a healthy dose of conservatism as opposed to narrow mindedness in our new generation. Raj Razdan said it was important to know and meet the peer group of the children.

Sujatha Reddy, who is very active in temple, social and community activities, said, “Teach them right from wrong, provide freedom and just trust them. Then see how their character and personality shapes up.”

Aparna Bhattacharya said sex education is a must. Rational and logical answers to all questions should be given. Ameeta Seth said that mothers had to break traditional barriers and even raise daughters to be financially independent; that sons should get no preferential treatment over daughters; that marriage should not be a do-or-die situation and that parental and community support should be present if women tried to break off an abusive relationship.

Madhavi Sethna felt the need for communicating with the other parents and other communities as the problem was not limited to Indo-Americans alone. She urged parents to make friends with and to keep channels open for communication with other children.

Dr. Uma Majumdar, who is now a grandmother, said there was a need to be friendly with children. Parents must understand what they really expect from their children and that issues needed to be discussed in an age-appropriate setting. Rational replies were needed to be provided to the youngsters' questions. Raju Gokarm said that by being open about one's own life, healthy communication can be initiated.

Uma Iyer said that a forum for Indo-American youth should meet on regular basis. Sometimes our children feel left out of mainstream activities; sometimes peer group does not include them; and sometimes in our effort to protect our children, we do not let them attend certain activities.

Sharmila Janakiraman said that a forum for a new immigrant is needed to assist in the acculturation process. She felt that more youngsters in India were getting into the wave of spiritualism and yoga. The same could be achieved here by arranging short and regular lectures or making booklets available (50-100 pp.) on topics like, significance of simple rituals, ways to increase confidence, concentration through age old traditional practices, collection of famous, relevant quotes and meaning from the *Vedas* and tips on how to prepare yourself to achieve high goals. Our *Vedas, Upanishads* and *Manusmiti* are invaluable sources, but we need to make these available in simple language.

In conclusion, the workshop agreed that the following was needed:

1. Regular family/parent workshops in local temples/ community centres.
2. Starting youth divisions on local community organisations.
3. Youth days, activities and executives in religious centres and community organisations.
4. Booklets about Indian values, rituals and traditions to be readily available through community organisations and temples.
5. Media to play an important role by writing positively about India and Indian traditions and its relevance to modem-day life.

Theme 3: Role Indo-American Women can Play in Educating Americans about India and Indian Heritage

Introduction

Indian culture still has not been properly introduced to Western civilisation. The success of Americans of Indic origin has opened with it a possibility of a vibrant dialogue with Western culture. The manner in which Indian families live, work and socialise in America is also a dialogue of civilisations. The particularly important role that Indian womanhood plays in holding a family together also empowers Indian women to be the best cultural ambassadors of our traditions. Indian women have not only been homemakers, but educated professionals, successful businesswomen and independent individuals with well-formed opinions. This is reflected in the traditional Indic culture as ascribing a female aspect of God as a goddess, or a Devi. This recognition of feminine divinity, on par with male divinity, is unique to Indian culture.

The development of Indic civilisation therefore is very critically dependent on Indian womanhood and its empowerment. There are many important ways in which Indian women could serve as ambassadors to American/Western culture. Some of these are:

Recommendations

1. Interacting and being involved with the community in which Indian families live, by being active in volunteering in schools and local civic groups, like local library, museums. Mrs. Raj Razdan, who is a very active in the Indian community and has worked incessantly to promote Indian cause, had the following suggestion:

- "It is imperative that we go and talk at churches, schools and at the PTA meetings about India and the Indian heritage. Participating at the school libraries and go and teach at the schools imply to the teacher that one would like to come and talk to the children about India. This is a very good forum. If the parents get involved as team mothers and fathers as coaches, the children will learn to accept the Indian figurehead. I have also been involved with the museums where we put up an Indian sari exhibition and another show was that of Indian jewellery. These exhibits have been very successful. We had about 600-800 people on the opening night. Participate with the people in the Congress and work at the election campaigns. These have been done before and it works."

2. Educating neighbours and friends about our culture and way of life in the process of socialising with them was one of the suggestions that could be practice by hosting a neighbourhood picnic.

- Ms Shashi Sidhaye had the following suggestion, "On this topic I had my suggestion that we should do volunteer service in neighbourhood hospitals and libraries. I used to volunteer in the hospital when it was close to my house and now I volunteer in local school libraries. I found school libraries do need help and we get satisfaction of volunteering; also we come know other Americans and we can spread the message in a subtle way. They appreciate help in whatever capacity possible very much."
- Ms. Shamila also had very good suggestions, "Only if we know exactly what Indian heritage is, then can we educate the Americans. We must have the answers regarding India and its heritage. Our best publishers are our kids as they mingle with at least 20 children every day. Tell them about India in positive terms so they are ready to share it with their friends. We can send gifts to schools on our special festivals, like Diwali. Maybe the kid could explain why we celebrate it in class. Americans are curious to know more about other cultures (I made my son do it. He was happy and proud to talk about India).
- We can make efforts to bring cartoon movies of the Jataka tales, *Panchatantra*, *Mahabharata*, *Ramayana* in the form of DVD or VHS and distribute to schools and libraries. Interactive VCDs on *Tenali Raman* stories now available in India and could be brought here too.
- An extensive Website addressing every aspect of our tradition and heritage (with links to already existing good sites) will be easily accessible to Indians and Americans than books. This website could have details about complex topics like Sanatana Dharma to day-to-day topics like *kolams* (*rangoli*),

Indian home medicine, Indian proverbs, *slokas* with meaning, and what not.

- So far all movies made in English on Indian lifestyle seem to defy Indian customs and heritage. Movies with a story line revolving around the core essence of Indian values could be made in English so that the youth of this country could learn more about India faster and in an interesting way.
- Public television stations can be urged to show cartoon films on Indian books, like *Panchatantra*; Something similar to the Chinese cat story *Sagwa*, which is telecast everyday. Through this story Chinese lifestyle, tradition, food, clothes, etc. are brought to our homes. Why can't there be a similar Indian story series?"

3. Never be apologetic about our background and traditions, and to politely, but persistently, counter misconceptions about our culture. To write to all the editors of textbooks and pursue the removal of incorrect material with a more current updated well-researched version.
4. Be active in networks of Indian interest groups to allow for concerted actions on issues of common interest.
5. Write letters to our local government, Congressmen and Senators about issues that affect the Indian-American community.
6. Above all, the best is there is no better ambassadorial activity than professional success.
7. The most critical thing to do is fundraising such that we are able to hire full-time and part-time professionals to do consistent public relations' campaign for India and matters related to Indian issues. Retired professionals can be approached to volunteer their services for this endeavour. They will be able to bring their skills which made them successful to this cause. Indian women will be especially great because they will bring their instinct, sensitivity and creativity.

Participant List

S. No.	Name	Occupation
1.	Asha Advani	Speech pathologist at Northside Hospital; active in Sadhu Vaswani Centre
2.	Neera Bahl	Law graduate from Emory University; doing legal research
3.	Sandhya Bhagat	M.A., B.Ed.; teaches at Bal Vihar; works at Target store
4.	Aparna Bhattacharya	Director, community organisation Raksha– workshops for law enforcement agencies
5.	Indu Dey	Occupational therapist; volunteer in Indian community activities
6.	Prof. Kamla Dutt	Professor, theatre/literature, Morehouse School of Medicine
7.	Dr. Indrani Dutta-Gupta	English professor at Kennesaw till 2000; VP of spouse's defence contracting firm
8.	Dr. Rajul Gokarn	Associate professor of accounting, Clark Atlanta Univ. School of Bus. Adm.
9.	Madhur Gupta	MA in music from India; Bal Vihar teacher; volunteer; accounting
10.	Monica Gupta	Dentist (DMD); will start pediatric post-doc., June 2004
11.	Rachna Gupta	LL.B, B.Ed.; JD; legal research; compiled NHRC human rights database
12.	Rashmi Gupta	M.A., English literature; running family daycare for 20 years
13.	UmaIyer	Accounting, small business; library assistant in county library
14.	Shamila Janakiraman	Home-maker; non-immigrant; freelance writer; B.E. (Elec. & Comm.). MBA

15.	Uma Majmudar	M.A. English; Ph.D. Emory thesis: Mahatma Gandhi; Forthcoming book: *Gandhi's Pilgrimage of Faith*; will teach in Religion Dept. at Emory, 2004
16.	Vimal Nikore	M.A .Psychology& Educ.; Ex- Pres. Raksha; counselling, public speaking
17.	Raj Razdan	M.Sc. Bio. & Geology; Ex-chairperson IACA; Exec. Dir. Sr Citizen's programme
18.	Dr. Sujatha Reddy	Psychiatrist; organises health fairs; Bd. Hindu temple of Atlanta
19.	Kalpana Rengarajan	Ph.D.fFrom India; working in Opthalmology Dept. at Emory Univ.
20.	Ameta Seth	Worked in a Bank in India, accounting exp.; M.A. Eco., Asso degree in accounting
21.	Madhavi Sethna	MBA-IIMA; MA-Columbia; MS-Clarkson; Faculty in IT; Ed. Din progress
22.	Dr. Paddy Shanna	President, IACA and in small business
23.	Preeti Sharma	Business
24.	Dr. Puma Sharma	Radiologist; breast imaging and image-guided breast intervention
25.	Shashi Sidhaye	Librarian
26.	Manju Tiwari	Hindi professor at Emory University
27.	Rani Varanasi	Retiree, worked for AT&T/Lucent
28.	Girija Vijay	Retiree; medical librarian; social activist; philanthropist
29.	Parveen Yusufji	Teacher; office &business manager in medical office

Workshop on Women's Issues (Baton Rouge)

March 4, 2004

Baton Rouge, Louisiana

Executive Summary

I. Context

The workshop titled 'Women's Issues: A Diaspora Perspective' is a part of an ongoing series of projects undertaken by the office of Ambassador-at-Large to accomplish its vision to network and study the issues concerning Indian diaspora. The workshops already undertaken by this office include 'Enhancing India's Image in the Western Media', 'Indo-Caribbean Leader's Forum', 'Indo-American Youth/Students: Their Contributions & Concerns', 'Meeting of the Inter-Religious Leaders', 'Improving the Quality of Financial services aimed at NRIs & PIOs', etc. The first workshop on women's issues was organised on February 1, 2004 in New York followed by another one in Atlanta on February 7, 2004.

II. Themes Discussed

The workshop's objective was to study the following:

1. Challenges and & Problems, if any, Faced by Indo-American women: Their Perspective &Experiences in American Society.
2. How Indo-American women can be Instrumental in Helping India Preserve Indian Value System in America and Guide the New Generation.
3. The Role Indo-American Women can Play in Educating Americans about India & Indian Heritage.

III. Participants

A representative group of leading women academicians, doctors, social workers, media professionals, etc. in the south-east region participated in the workshop. The workshop has put forward suggestions, recommendations and an action plan which are included in this report.

IV. Key Recommendations

1. Learn the laws of the land, both in America and India.
2. Be more involved in community service projects and the

political system of America.

3. Promote more organisations for Indo-American senior citizens in the metropolitan areas in the US.
4. Create awareness about India, its culture, clothes, festivals and diversity in community and schools.
5. Overcome isolation and unfamiliarity.
6. Take children to India often and help them connect with their roots through travel and visits to their extended families.

V. Next Steps

1. Last such workshop is scheduled in San Francisco on April 16, 2004 followed by a national conference on May 22, 2004 in University of Hartford, Connecticut to discuss the concerns that emerged during the series of workshops and formulate a course of action to address them.

Highlights of the Workshop

Introduction

The workshop titled 'Women's Issues: A Diaspora Perspective' in Baton Rouge, Louisiana was chaired by the Ambassador-at-Large for NRIs and PIOs Dr. Bhisma K. Agnihotri on March 4, 2004. This workshop was a continuation of the office of Ambassador-at-Large to accomplish its vision to network, study the issues, highlight the common needs, concerns and recommendations of the Indo-American diaspora women and to relay the same to policy makers in India for further action. The workshop was attended by 50 representatives of various women's organisations, community leaders, academicians, professionals and students from the north-east region of the United States.

The project involving the Indo-American women and as part of the preliminary workshop aimed at identifying and trying to address the challenges faced by women and their contributions to society and was developed around three themes of 'The Challenges &Problems, if any, Faced by Indo-American Women: Their Perspective and Experiences in American Society'; 'How Indo-American Women can be Instrumental in Helping India Preserve Indian Value System in America and Guide the New Generation' and 'The Role Indo-American Women can Play in Educating Americans about India and Indian Heritage'.

Initiating the meeting, Dr. Agnihotri, Ambassador-at-Large

highlighted the details of various projects developed and being undertaken by his office covering different segments of the diaspora and which have resulted in formulation of study papers, proposals and recommendations on various issues, including the concerns of the Indo-American student/youth, enhancing the image of India in the Western media, complaints and grievances of the diaspora, Indo-Caribbean community leadership and inter-religion and inter-faith issues, etc. He added that these projects resulted in crystallisation of perspectives and issues concerning the diaspora and helped in articulating these to policy makers in India for further consideration and implementation.

Theme 1: Challenges & Problems, if any, Faced by Indo-American Women: Their Perspectives & Experiences in American Society

The discussion leaders were Dr. Sharda Kumar, Mrs. Madhu Shah and Mrs. Jyoti Shah.

Highlights

Dr. Sharda Kumar spoke about challenges faced by Indo-American women due to their differences, such as that of skin colour, dress, accent, etc.; discrimination against Indo-American women from mainstream America, including dominant minority groups; the challenges faced at home, such as good parenting and informing future generations about Indian culture and values; and finally about the need for the Indo-American community to address these issues by investing in organisations that specifically cater to the needs of the young Indo-American generation and the senior citizens community.

Mrs. Madhu Beriwal discussed the challenges Indo-American women faced in the workplace due to glass ceilings and at home due to a lack of economic independence, for those who are homemakers. She felt that Indo-American women should accept challenges head on and work towards solutions. Involvement within the local community and the need to explain Indian culture in simple terms to non-Indians was another point that was made.

Ms Jyoti Shah expounded on the challenges faced by Indo-American women due to the various responsibilities towards family, work, children and parents. Several participants also spoke about their own experiences while facing the above-mentioned challenges.

Theme 2: How Indo-American Women can be Instrumental in Helping India Preserve Indian Value System in America and Guide the New Generation

The discussion leaders were Dr. Vinita Hingorani and Dr. Mary Joseph.

Highlights

Dr. Hingorani said that Indian culture and values were a part of the reason that the first-generation Indo-Americans were successful and appreciated in America and these values needed to be passed on to the future generations. This task requires Indo-American women to preserve Indian culture at home, participate in temples or cultural centres and to educate the local community about India and its culture. Such steps would help the younger generation know more about their Indian roots as well as instil pride in them about the same.

Seemingly simple things, such as speaking in one's mother tongue at home or cooking Indian food will help. Sunday schools that may impart education about language, religion, history, music, dance, etc. also need to be encouraged.

Indo-American women also need to actively engage within the local community through voluntary work and the schools of their children to bring the diversity of India to the American mainstream.

Mrs. Mary Joseph spoke about the need to respect and take care of the elderly and the importance of extended families. She also felt that Indo-American women should save symbolic things that help identify them distinctly, such as the sari and dot (*bindi*) from becoming extinct. Concern was expressed at the rate at which culture in India was becoming 'Western' as well, for example, in clothing habits.

Theme 3: The Role Indo-American Women can Play in Educating Americans about India and Indian Heritage

The discussion leaders were Mrs. Naumi Kak and Mrs. Sumir Chel.

Highlights

Mrs. Chel felt that Indo-American women needed to identity some of the major reasons that in the past had been a problem in letting the Indo-Americans play a role in educating Americans about India and Indian heritage. So to address this context, it was necessary to assess the 'real situation on the ground'.

There is a need for Indo-American women to engage with the mainstream at various levels, increase knowledge and appreciation about both Indian as well as American values and also know enough about India to be able to correctly educate Americans about it. A list of seven recommendations was generated which includes among other things, educating Americans about India's spiritual heritage, educate the media and invite coverage, make cultural presentations and promote the concept of 'visit-India'.

Each topic generated considerable discussion and many suggestions were made.

Theme 1: Challenges & Problems, if any, Faced by Indo-American Women: Their Perspective & Experiences in American Society

Reports submitted by: Dr. Sharda Kumar, MD and Mrs. Madhu Beriwat and Mrs. Jyoti Shah, Discussion leaders

Report by Dr. Sharda Kumar

1. Challenges and Problems due to their Differences

The Indo-American women look different, act different and speak with different accents as compared to other Americans. The younger women, who are coming to the USA from India in the recent years, are facing almost the same problems as those by the early immigrants. New Indo-American immigrants, not being completely accepted in the American society because of their unusual accent, looks and way of living, become very frustrated at times. The new generations of Indians, who are born and raised here, seem to be compatible with the American lifestyle. Nonetheless, they, with perfect American accents and partially isolated from Indian heritage, are still recognised as part of a minority (Asian-Indian) group rather than the mainstream American society. In other words, some of us who may have lost our cultural identity as Indians just to become Americans are still treated as Indians, not as Americans. Such being the case, our youngsters should be taught to be proud of their Indian heritage and cultivate the Indian values while learning about the American way of life. Indo-American children should realise and appreciate that different kinds of boats and ships can and do sail in the same ocean. They must not lose their character as Indian-Americans.

2. Discrimination in Varied Forms

We came to America dreaming of the New World as the land of opportunity, but we quickly experienced the reality that it is a land of discrimination as well. We experience this at workplace, restaurants, hospitals, hotels, highways and elsewhere. The irony is that we are neither counted in the minority nor the majority. The black and the white tend to discriminate against us the same way. While the American society is changing, discrimination exists in varied subtle forms to which we fall victim and suffer. We, as professionals, have to work harder than our American counterparts.

3. Family Problems

As professionals or non-professionals, most of us go to work and when we return home, we have another full-time job to do at the household because help is not available, as in India. Childrearing is a real challenge. Most of us have to keep our children at day-care centres where the kids cannot learn the Indian values. Adolescents and teenagers present formidable problems for the Indian-American parents. We, the Indo-American mothers, have to struggle very hard to shape the character of children while protecting them against the negative influences of mainstream society.

4. Recent Trends

The American dollars are flowing into India to sustain religious groups, temples, churches, *ashrams*, hospitals and other numerous institutions, but, we hesitate to dedicate funds for similar projects in America. We directly need to establish and run organisations in the US for the proper growth and cultural education of our children, *ashrams* and shelters for the Indo-Americans in need or distress, and retirement centres for our aging population. We also need to have some NRI centres in different parts of India where we can feel at home and are not exploited.

Additional valuable suggestions from the workshop participants

1. Learn the laws of the land, both in America and India.
2. Be more involved in community service projects and the political system of America.
3. Communicate to help each other.
4. Older generations should get involved with younger

generations, whether they are newcomers or grownups here.

5. Facilitate educational group trips for the younger generation of Indo-Americans to India.
6. The office of the Ambassador-at-Large should provide aid to take care of properties of Indo-Americans in India.
7. Adopt measures to assist parents who come here.

Report by Mrs. Madho Beriwal

Imagine that you are on a balance beam, not just walking but trying to jump. Also, imagine that there is a glass ceiling above you –if you jump too high, you will hit it. There is no net below you to break your fall if you slip. The team standing to the side is often not supportive. These are some of the challenges that Indo-American women may face in sharper focus.

They must maintain a balance between work and home and there is a glass ceiling limiting upward movement. For women that do not work, there is the additional problem of lacking a safety net. If they are widowed or divorced, or if they are faced with a catastrophic illness, their ability to survive economically is in jeopardy. If they don't work, they lack an economic net – one that can support them and their children. Also, often they do not have the support of other women. Women tend to polarise themselves into the 'working mothers' and the 'stay at home moms' and, regardless of which label we fall under, we tend to create stereotypical responses against the other.

These challenges, however, are the same for most women. As first-generation Indo-American women, some of these challenges are in sharper focus. The difference is one of magnitude.

2. Founder-president and CEO of IEM, Ms Madhu Beriwal is an emergency management expert with over 17 years of experience, managing high-technology research activities. With a background in urban planning and transportation engineering, Ms. Beriwal is a recognised expert in evacuation modelling. She received a Special Merit Award from the Louisiana Emergency Preparedness Association for "her outstanding contribution to the civil defence agencies of southeast Louisiana in the development of Hurricane Survival Piao." A gifted speaker, who has written numerous articles, Ms. Beriwal was also named a regional finalist for national 1999 Working Women Entrepreneurial Excellence Awards.

There are challenges and problems, but we are shaped by how we cope with and handle our challenges and problems. The first and most important issue, in my experience, is to not allow the problems to become a crunch. Each of us has a challenge to overcome. A little story from my own experience illustrates this. I often work with military people. One of them mentioned one day: "When I brief, people assume that I know what I am talking about, but I do not care. When you brief, people think you care but do not know." He had to show he cared; a woman has to show she knows. We all have our own personal challenges and we need to work hard to overcome them without blaming our ethnicity, others' perceived reactions to us, or our gender.

Another important factor is to find connecting experiences with others. It is harder when you do not have the formative high school-college experiences, sports analogies and other background to form a bond. But, it is often surprising to find the connecting links, if you look for these links. People respond to things that interest them. Working at finding these common interests is useful.

One of their interests may be a better understanding of your background and ethnicity. Indians have a love of complexity, but when asked about our background, we need to simplify, simplify, simplify. People are busy and distracted; information needs to be in bite-size chunks. It is useful to develop a set of simple statements to explain the common items that people ask about.

Finally, women need to have some control over their own destiny. We cannot allow ourselves to be wholly dependent on others for economic support. It would be prudent to take risks when the sun is shining, rather than be forced to take risks during great urgency, during a storm.

Report by Ms Jyoti Shah

Introduction

The Indo-American women feel that they are sort of a 'sandwich generation' because of multiple burdens of caring for their own family, maintaining a career in their chosen profession, and caring for their elderly parents and/or in-laws either in the US or in India. If the latter, then the burden becomes overwhelming.

Several participants gave personal examples of their own experiences in managing the emotional and financial needs of their loved ones, and the toll it takes on them (emotional and financial) and their families in meeting their obligations.

Suggestions

1. Promote more organisations for Indian senior citizens in metropolitan areas in the US.
2. Ms Jyoti Shah is a community leader
3. These organisations, if encouraged to be managed by senior members, can provide the needed social, cultural and emotional stimulation to cope with the problem of loneliness in old age. This in turn would also minimise some of the responsibilities faced by the 'sandwich generation'.

Theme2: How Indo-American Women can be Instrumental in Helping India Preserve the Indian Value System in America by Guiding the New Generation

Report Submitted by Dr. Vineeta Hingorani, Dr. Mary Joseph - discussion leaders

Report by Dr. Vineeta Hingorani

Introduction

The Indo-American community is recognised as one of the influential ethnic communities in the United States and is often referred to as a model community as per the Report of the High Level Committee on the Indian diaspora. The first-generation immigrants are appreciated for being successful by working hard and for being able to adapt to the local conditions. We are able to do this because of the values that we learnt when we were growing up in India.

We have to work even harder in order to instil the same values in the second-generation immigrants, our children. It was easy for us because we were exposed to the culture, traditions and religion as it was all around us. We just imbibed all of it in, without having to make a special effort. We can inculcate these values by following the same pattern.

1. Give children the best education that is possible. Along with academics, they also need to have other talents in order to succeed, such as music, art, etc.

But in order to be successful, be appreciated and be content in a society of people with white skin, they need more than just education and skills. They need to know who they are and where they come from.

At Home

2. Try to speak your mother tongue.
3. Cook Indian food.
4. Wear Indian clothes for festivals and get-togethers.
5. Watch some good shows on the Indian TV channels.
6. Visit India at least once every two years and keep in touch with extended families.
7. Let them know that it is important to respect their elders and take care of them in their old age.

At Temples or Cultural Centres

8. The kids should go to Sunday schools like BalVihar where they learn about their religion, Indian history, Indian music, Indian dance, etc.
9. Learn Hindi, our national language.

In the Community, such as the Kid's School

10. Create awareness about India, its culture, clothes, festivals and diversity.

The emotional insecurity and stresses caused by an alien environment play an important role in the psychological make-up of Indian-Americans. Having a religious and cultural centre is one way of affirming our proud cultural heritage and roots.

Recommendations & Suggestions

1. Show good Indian movies to kids. Also let them see *Ramayana* and *Mahabharata* series. Play *bhajans* and Indian music.
2. Read books by Indian authors.
3. Roots are important.
4. Teach them to respect their elders.
5. Take them to India often and let them know the extended families.

Report by Mrs. Mary Joseph

Introduction

Challenges and problems facing Indian women, in many ways are the same as those faced by all new immigrants to this country. The problems may be understood in the light of a term coined by the great African American sociologist and thinker, W.E.B. Dubois to identify the condition of the African- American in this country. Dubois appropriately characterised the ambivalence of the African-American as 'double consciousness'– two ways of looking at oneself – as an American and as a Negro. 'Always looking at oneself through the eyes of others' is another way Dubois defined double consciousness. For people of Indian origin, it is two ways of looking at themselves, as Americans and as Indians.

Preserving Indian Value System

'Easier said than done' would be my first reaction. Then I realise that preserving our traditional values in India is getting increasingly difficult. The break-up of the extended family system and the large-scale migration to the cities and overall urbanisation have made preserving our old world values in India a challenge. I consider respect and concern for elders and hospitality to be the hallmarks of our value system. In the extended family system, taking care of the elderly was almost an automatic process. Without looking at official statistics, I would say that at present, the number of nuclear families far outnumber the number of extended families, making the care of the elderly very difficult. Many of the care-giving generation, living in cramped quarters in urban areas, often without the help of servants, find taking care of the elderly a challenging and taxing job, if not a downright impossible one. Many of us are trying to take care of our parents in this country and the problems are multiplied several times here. Even when proper care is given by family members, the elderly face severe emotional problems because of isolation from their peers.

In this country, two things that help identify an Indian woman are the sari and the dot on the forehead. In recent years, two famous women gave high international visibility to the sari – Indira Gandhi and Mother Teresa. The sari now appears to be almost headed toward extinction. Young people coming of age in India these days are Westernised in their clothing. Even older people are giving into convenience dressing. For example, until recently, Kerala women were noted for their unique white apparel. These days, a modified version of the nightgown has taken over. Women, even older women, and even in the villages, have discovered the comfort of wearing full length cotton kaftan for the house. The change in clothing style, when it came to India, came very fast. In Western countries, the evolution from the hoop skirts and other full-length dresses to the modem, especially uni-sex kind of dressing, took much longer.

Recommendations

1. Encourage our younger generations to maintain their ties with the peers of Indian origin, without isolating themselves from the mainstream. Maintain these value systems in our homes, and most of all, practice them in our lives.
2. Encourage socialising with mainstream America. A mistake many of the Asian-Americans, including the Indians, make, is in regard to social life. We often tend to socialise almost exclusively among ourselves. Our work ethic allows most of us to make rapid advances in the workplace, but to our colleagues, we are often a mystery. Inviting them to our homes and to our celebrations and letting them freely observe us in our own surroundings, will help increase understanding. This, in turn, will help our young people to see that it is possible to have the best of both worlds.
3. Provide help to women of Indian origin to get assimilated into the mainstream without losing their cultural identity and encourage them to give back to the community by getting involved and through volunteerism. This will influence Americans in general to take us and our values more seriously.
4. Encourage the wearing of our native clothes.

Theme 3: Role Indo-American Women can Play in Educating Americans about India and Indian Heritage

Report submitted by Mrs. Sumir Chehl

Introduction

The discussion was interesting and women were quite vocal about the subject. There seemed to be a common consent that in order to educate Americans about India and the Indian heritage, it must be acknowledged:

- The first generation Indian immigrants, in general, keep themselves isolated from the mainstream America. There is a need for improved involvement in the social and political arena.
- There are adverse experiences, personal misconceptions and consequent fears and apprehensions which keep Indians from mingling with the mainstream.

- To teach the American about the India and Indian heritage, American interest must be drawn.
- Indians need to be educated about the American and American heritage to be able to converse, compare and contrast with understanding and promote familiarity and thereby the exchange of goodwill.
- Education is necessary for the Indians to realise that each one represents many Indians within India. India is a vast country with a rich and diverse heritage. There are cultures within a culture. There is a multiplicity of religious beliefs and practices. There are many languages and dialects and multitude of festivals and traditions, regional cuisines and colourful costumes and attires. Indians need to understand a broader India to be able to represent and promote India and Indian heritage.
- Indians in America, have much to be proud of. Indians have an image of educated, professional, progressive businessmen and women, hardworking, dependable and honest people. They need to protect that image and use that advantage to promote the root principles. Arrogance, petty tricks and manipulative behaviour, stereotype and damage the image. Progressive and high-profile affluent image generates jealousy.

A few suggestions and recommendations are given below to help promote India and the Indian heritage in America.

Suggestions and Recommendations

1. Break barriers: Identify Reasons for Isolation

Experiences, conceptions and misconceptions

Fears, apprehensions, etc.

2. Overcome Isolation and Unfamiliarity; Know to be Known

- Education and awareness are the strongest tools to break the barriers of ignorance. And, learning and teaching go hand in hand. Create a multifaceted, bilateral familiarity.
- Know America and the American counterpart. Learn about the history, geography, heritage, culture, arts, religion, racial diversity, racial history, racism. Similarly, know India and the Indian: India has cultures within a culture, diverse yet intermingled and co-mingling. Learn and understand the

Indian diversity in history, geography, heritage, culture, arts, religion, racial diversity, caste system, etc.

3. **Have Pride in Indian Heritage and have a High Cultural Esteem and Self-esteem**

   Indians are highly educated, professionals, progressive businessmen and women, hardworking, dependable, honest and more. Use this advantageous image of the Indian face to promote India and Indian heritage.

4. **Present and Represent the Rich and Diverse Cultural and Spiritual Heritage**

   Represent diverse India in all walks of the daily American life. Use the appearance, attire, accent, etc. to complement Indianness and invite enquiry.

5. **Contribute to the Community and Society**

   Give and take, in that order, both services and money. Be ambassadors of goodwill, participate and interact; be educated and educate!

- Understand similarities and differences, caste system, races and the racism, social, cultural and religious diversity; create a cultural and political awareness; show civic involvement in various civic organisations, volunteer services, neighbourhood clubs, auxiliaries of schools, hospitals and nursing homes, attend political events at neighbourhood, city, state and national level.

6. **Express and Expose, Create Awareness**

   Get involved, be visible and speak up and invite media coverage. Presentations be made of cuisine, fine arts and performing arts, religion, way of life. Visit schools, join social clubs, religious and civic organisations. Invite non-Indians, political and civic leaders to your special events or stage special events for them.

7. **Promote 'Visit-India'**

   India is the largest democracy; it is among the oldest civilisations of the world and offers unique ancient architectural treasures, powerful spiritual and cultural experience. Invite your friends to visit your family.

Participant List

1. Mrs. Neela Adhvaryu
2. Mrs. Anju Ahuja
3. Mrs. Suneeta Ahuja
4. Mrs. Meena Ajmera
5. Mrs. Vasundhara Arimilli
6. Mrs. Sunitha Bachireddy
7. Mrs. Madhu Beriwal
8. Mrs. Sharmishta Brahmbhatt
9. Mrs. Urmila Choksi
10. Mrs Bhavna Desai
11. Dr. Prem Mohan Sharma
12. Mrs. Sadhana Gera
13. Mrs. Nirmla Gopu
14. Mrs. Sunita Gupta
15. Mrs. Swaraj Gupta
16. Dr. Vinita Hingorani
17. Mrs. Mala Jain
18. Mrs. Simi Jaisinghani
19. Mrs. Anita Jhunjhunwala
20. Mrs. Raj Jindal
21. Mrs. Priti Juneja
22. Mrs. Nawni Kak
23. Mrs. Uma Kikkeri
24. Mrs. Veena Kumar
25. Mrs. Sangeeta Mathur
26. Mrs. Rekha Parikh
27. Mrs. Radha Ramachandran
28. Mrs. Sudha Rawal
29. Mrs. Upendra Reddy
30. Mrs. Jhama Sengupta
31. Mrs. Jyoti Shah
32. Mrs. Sandhya Shah
33. Mrs. Jyotsana Shah
34. Mrs. Asha Sharma
35. Mrs. Shandan Sharma
36. Mrs. Anita Singh
37. Mrs. Aruna Sura
38. Mrs. Sudha Vaidyanathan
39. Mrs. Nirmala Verma
40. Mrs. Ila Vora
41. Mrs. Ela Patel
42. Mrs. Nisha Valsaraj
43. Mrs. Geeta Modha
44. Mrs. Renu Seth
45. Dr. Mary Joseph
46. Mrs. Meena Sachdeva
47. Mrs. Madhu Shah Beriwal
48. Dr. Sharda Kumar
49. Mrs. Sumir Chel
50. Mrs. Jyoti Vora
51. Mrs. Naz Jafri
52. Mrs. Manjari Patel
53. Mrs. Pinki Diwan
54. Prof. Krishna Agnihotri
55. Mrs. Sahil Chehl
56. Mrs. Janaki Vaidyanathan
57. Mrs. Aruna Mordgil
58. Mrs. Lakshi Joshi
59. Mrs. Ved Diwan
60. Mrs. Darshan Kherry
61. Mrs. Monica Kherry

Workshop on Women's Issues (NEW YORK)

February 1, 2004
New York

Executive Summary

I. Context

The workshop titled 'Women's Issues: A Diaspora Perspective' is part of an ongoing series of projects undertaken by the office of Ambassador-at-Large to accomplish its vision to network and study the issues concerning Indian diaspora. The workshops already undertaken by this office include 'Enhancing India's Image in the Western Media', 'Indo-Caribbean Leader's Forum', 'Indo-American Youth/Students: Their Contributions & Concerns', 'Meeting of the Inter-Religious Leaders', 'Improving the Quality of Financial services aimed at NRIs & PIOs', etc.

We think it is important that Indo-American women in the professions and as homemakers should discuss women's issues for a better understanding and meaningful guidance to the women's section of the diaspora. This workshop is an effort by women to highlight these common concerns as immigrants.

II. Themes Discussed:

The workshop's objective was to study the following:

1. Challenges & Problems, if any, Faced by Indo-American Women: Their Perspective &Experiences in American Society.
2. How Indo-American Women can be Instrumental in Helping India Preserve Indian Value System in America and Guide the New Generation.
3. Role Indo-American Women can Play in Educating Americans about India and Indian Heritage.

III. Participants

Representative group of leading women academicians, doctors, social workers, media professionals, etc. in the north-east region participated in the workshop. The workshop put forward suggestions, recommendations and action plan for addressing concerns of national agenda which are included in this report.

IV. Key Recommendations

1. To start daycare and/or baby-sitting centres for Indian families with Indian environment by involving senior citizens and women coming on H4 visa status.
2. Sunday schools for children to teach Indian languages, arts and cultural heritage by involving community people through funds coming from within the community. The Government of India, embassies, consulates and the office of Ambassador-at-Large can be instrumental in generating funds for such efforts.
3. The Indian government must improve its public relations efforts in America, as a better image of India will not only benefit India but also the Indo-American women.
4. Indo-American community can remain connected with the mainstream in America and provide support for cultural diversity through outreach in schools, by acting as guest speakers, resource persons,, etc. Indian culture can also be brought to schools through cultural shows about Indian music and dance.
5. Indo-American women can also lobby for the inclusion of Indian languages within the American school curriculum, especially where the Indian community is in significant numbers.
6. To use the Indian media (papers and lease time programmes on the cable channels and radio programmes) for the portrayal of correct image of Indian civilisation.
7. To make an effort to correct any wrong depiction about the status of Indian women in India. The best defence would be a good offence.

V. Next Steps

I. Similar meetings/workshops are scheduled at Atlanta and Louisiana in the months of February and March, 2004. A national conference is being scheduled later this year.

2. To involve young professionals, both male and female as next generation, will be raised by both the parents.

Programme Schedule

- Welcome- AmbassadorBhishma K. Agnihotri
- Introductions
- Discussion on the following issues:

Theme 1: Challenges & Problems, if any, Faced by Indo-American Women: Their Perspective &Experiences in American Society. Discussion leaders: Dr. Bharti A. Palkhiwalaand Mrs. Uma Shah

Theme 2: How Indo-American Women can be Instrumental in helping India Preserve Indian Value System in America and Guide the New Generation. Discussion leader: Dr. Anjana Sandhir

Theme 3: Role Indo-American Women can Play in Educating Americans about India and Indian Heritage. Discussion leader: Dr. Kamlesh Kapur

- Suggestions & Recommendations
- Summation - Prof. Krishna Agnihotri
- Closing: Ambassador B.K. Agnihotri

Highlights of the Workshop

Introduction

The office of the Ambassador-at-Large for Non-Resident Indians and Persons of Indian Origin, as part of its ongoing project activities involving various segments of the Indian diaspora, organised a workshop on 'Women's Issues: A Diaspora Perspective' on February 1, 2004 at the Shaan Restaurant in New York City. The workshop was attended by 75 representatives of various women's organisations, community leaders, academicians, professionals and students from the north-east region of the United States. The Workshop was chaired by Dr. B.K. Agnihotri, Ambassador-at-Large for NRIs and PIOs.

The project involving the Indo-American women and as part of the preliminary workshop, aimed at identifying and trying to address the challenges faced by women and their contributions to society, was developed around three themes – 'The Challenges &Problems, if any, Faced by Indo-American Women: Their Perspective and Experiences in American Society'; 'How Indo-American Women can be Instrumental in Helping India Preserve Indian Value System in America and Guide the New Generation' and 'The Role Indo-American Women can Play in Educating Americans about India and Indian Heritage'.

Initiating the meeting, Dr. Agnihotri, Ambassador-at-Large highlighted the details of various projects developed and being undertaken by his office covering different segments of the diaspora and which have resulted in formulation of study papers, proposals and recommendations on various issues, including the concerns of the Indo-American students/youth, enhancing the image of India in the Western media, complaints and grievances of the diaspora, Indo-Caribbean community leadership and inter-religion and inter-faith issues, etc. He added that these projects resulted in crystallisation of perspectives and issues concerning the diaspora and helped in articulating these to policy makers in India for further consideration and implementation.

Theme 1: Challenges & Problems, if any, Faced by Indo-American Women: Their Perspectives & Experiences in American Society

Introduction

The first theme was presented by Dr. Bharti A Palkhiwala and Mrs. Uma Shah. Dr. Palkhiwala approached the topic by outlining the challenges faced by Indo-American women at different times as part of the immigrant experiences of the community. She felt that the early Indo-American immigrants, particularly women, had various challenges of living with emotional isolation due to an immediate lack of family and friends while trying to assimilate into the mainstream and its various institutions, such as colleges and the corporate workforce.

Highlights

- Many of the Indo-American women who came to the US during the early 1960s to the late 1970s were educated professionals. However, their adjustments to a new environment and society in America was an uphill task. There were the obvious adjustment issues of language and economic stability; additionally, Indo-American women had to assimilate and adjust culturally into the workforce. Such adjustments led to identity crises at different levels.
- Mrs. Uma Shah added to what was said by reviewing the challenges of the Indo-American women who came to the US

from the early 1980s to the present. Many of these women were IT professionals, students and family members of early immigrants. Mrs. Shah felt they had some advantages vis-a-vis the Indo-American immigrants of earlier decades. These included certain clear advantages associated with globalisation. Comparatively, they have had more exposure to Western culture and society; also there is the advantage of the Indian educational system today, which better prepares them with the necessary tools to succeed in America.

- Support structure for Ind--American women, i.e. women organisations, community organisations, the Government of India, etc. have developed dramatically over the last 40-50 years. The increased number of organisations as well as the highly motivated and achievement-oriented Indo-American community do provide certain assistance for Indo-American women.
- However it was observed that improvements in two areas are needed – first, there is a need for the different Indo-American women organisations to develop networking and co-operating with each other. Avoiding re-inventing the wheel will free the resources for use to serve the community more effectively. Second, awareness must be developed about the different services provided by the Indo-American women organisations to enable the community to reach out and take advantage of them.

Follow-up Discussion and Interactive Issues

- Follow-up discussions on the presentations made by the discussion leaders, a session of comments and discourses followed. The participants articulated various challenges in further detail and some recommendations were also made. Some of the important ones are detailed in this report.
- The challenges of Indo-American women at the workplace are not limited to cultural adjustments, but extend to issues of promotions and glass ceilings. They feel as though they are faced with the double jeopardy. They are faced with the

challenges associated with womanhood but also by being Indo-American women, the challenges are greater.

- Indo-American women also have to balance their time between the workforce and caring for the family and children, which is expected of them as part of their traditional role in society. Here again their challenges are greater than their fellow-women. Not only do they have to care for their children and spouses with basics, such as education and food, but they have an added responsibility of maintaining and passing on the cultural values to the next generation.
- Many participants felt that the stereotypical images of India impacts mainstream personal and professional relationships negatively and therefore, more efforts are required at creating awareness about India and its culture. The participants felt that the racial and religious discrimination they faced stemmed from ignorance about India and Indo-Americans among the mainstream.
- The lack of participation and presence in the civic and political arena are other challenges that need to be overcome to make a difference. As such, long-term investment, nevertheless volunteering at the local PTAs and libraries, was considered indispensable by those present.
- Not all of the Indo-American women are professionals. Indo-American women, in some instances, also have to deal with domestic violence and substance abuse within the family. There is the need to provide non-professionals with assistance on pertinent issues, such as poverty and language. Information about the educational system, healthcare system, family welfare system, the legal system, the social service system, etc. in the US will be of use and appropriate application to many of the Indo-American women.
- A section of the Indo-American women face challenges that are yet different. These are the children of the early immigrants, who in some instances have missed out on the opportunities of connecting to their Indian roots in the initial struggles

of assimilation. There is a need to network the second- and third-generation Indo-American women in order to identify and provide them with the opportunities and support that they may have missed, but is since available.

- In some instances, Indo-American women or their family members are part of mixed marriages. In such cases, the challenge is to reconcile the identity of themselves and the children involved and also create a proper understanding among the families involved. So the Indo-American women do not have to shy away from introducing Indian cultural heritage within their families.
- However, most Indo-American women, regardless of mixed marriages, identified their biggest challenge in instilling Indian values in their children growing up in America.
- The generational gap seems to be widening as more and more Indo-American youth grow disconnected from their older generations of parents and grand-parents. The need to reconcile identities poses another challenge of maintaining the religious identity of the children of Indo-American women as well.
- As working women, Indo-American women have less time to spend with their children, which can at times lead to emotional stress and developing guilt for both, the mother and the child.
- A unique and growing problem discussed was the untapped potential of the dependent Indo-American women who cannot work in America for money. In many instances, they happen to be professionals and their careers have to suffer as a result of American laws. While there was a desire among the participants to engage this section of women in community activities, they also hoped that the Government of India and office of the Ambassador-at-Large could assist in pushing for a change.
- Innovative ideas are required to deal with this and other challenges faced by the Indo-American women.

Theme 2: How Indo-American Women can be Instrumental in Helping India Preserve Indian Value System in America and Guide the New Generation

Introduction

Indo-American women have a role to play in helping India and in preserving the Indian value system in America. How can the Indo-American women accomplish this? How can the Indo-American women help in guiding the new generation? Dr. Anjana Sandhir led this discussion by stressing on the need to take pride in the Indian cultural traditions, including language and celebrating and sharing Indian diversity with the American mainstream.

Highlights

- The participants felt that it was very important to maintain our linguistic heritage and that our younger generation was capable of being multi-lingual. The Indo-American women present at the workshop felt that they should take the lead to ensure that Indian languages are spoken within the families and passed on to future generations.
- It was important not just to ensure that the younger Indo-Americans learned the languages of their ancestors but also maintained connectivity to India and felt more at home when they visited India.
- The participants also believed that along with Indian languages, Indo-Americans should take pride in their ethnic attire. American co-workers, neighbours, etc. are more open today than they were before to diversity and would welcome a greater pride in such cultural traits. Indo-American women should feel comfortable with Indian attire in American society. Such comfort would come with a greater understanding.
- Specifically on the question of Indian cultural and family values, they are an asset to the Indo-American community. Many prominent Americans have commended the Indian value system and the Indo-American women are the fountainheads of these values.

- Celebrating Indian festivals at home and also sharing their significance with fellow-Americans would be required to create a more appreciative and understanding environment.
- Inda-American parents should give their children Indian names as it would form part of their Indian identity.

Follow-up Discussion and Interactive Issues

- Some of the participants shared their experiences in celebrating Diwali at their workplace, significantly in colleges and schools.
- For this healthy exchange to take place it was considered important to realise that we are ethnically and culturally different.
- Even though Indian names oftentimes get distorted, compromising on the question would not help the problem. Because the issue is related to cultural pride as well as identity, it should not be compromised.
- There are a number of challenges here as well; some which have already been described, such as balancing the Indian and American identities.
- Additionally, there is a need to identify and counter resistance to multi-cultural diversity from segments of the system, to counter the negative images of the status of women in India and the Indo-American society, to identify the problems of Indo-American women and redraw the line between freedom and responsibilities.
- The Indo-Caribbean women pointed out their experiences and efforts to hold on to the Indian value system. Pundita Indrani recited a short poem about India for the participants as an expression of her pride on her heritage.
- Assistance in the form of information dissemination by Indian government offices, embassies and consulates as well as the office of the Ambassador-at-Large was deemed critical.
- The Ambassador briefly talked about his trip to the Caribbean and congratulated the Indo-Caribbean community on their success and commitment to India as well as the diaspora.

Theme 3: The Role Indo-American women can Play in Educating Americans about India and Indian Heritage

Introduction

The final theme taken up for discussion among the participants at the workshop was preceded by a slide show by Dr. Kamlesh Kapur. The presentation set the stage for an intense discussion on the third theme of the workshop that is cited above. Dr. Kapur felt that pride for Indian culture and values can stem through education. To that end, she proposed taking information about India to the schools and colleges in the form of presentations.

Highlights

- Dr. Kapur highlighted the fact that Indian religions and culture were being demonised/misrepresented in American schools and textbooks.
- The Indo-American community faces many negative stereotypes about things like *sati* and the caste system and other repercussions as a result.
- It was highlighted that information available within the community, especially among the second- and third-generation Indo-Americans about India and its heritage was limited.
- As a direct consequence, Indo-American generations may suffer from a lack of pride, self- confidence and shyness about their heritage.
- It was suggested to pick a few battles and focus by preparing lesson plans for different age groups.

Follow-up Discussion and Interactive Issues

- Dr. Kapur suggested that myths need to be separated from Indian history to provide the mainstream with an appropriate picture about India and its culture.
- During the discussion, it was pointed out that where textbooks are misrepresenting India, Indo-American women should actively approach authorities at educational institutions and the publishers of those books to correct their mistakes.
- Parallel efforts need to be made by the Indo-American

community to educate the younger generations about India and its heritage.

- Parents should also be sympathetic to the challenges of Indo-American children and communicate with them about their problems.
- The participants felt that young Indo-Americans should be encouraged to visit India more often as such trips would help them learn firsthand.
- Another issue of concern was managing the perceptions of the mainstream about India. On this topic, the participants felt that there was a need to stress the Indian identity, instead of accepting the 'South Asian' brand being imposed.
- The need to speak out against misrepresentation in the Western media about India in general and Indian and Indo-American women in particular, was also stressed.

Suggestions/Recommendations

To help realise the outlined objectives, the following suggestions were made:

1. Baby-sitting facilities with an Indian environment - senior citizen community as well as the dependent women who cannot work can be tapped into for equipping the coming generation with the needed cultural guidance as well as support they need to become successful.
2. Sunday schools for children to teach Indian languages, arts and cultural heritage were deemed as necessary. The participants hoped that the office of the Ambassador-at-Large and the Indian government would consider providing qualified teachers to meet this growing demand.
3. The Indo-American community should also look into setting up Indo-American community centres or India Centres. Such centres can serve as a central place for the community and cater to the needs of various sections of the society, including Indo-American women, children, senior citizens, etc. Courses on yoga and meditation in such centres would help maintain elements of Indian

cultural heritage being emulated the world over.

4. In order to strike a balance between corporate culture and an Indian home, it was suggested that Indo-American women should try to study the Jewish community model.
5. Indo-American community needs to work in harmony and with unity on the issues of the Indo-American women.
6. Indo-American women should get involved with the mainstream. Participation through volunteer work in the local communities would help generate goodwill and a better understanding for the community. In addition it would open up necessary doors for involvement in grassroots civic and political activities.
7. The participants felt that the Indian government must better its public relations efforts in America as a better image of India would benefit not only India, but also the Indo-American women.
8. There is a need to remain connected with the mainstream in America and provide support for cultural diversity through outreach in schools, by acting as guest speakers, resource persons, etc.
9. As concerned parents, it was believed that Indo-American women must care for the self-esteem of the Indo-American children in schools and fight for it aggressively where it was being compromised.
10. Indo-American women can also lobby for the inclusion of Indian languages within the school curriculum of America, especially where the community is in significant numbers.
11. Indian culture can also be brought to schools through cultural shows about Indian music and dance.
12. With regard to the contribution of Indo-American women to India, it was suggested that they help fight social ills, such as dowry and illiteracy among women in India.
13. Educating women and the rest of society being the key, it was recommended that Indo-American women proactively support projects in India which are working towards these goals.

14. In developing a strategy to combat the ignorance about the status of women in Indian society, some participants felt that the best defence would be a good offence.

Theme 1: Challenges & Problems, if any, Faced by Indo-American Women: Their Perspective & Experiences in American Society

Introduction

Coming to USA during the early years of 1960s and 1970s, the first-generation women faced the major challenges of assimilation and acculturation. There was a lack of family and social support system with a feeling of loneliness. They faced all the classic challenges faced by any new immigrant community.

Today, the immigrants coming to the US do not have the acculturation and assimilation problems of the same magnitude. Even before they migrate, they are more exposed to the Western lifestyle and are more prepared to assimilate without much of a cultural shock. The community has grown with large numbers living in close proximity with many Indian organisations catering to the community needs. Local awareness of Indian community and culture is better. Availability of Indian goods and services do ebb the pain of being away from home to some extent. Improved technology has made communication easier with family and friends back home.

1. Dr. Bharati Palkhiwala is a psychiatrist and has her practice in New Jersey.
2. Uma C. Shah is a financial planner, providing full range of financial services in New York, New Jersey, Connecticut and Pennsylvania.

The workshop focussed on the issues that are faced by Indian women, first-generation and the new immigrants alike. Specifically, the following concerns and issues emerged:

1. Indo-American women face double jeopardy at the workplace. Indo-American women in the mainstream workplace face double jeopardy of being a woman (a minority) as well as an Indian (a minority community). There still exists a glass ceiling in promotions and playing leading roles.

2. Challenges faced in trying to fit into the expectations of the American society and yet maintain the Indian heritage and values in the family. Women are equals at the workplace but not much has changed at home. Although tremendous progress has been made but there is still a need to teach Indian men about equality. There is a need for shared responsibilities of parenting and housework.
3. Challenges of child care while mother is a working woman. There is a tremendous need for daycare and baby-sitting facilities that are reliable and also impart Indian culture and values.
4. Challenges in maintaining the Indian heritage and values through the second- and third-generations. As the community grows and becomes more mature, maintaining our heritage and values is becoming a major challenge, especially so, as the younger generation does not have the advantage of being brought up in India.
5. Lack of full knowledge and familiarity with the laws of the land pertaining to healthcare, family welfare system, legal system, social security system, estate tax and estate preservation, etc. Majority of Indo-Americans are still not fully familiar with the laws of the land and the rights. This lack of knowledge is much more prevalent among women. Thus, when women are faced with problems, they often do not know how and where they can obtain help.
6. Lack of participation and presence in the civic and political arena. Although we have entered the workplace and have made our presence felt, we have stayed out of civic and political arena. We do not participate in school activities, like PTA, county or town councils, public libraries, sports, scout and such service organisations. These are crucial for guiding our younger generation in becoming more mainstream-oriented and yet maintain Indian heritage and values.
7. Indian presence is still fragmented and not unified.

We have formed Indian organisations, groups and support system along the lines of regions and languages of India and have not crossed over those boundaries yet. This fragmentation may be one of the causes of our lack of presence in the political and civic arena.Without forming and projecting a cohesive Indian image, retaining our younger generation in the Indian values and heritage will be difficult. This impacts the formation of a strong Indian-American identity amongst the second-generation and the third-generation Indians.

The discussion that brought out these concerns was very lively. Participants were very articulate and assertive about their viewpoints. Not only the concerns were expressed, but also the participants offered various recommendations for dealing with them.

Recommendations

1. Set up a support system to deal with workplace concerns. Educate women about their rights in the workplace. Find and teach ways of making the double jeopardy into a positive impact.
2. Can we start daycare/baby-sitting centres for Indian families? Can the women coming on H4 Visa status be utilised in such centres? Can they be compensated differently? Can we utilise the potential of senior citizens in such centres? With their experience such centres can become conduits to instil and maintain Indian values in our kids.
3. Need support group for the first-generation women to deal with issues and stress of dealing with two generations – we are the sandwich generation that deals with the expectations of the seniors and the demands of children.
4. Conduct seminars and workshops regarding healthcare, family welfare system, legal system, social security system, estate tax, estate preservation, etc. Some of these educational seminars and civic education can be done through the radio and TV media. Indian embassy and consulate can sponsor periodic workshops/seminars educating the women, in particular and the community, in general.
5. For a cohesive and positive image of being Indian to emerge, one of the most important factors is as to how an Indian is

presented and perceived in the media. In this regard the Indian government can do a lot. Sure there is an increased effort from the Indian government in this regard, but it is not enough. There should be more vocal, visual and loud protests every time India is misrepresented and misquoted. India should take a strong position in voicing its displeasure, which would give the support and confidence needed by the local Indian community to do the same.

6. Indian embassy and consulate should become centres of resources about India, its history and its culture. They can and should become the sources that one turns to when in need of information about India. They should be equipped with the right resources about India - books, audio and video presentations and speakers. They can also organise educational seminars, workshops about India, open to public and in the universities throughout America.
7. More Indians, especially women, should start taking an active part in schools and community events. The younger generations need to see the first- and second--generations retain their Indian identity and values while being active in the mainstream civic and political arena.

Theme2: How Indo-American Women can be Instrumental in Helping Preserve the Indian Value System in America by Guiding the New Generation

Report Submitted by Dr. Anjana Sandhir, discussion leader

Introduction

A women's workshop entitled 'Women's Issues: A Diaspora Perspective' was organised by the office of Ambassador-at-Large on February 1, 2004 in New York. The topic of discussion was as given above. As a discussion leader, I raised some issues and they were well supported by the participating women.

Issues & Recommendations

1. We must speak our language at home as the language is the carrier of our cultural values. To save our values, we have to talk in our mother tongue as it develops self-respect and self-confidence among

children. It is said by many language scholars that if a child knows one language fluently, he can easily learn another language. If the child knows the mother tongue, clarity of thoughts and confidence in performance is found in his behaviour. It is said that you think the best in the language which is your very own.

Our mother tongue may be Punjabi, Gujarati or Bengali but Hindi is our national language; hence it must be spoken in our homes and community gatherings. Hindi should be our common language. Working with other people, English can be used. This will develop self-respect and national pride too.

Suggestions

- Indian government must provide some help in this regard. Some well-trained teachers should come from India through help of the government for this purpose. These teachers must be trained to teach, not only Hindi, but Indian culture too.
- Not sufficient information of Indian culture/ history is given in the school textbooks and whatever is printed, is damaging our picture. We need to unite on this issue. We must try to supply correct information. There is a need to provide small books for schoolchildren that present the real picture of India and its cultural values. The people who are already working for this cause must be supported. Our government has done nothing in this regard.
- We must supply free books about India to the libraries.

2. Our children should have Indian names. Name is the first gift to the child by his parents and it is forever and it works as his identity. In childhood, they do not know much but as they grow, they try to find their roots– a great change is seen in their behaviour-hood, A child must know the meaning of his or her name to tell others and to pronounce it correctly. This will give him a great confidence.
3. Mother is the first guru of the child. A child learns what he or she sees at home. The responsibilities of women are more as they work both in and out and they work without domestic help. There is a need to help them, specially if there is domestic

violence, to solve the problem of babysitting as well as older people in the house as they need attention too.

4. Celebrate festivals at home. We must celebrate festivals like Diwali, Holi and others at home. Tell our children about Diwaliaknd why it is celebrated, what should be done on this day and invite children's friends and decorate the house with lights. We will have to keep on doing this at our homes. If we do not celebrate festivals at home, how would our children know about them? As a result of Diwali celebration every year at South Seaport, at least American people also come to know that Indians have a festival of lights called Diwali. This kind of celebration should be done at the personal level, at the school and volunteers should talk about it.
5. Wear your traditional dress, which is our identity too. In the name of assimilation, we have forgotten what we are. If it is possible, we all should wear our traditional dresses at work on festivals, if not everyday. We have to develop this in our mind that we are different. How can we cover the colour of our skin or hair? Just by wearing Western dresses we cannot change our faces. People respect and accept the people the way they live. There is no need to live with an inferiority complex. Dr. Sandhir cited her example by saying that she goes to her university in her traditional Indian dress, the *salvar-kameez* and so far nothing has happened.
6. Take your children to India every year or two. This creates a real bond between their relations. There should be some cultural exchange programme at government level.
7. Respect your motherland and the rich culture you belong to. The following suggestions were made:

(a) Some Indian people talk ill about India. We have to be very careful of these people and stop them strongly.

(b) A data bank and some awareness centres about India should be created so that correct information about India can be provided immediately if such a need arrives. Indian embassy should help and support such organisations.

(c) From time to time such workshops should be organised with other community people to tell them about India and Indian culture. We have to do this practically, with or without any help.

8. Cook Indian food at home. Sit and try to eat with your family members together. This is very important.
9. Spend at least half an hour to one hour with your children. Do not only buy toys for them but talk to them, share their feelings, answer their questions and do not always leave them with baby-sitters or with grand parents. They are your children and they need you and your time.
10. Narrate stories of your religious faiths to your children. Do not force them to follow what you want them to learn but just create an atmosphere at home. Watch *Ramayana* or *Mahabharata* or other TV serials together and tell them about our cultural heritage.

- It is suggested that more and more cultural-heritage-awareness programmes should be organised.
- Summer camps of short durations for children will be helpful to learn about their cultural values.
- More schools, like Ekal Vidhyalaya are needed.

Hence language, traditional dress, food and celebration of festivals bring the pride of cultural values slowly. We have to keep on doing this, even though it may seem like a long way.

Theme 3: Role Indo-American Women can Play in Educating Americans about India and Indian Heritage

Report submitted by Mrs. Kamlesh Kapur, discussion leader

Introduction

Several years back many students of Indian origin started dubbing themselves as ABCDs (American Born Confused Desis). In the past decade, many of the students have selected a label for themselves as South Asians and, many still are fighting with labelling their identities. The workshop served as a platform to focus on the issue of confusing identity of Indo-Americans, their self-perception and their perception by mainstream Americans. The workshop also served as a forum to chart out a long-term plan to find out solutions to improve the image of India's heritage and the contributions of Indian civilisation to the progress of mankind. Heritage provides roots to a person the same way as roots provide to trees and plants their very existence. History, culture, social practices and religion overlap and most of the times submerge.

Specifically, the participants during this session outlined the following concerns about portrayal of India, its people, its culture and diverse religions:

1. Here are some problems with American textbooks the way these project India and Indians.

(a) The textbooks are written around assumptions, sensational stories and anecdotes from works of fiction. The compilations of history stereotype India and confuse the students with partial truths, lies, misrepresentations and out-of-context anonymous quotes. Will Durant's famous words in his *History of Civilisation*, vol. 1: "History is partly guessing, the rest is bias" echoes in the pages of these compilations.

(b) Myths about India

- India is a Third World country.
- Third World countries are underdeveloped and poor.
- India is a poor country mostly because of its culture and religion.
- Excepting the Taj Mahal and the British Raj, nothing glorious ever happened in India.
- Illiteracy, poverty, food insufficiencies, cows are integral part of Indian scenario.

2. To the extent Indian people and their culture are demonised in the media and the American textbooks, our children will try to de-Indianise themselves. To the very same extent, mainstream Americans with whom our children are going to work and live will denigrate them. No child or adult in this age and times should live being misunderstood and being discriminated for his roots.
3. While this tirade against Indian traditions has been going on

for three decades, our community has been totally ignorant about these developments.

4. Any time these were brought to the attention of the community leaders, all they showed was apathy. People either pretended their ignorance or professed their inability to do anything; mostly they held the shield of secularism. Hypocrisy and self-deception on the part of the diaspora has led to the situation where negative portrayal has now become malicious in several books. Denying that there is a problem going around will not let the problem go away.
5. Any positive art or event is labelled as South Asian.
6. Anything remotely true or an occasional abrasion is labelled Indian.
7. Totally imbalanced portrayal of Indian civilisation is given–dismal and confusing. The heights it reached, the diversity it accepted, the cultural diffusion and enrichment that was created as a result of assimilation and coexistence (a direct result of and example of Hindu tolerance) is blacked out.
8. What we find is a picture of differences, divisions and conflicts zoomed manifold. Myths are created on biased assumptions and ballooned to a reality, thereby creating more myths. A picture of two small emaciated kids adds to the myth what is called India. No wonder as a group we are the most misunderstood and a downplayed ethnic group.

One of the main concerns is the fragmented approach of the community towards issues of assimilation while keeping the Indian value system. What can we as parents and educators do? More importantly, what can we women do to improve the perception of Americans about our diverse culture and rich heritage?

Recommendations

Through the discussion, the following steps were suggested by way of solutions:

1. Women may perhaps be instrumental in getting rid of hypocrisy and self-deception on the part of the diaspora.
2. A correct knowledge of our own history through turbulence

and sublimity is a prerequisite. Procuring books written by Indians with academic honesty and placing these in the libraries is essential and is possible too. The libraries in this country are required by law to procure the books even if one person needs these for research. Let us learn to use the system to promote correct version of India and its culture. When we stop de-legitimising our civilisation and its heritage, others (including our own kids) will respect us for who we are and where we come from.

3. The American ethos to understand and accept Indian ethos, some suggestions were made:

(a) The best way to counter prejudice is to promote and highlight India's achievements.

(b) India has had women Prime Minister and presidents from all different faiths. Those who give slants can they really boast of the same?

(c) Being on the defensive does not always work. Sometimes question can answer a question. For example, gender discrimination in Indian history is stressed; we can ask which country, five thousand years back, gave voice to women in any matter at all? Please give an example of that country. At the same time, we can give the names of Gargi and Lopamudra, etc.

4. Outreach programmes through community groups may be arranged for the mainstream Americans, adults as well as children. Some of the educators have started outreach programmes. Correct knowledge about India and its heritage has been well received by those participating in the programme. The participants agreed that this may be tried in other places as well.

5. Women can get involved in schools as guest speakers.

6. Grandparents may give glimpses of Indian history to their kids because in the emerging social scenario of two parents working, they would be contributing to the raising of grandchildren.

7. Anthology of diverse Indian art forms and literature may be prepared and placed in the libraries.
8. Many participants in the workshop were teachers and they agreed that lessons should be prepared and handed out to various community centres. These lessons can be used by various people– both teachers and parents.
9. Anthology of contributions of Indian civilisation given in the booklet titled, *India: A Cultural Millionaire* can be posted on Websites and circulated through community groups.
10. During a lively discussion that ensued, many participants suggested that we may approach publishers and the education departments to revise the books. Laudable as it is, many others agreed that this may not be possible because so many vested interests are involved.
11. Another suggestion was to use the Indian media (newspapers and lease-time programmes on the cable channels and radio programmes) for portrayal of a correct image of Indian civilisation.
12. Websites may be created to post material which may be accessed by the teachers. It was further pointed out that through teachers' associations, seminars may be arranged.
13. Almost all agreed that decoupling between Dharma and current social practices (which are usually the result of historical events and disasters) must be done and pointed out to others.

Participant List

S.No.	Name	Occupation
1.	Dr Urmilesh Arya	Physician, president, AIA, New York chapter
2.	Dr Ujwala Shah	Physician, secretary, Gujarati Samaj
3.	Ms Kalpana Rao	Vice president of Regulatory Affairs at Taro Pharmaceutical
4.	Ms Pam Kwatra	CEO, Kripari
5.	Dr Maya Chadda	Academician, International Relations, Peterson University
6.	Dr Bharti A. Palkhiwala	Physician, president, Women's wing, AAPI
7.	Ms UmaShah	Insurance agent
8.	Ms Bhavna Desai	Microbiology supervisor at Barnert Hospital, Paterson, NJ
9.	Mrs Sudha Desai	Senior immunologist at Boehringer -Ingleheim in Danbury, Connecticut
10.	Dr Sushila Gidwani	Treasurer, GOPIO and president, TOUCH
11.	Ms Rupa Ranganathan	Senior vice president, Ethnic Strategist, SRI Institute
12.	Mrs Kamlesh Kapur	Former I.A.A.S. cadre in India; educator for over two decades and writer for several books in Hindi and English
13.	Dr Manjari Bhatt	Physician
14.	Mrs Sudha Sharma	Food drive
15.	Ms Ritu Sharma	Executive director, TBWA
16.	Dr Seema Singh Zokarkar	COO, Desi Match Maker
17.	Mrs Kirtida J. Bhatt	Vice president, J.P. Morgan Chase
18.	Dr Anjana Sandhir	Hindi professor at Columbia University, Department of Middle East & Asian Languages & Cultures; poetess & writer; journalist of Hindi periodicals
19.	Pandita Indrani Rampersad	Academician and Hindu priest
20.	Ms Devika Kapoor	Student

S.No.	Name	Occupation
21.	Dr Bhawani Srinivasan	Physician, president, India Association of Long Island; treasurer, AAPI Queens/LI chapter; past president, Suffolk PED. Society
22.	Dr Anila Midha	President, Five Towns Indian Association; executive member of India Association of Long Island; editor of newsletter of IALI
23.	Mrs Hansa Ashar	Social activist
24.	Mrs Prajna Khisty (Vandana)	Financial advisor, AXA advisors, LLC
25.	Mr. Marinal Chopra	Student
26.	Ms Sabeena Jindal	Student
27.	Mr. Manu Chopra	Working at Morgan Stanley
28.	Ms Kavita Mehra	NYU, student
29.	Mrs Mridula Patel	MILAN,NJ
30.	Dr Madhu Ahluwalia	Psychiatrist
31.	Prof Gargi Chattopadhyay	Founder director, OMNA ancient art
32.	Mrs Falguni Bhatt	Office manager, Anthem Technologies
33.	Mrs Rachita Singh	President, International Hindi Association, NJ chapter
34.	Mrs Sudha Acharya	Executive director, South Asian Council for Social Service; representative of All India women's conference at the UN
35.	Dr Uma Mysorekar	President, Hindu temple
36.	Mrs Najma Sultana	Ex-president, Federation of Indian Muslims, TV Asia
37.	Mrs Sushila Palan	VP,HSBC
38.	Mrs Smiti Khanna	AIA,member
39.	Ms Veena Shetty	Documentary filmmaker
40.	Ms Mohini Sarin	Businesswoman
41.	Ms Chetna Shah	Businesswoman, writer/social worker

S.No.	Name	Occupation
42.	Mrs Dolly Hassan	Director, women's affairs, Indo-Caribbean Council, NY
43.	Mrs Janet Maragh	Assistant secretary, Indo-Caribbean Council, NY
44.	Mrs Bhagmanee Pooran	Treasurer, Indo-Caribbean Council, NY
45.	Dr Sudha Parikh	Physician
46.	Mrs Seorie Autar	Presenting Indian classical music show at BBC Radio
47.	Mrs K. Bhuvaneshwari Bhagat	Marriage counsellor
4K	Dr Raghuwinder Bajwa	Physician
49.	Mrs Uma Swaminathan	Information Technology professional
50.	Mrs Shalini Sharma	Entrepreneur
51.	Dr Jameela Yusuf	Physician; Member, Indo-Caribbean Council
52.	Bhagwatie Bhanu Dwarika	Co-chair, Asian Heritage Committee, District Council 37; Executive director, Shandanaresource Centre; member, GOPIO
53.	Ms Manju Masad	
54.	Ms Ambalika Misra	Voice of America
55.	Ms Rama Sood	
56.	Ms Suchi Sood	
57.	Ms Shurtha Karnath	
58.	Ms Mohini Sood	
59.	Ms Vimisha Dubai	
60.	Ms Reshma Roshania	
61.	Ms Sheena Raja	
62.	Ms Sneh Sharma	
63.	Ms Deepali Vyas	
64.	Ms Madhuri Mittal	
65.	Dr Shanti Sharma	
66.	Ms Deepa Kataria	Student, Rutgers
67.	Mrs Neena Sahani	

S.No.	Name	Occupation
68.	Ms Surekha Vijh	Journalist
69.	Pro£ Krishna Agnihotri	Mrs Ambassador
70.	Ms Nishi Kohli	Community relations, office of Ambassador-at-Large for NRIs/PIOs
71.	Dr Panchali Dhar	Active community leader
72.	Mrs Veena Modi	
73.	Mr. Devag Vyas	Community assistant, office of Ambassador-at-Large for NRIs/PIOs
74.	Mr. Subhash Chander	Attache, OAAL
75.	Mr. Suresh Sharma	President, Milan

Appendix-II

AMERICAN ASSOCIATION OF PHYSICIANS FROM INDIA

8725 Bridgewater Lane, Cincinnati, Ohio 45243

MINUTES OF THE EXECUTIVE COMMITTEE MEETING OF AAPI
November 28, 1986
The Palace Hotel, Philadelphia, Pennsylvania

ATTENDED BY: All Executive Committee Members
Three Regional Directors
Region 5 - Dr. Kulkarni
Region 6 - Dr. Navin Nanda
Region 9 - Dr. Rakesh Arora

Several active and friendly members from the host association--The Association of Indian Professionals, Inc., Philadelphia, also attended and gave their valuable ideas and opinions.

The Meeting was called to order by the President at 9:30 a.m. The first item on the agenda was CME India. Dr. Navin Shah presented details of his recent visit to India. These have already been circulated to all members in a separate communication. Mr. Rao, Minister for Health and Human Resource Development has agreed to create a separate office in the Indian Embassy in Washington to oversee Continuing Medical Education Exchange between USA and India.

Dr. Shah also discussed plans to invite Deans of Medical Schools. Alumni get-togethers will be organized during these visits and members would be encouraged to donate equipment, etc. to their alma mater.

In response to a question, Dr. Shah stated that packing, storage and shipping up to the exit port is the donor's responsibility.

At this point Dr. Kakarela admonished that CME and Charitable foundations are separate issues.

Dr. Roshan Lal: Can leaders from the USA side select the site for their seminar?

Dr. Navin Shah: Suggestions are welcome. But the final decision should be left to the Indian counterparts.

Physicians interested in attending these meetings should get in touch directly with the chairman of the specialty.

AAPI Congratulates

Honorable Ambassador B.K. Agnihotri

for his Appointment as Ambassador-at-Large.

Mr. Agnihotri has provided visionary leadership and given selfless service and guidance to AAPI, since its inception, and to various other organizations.

S. 'Jay' Jayasankar, MD
AAPI President

Past Presidents

Ujamlal C. Kothari, MD (Late)	1982-85
Navin Shah, MD	1985-86
Roshan Lal, MD	1986-87
Jagan Kakarala, MD	1987-88
Suvas Desai, MD	1988-89
Navin Nanda, MD	1989-90
Sarjit Singh, MD	1990-91
Vijay Kulkarni, MD	1991-92
Apparao Mukkamala, MD	1992-93
George Thomas, MD	1993-94
Gopal Lalmalani, MD	1994-95
C. Venkata S. Ram, MD	1995-96
Vinod Sawhney, MD	1996-97
Ranga Reddy, MD	1997-98
Kalpalatha Guntupalli, MD	1998-99
Satya Ahuja, MD	1999-00
Dayan Naik MD	2000-01

Past Chair BOT

Jagan Kakarala, MD	1990-91
Enas A. Enas, MD	1991-92
Srikrishna Nuthi, MD	1992-93
Chander Kapasi, MD	1993-94
Radhu Agrawal, MD	1994-95
Bhimsen Rao, MD	1995-96
Krishan Aggarwal, MD	1996-97
Raghavendra Vijayanagar, MD	1997-98
Surendra Purohit, MD	1998-99
Dharmapuri Vidyasagar, MD	1999-00
Surekha S. Rao, MD	2000-01

AAPI would also like to thank the Honorable Prime Minister of India Mr. Atal Behari Vajpayee for appointing Mr. Agnihotri to this prestigious position.

Executive Committee 2001-2002

S. 'Jay' Jayasankar, MD	President
Kiran Patel, MD	President Elect
Sharad Lakhanpal, MD	Vice President
Jagan Ailinani, MD	Secretary
Akshay Desai, MD	Treasurer
Rajam Ramamurthy, MD	Chair BOT
Ruchi Gupta, MD	President YPS Section
Majid Basit, MD	President MS/R Section
Sudeep Kukreja, MD	Pacific Regional Director
Rachakonda Prabhu, MD	Mountain Regional Director
Elly Bhuyan, MD	Northwest Central Regional Director
Sanku Rao, MD	Southwest Central Regional Director
Birinder Marwah, MD	Northeast Central Regional Director
Sampat Shivangi, MD	Southeast Central Regional Director
Ram Upadhyay, MD	New England Regional Director
Hemant Patel, MD	Mid Atlantic Regional Director
Suresh Malhotra, MD	South Atlantic Regional Director

THE WHITE HOUSE

WASHINGTON

May 5, 1995

Bhishma K. Agnihotri
Chancellor
Southern University Law Center
Post Office Box 9294
Baton Rouge, Louisiana 70813

Dear Chancellor Agnihotri:

Thank you for inviting President Clinton to address the American Association of Physicians from India at its 1995 Annual Convention. The President has asked me to convey his appreciation for your kind offer.

I am pleased to inform you that the President will be able to join you for this important event on June 30.

On behalf of the President, thank you again for your offer. Please do not hesitate to contact my office if we can provide you with any further assistance.

Sincerely,

William M. Webster, IV
Director of Scheduling and Advance

WMW/lab

ॐ

Form No. [illegible]
March [illegible]

SURAJ BHAN
M.A. (Panjab & London) M.L.C.
PRINCIPAL

D. A. V. COLLEGE
JULLUNDUR CITY.

Dated 23-3-55.

It gives me great pleasure to put on record the high opinion I have formed of the ability and character of Shri Bhishma Kumar Agnihotri who has been the student of this institution for two years.

He has been admittedly one of the best students of the college and ~~xxxxxxxx~~ invariably achieved distinctions in the various examinations. He impressed his teachers greatly by his scholarship, high sense of duty and gentlemanly deportment. He has a personality about him and throughout his stay in the college, greatly enjoyed the respect and esteem of all those with whom he came in contact.

Shri Bhishma Kumar is extremely smart and well-behaved. It is no superficial smartness I am referring to. This youngman has got a quickness and vitality that indicates that he is bubbling all over with life. In these days, we have a lotof intellectual inanition about us and it is extremely refreshing to come across a living youngman, and Shri Bhishma Kumar, I am sure, is one of them.

Shri Bhishma Kumar also weilded great influence

-2-

with the students and was very popular with them. He was elected the President of the Student Council of the college for 1954-55-- a rare honour for a student--and as such discharged his duties with great devotion and loyalty for the cause of those he represented.

Shri Bhishma Kumar is an eloquent speaker and possesses outstanding debating talents. He represented the college in a large number of debates and almost invariably won prizes and trophies. The following is the list of the prizes and trophies he won:-

1. All India Debate, Hans Raj College, Delhi. First Prize and Trophy.
2. All India Debate, Meerut College, Meerut, First Prize and Trophy.
3. All India Debate, Birla College, Pilani, Second prize.
4. All India Declamation Contest, Simla. First Prize-Trophy.
5. All India Debate, Simla. First prize- trophy.
6. All India Debate, Simla, 1st prize.
7. Inter-collegiate Debate, D.M.College Moga. 1st prize-trophy.
8. Inter-collegiate Debate, Batala. First prize.
9. Inter collegiate Debate, Hoshiarpur. 2nd prize.
10. Inter collegiate Debate, D.A.V.College,Jullundur. 1st prize.
11. Inter-collegiate Student Congress debate. 2nd prize.

ॐ

Form No. 13-3000
March 1953.

SURAJ BHAN
M.A. (Punjab & London) M.L.C.
PRINCIPAL

D. A. V. COLLEGE
JULLUNDUR CITY.

--3--

Dated ____________

12. Inter Collegiate Debate, Rajindra College Bhatinda.
1st prize and Trophy.

13. Inter-collegiate Debate, Randhir College, Kapurthala.
1st prize Trophy.

14. All India Youth Festival-University Eloquence Competition
2nd position.

15. Inter-collegiate Debate, Qadian, 1st prize.

Shri Bhishma Kumar led the students' goodwill mission to Kashmir in 1954 and represented the Punjab at UNSA Seminar at Delhi.

Shri Bhishma Kumar is a charming youngman of high moral character and exceptional ability. I can confidently recommend him for any position requiring high intellectual capacity, mature experience, sound judgment, quick mind and hard work.

PRINCIPAL.
RG
D. A. V. College, Jullundur

Appendix-III

No. 89-1399

In The

Supreme Court of the United States

October Term, 1989

INTERNATIONAL SOCIETY OF KRISHNA CONSCIOUSNESS OF CALIFORNIA, et al.,

Petitioners,

v.

ROBIN GEORGE AND MARCIA GEORGE,

Respondents.

On Petition For Certiorari To The Court Of Appeal, State Of California Fourth Appellate District, Division One

MOTION FOR LEAVE TO FILE BRIEF AMICUS CURIAE AND BRIEF AMICUS CURIAE OF THE WORLD HINDU ASSEMBLY OF NORTH AMERICA (VISHWA HINDU PARISHAD), COUNCIL OF HINDU TEMPLES OF NORTH AMERICA, NATIONAL FEDERATION OF INDIAN AMERICAN ASSOCIATIONS, GITA FORUM, GREATER ATLANTA VEDIC TEMPLE SOCIETY, HIMALAYAN ACADEMY, HINDU SWAYAMSEVAK SANGH, THE HINDU TEMPLE OF GREATER CHICAGO, INDIA ASSOCIATION OF NORTH TEXAS, INDIA HOUSE OF WORSHIP, INTERNATIONAL SWAMINARAYAN SATSANG ORGANIZATION, SATCHIDANANDA ASHRAM - YOGAVILLE, SATYA NARAYAN MANDIR, SRI VENKATESWARA SWAMI TEMPLE OF GREATER CHICAGO, VEDANTA SOCIETY OF SACRAMENTO, VEDANTA SOCIETY OF SOUTHERN CALIFORNIA, VEDIC CULTURAL SOCIETY, VEDIC DHARMA CENTER, and VIVEKANANDA VEDANTA SOCIETY, AS AMICI CURIAE IN SUPPORT OF GRANTING CERTIORARI

BHISHMA K. AGNIHOTRI
Chancellor, Southern
University Law Center
P.O. Box 10837
Baton Rouge, LA 70813
(504) 771-2552

D. S. SASTRI
Counsel of Record
9881 Broken Land Parkway,
Suite 400
Columbia, MD 21046
(301) 381-6000

COCKLE LAW BRIEF PRINTING CO., (800) 225-6964
OR CALL COLLECT (402) 342-2831

Baton Rouge proudly hosts . . .
The Eighth Annual World
Hindu Conference
July 5 and 6, 1980 at the Riverside Centroplex in
Baton Rouge, Louisiana.
Registration will begin at 8:30 a.m.
July 5th.
Renowned scholars, philosophers and religious leaders
will participate in the deliberations.
The topics will include–
yoga, meditation and health, self-realization,
the Bhagwat Gita, Buddhism, etc.
For further information call–
(504) 766-0458
(504) 923-4234
293
All are invited to attend

Press Conference, December 20, 1976

DEAN B.K. AGNIHOTRI

CO-CHAIRMAN--WORLD FELLOWSHIP OF RELIGION

STATEMENT:

"I am not a member of the International Society for Krishna Consciousness. I may not believe in every aspect of this movement. I am here in the capacity of the co-chairman of the World Fellowship of Religions. The World Fellowship of Religions stands for good will and understanding amongst all faiths for mutual benefit and development. I am concerned and, in fact, deeply distressed, as one from the World Fellowship, as a Hindu, and as a person of Indian origin, to witness the recent attack on one of the main faiths of Hinduism-- the Hare Krishna movement.

This country is a pluralistic society in religion. The first amendment of the Constitution lays the foundation of the full play and interplay of all faiths. The freedom of a religion is not to be abridged only because it is unconventional in its beliefs and practices, or because it runs against the likes and dislikes of the main stream. Without this proliferation and variety of approaches to God, the freedom of religion will be a meaningless right in the Constitution.

Attacks, direct and indirect, subtle or obvious, on the Hare Krishna movement are attacks on this fundamental right of all religions. A hundred years ago the target was the Jews, 50 years ago the target was the Mormons, 10 years ago the target was the Black Moslems and now the target appears to be centered on religions of eastern origin. I do not, and the Constitution does not, sanction illegal activities on the part of any Faith. If any group is involved in any illegal practices in the name of any religion, no protection can be extended to that group. But the Hare Krishna movement is one of the purest forms of traditional Hindu faith, trying to inculcate in its followers the teachings of the Bhagavad-gita (the bloodline of Hindu religion) and other holy scriptures. Their followers lead a life of austerity, self-dicipline and self spiritual improvement. Their movement has been a source of great inspiration and strength for Hindus of America because in it they see a resurgence of their traditional values and faith. Many of them make use of the temples of the Hare Krishna movement for regular worship.

It appears, sometimes, some over-conscious parents get concerned about the changed "Dress Style" of their sons and daughters on their joining the society. Their apprehension is unfounded and misplaced. The authorities in the society cannot judge the quality of a faith on the superficial exterior. I think this country should thank the Hare Krishna movement and other such faiths who have taught the west to search for the real self in the human being, minus his possessions, his wealth and wardrobes.

I understand one of the charges against some persons in the movement is branded as "brainwashing'. Every religion has a right to present its principles and beliefs with some persuation, and every religion does engage in some sort of persuation. That by itself would not amount to brainwashing. If every act of group activity and persuation is brainwashing, then every religion in the world would be exposed to that charge. I only wish that the Hare Krishna movement, by becoming over-conscious may not step back of its ceremonies, thereby depriving the country of the cultural nourishment it has brought.

I therefore, on behalf of all the religions, request all the persons of all the faiths to join us in educating the people so that the wave of suspicion and possible persecution against one of the main faiths of Hinduism is checked."

INTERNATIONAL SOCIETY FOR KRISHNA CONSCIOUSNESS

Founder - Acarya HIS DIVINE GRACE A.C. BHAKTIVEDANTA SWAMI PRABHUPADA
Sri Sri Radha Govinda Mandir · Radha Damodar Traveling Parties
Hare Krishna Center, 340 West 55th Street, New York, N.Y. 10019
(212) 765-8610

April 18, 1977

Dean Agnihotri
Southern University School of Law
Baton Rouge, LA 70813

Dear Mr. Agnihotri:

I noticed a very interesting thing in Judge Leahy's decision that is worth your noting--on p. 10, paragraph 3, the good Judge is quoting almost word for word your statements from the Press Conference in New York. I was told that you and the Judge had conferred by telephone prior to his decision, but I had no idea that he would be using word-for-word practically the same wise words you spoke. So, as it is evident, your appearance here was a well spent trip.

I wanted to take this opportunity also to inform you of the upcoming Rathayatra Festival scheduled July 23 and July 30 of this year. The enclosed press clippings give you some idea of the festival and its reception last year. On July 23 we are planning to have various guest speakers speak something about our Krishna Consciousness movement, this being the larger of the two festival days. We would be greatly honored to have your presence if you planned to be in New York at that time in the summer. Quite frankly the extensive legal expenses covering the court case has more than exhausted our treasury, but if you were planning to make trips to New York in the summer anyway and could arrange for this particular weekend to fit into your plans, we would be happy to be your host for the duration of your stay in New York and arrange for your participation in the Rathayatra festivities. I hope that you can appreciate the sincerity of this invitation and will overlook the meager means presently at our disposal.

I look forward to hearing your reply as soon as you can confirm or deny this invitation.

Very truly yours,

Romapada das

Romapada das,
Director of Publis Affairs
ISKCON - N.Y.

RD/jd
encls.

WORLD FELLOWSHIP OF RELIGIONS

Founder: H.H. MUNI SUSHIL KUMARJI
777 UNITED NATIONS PLAZA
NEW YORK, NEW YORK 10017, U.S.A.

Patron
Hon'ble Shri Fakhruddin Ali Ahmed
President of India

Hon'ble Shri B. D. Jatti

Chairman: H.H. Muni Sushil Kumarii
Directors: H.H. Shri Chitrabhanuji Muni
H.H. Swami Chidanandaii Maharai
President: Edward Gottlieb
Vice President: Michael Shoemaker
Secretary-General: B.K. Agnihotri
Secretary: Lawrence T. Lowen
Assistant Secretary: V. Pandhi
Treasurer: Padam Dhakad

Spiritual Patrons:
H.H. Jagadguru Shankaracharya Sringeri
H.H. Jagadguru Shankaracharya Dwarka
H.H. Acharya Anand Risshiji
H.H. Acharya Samudra Vijayji
H.H. Acharya Desh Bhushanji
H.H. Acharya Tulsiji
H.H. Delai Lama
Ven. Mahasthavira N. Jinaratna
Archbishop Angelo Fernandes
Most Reverend Eric S. Nasir
Maulana Mohammed Tyeb, Deoband
Giani Sadhu Singhi .S. Akal Takhat, (Amritsar)
H.H. Sant Darshan Singh
Dr. Norman S. Lunde, U.S.A.
H.H Swami Chidanandaji (Rishikesh)
Baron Frary Von. Blomberg (U.S.A.)
H.H. Dr. Pir Wilayat Khan Inayat Khan (Paris)
H.H. Shri Yogi Bhajan
Dr. H.K. Billings (U.S.A.)

Regional Representatives

Joseph Wardell—Texas
T.S. Khanna—Virginia
Dr. Edward v. Rothkirch-Panthen—D.C.
Payare Lal Jain—Buffalo
Richard Blum—California
Sulelh Chanda Jain—Boston
Ma Parm Puja—Chicago
Swami Harihar Dass—New York
Om P. Gaur—New York
Ramesh Jain—New York
Surender Jain—New York
Dr. K. C. Bhaiji—South Carolina
Dr. K. C. Bhaiji—Cleveland
Shri T.K. Venkateswaran—Detroit
Frank Gessner—Monroe, N.Y.
I.L. Kapoor—Conn.

Appendix-IV

The following documents represent the presentations, etc. made on the occasion of the Vancouver meeting with the Sikh community.

1. Press Release: 8/28/03,community meeting
2. R. Paul Dhillon, article
3. Raghbir Singh Bains, Article: Removal of Foreign Sikhs' Names from blacklist announced by the Government of India
4. B. K. Agnihotri speech notes

---

1. Press Release: 8/28/03, Community meeting

Dr. B.K. Agnihotri, Ambassador-at-Large for NRIs and PIOs at the invitation of the South Asian human rights group of Canada, comprising Sikhs, Hindus, Muslims and Christians, visited Vancouver, Canada to meet the local Sikh leadership and to address a meeting of the community on August 28, 2003. This historic meeting was attended by almost all the major South Asian organisations, especially that of the Sikh community in Canada. Among others, the meeting was attended by a large number of Canadian, Indo-Canadian and South Asian Canadian politicians, including Dr. Gulzar Singh Cheema, State Minister for Mental Health, British Columbia, Mr. Joe Peschisolidio, parliamentary secretary of Inter-Provincial Government Affairs of Canada, Mr. Svend Robinson and Mr. Gunnant Singh Grewal, members of Canadian Parliament.

On the previous evening, representatives of all the major Sikh organisations and associations held a lengthy meeting lasting for a period of over three hours with Dr. Agnihotri and the open discussion during the meeting covered all matters of concern and pending issues pertaining to overseas Sikh communities.

Dr. Agnihotri addressing the banquet meeting as the chief guest highlighted the contribution of the Sikhs to the freedom movement of India, starting from 1857 and the sacrifices made by the community to retain the values and spirit of the freedom. Ambassador-at-Large added that the Sikhs have contributed immensely to the prosperity of national unity and globalisation of India as a whole and their contribution is not limited only to the state of Punjab.

Dr. Agnihotri highlighted the leadership role of the Prime Minister Shri Atal Bihari Vajpayee and stated that the Prime Minister is committed to the cause of national unity of India and had special feelings for the Sikh community.

Dr. Agnihotri stated that his office is only a vehicle through which articulation of the grievances of the Sikh community has been communicated to the policy makers at all levels in India. He would continue performing this task in the future.

Dr. Agnihotri also announced that the Government of India as of August 28 had itself removed all the 22 names from the blacklist provided to him by the community leaders in June 2003.

Dr. Agnihotri also congratulated the Sikh associations of the Vancouver for starting such a process. This is beneficial to the Sikh community and their motherland, India. Dr. Agnihotri added that he would continue a similar interaction process all over the world, reaching out to the Sikh communities everywhere. He believed that through this process of interaction, dialogue and communication between the diaspora and the Government of India, all the pending issues could easily be worked out.

Dr. Agnihotri was honoured with the Humanitarian Award at the banquet in recognition of his outstanding services towards unity, peace and mutual harmony.

---

2. R. Paul Dhillon article

Historical meeting between Sikh groups and Indian Ambassador for NRIs. In a ground-breaking meeting between Dr. Bhishma Agnihotri, India's Ambassador-atLarge and many traditionalist Sikh organisations, it was declared that the Government of India is prepared to lift the ban on the travel of those blacklisted following Operation Bluestar. And as an added effort to heal the wounds, it will also look into other issues facing the NRI Sikhs, such as doing business and owning property in India.

By R. Paul Dhillon

Vancouver: Many Sikh groups were blacklisted and refused entry into India for criticising the Congress government after Operation Bluestar which forced Indian troops into Sikhs' holiest shrine in Amritsar in1984.

But this week, India's newly appointed Ambassador-at-Large Dr. Bhishma K. Agnihotri, who is responsible for the entire Indian diaspora, came bearing gifts in the form of reconciliation and a promise to undo the wrongs of the past by granting entry to those blacklisted to their homeland so that they can visit their relatives and friends, many of whom they have not seen for more than two decades.

On Wednesday evening, groups, such as the World Sikh Organisation, Khalsa Darbar Society of Vancouver, Kalghidhar Sikh Society of Abbotsford, Rode Federation and a number of other traditionalist Sikh representatives met Agnihotri in Vancouver fora lengthy discussion on their concerns in a meeting arranged by South Asian Human Rights Group of Canada.

In an exclusive interview with *The LINK* on Thursday at his downtown Vancouver hotel suite, Agnihotri described he discussion as extremely fruitful and productive, saying this is the reason he decided to take the NRI-ambassador position so that he could hear the concerns of all of them because after all they are Indian.

"Discussion is knowledge and only through dialogue can we increase mutual knowledge and that is what happened during my meeting with people in Vancouver," said Agnihotri, who is a former Indian magistrate and a former Chancellor of Louisiana University in America.

During the visit, Agnihotri was able to clear the cases of 22 affected individuals, who had been denied entry into India until this week. He said more work is needed on this issue but he feels this is a good start in mending the fences between India and the Sikhs, especially those living abroad.

"Yesterday (Wednesday) it was as a big family meeting and we were all talking and discussing – and if I can be very honest – it was very emotional because so many of these people have not been able to visit India and in the meantime, they lost loved ones – parents, brothers and sisters – and they couldn't even attend their funerals," Agnihotri said. "Whatever has happened in the past is the past and we cannot change that. But we can affect the future and I hope this is a starting point for improved relations between India and its Sikh family abroad."

For those critical of these developments and wanting to categorise these efforts as political, Agnihotri had a clear response. He said that

Indian Prime Minister (Atal Behari) Vajpayee has never played politics with the Sikh community.

"For him (Vajpayee), this is not a matter of politics or strategy; in fact, this is how he felt in 1984 and he feels the same way today," Agnihotri said. "We will welcome these people with garlands when they come home."

Agnihotri said India belongs to the Sikhs because they have made great contribution to its history, from Guru Gobind Singh and Guru Tegh Bhadhur to Kookas, who began India's freedom struggle in 1857 and to the Ghadhri Babas who took the freedom struggle from North America's shores to India and were later followed by great freedom fighters like Kartar Singh Sarabha, Udham Singh and Bhagat Singh.

"We can't underestimate the contributions the Sikhs have made to India and its struggle to win independence," he said. "If we look at the past century, there is no doubting the great role they have played in India's Defence and Armed Forces. Even today, they are the cream of Indian society."

Agnihotri was impressed with the people he met in Vancouver and said the interaction was emotional and affectionate and very real. He will take all their concerns, including such issues as the execution of Prof. Bhullar, to the Prime Minister. A delegation of Sikhs is also expected to visit India to meet top government officials. Agnihotri said that the Union Home Ministry is all set to remove the names of these 22 Sikhs from the blacklist issued after Operation Bluestar. Agnihotri's visit comes after several high-level meetings held at the Union Home Ministry in India and a recent meeting between Sikh representatives, including Jatinder (Jay) Minhas, vice-chair of South Asian Human Rights Group of Canada and India's No. 2, Union Home Minister L.K. Advani.

Agnihotri, along with Rulda Singh, a senior leader of the Rashtriya Sikh Sangat from Patiala, held meetings with Home Ministry officials and Union Home Minister L.K. Advani in this connection.

During Advani's visit in June to New York, certain organisations of NRI Sikhs asked him to review the blacklist. There are about 400 names on the list. Many among them are in Germany and other countries, including Pakistan.

"The journey begins with Ottawa, India and New York and lot more," said Minhas, who has made much sacrifice and effort for this cause. "It takes so much time, energy and effort but it's worth all the trouble."

Agnihotri was appointed in the Indian mission in Washington in September 2001 with the rank of Ambassador to advise on the affairs of the Non-Resident Indian community and the people of Indian origin in the world.

---

3. Raghbir Singh Bains Article: Removal of foreign Sikhs' names from blacklist announced by the Government of India

Vancouver, August 28, 2003: Dr. Bhishma K. Agnihotri, India's Ambassador-at-Large (USA) announced today the abolition of the blacklist of the Sikhs prepared by the then government of India after attack on Sri Harmandir Sahib in 1984. He was addressing an overwhelmingly large congregation and dinner meeting of four elite communities of Canada, arranged by the South Asian Human Rights Group of Canada. The group comprised Sikhs,Hindus, Muslims and Christians.

After the tragic episode of desecration and demolition of Sri Harmandir Sahib, and Sri Akal Takht Sahib at Amritsar on June 5, 1984, many of the Sikh youth were put behind bars in Indian prisons as they had protested against the excesses of the then government. Many of the Sikhs living abroad grew bitter over this assault and as such, their leaders were picked up to be banned from visiting their families in India. The bleeding psyche of the foreign Sikhs has been simmering against the Government of India for a long time. Mutual trust was lost and this created wedges and fissures. Mediators were working for decades to lessen the tension and they were looking for an opportunity to re-build the lost confidence and repair the saddened relationship between the Sikhs and the present Government of India. It was after two decades that a person of the stature of Dr. Agnihotri dared to jump into the distressed arena to solve the boiling issue of the Sikhs.

The dialogue to find a mutual and honourable solution was already underway behind the doors through good offices of Dr. Agnihotri, who worked very hard to smoothen the rough turf and dilute anguish and anger growing in the Sikh minds. The ground was prepared at a meeting held between the Deputy Prime Minister of India Shri L.K.

Advani with the South Asian Human Rights Group of Canada at New York on June13,2003.

To pave the way for the new era of peace and harmony, Dr. Agnihotri announced that all the 22 names of the Sikhs from British Columbia which was handed over to him by different organisations, have been cleared from the blacklist by the Government of India."Now those blacklisted NRI Sikhs can visit their homeland freely," Dr Agnihotri said.

Dr. Agnihotri added that the other demands of the South Asian Human Rights Group of Canada are under active consideration of the Government of India. He said, "I respect the Sikhs who are strong supporters of universal peace. They believe in brotherhood of the entire human race.We know that they preserved the rich heritage and laid down their lives for dignity, honour and freedom of India.Our Prime Minister Atal Bihari Bajpai was the only strongest person who voiced loudly in favour of the Sikhs during their turbulent times. He is very eager to settle the issues of the Sikhs and re-establish their honour."

Mr. Agnihotri further emphasised, "The conflict resolution is the priority of the Government of India and my job is to build bridges. We will do our part earnestly." Talking about the death penalty case of Prof. Devinder Pal Singh Bhullar, Dr. Agnihotri said vigorously that people know much better the latest position. Positive results are expected soon. Dr. Agnihotri was applauded many times by the audience for his sincere approach.

Harpal Singh Nagra, chairman of the South Asian Human Rights Group of Canada, who played a major role in bridging the broken gaps, applauded the Government of India for taking the groundbreaking step to deal with the sensitive issues of the Sikhs in their entirety. He urged upon the Government of India to immediately release the Sikh youth detained in the Indian prisons, including the army personnel who abandoned their barracks under sway of emotion and respect for their nerve centre Sri Harrnandir Sahib. He demanded that Sikh identity be recognised legally in India through a constitutional amendment. He strongly stressed the need for mutual negotiations with honest approach on both sides so that peace and harmony could prevail in the minds of people living in India and abroad. He thanked Shri Anil Anand, acting consul general of Vancouver and all other organisations for their presence and for extending full support to the cause.

Dr. Guizar Singh Cheema, State Minister for Mental Health of British Columbia. Joe Peschisolidio, parliamentary secretary of Inter-provincial Governmental Affairs or Canada, Svend Robinson and Gurmant Singh Grewal, members of Canadian Parliament, ML.As and other politicians including the Canadian mainstream people, who attended the gathering, supported the demands. They emphasised during the dinner meeting, that the Government of India, which has a legacy of fairness and equality, must guarantee human rights to all the communities in India, irrespective of caste, colour and creed. They said with one voice that Canada has a friendly relationship with India and they want their friend to protect democratic values and provide justice to the Sikhs. They wished success to Dr. Agnihotri, who had started a new era to find solutions to the long-standing issues of the Sikhs. They demanded abolition of death penalty to Prof. Devinder Pal Singh Bhullar.

Dr. Agnlhotri was honoured with 'Humanitarian Award' by the South Asian Human Rights Group of Canada. Participating organisations of Hindus, Sikhs, Muslims and Christians along with ethnic media, were recognised for their outstanding services towards unity, peace and mutual harmony. The plaques of appreciation were presented by Dr. Agnihotri.

---

4. B. K. Agnihotri speech notes

1. The volunteers – SEWA and value of SEWA

2. Human rights – Manav Dharam for the people of India. Rights and duties of every human being are basic/inherent in the very nature of existence. Indians go beyond that as they respect the rights of even all living entities and the majority would not like to harm even animals, for example, the place of cow in the ancient society.

3. I am pleased to be here amongst the people I know, the people of Punjab, the people whose every drop of blood speaks of the great sacrifices of the great gurus – Guru Teg Bahadur's sacrifice can never be forgotten, who preferred to give up his life than to give up his religion and principles; Guru Gobind Singh, who sacrificed his four sons, wife and mother for upholding the principles of Dharma. As a true patriot he fought against the tyranny (of a foreign ruler). The history of Sikhs

in Punjab is a history of sacrifices and commitment to the cause of India's heritage.

4. Immediately after the first War of Independence in 1857, Kooka Ram Singh and 66 associates were executed for revolting against the British empire. The second War of Independence started right here on the western part of USA and Canada in 1913 and 1914. Most of the people living in America and Canada were Punjabis. They organised along with some others, a GhadarParty for liberating India. The history of Ghadar Party is a history of unparalleled patriotism and passion for the freedom of India; 8,000 of the then Indians living in the Western world decided to go back to India to fight the British. There were a lot of young people amongst them; they had come from India after selling everything a few years earlier and now they were going back to India after selling everything in America and Canada because they thought that India needed the mat that time.One of them was Kartar Singh Saraba, 19-year old young man, who left the prestigious University of California in Berkeley to go back and organise an army against the British. Unfortunately they could not succeed because of inside information against them and 45 of them were hanged to death; others were sent to Kala Pani. When you read the saga of those people, it is unbelievable that such people existed. When Kartar Singh was being hanged, he said "Why are you delaying? I want to come back to fight for India's freedom, so don't delay my death."In their clarion call for the *ghadar* recruits, they urged "Come brothers, you have plenty of dollars; come, let us go back to our motherland and raise the banner of *ghadar*. . . don't delay; only he is a brave fighter who fights for his country; even if he is cut into pieces, he does not leave the battlefield." This was the spirit and this is part of our heritage. We cannot go away from that, however hard we may try. Out of that spirit, came people like Bhagat Singh and others, who paved the way for the freedom of India.

5. Sikhs were most prominent in the INA Army of Subhash Chandra Bose. Mohan Singh Dhillon was one of the commanders. Therefore, if anybody says I want Punjab, I want to tell them that India is yours; why do you want only one part? Of course Punjab is in India, so Punjabis in India . . ..In the wars after independence in 1965 and 1971, of course Sikhs were at the forefront and were responsible for saving our country.

6. So it is my privilege to be here where I find so many people from Punjab because this fills me with great pride.

7. Certain things happened which were unfortunate and they should not have happened. Lot of people suffered lots of pain. Punjabis suffered lot of pain but I think this is a time to move on. Punjabis are warm, gracious and committed individuals; therefore, they have the capacity to contribute, as always, more successfully to the development of India. Government of India is cognisant of the greatness of the Punjabis. Our Prime Minister has expressed again and again his anguish over the happenings in Punjab in the past. In 1984 he expressed his dismay at what happened. His government allocated Rs 300 crores for tricentennial celebrations in Anandpur Sahib; now they are committed to bringing all the family together. Let me explain my role at this time.. I am Ambassador-at-Large for NRIs/PIOs based in New York . . .My job is to build bridges to cut short the distances so that we can all unite as one in the service of our motherland. When we start looking into the various requests made by this group, I find everybody to be very sympathetic. It is not a matter of convenience or political expediency; this is a matter of faith with these leaders. They believe in concrete results, wherever they may be, in Kashmir or Nagaland. So if Punjabis or Sikhs living outside India have some concerns, believe me our Prime Minister is equally concerned. He is concerned about NRIs/PIOs. That's why he has initiated various moves for expanding and uniting Indian families all over the world, for example, my appointment, PravasiBharatiya Divas and dual citizenship in the near future, so, that when your group approached me and I talked to the Deputy Prime Minister, he agreed to meet the group and we have been working since then on the various concerns expressed by them. I can say today that one of the concerns was the blacklisting of 22 people. You will be pleased to know that phase by phase, we have now cleared all the cases. So far,16 orders have been issued; six orders will be issued before I leave tomorrow. Decision has been made. We want all people of Indian origin to feel that they are welcome in India. Past has no connection with the future behaviour. We have to forget, have to forgive and move forward. This is just a beginning; all other issues will be looked into. This is also a beginning in terms of resolving similar issues in other parts of the world also. You are lucky that the process

is beginning from here; from Vancouver, it will go to other parts of Canada, to USA, England, other places in Germany and we are not going to stop till all genuine concerns are adequately addressed. We want the people who loved India, who love India and who shall love India to feel good about India and promote India's welfare and all that is what our expectation is.

POINT: Education of other Canadians regarding Sikhism. You should all take upon yourselves to educate non-Punjabis/ Sikhs regarding Sikhism. There is so much misunderstanding, I think this should be one of the major projects. Based upon my experience in USA and other countries, unless we do it, we will not be further subjected to harassment and misunderstandings.

□□□